THE PROTECTOR'S SACRIFICE

BOOK FOUR OF THE TALES OF CALEDONIA

PETER WACHT

The Protector's Sacrifice
By Peter Wacht

Book 4 of The Tales of Caledonia

This book is a work of fiction. Names, characters, places, and incidents are the product of the author's imagination or are used fictitiously. Any resemblance to actual events, locales, or persons, living or dead, is coincidental.

Cover design by Ebooklaunch.com

Published in the United States by Kestrel Media Group LLC.

ISBN: 978-1-950236-24-4

eBook ISBN: 978-1-950236-25-1

Library of Congress Control Number: 2022903166

Created with Vellum

ALSO BY PETER WACHT

THE REALMS OF THE TALENT AND THE CURSE

THE TALES OF CALEDONIA

*Blood on the White Sand (short story)**

*The Diamond Thief (short story)**

The Protector

The Protector's Quest

The Protector's Vengeance

The Protector's Sacrifice

The Protector's Reckoning (Forthcoming 2022)

The Protector's Resolve (Forthcoming 2023)

The Protector's Victory (Forthcoming 2023)

THE TALES OF CALEDONIA: THE TERRITORIES

Death on the Burnt Ocean (Forthcoming 2023)

THE SYLVAN CHRONICLES

(Complete 9-Book Series available at Amazon)

The Legend of the Kestrel

The Call of the Sylvana

The Raptor of the Highlands

The Makings of a Warrior

The Lord of the Highlands

The Lost Kestrel Found

The Claiming of the Highlands

The Fight Against the Dark

The Defender of the Light

THE RISE OF THE SYLVAN WARRIORS

*Through the Knife's Edge (short story)**

* Free short stories can be downloaded from my author website at www.kestrelmg.com

YOUR FREE SHORT STORY IS WAITING

THE DIAMOND THIEF

This short story is a prelude to the events in my series *The Tales of Caledonia* and is free to readers who receive my newsletter.

Join Peter's newsletter at www.kestrelmg.com to get your FREE short story.

SETTING THE STAGE

The Protector's Sacrifice, Book 4 of *The Tales of Caledonia*, is set more than one thousand years before the events that occur in *The Sylvan Chronicles* and takes place in a separate land of *The Realms of the Talent and the Curse*. Caledonia, though a monarchy, functions more like a loose confederation of Duchies, especially now that Marden Beleron is dead.

During this time, some of the more adventurous and grasping members of the Caledonian nobility accept King Corinthus Beleron's territorial grants and begin to colonize the Territories, often called New Caledonia, far to the west on the other side of the Burnt Ocean. These Territories will eventually become the Kingdoms of *The Sylvan Chronicles*.

In Caledonia, as in the other realms, the ability to use the Talent sets apart the person gifted with this unique skill. But being able to use the Talent is only part of the dynamic. For if a Magus chooses to follow a darker path, the Talent becomes the Curse.

1

THE TRUTH REVEALED

Killen Sourban, the Captain of the Royal Guard, shook his head in resignation as he stepped out onto the plaza that encircled the Colosseum. If only the King had listened to him, thought Killen. If that stupid, stubborn ass had demonstrated even a modicum of judgment and reserve, this ridiculous rebellion would have ended before it had gained any traction among the people. The King's rule would never have been put in such jeopardy. But Marden listened to no one except for Tetric, and the King's Advisor had supported every single one of the King's decisions, helping to put him on the path that led to his bloody demise.

Now, King Marden Beleron, the last of a dynasty more than three hundred years old, was dead ... or soon would be. Long live the new ...

Sourban wasn't certain who would assume the Caledonian throne. He was certain of the outcome of the combat before the King of Caledonia stomped onto the white sand.

It was a given. There was no doubt. He knew this gladiator. He had seen him fight many times in the Colosseum. He had won several bags of golds by betting on him more times than he could remember.

No matter what Marden Beleron and his fool Advisor believed, no one and nothing could kill the Volkun on the white sand.

Despite his repeated attempts to change Marden Beleron's mind, the King had ignored him and walked into the Pit. The King was so eager to prove himself. He was so eager to be what he thought his people wanted him to be, visions of the loved, benevolent lionheart dancing through his head. Those visions would do little for him when he faced the steel of the Wolf's double-bladed spear.

What a complete and utter fool, thought Sourban. The King had never realized that he could never be anything more than what he already was. He had shown such promise when he had taken his father's place on the throne. Intelligence. Drive. Cunning.

Yet all for naught. Because of his arrogance and recklessness Marden was a failed king. And now Sourban suspected a dead king as well, because there was no way Marden was going to escape the Volkun.

Of course, Sourban was not a fool. He understood that the second that Marden died at the hands of the Volkun, his own time in the capital would be coming to an end. Fast. His enemies would be looking for him.

With some justification, he admitted. So he had waited through several agonizing minutes until the combat between the King and the Volkun was well underway before sneaking out of the only accessible tunnel that led away from the Colosseum onto the square, his primary concern escaping Tintagel as quickly as possible.

The merit of his decision was confirmed when he saw the Guards from Murcia, the Three Rivers, Roo's Nest, and the Southern Marches lined up in formation across the plaza. The companies of Royal Guard he had dispersed around the square were nervous, perhaps even a little frightened, by the arrival of these soldiers because these troops from the Duchies outnumbered them by at least two to one.

So far nothing had happened, the soldiers of the Royal Guard eyeing with a good amount of trepidation these potential adversaries. Sourban could see it just as well as they could. The Captains of the Duchy troops had positioned their fighters in overlapping ranks, one company always in support of another, ensuring, right from the start, that any fight on the plaza ended rapidly and in their favor, assuming, of course, that any of the soldiers would be willing to risk their lives for the not very well liked and soon-to-be-dead King.

Sourban shook his head in resignation once again. It wasn't his problem anymore. The city was lost the second the Duchy soldiers passed through the gates, and the Crown would be lost in a matter of minutes as soon as the Volkun turned the white sand red with the King's blood.

Resigning the soldiers under his command to their fates with nary a feeling of remorse, Sourban started walking across the plaza in a small lane that separated a company of the Royal Guard from a company of the Murcian Guard and provided the most direct access to the alley that beckoned to him at the far end of the plaza. With all that was going on in the square, the tension palpable and intensifying, no one bothered him. No one really paid any attention to him.

He was almost to the edge of the plaza, just a few dozen yards from the anonymity of the maze of streets that surrounded the Colosseum, when he heard a commanding shout at his back that sent an involuntary shudder up his spine and immediately brought back memories of all the time that he had suffered in the practice yard in the Corinthian Palace.

"At least Marden had the good grace to fight in the Pit before he died, yet you would slink away like a coward? I can't say that I'm surprised. You always preferred the easy way out, didn't you, Killen?"

Sourban, his long blond hair tied at the nape of his neck with a black leather band, stopped short, then reluctantly turned back in the direction from which he had come. His ice-cold blue eyes, normally free of emotion, revealed a hate that he couldn't hide. The tight smile that he offered his former mentor twisted into a sneer.

"The tide has turned, old man," said Sourban, ignoring the insult even though it burned deeply within him. "It's time for me to move on."

"Yes, and you were always one to follow the whims of the tide, weren't you?" challenged Jurgen Klines, Blademaster of the Royal Guard. Tall and thin, he appeared austere, almost ascetic when you took in his thin mustache and pointed beard, his cheeks free of whiskers. His thinning grey hair was pulled back and kept out of his bottomless green eyes thanks to a leather strap tied at the base of his neck that looked very similar to the one Sourban wore.

"I simply try to go in the direction of the current, old man, and right now the current is leading me this way," he said, motioning to the crowd of people at the border of the square and filling the alley just beyond.

Many of those people, drawn to the Colosseum by the conflict between the gladiators and the Royal Guard, now had begun to take notice of the confrontation occurring right in front of them, as did the soldiers standing in ranks on both sides.

"That will have to wait, Killen. We have unfinished business, you and I."

"You were better than me in the practice ring, but that was years ago when I was young and impetuous. Time hasn't been kind to you, Klines. Older. Slower. More emotional if you're still holding on to your grudges." Sourban chuckled, though it came across as somewhat forced. "Are you sure you want to do this, old man?"

"Dying to, Killen," replied the Blademaster. "You know that. You've known it ever since you took her from me."

"She chose me," Sourban replied heatedly, unable to keep the emotion from his voice.

"She didn't know the real you. Neither of us did. And we both paid for it, though her price was beyond imagining."

For almost a full minute, Sourban stared at the Blademaster, his escalating anger stoking his hate. Yet at the same time the voice in the back of his head that had proven so useful to him as a soldier, that warned him of impending danger, was telling him to ignore the old man, turn on his heel, and disappear into the crowd.

The Captain of the Royal Guard considered that option for just a moment, then discarded it. He couldn't do that. He had never been able to walk away from a challenge before, and the one that the old man offered to him now was too enticing to pass up.

Because the old man was right. There was unfinished business between them, and this might be his only chance to close accounts with his former mentor and friend. It certainly would be a satisfying way to end his time in Tintagel.

Even so, he still appreciated the risk associated with this challenge. Yes, the Blademaster was older, probably slower, yet he was still a dangerous opponent. So Sourban decided to take the approach that he believed would offer him the best chance at success. Smiling, Sourban nodded his head, and then gestured in a way that suggested that he had something else to say.

Then, he launched himself forward, closing the twenty feet to the Blademaster in just three bounds, pulling his sword from the sheath on his hip as he did so and slashing through the air with a cut that would have taken the Blademaster's head from his shoulders. If it had connected.

It didn't. Klines sidestepped easily, assuming his former pupil would make such a play. When he ducked out of the way Klines gave Sourban a slight nudge with his hip that threw him off balance.

Sourban fought to stay on his feet, fearing that he would cede the advantage to his opponent. That effort to recover gave the Blademaster the time to pull his sword from its sheath and face off against Sourban with an almost unnatural, definitely unnerving calm.

Growling in anger because of the ease with which Klines had avoided his surprise attack, Sourban leapt once again toward the Blademaster. Sourban brought his blade above his head, thinking to cut down into the flesh between the Blademaster's neck and shoulder blade. He realized midswing that his attempt would fail. The Blademaster already was moving out of the way. So Sourban turned the blade in his hand, instead seeking to slash his steel across Klines' hip.

That improvised effort at least forced the Blademaster to use his sword to defend himself, the ring of metal echoing in the plaza as the Blademaster parried Sourban's attack. The Captain of the Guard's assault didn't stop there. The clang of steel meeting steel sounded with a discordant tone as he tried to keep the Blademaster engaged and on the defensive, seeking the slightest of openings that he could use to slide his blade into Klines' flesh and overpower the old man quickly.

Sourban knew how good Klines was with a sword. The man wouldn't have earned the position of Blademaster otherwise. And he knew that the longer the combat continued, the greater the odds that he would be the one to die.

He had experienced the Blademaster's skill with a blade firsthand many times in the past, having sparred with him for what seemed like endless hours in the training circle. Sourban had learned a great deal from the old man, and he had viewed the Blademaster as someone he could learn from and emulate at the beginning of their relationship.

That all had changed over time. So much so that for the last several years Sourban had been seeking an opportunity to kill his former friend. He had spent most nights dreaming about it. About how he would do it. About the look on the old man's face when he realized that Sourban was the one who was about to punch his steel through his throat.

As he continued his incessant assault, blade whipping through the air with a speed that would be the envy of most any other sword fighter, a touch of fear settled in his stomach. He was beginning to comprehend that turning his dreams into reality might prove impossible.

The old man was defending his attacks with an irritating ease. It was as if the Blademaster could read his mind, his steel already occupying the space that Sourban's blade was about to before Sourban had even decided what he was going to do. That realization fed his fear, which quickly threatened to spiral out of control when he concluded that the old man was simply playing with him.

Sourban tried one more series of attacks, his blade a blur as it sought the old man's thigh, then shoulder, then hip, then hamstring. Despite his best efforts, Sourban's steel never scored the old man's flesh. It never even came close.

The Blademaster stood there calmly, barely moving his feet, oftentimes just flicking his wrist so that he could deflect Sourban's lunge or stab, tilting his body out of the way or pivoting to the side to avoid a slash or a cut, allowing Sourban to tire himself out while he conserved his energy. Sourban would have been impressed by the display if it wasn't his life that hung in the balance.

As his rising fear slowly turned to terror, Sourban sought desperately for some solution to his problem. It seemed that his impetuousness was still too much a part of his decision-making. Now, to counter that, he had to find a way to win this combat that he had so foolishly engaged in. He could have walked into the crowd and lost himself in the city. But he hadn't.

Just like the King and his doomed combat with the Volkun, Sourban had fallen into the same trap, allowing his ego to reign. And now that hubris was going to cost him his life. Unless he could find some way to distract the old man.

Stepping back to catch his breath, Sourban wasn't surprised to see the interest the duel had garnered. The soldiers standing in formation on the plaza closest to them, those of the Royal Guard and those of the Duchy Guards, watched the contest intently. Yet none demonstrated any desire to intervene.

For just a second, Sourban thought to order the soldiers of the Royal Guard to come to his aid. He scrapped the idea immediately. He could see that wasn't going to happen. Not with the looks of contempt and disgust on the soldiers' faces. They sensed how the combat was going to conclude, and it didn't bother them in the least. Rather, they seemed to think that it was the right ending for this story. The deserved ending.

Sourban turned to the only other course of action that came to mind that might actually allow him to live through this combat. He needed to make the old man angry, because only then would he find an opening. Only if the old man lost his focus, even if just for a heartbeat, would he stand a chance.

"You were right from the beginning," said Sourban with a malicious grin. "All those years ago, you were right. I killed Arisel."

Klines, who had been preparing to launch his first attack of the combat, one that he suspected would end the duel, stopped in his tracks, Sourban's admission freezing him.

Seeing the effect that his revelation had on the old man, Sourban continued, hoping that he could use the truth that he had kept hidden for years to his advantage now.

"She thought that she could break it off with me without any consequences. She thought that she could embarrass me like that without paying a penalty." Sourban's voice was soft, then he chuckled with a quiet fatalism. "She was wrong. She was mine. She will always be mine."

"You killed my daughter because you didn't want to be embarrassed? Because she was smart enough to see you for who you truly were?"

Recognizing the anguish in the old man's expression, Sourban's eyes flashed brightly. It looked like his play might be working. His opportunity would come, he believed, so now he just needed to be ready. He took a few steps closer to the Blademaster, who had lowered his sword so that the steel tip rested on the cobblestones.

"Yes, I killed your daughter," he said, the malice clear in his voice, "but not because of how she saw me. I killed her because she didn't see me for what I could become. And she didn't realize what that could be until my dagger had slid into her heart and I watched the light leave her eyes. But by then it was too late. She was gone, and she had gotten what she deserved."

Sourban struck when he recognized the look of devastation that appeared on the Blademaster's face, lunging at the old man, his sword aimed for his gut. Yet just as the Captain of the Guard had done so many times when he was younger and training with the Blademaster, he had miscalculated. Sourban's admission shocked Klines. It also freed him from the bonds of his tortured past.

Listening to Sourban's confession, a cold anger surged through the Blademaster, giving Klines a clarity and focus that for most was difficult to attain. It was as if Sourban attacked him in slow motion, and in response Klines turned on his heel and spun out of the way, Sourban's blade missing him by more than a dagger's length. But the Blademaster didn't miss. Klines drove his blade backward with two hands, slicing through Sourban's back, the tip sliding out of his gut.

The Captain of the Guard slipped off the Blademaster's sword and landed in a sprawl, his dark red blood staining the white stone of the plaza, his face revealing his shock at failing to kill the Blademaster. He had been so certain that his ploy would work, just as he had been so certain about so many things.

That misplaced arrogance had cost him his life.

Klines stared down at Sourban without remorse. He took no particular pleasure in killing, though he did feel some satisfaction and vindication with Sourban's death. His daughter's killer, as he had suspected but had never been able to confirm, had finally been brought to justice.

He watched the dying man try to murmur something with his last few breaths. He didn't care what Sourban had to say. Rather, in that moment Klines was thinking of his daughter. Of what she could have been if she had not met Sourban. Of how much he missed her. And of how much the Lady of the Southern Marches reminded him of her. He promised himself then that even though he had failed to do everything that he could to protect Arisel, he would do all that he could to protect Lady Winborne.

Klines turned away from Sourban to go back into the strangely silent Colosseum so that he could keep his newly made promise. Instead, he found Benin and several other Sergeants standing at attention.

"The Royal Guard stands with you, Blademaster," said Benin, pulling his blade from his scabbard and touching it to his forehead in a sign of respect, the other men with him doing the same. "Your orders ... Captain?"

Klines smiled wistfully, then nodded. With Sourban dead, he was the only other Captain in Tintagel with the rank and authority to command the Royal Guard. It seemed that the death of his daughter's murderer had just given him an added tool that he could use to assist Lady Winborne and the Volkun. And he meant to do just that.

2

TOGETHER AGAIN

They stood no more than six feet apart.

Aislinn Winborne, Lady of the Southern Marches, stared across the space at her Protector. She had not seen Bryen since she had freed him from most of the restraints of the silver Protector's collar that still circled his neck. Right before she had left the Southern Marches for Tintagel, intent on rescuing her father from King Beleron's grasp while avoiding her own planned nuptials to the man who had become her captor. The man who was now dead.

Somehow everything had worked out exactly as she wanted. Marden Beleron removed from the throne. Tetric gone, though not in the way that she had imagined. Her father safe.

How much of a role she played in it all, she couldn't say for sure. Because from what she had seen and heard the catalyst for the massive change that had swept through the Caledonian capital was the young man standing in front of her. Her Protector.

Bryen looked no different than when she last saw him. His prematurely white hair with just a few specks of brown left was a bit longer than it had been, now down past his shoulders. His grey eyes were just as sharp as always, though she did detect an unexpected spark there that she had never seen before.

He had walked up from the Pit, having cleaned the gore from his double-bladed spear. The same could not be said for himself.

His battered leather armor, covered in blood and nicked in dozens of places, testified to the brutality of the insurrection and the combat that he had just fought, and he carried at least a half dozen wounds on his arms and legs. She couldn't tell how many for sure because of all the grime and dirt mixed in.

Still, his injuries didn't seem to affect him. He was just as stoic and imperturbable as always.

Aislinn had already dueled Marden in the Pit, so she hadn't been worried for Bryen during the combat. At least that's what she kept telling herself while she watched, her heart in her throat several times until finally the King of Caledonia crumpled to the ground and stained the sand beneath him.

Aislinn wanted to say something as she stared at Bryen, she just wasn't sure what. She had never expected to see Bryen again. She had hoped that she would, but she had assumed that he would have taken full advantage of her having given him his freedom. He had spoken of wanting to see the Territories, of leaving Caledonia and the slavery that had been forced upon him and starting fresh where there were no expectations and memories were short.

Yet here he was. Rather than leaving the Kingdom as he could have, as he said he planned to do, he had come here instead.

Needing time to gather her thoughts, she allowed herself

to be swept up for a moment by the rush of activity all around her. Wounded gladiators and soldiers of the Royal Guard were being cared for by the physicks, Rafia and Sirius assisting. Noorsin Stelekel, the Duchess of Murcia, stood by the tunnel leading away from the Pit. From what she could hear, she was asking Cornelius Stennivere, Duke of the Three Rivers, and Wencel Roosarian, Duke of Roo's Nest, to work with the Blademaster so that the Royal Guard could leave the plaza and return to their barracks, escorted by the Duchy troops of course, to ensure that nothing untoward happened now that the Kingdom had lost its monarch.

Duchess Stelekel then asked the Blademaster to deal with the soldiers, not more than a few hundred, who had tied themselves to the King's Advisor. Tetric had been revealed for all to see while fighting Sirius. The man who he had been was no more, taken by the creature who had threatened the Kingdom since the First Ghoule War. Duchess Stelekel wanted to make sure that none of the soldiers who had aligned themselves with Tetric had been corrupted in a similar way.

In a surprisingly subdued manner, the Blademaster confirmed that the Captain of the Guard, Killen Sourban, and the greatest danger to maintaining peace in the city, was no longer a problem. So matters were proceeding apace.

Once the Royal Guard returned to their barracks, Duke Stennivere and Duke Roosarian were to position their troops around the capital in all the plazas and at other key locations in order to prevent any unrest, hoping to ensure that the riots of the last few months were a thing of the past. The Volkun's victory over the King certainly helped in that regard, sending a wave of jubilation through the city, the residents of Tintagel feeling as if a yoke had been lifted from their shoulders.

Nevertheless, the Blademaster also would ensure that his most trusted soldiers assumed responsibility for guarding the city wall and the gates. Then, the Blademaster would take several companies of soldiers to the grain silos and begin distributing what remained of that dwindling supply to those in need.

Duchess Stelekel already had put a plan in place for getting the bakeries started again, the cost to be paid for by the Crown. Such an effort should be enough to feed the city for a few days. By the time the grain ran out, more shipments of that and other needed foodstuffs would arrive when the first caravans began to appear in the next three days, Duchess Stelekel having made the arrangements before leaving Murcia for Tintagel.

"You've been busy," said Kevan Winborne with a deep laugh.

The Duke of the Southern Marches had come to stand behind his daughter after speaking with Tarin Tentillin, Captain of the Battersea Guard, and providing assistance to some of the injured gladiators. Kevan looked across at Noorsin Stelekel who, having given all the orders that needed to be issued, had walked over and now stood next to Aislinn's Protector.

The bloody, gore-splattered young man who had played such an integral role in freeing him and his daughter remained a challenge for Kevan that he was not ready to address. He did make an effort, however, giving the Protector a nod of respect, which was the best that he could do in that moment as his attention shifted to the woman who had begun to mend his broken heart.

The Duchess of Murcia was known for her keen mind. She was also exceedingly beautiful. Stepping forward, Kevan wrapped her in a hug, then kissed her, ignoring the shock that some of the people around them demonstrated at such an open display of affection from the usually reserved, taciturn Duke of the Southern Marches. In that moment, he realized how lucky he was to have a second chance, and he was not going to let the opportunity pass him by. His time as a captive taught him how fickle fate could be.

"I couldn't just pine for you as I made my way here," she replied with a smile, once Kevan reluctantly released her from his arms. "Besides, this uprising has been in the works for quite some time. Since I began receiving secret correspondence from your daughter, in fact."

Noorsin finally felt as if she could breathe once more when Kevan gave her a devilish grin that she never thought she'd see again. Her fear for him while he was held prisoner by Marden had become an unwelcome guest within her, and she was glad to finally let it go.

"Yes, Aislinn has certainly demonstrated her very unique skills during my incarceration," replied Kevan.

"So I've heard," said Noorsin. "I'm intrigued to learn more."

"You are being far too kind, Duchess Stele..." Aislinn started and then stopped, noticing Noorsin's raised eyebrow. "Noorsin," corrected Aislinn, remembering the Duchess' wish to remove the formality between them. "You are being much too kind, Noorsin."

"I'm being honest," Noorsin replied. "Don't sell yourself short, Aislinn. The information you provided was critical to our success, and you gaining the trust of the Blademaster and a good number of the Royal Guard proved invaluable by ensuring a minimum of bloodshed here and when we took the city."

Noorsin would have said more, but she could tell that

Aislinn's thoughts were on other matters. "And congratulations to the Volkun," Noorsin said, turning to Bryen. "Well done, young man. Well done, indeed. You never cease to impress me."

"Thank you, Duchess Stelekel. And thank you for your assistance. Without your timely arrival, my gladiators would have faced a grim future opposing the King and his Guard on our own."

"I don't know about that, Protector. From what I've seen while making my way here, you and your gladiators were more than a match for the King and Tetric, even with the steep odds against you." Noorsin then motioned for Kevan to take her arm. "Would you please join me, Kevan? The next conversation is not ours to be had."

The Lady of the Southern Marches nodded her thanks to Noorsin as the Duchess of Murcia led her father out of earshot, her eyes never leaving her Protector.

"Why haven't you gone to the physick?" asked Aislinn. There was so much that she wanted to say, yet her anxiety led her to the most obvious topic. The safest topic.

"It looks worse than it really is."

Bryen's voice was quiet and unexpectedly soft for someone so tall and imposing. He smiled, feeling a warmth and a familiar sense of connection upon seeing Aislinn again. Anyone could tell that she was beautiful with her long auburn hair, quick smile, and captivating dimples. He knew also that Aislinn's beauty hid the fighter just beneath the surface, as well as so much more.

"You say that every time you're hurt," Aislinn replied. "I know you have an incredible ability to heal but those wounds look like they might need a physick."

"I'll go in a minute. There are gladiators who are injured worse than I am." Bryen hedged for a moment, looking away from her so that he could recapture his thoughts. For more than six months, he had spent every waking moment with the Lady of the Southern Marches. So why did now feel so awkward? He turned his gaze once more to Aislinn and decided that there was no point in dancing around what he wanted to say. Better to just be honest. “I just wanted to make sure that you were all right.”

Aislinn didn’t know what to say upon hearing that. Her own emotions threatened to overwhelm her as she looked into Bryen’s eyes, which were usually cold grey orbs, yet now were soft, almost uncertain. She stepped forward and hugged him, pulling him in close and holding him tightly despite all the activity around them, then she stepped back suddenly.

Bryen didn’t know what to make of Aislinn’s action. Despite their time apart, there was still a closeness between them. There also was an unexpected distance that hadn’t been there before. Why that new, unwanted feeling had worked its way between them, he didn’t understand.

“You came to have the collar removed?” asked Aislinn, seeking to avoid the subject that she really wanted to discuss, yet at the same time didn’t.

“I came for you,” he replied in a moment of uncommon honesty.

Aislinn felt like all the emotions roiling within her were stuck in her throat, preventing her from responding. Despite the cool temperature that accompanied the falling night, a cold sweat dripped down her back and her hands had a mind of their own, twisting the fabric of her riding skirts, both clear signs that her nerves were on edge.

She didn’t know what to say. She corrected herself. She did know what she wanted to say. She just didn’t have the courage to say it. Not yet.

"It took you long enough," she replied, unwilling to reveal what was going through her mind, instead trying to extricate herself from an uncomfortable situation with humor.

Bryen smiled sadly, realizing that she wasn't ready for the conversation that they needed to have. So he looked down at himself, a few cuts here and there though nothing too deep or too serious. Most of the blood on him wasn't his own.

"It's been a long day. I'm a bit slower than I should be," he said with a tentative grin.

Rafia, who watched the entire exchange with great interest, nudged Sirius with her elbow. After helping with the wounded, the two Magii had come looking for Bryen. The capital was theirs, the gladiators were free, but there was still so much more to do.

"That was more awkward than when you found me naked in that swimming hole, Sirius."

"That was not my fault!" Sirius protested, grumpy after the stress and strain of the last few days, his failure to kill the Ghoule Overlord on the white sand leaving him seething in anger. "I didn't know you were there."

"I'm still not buying it, Sirius, even after all these years. You knew I was there. You had no other reason for being there than to catch me like that. You could have joined me from the beginning if you had just asked."

Sirius groaned in frustration as he once again allowed the Keeper of Haven to get under his skin. Why he permitted her teasing to affect him as it did, he couldn't explain, as it simply added to his already considerable frustration. She never failed to rile him up when she put her mind to it. And her latest comments forced him to look away. He was blushing profusely as he remembered that never-to-be-forgotten incident, and then his grimace turned to a smile as he recalled how much he had enjoyed it.

When he finally looked back at Rafia, her arched brow made the old Magus blush even more. A shout from Noorsin saved him from further embarrassment. The Duke of the Southern Marches had collapsed just a few feet from the entrance to the tunnel, a spiderweb of jet-black veins sprouting from beneath his collar, turning his neck a ghastly color.

"It's the collar," said Noorsin, who knelt down next to Kevan and immediately ripped open his shirt to confirm her suspicions, Aislinn there in an instant on his other side. Both women gasped in fear and shock. The tendrils had already begun to spread up the side of Kevan's face and down his chest, the threads pulsing a deep black with the taint of the Curse. "With Tetric gone, the Dark Magic is forcing its way into your father. Killing him. We need to get this collar off."

Rafia knelt down next to Aislinn, placing her hand on Kevan's chest and allowing the Talent to run through her fingers and then into him. Her frown deepened as she sensed the evil flowing through the collar and consuming the Duke.

"I don't know how to remove the collar, and even if I did, he could still die."

"He'll die if we don't," whispered Aislinn, her fear for her father's life revealed through a shaky voice.

"I know, child. We will try to remove the collar, and we will do all that we can for him. But it will not be easy."

"Blademaster!" called Noorsin, who pushed herself up off the ground.

Klines had come back into the Colosseum, several dozen soldiers at his back. He had gotten there right before the

Duke of the Southern Marches had dropped to the ground, and he understood without being told exactly what was needed.

"Six men and a stretcher," Klines ordered. "We need to get him to the Palace."

3

ON THE EDGE

Aislinn grasped her father's hand tightly, trying to will her own strength into him, her terror increasing by the second. As the soldiers attempted to lay the Duke onto a makeshift stretcher, he began flailing about, clearly in agony as the Dark Magic ravaged him. The web of black continued to spread up and down his body, strands of corruption now appearing on his throat and cheeks as well as his arms and abdomen.

"Please, we need to help him," begged Aislinn of anyone who might be able to assist.

Tears streaked down her cheeks as she stared at her father. She had reached for the Talent as soon as Noorsin had ripped open his shirt to reveal the expanding gossamer of darkness raging through him. Yet her attempt at helping her father was short-lived. Her skill in the Talent lay in directions other than healing.

Even recognizing that, the Dark Magic already coursing through her father's blood had repelled just her light touch as she attempted to locate and destroy the source of evil. Crestfallen, she realized that to take the approach that she had in mind, fighting the Curse within her father with the Talent, would lead to only one result. Her father's death.

"This wound appears similar to the one your young Protector overcame after his fight on the coastal road," said Noorsin. "So let's see if an approach similar to what I did then proves effective now."

Noorsin reached for the Talent. Usually, when the power of the natural world filled her, she felt an exhilaration, a charge of invigorating energy cascading through her that offered greater clarity, the colors of the world brighter, the sounds clearer, the smells sharper. Not this time. Now, she felt only purpose as she stared down at the man she loved, something that she only just admitted to herself.

"But I must warn you," continued Noorsin. "When I helped your young Protector, I was only helping, not healing. He used the Talent that I shared with him to heal himself. This Dark Magic your father battles right now is more insidious, more pernicious, and I don't know that I can heal him."

"All I ask is that you try," whispered Aislinn, who continued to maintain a strong grip on her father's hand so that he would know that he wasn't alone.

With her training at the Royal Medical School and strength in the Talent, the Duchess of Murcia was likely the most proficient healer in the Kingdom. So she began to apply her knowledge and skill to the obviously worsening Kevan as the web of black continued to expand. She had never seen Dark Magic advance so aggressively before. Usually, it would take hours rather than minutes to reach this point of infection.

Kevan's face had become paler in just the last few seconds, the tendrils of black reaching his neck, then his forehead, which coincided with him beginning to struggle for breath, his gasps for air now no more than a rattle in his throat. After a long wheeze, the Duke suffered a bout of choking that Noorsin feared would rip him in two. When he finally settled back on the stretcher, the shivering and shaking came to an end, though his skin had taken on a greyish cast and a thin stream of putrid black fluid oozed from his mouth and his eyes.

The calm that was so much a part of Noorsin's character began to waver as she watched his struggles worsen. Still, she began her work, attempting to burn away the filth of the Curse by sending tiny streams of the Talent into Kevan, as if she were a physick seeking to cut away befouled flesh. Much to her disgust and fear, she learned within seconds that her approach wouldn't bring the success that she so desperately wanted.

Incredibly the Dark Magic defended itself, blocking Noorsin's efforts. It was as if someone or something was controlling the Curse from afar, fighting her with it, keeping her from doing anything that could remove the rapidly worsening corruption. She realized, just as Aislinn had discovered, that to fight the Dark Magic as she wanted to would simply accelerate Kevan's demise.

So she tried a different approach, seeking to grab hold of the Dark Magic and draw it like poison from a wound. She focused her efforts first near Kevan's neck, where the source of the Dark Magic lay against his skin. Time after time she failed to seize it with the Talent. The Curse dodged every effort she made to grasp it and pull it free.

She decided to try the same approach somewhere else, selecting a tendril on his forehead. Yet again the Curse easily wriggled away from her. It was the most remarkable thing she had ever seen, and under other circumstances would have incited her intellectual curiosity and desire to learn why it was happening. Now all she wanted was to destroy the Dark Magic.

Nothing she tried was working, and she was quickly running out of ideas. It was as if the Curse was teasing her. It was testing her abilities and finding them lacking. Her all-pervading calm began to twist into panic. Her composure threatened to shatter as she continued unsuccessfully to use the Talent to cleanse Kevan, the Curse immune to her efforts and now spreading down his legs, his heart rate increasing to a dangerous level as his body fought a desperate but losing battle.

"Rafia, I need your help. Now."

The Keeper of Haven knelt beside Noorsin, reaching for the Talent as she did so. "What is it? Can't you burn it away?"

"Nothing that I would normally do in a situation such as this is working," Noorsin explained rapidly in tight, clipped sentences. "The Dark Magic is resisting whatever I do to cure Kevan. It's almost as if someone is controlling the Curse from afar. I can't even destroy a speck of the infection. It's playing a game with me. This has never happened before. Yes, the Dark Magic has resisted when confronted with the Talent. It has never actively escaped the Talent as if it has a mind of its own. Nothing I have tried has worked, and I don't know what else to try."

Rafia swept the Talent over Kevan, who was now completely unresponsive, sweat pouring from his body and mixing with the thin black streams oozing now from his nose and ears.

"I can see it," Rafia said through gritted teeth. "The Curse is coming from the collar. I knew it would be linked to him since this collar functions similarly to that of a Protector's, but this blasted metal is different."

Rafia pulled in more of the Talent as she continued to explore the Dark Magic that was consuming Kevan.

"The Curse is shielded somehow, and you're right. It appears to have a sentience tied to some other creature. I can only assume the Ghoule Overlord since he's the one who likely created this monstrous tool. That's why this is so difficult. The Dark Magic in the Duke is responding to the commands of the Ghoule Overlord, which the beast may have set within the Curse when the collar was affixed around Kevan's neck. And that's only part of the story. The shield protecting the Curse is the main problem. We need to penetrate the shield to get through to the Dark Magic, but I worry that the Duke doesn't have the strength to survive a fight like that. He's been afflicted by the Curse for too long, and he's too weak."

"Try, Rafia," said Noorsin, tears beginning to stream down her cheeks as the full import of what was likely about to happen struck her a vicious blow. "You must. He dies if we don't."

Rafia simply grunted in response, seeking to find some crack that she could manipulate in the shield surrounding the Dark Magic. Her aggravation and worry increased, though she kept both under control. She couldn't locate a weakness. That wasn't unexpected considering the likely source of this Dark Magic, so she didn't allow that discovery to faze her.

She then sent several concentrated streams of the Talent into Kevan, seeking to break the shield with a focused force, much like a miner who based on years of experience could identify the perfect place to strike a wall with his pick-axe and cause the entire face to shatter as a result. Again, nothing. The Curse was too strong within Kevan and too well guarded.

So she took the same approach as Noorsin did when she first tried to help Kevan, hoping that she would have better luck than her former student had. Using the Talent, she reached for the Curse, trying to grasp it as she would a loose thread and then pull it free.

It was like trying to grab onto a slimy eel. Every time she thought she had the Dark Magic between her fingers, the Curse simply slipped away. Through it all, as the seconds passed, Kevan's condition worsened, his breath becoming more ragged and weaker, as if there was some tremendous pressure on his chest caused by the Dark Magic raging within him that was slowly and mercilessly crushing him.

"I'm not doing any better than you, Noorsin," grumbled Rafia in irritation. "This is not just the Curse. It's something more as you said. Something more powerful. Tetric didn't do this. If what we saw in the Pit was real, this evil was placed upon him by the Ghoule Overlord. It's like the Curse combined with the very essence of that beast, as if we're fighting him and not just his Dark Magic." She looked up from Kevan to Noorsin, the look of anguish on the Duchess' face confirming her true feelings for the Duke of the Southern Marches. "I'm sorry, Noorsin. I don't know how to combat this."

"Please, you have to do something," pleaded Aislinn, tears streaming down her cheeks as she watched quietly and with growing apprehension as the two Magii tried to save her father yet demonstrated little success. "You must. Please, you must."

Bryen had watched dispassionately as Rafia and Noorsin strove to help the man who had continued his enslavement by bringing him from the Pit to the Southern Marches. He had no love for the Duke, though the misery and fear that Aislinn was experiencing tore at him. As the scene unfolded before him, for some unknown reason, another of Declan's many, often irritating sayings kept playing through his mind: "You must do what you must do."

So instead of simply waiting for the Duke's inevitable end, from where he was standing Bryen used the Talent to study the collar encircling the Duke's neck. He could certainly appreciate the irony of the situation. The man who had collared him now wore a collar himself and likely was dying because of it.

Rather than acknowledge the unbecoming sense of comeuppance that trailed through Bryen's mind, he began to think about what had been done to the Duke of the Southern Marches. He assumed that if this blackened steel collar functioned in a fashion similar to the Protector's collar around his neck, then proximity to the holder of the collar was essential.

With the Ghoule Overlord having disappeared -- and he was certain that this was not Tetric's work after having judged the power within him, which didn't measure up to the strength required to do something like this -- Bryen assumed that connection had been broken, which in turn had released the Dark Magic that had been infused within the collar.

He had read about something like this when he was in the Library of the Magii on Haven, so he agreed with Rafia's assessment that a hidden hand played a role in what was happening to the Duke. A final bad twist of fate, a poisoned pill essentially.

The collar was impressive in its design, and it demonstrated a knowledge of Dark Magic that was frightening when fully contemplated. Then Bryen realized the trick. Focusing on the person infected by the Curse, in this case Duke Winborne, would do little good.

Rather, you needed to focus on the source, on what was guiding the Dark Magic. You needed to concentrate on the artifact that managed the flow of the Curse into the victim. The only way to overcome the Curse was to destroy the blackened collar or drain the Dark Magic from it.

"Rafia, Duchess Stelekel, please move back."

Before either Magii could respond, Bryen knelt next to the Duke, Aislinn still holding her father's clammy hand, knowing with a growing certainty that she was about to lose him. Bryen gave Aislinn a brief nod, attempting to say with the gesture that everything would be all right, even though he wasn't sure that it would be. Then he placed his hand on the collar, which continued to pulse a deep black, as if it was feeding off of Duke Winborne, which Bryen believed that it actually was.

Recognizing the danger presented by the collar, Bryen took several seconds to confirm what he had thought he had seen during his initial examination of the artifact with the Talent. The collar crafted by the Ghoule Overlord was slightly different than the one he wore, as a tiny pin hidden beneath the front of the collar pierced the Duke's flesh, serving as the means by which the Dark Magic contained within the collar flowed into him. Ingenious in a horrendously malicious sort of way.

That was the key, Bryen realized. That was the weakness. Rather than having the Dark Magic continue to flow into the Duke, Bryen needed to give the Curse another outlet. So he did. Opening himself to the Seventh Stone within him, he used the Talent to fasten onto that single sharp point that was hidden from view.

The depth of the Dark Magic that he encountered sent a wave of revulsion through Bryen. He almost collapsed next to the Duke, never expecting so much of the Curse could be placed in such a small artifact. Before he dropped to the ground, Rafia grabbed onto his shoulders, helping to hold him upright, Bryen keeping his hand on the collar so that he could maintain the connection that he needed.

Once he regained his equilibrium, having mastered the skill of manipulating Dark Magic behind a thin layer of the Talent, Bryen did that now, allowing the Seventh Stone to pull on the Curse contained within the collar. At first, the Dark Magic resisted. That resistance rapidly disappeared, even the huge amount of the Curse contained within the collar no match for the strength of the Seventh Stone. Once the artifact had gotten a taste of the Dark Magic, it drew on the corrupted energy hungrily, pulling it faster and faster into Bryen, who paid careful attention to ensure that the Ghoule Overlord's power remained safely behind the barrier that he had built within himself to guarantee that he avoided even the slightest touch of the Curse.

As he did so, Rafia gripped his shoulder with a stronger hand, offering her support and understanding the difficulty involved in what he was doing, while Noorsin stared in amazement as she sensed what was required of the Protector to drain the artifact of its tainted energy.

Finally, after several long minutes, Bryen completed the first part of his assignment. He had extracted the Dark Magic from the collar, which had been reduced to nothing more than a cold piece of metal. Yet Bryen still had more to do.

He needed to remove the remnants of the Curse from within the Duke without killing him. So how to shatter the shield that protected the Dark Magic that had already flowed into Aislinn's father? Attacking it with the Talent had done nothing but provoke a response. What could he do that hadn't been attempted already?

After thinking about his dilemma for a few seconds, using the Talent, Bryen searched for the weakest point of the infection, much as he did when he healed Duchess Stelekel after Tetric had attacked her in the Broken Citadel. He scanned as quickly as he could, understanding that time was running out for the Duke. Thankfully, he found what he was looking for.

The newest strand that had appeared, running straight up the Duke's forehead. He had watched it spread. As the Dark Magic expanded, it stretched the shield, weakening it for a split second in the very space where it grew. So Bryen waited as patiently as he could for his chance, fixated on that pulsing strand.

When that thread began to inch higher up the Duke's forehead toward his scalp, Bryen struck with a stream of the Talent thinner than that of a hair, shooting the needle into the strand and piercing the shield at its weakest point. What happened next was much like what occurred when a water bag was pricked with a pin, a tiny stream of liquid shooting out with great force. In this case it was the Curse that burst from the minute hole, the Seventh Stone within Bryen absorbing the tainted power greedily.

It didn't take long for Bryen to complete his work. As the Seventh Stone took in the Dark Magic, the web of black that had spread across the Duke's body slowly receded. As it did, the sable substance oozing from his eyes, ears, and nose dried up and flaked away, the Duke's breathing and color improving.

When the last of the Curse had been removed, Bryen released the Talent and took his hand from the Duke's chest, satisfied that Aislinn's father was healed now that he was breathing regularly and a missing warmth had returned to his body.

As Bryen rose to his feet, feeling more exhausted than he did after fighting in the Pit for several hours, he caught the look that passed between Rafia, who remained at Kevan's side next to Aislinn, hugging her father with unrestrained joy, and Sirius, who stood on the other side of their small gathering with a large smile marring his usually crabby expression.

He couldn't say with any certainty what the look that passed between the two Magii meant, though he could guess. With Tetric no longer a concern and Bryen in better control of the Dark Magic contained by the Seventh Stone thanks to his acquisition of the Spear of the Magii, he believed that their thoughts had turned to larger and more pressing issues.

With the Ghoule Overlord now revealed, no one had any doubt that his Legions would attempt to break through the Weir. The only way to prevent those attacks, which would threaten the very existence of Caledonia, was to repair the barrier created by the Ten Magii. Bryen had seen it in Sirius' eyes, having learned to read the old Magus quite well after spending so much time with him during the last few months.

He had used the Seventh Stone to heal the Duke of the Southern Marches. At the same time, he had passed an unexpected test, at least in the eyes of Rafia and Sirius. The collar contained a large amount of Dark Magic, though certainly not what would be required if Bryen were to attempt to rebuild the failing magical barrier. Even so, they already knew his strength in the Talent, augmented by the Seventh Stone, and they had assumed that strength would transfer to his manipulation of the Curse.

No, what had impressed the two Magii was what would also be required if he were to reconstruct the Weir. A deft, light touch. Precision. Something that had been a challenge for him as he learned to apply the Talent. Something that he had just demonstrated while saving the Duke's life.

"Why would you do this?" Aislinn asked, who could barely get the words out. "After everything he put you through. After he put a collar on you."

"He didn't deserve to die this way," Bryen replied simply, distracted from his thoughts by Aislinn's question. "Besides, it was the right thing to do."

With nothing more to say, Bryen walked toward the Pit and the gladiators' stockade where he could clean and heal his wounds and maybe find some clothes not covered in blood.

4

TWO SEPARATE PATHS

Even though it was late summer, there were already a few inches of snow on the ground, and the dark grey clouds, heavy and leaden, promised several more hours of a hard snowfall. This wasn't unusual. Not at the northern edge of the Shattered Peaks. Here where the mountains soared several miles into the air and the Lost Land fell away on one side and the Winter Pass pointed to the south.

It would have been strange to not have snow now. In fact, there were only a few months during the year when the Winter Pass was navigable because of the harsh weather and winds.

That's why the thousands of Ghoules stood patiently on the northern side of the flickering Weir. The time for entering the lands of man and making it through a gap not obstructed as it usually was by snow a hundred feet deep was now. Much of the snow that had piled up during the past year had melted, feeding the dozens of streams that snaked through the land and emptied onto the Breakwater Plateau.

The Ghoules would have two months at most, probably

a bit less. Still, that should give them enough time to begin feasting on their prey. Assuming, of course, that they made it through the magical barrier and the danger that lurked within it.

The Ghoules who stood among the gullies and fissures that led to this preferred spot among the mountains where the Elders created the portals that would allow them to brave the Weir knew the cost that some of them would be required to pay. There were never any guarantees when trying to cross the Weir other than the fact that some of them would die.

Because though the Weir was weakening, the usually greyish cast to the barrier replaced at times by an inconsistently flashing white and black that reflected the two powers it had been constructed from, the magical barricade still ensured that any creature of Dark Magic trapped within it would die an excruciating death.

Some of the Ghoules called traversing the Weir walking the firepit, as they sprinted through the ashes of all the Ghoules who had tried to cross before them who were unfortunate enough to be caught by the power of the Magii.

The white-hot energy of the Talent would char the Ghoules to a crisp, but slowly. First, they would be caught by a tendril of that blasted energy, fixed in place, unable to move a muscle. Then their flesh would begin to burn, then char, then flake off as it turned to ash. Their muscles and organs would follow, and then all that would remain would be their bones, which wouldn't last long, the heat of the humans' magic leaving nothing but cinder in its wake.

They knew what to expect. Many Ghoules had seen it happen with their own eyes.

It was inevitable. Despite the skill of the Elder Ghoules at creating temporary paths through the Weir, there was always a cost to bear. A third of the Ghoules who braved the passage were certain to die, and a quarter of the Elders giving them the opportunity to either die or enter the lands to the south would lose their lives as well, the Weir lashing out arbitrarily at those seeking to manipulate it.

Yet despite the strong likelihood of death, still the beasts came. They had been summoned here. And they would never refuse the demands of the one who required so much of them, for to do so promised a death worse than the one that could be found if caught in the Weir.

So they stood there in the wind and the snow. Waiting. Ignoring the cold and the wet. Anticipating the glory and the prey to be taken. Because there was only one reason why they had all been summoned to this desolate, treacherous place.

They were to be sent into the lands of the humans, whose skill with the blade was poor and whose flesh was soft and sweet. If some of them were to die in order to partake of that opportunity, to finally make a bone knife and claim their place in the Ghoules' warrior society, then it was a risk that they were willing to take.

The snow was almost three inches deeper by the time a spinning mist of black appeared right in front of the Weir. The Dark Magic expanded quickly until it was large enough for one of the massive Giants of the Rime to walk through.

Instead, a Ghoule more than eight feet tall appeared, his anger wafting off him and melting the snowflakes that tried to settle on his flowing brown robes. In his right claw he gripped his staff of twisted black ash that was taller than he was, the smooth wood curling around a black diamond the size of the creature's fist. Besides his height, the primary distinction between this beast and the others assembled below him was the carving in his forehead. A black diamond to match the one set upon his staff. The mark of the Ghoule Overlord.

In a flash of black the portal disappeared. The commander of the Ghoule Legions had returned to his full height upon revealing himself in the Pit, though pieces of the fleshy shell that had been Tetric still clung to him. Disgusted that the remnants of the weak human remained to remind him of his failure, the Ghoule Overlord waved his staff above his head in a strangely gentle motion, a thin mist of the Curse spinning out and wrapping itself around the huge beast. The Dark Magic spun faster and faster, no more than a blur to the eye for several seconds, before it calmed and slowly faded away.

The Ghoule Overlord smiled broadly as he stretched his back, revealing his sharp, serrated teeth. He felt good. He felt like himself again. Forcing himself into Tetric's skin had been a challenge to begin with and had proven to be exceedingly uncomfortable. Still, it had served its purpose. And he was glad that now all that remained of the King's Advisor was a memory.

He didn't achieve all that he had wanted to while in the land of his quarry, though his time there had been well spent. He had learned a great deal about his enemies. About those who would oppose him. Their strengths. Their weaknesses. How to exploit both.

He had hated having to wear the skin for so long, although he could have benefited from more time playing the role of Tetric. He admitted that reluctantly.

Despite his best efforts, the charade had come to an end. All because a Magus somehow had sniffed him out.

The Magus who had challenged him in the Colosseum had looked familiar. After the combat with the wild-eyed human and then the Protector, followed by his escape from the Colosseum, he remembered him. Vaguely, since it had been so long ago. That Magus had fought him during the Ghoules' first invasion of the lands of the humans.

As a younger man, the Magus had gotten lucky in that he had survived his Elders' onslaught, many of the members of the Order of the Magii dying during that war. And the old man had gotten lucky once again. Lucky that the boy had appeared when he did to fight for him on the white sand of the Pit.

The boy he had met before in the Sanctuary and had thought would be an easy kill after that encounter. But the boy wasn't an easy kill as he had thought would be the case, and now that worried the Master of the Ghoules.

Of course the boy wasn't really a callow youth, was he? The Ghoule Overlord was familiar with the customs and practices of the humans. He had studied them for centuries, wanting to understand them so that it would make his conquest of their lands an easier task. He had recognized the collar of the Protector around the boy's neck. So the Overlord's opponent really wasn't soft like most of the other humans.

He couldn't be. Not having been made a Protector. Not having so much of the Talent surging within him. A quantity of power that dwarfed that of any of the Magii the Ghoule Overlord had faced before.

But it wasn't just the Talent that the Ghoule Overlord had discovered while fighting the Protector. No, he had identified a deeper power. A more devastating power. A power that sang to him.

Clearly, the Protector was a problem. He needed to be removed. But the Protector was also what the Ghoule Overlord wanted. What he needed. Because the Ghoule Overlord knew it now. He understood now what had happened. He had confirmed his suspicions when he fought the Protector on the white sand.

At the beginning of the combat, the Overlord had thought that the Protector had the Seventh Stone in his possession, and that once he killed the Protector, he could take the Seventh Stone and be gone. Then he realized that he was mistaken.

The Protector didn't have the Seventh Stone in hand.

The Protector was the Seventh Stone.

And the Ghoule Overlord had to have the Seventh Stone. His Ghoules needed the Seventh Stone. Gaining the Seventh Stone was the only way to destroy the Weir and open the path for all his Legions to march on the lands of men.

Having stared long enough through the Weir toward the gap that led through the Shattered Peaks all the way down to the Breakwater Plateau, the Ghoule Overlord turned away from the magical barrier and looked back down the slope that ran to the north.

The Ghoule Legions waited for him. Thousands of Ghoules for as far as he could see.

Eager. Expectant. Hungry.

The Overlord issued a quick command in the guttural Ghoule language of hisses, barks, and grunts that accommodated their teeth and the shape of their mouths. A handful of Elders trotted up to him, bowing their heads in respect.

"The humans are weak at the moment, weaker than they ever have been in the past."

"How so, Master?" asked Nibli, the Elder, taller than all the others by a head, serving as the Overlord's second in command.

"Their King is dead."

"You killed him, Master?"

"No," replied the Ghoule Overlord with a vicious grin. "The Seventh Stone did before I had the chance."

The Elders stared at him in disbelief.

"How did that happen, Master?" asked Nibli.

They understood the ancient artifact's properties. They did not comprehend how it could do such a thing on its own.

The Ghoule Overlord took a moment to explain. "The Seventh Stone has merged with a human. I could sense it. The Seventh Stone and this human are one."

"How is that possible?"

"I don't know, Nibli. What occurred doesn't matter. What does matter is that we obtain the Seventh Stone. Kill this human and we can extract the Seventh Stone from him."

"How will we take this human, Master? Finding him is certainly possible, we can track the Curse within him, but I assume that he will be surrounded by guardians. The humans must know the importance of the Seventh Stone."

"This human will come to me. I will nudge him in the direction that I want him to go, and he will come to me."

Nibli nodded, beginning to understand. "Yes, Master. Even so, if the armies of the humans come with him ..."

"The armies of the humans will have their own concerns," said the Ghoule Overlord, cutting in as he struggled to maintain what little patience he still had left. Nibli was excellent at following his commands, but he was not very creative with his thinking and had a difficult time with strategy. That didn't bother the Overlord so long as Nibli didn't test his patience too often. The Elder was not a thinker. He was a hunter and a killer. Point him in the right direction and he would do what was required of him. Just don't ask him to figure out in which direction he should be pointed. "While I meet the Seventh Stone and make him mine, you will lead the Legions through the Winter Pass."

Nibli nodded, his comprehension improving slowly. "We are the threat that will draw the human armies while you lure the human who is the Seventh Stone to a different location."

"Correct, Nibli. Besides, there is only one place the Seventh Stone will go."

The Ghoule Elder gave the Overlord a satisfied grin.

The Overlord then continued to explain what would be required of the Elders and their soldiers for his plan to work.

"The weather will remain good for two months, no more. The snows will lessen. The winds will ease. The pass will be open for those willing to risk its dangers. We must take advantage of that break. We must have the Legions through the Weir then down into the Pass before the weather worsens. To pull their armies and their attention here, the Legions must be through the Weir and be in a position to threaten the human lands."

Nibli and the other Elders nodded that they understood what would be required of them and their warriors.

"We must have as many of the Legions gathered here through the Weir within the next month to have any hope that our Ghoules are far enough south to attract the humans' interest."

"Yes, Master," said Nibli, though his scrunched up face demonstrated his concern. "Master, even with the Weir weakening, it will cost us a huge number of fighters and Elders to force through so many at one time."

The Overlord ignored his second's concerns. "Based on the time frame that I gave you, Nibli, how many Legions can we get through the Weir?"

"Master, remember the cost ..."

"I know the cost, Nibli. The cost is not important. What is important is that we take advantage of the opportunity that has been presented to us. The Caledonian Kingdom is leaderless. The various Duchies will be vying for power. The humans' attention will be diverted just by that. We will make their problems worse. We will distract them even more and divide their attention. They will focus on the Legions here, which means that I can focus on guiding the Seventh Stone where I want it to go. And once I do, I will take the Seventh Stone and use it to our benefit. This cursed barrier will no longer keep us from achieving what we set out to do a thousand years ago. We will conquer the lands to our south, and we will feast on the humans. But to do that we must have as many Legions south of the Weir as we can before the weather turns against us. Now tell me, Nibli. How many Legions can we get through the Weir in the time frame that I've given you?"

The Elder Ghoule knew that now was not the time to protest or dissemble, not if he wanted to keep his head on his shoulders. "Ten Legions, Master."

The Ghoule Overlord thought about that for a moment. Ten thousand Ghoules. Even if the humans brought twice as many soldiers to challenge his Legions, it would not be enough. It would not be enough if they gathered thirty thousand to contest against his fighters. His Ghoules were too fast, too strong, too deadly. Any of his Ghoules could kill half a dozen humans in less than a minute, no matter how skilled the humans might be. He nodded his head slowly, then looked at Nibli with a feral grin.

"Make it happen, Nibli. Ten Legions in the time that I told you. Ten Legions in one month. They must be through to the southern tip of the Winter Pass a month after that.

They are to hold there. They are not to go beyond. The humans will learn of the Legions and meet you in the Pass. You are to hold them there. Keep them busy. Give me the time that I need to make the Seventh Stone mine."

"Yes, Master. It will be as you command."

"Do not disappoint me, Nibli. You know the cost of failure."

"I do, Master. Ten Legions by the end of the month. Ten Legions through the Winter Pass before the snow falls."

"Good," replied the Ghoule Overlord. "Before you begin, give me a dozen packs of our best fighters. While you are preparing the way for our invasion, I will need some help in making sure that the Seventh Stone goes where I want him to. And who knows, perhaps I can kill him along the way. Perhaps I can end this sooner than I expected."

5

FINALLY FREE

"You know, I never expected that this scheme would work," said Sirius. "I must say that I'm quite pleased with the end result."

"Why ever not? Why would you ever doubt that the Volkun could start a rebellion by engaging the services of only a few hundred slaves who would topple in just a day a dynasty three centuries in the making?" asked the Magus who walked by his side, her curly black hair constantly breaking loose from her scarf and falling across her eyes. Sirius watched as she tucked the loose strands behind her ears, always captivated by the habit. "Why would you ever doubt that the fastest and most efficient revolt in the history of Caledonia would also help us to discover that the Kingdom's worst and most deadly enemy had a hold on the Crown? Looking back on it now, it was child's play."

"You can't be serious," protested Sirius, his ancient eyes crinkling in sarcastic disagreement. "It was a long shot to begin with."

"I'm not being serious, Sirius," replied Rafia with a mischievous smile. "You should know me better than that.

This plan of ours had little chance of success. And yet we made it work. We have the Volkun to thank for that as well as the unexpected assistance of several others who all contributed at exactly the right time. Sometimes things work. Sometimes they don't. And sometimes, very rarely, they work perfectly."

"Then why are you mocking me?"

"I'm not mocking you," answered Rafia in what she hoped was a placating tone. "I'm just having a little fun. It's what we do. Tease one another."

"I must say that you are the most difficult woman I have ever met," said Sirius, his smile betraying the fact that he was enjoying the banter and the challenge of their engagement.

"You've said that many times, Sirius," Rafia confirmed with a smile and a nod. "Yet here we are, still working together after all this time."

Aislinn, who walked with the two Magii, bit her lip to prevent herself from laughing. The night before, she had told Rafia and Sirius what she wanted to do. Although they argued strenuously against her decision, there was no changing her mind. So they had agreed to accompany her.

As the three Magii walked into the gladiators' compound, Aislinn was content to allow the muted disagreement between Rafia and Sirius to continue, knowing that this was the most common way that they interacted, the constant squabbling a necessary part of their relationship. Her thoughts turned to the person she had come to visit as their wrangling carried on.

The last time that Aislinn had been here, she had been greeted by the steady drumbeat of motion, the gladiators preparing for their combats that would occur on the week-end. She had found it difficult to enter the practice yard then, despite the Blademaster accompanying her, the soldiers stationed at the gates unwilling to grant them passage until the Master of the Gladiators appeared.

But now, just a few months gone, they had walked right through the open gates and onto the training ground with barely anyone in sight. Somewhat astonished by how quiet the yard was, Aislinn led Sirius and Rafia into the small tunnel that led toward the Colosseum, the massive arena placing the gladiators' barracks in shadow for much of the day.

Every other time that she had set foot in the arena, there had always been a buzz of activity partnered with an undercurrent of noise. Now, a few days after the revolt that had toppled the Crown, there was nothing but silence. The combats had come to an end and the gladiators had been freed, many taking up residence in the soldiers' barracks in the Corinthian Palace, though a few still remained here, trying to decide what they would do next or simply not comfortable anywhere else.

As she exited the tunnel and walked out into the Pit, Sirius and Rafia still contesting with one another behind her, Aislinn wasn't surprised to find Bryen here, her Protector standing on the white sand, lost in thought.

Although all of the gladiators detested the Pit, it was still familiar to them, offering them some strange comfort despite the blood that they had lost and the pain that they had experienced here. In consequence, the enclosed space often helped to settle them. Aislinn knew that Bryen was struggling with something, a decision that needed to be made. Though he hadn't shared with her what the matter involved, she could guess.

She ran her eyes over him, a bout of nerves almost making her change her mind about why she had come. Of course, now was not the time to be afraid. Now was the time to demonstrate strength and confidence. Otherwise, what she was about to propose would fail before they even began.

"I wanted to return this to you," said Aislinn, holding out a small item, the movement breaking Bryen's train of thought.

He looked down, then took it from her, smiling. *The Revenge of the Lost Count*. His favorite book.

"How did you know?" asked Bryen, who slowly came back to himself, his eyes fixed on the rubble littering the stands above him, seeing everything and nothing both at the same time.

"When I met Declan for the first time, he gave this to me," she said with a gentle smile, the two Magii still arguing behind her now more of a distraction than a form of amusement. "So did you obtain your revenge?"

She thought that perhaps he had gained it now that he had freed the gladiators and removed Marden from the throne. When he frowned, she wasn't surprised by the answer that she received.

"Not quite," Bryen said. "I still have some unfinished business."

He chose not to tell her that as he stood in the Pit, he had been replaying in his mind his combat against the Ghoule Overlord, trying to determine if he could have done anything differently that would have aided his efforts to kill the beast. So far, he believed that he had approached the duel the right way, identifying little that he would have changed with respect to his approach.

Bryen admitted grudgingly that the Ghoule Overlord had escaped him because of his skill with the Curse, something that he needed to be prepared for the next time that they met. And he was certain that they would meet again.

The Ghoule Overlord wanted him. He wanted the Seventh Stone.

Bryen wanted another chance at the beast. His business wouldn't be complete until he had killed the monster responsible for the death of his parents.

"Thank you," said Aislinn, still avoiding the subject that sent a slight shiver of fear through her and hoping to remove the strange look from Bryen's eyes. She assumed it was an expression that he wore when he fought in the Pit, because it was quite intimidating.

"For what?" asked Bryen, not understanding.

"For saving my father. You didn't have to do that."

Bryen simply nodded in response. He could have been honest with her and told her that he didn't do it for her father. He did it for her. Even though he sensed that she knew why he really did it, he wasn't ready to tell her that. He didn't know if he ever would be. That was in large part because he could tell that she wasn't ready to acknowledge what it would mean if he told her his true feelings.

To prevent the conversation from continuing in a potentially uncomfortable direction, he turned his attention to the two Magii standing a few feet behind Aislinn, bickering as was their wont. After having spent so much time with Sirius and Rafia, it would have been strange to not have them act in this way. The ceaseless back and forth could be entertaining, at least in the beginning. After a while, it simply became annoying.

"I take it that this isn't a social visit," Bryen said.

"Not from our perspective," said Sirius, who stepped forward, Rafia right behind him.

"No, I wanted to talk with you about something," said Aislinn, cutting in before Sirius could continue.

"What did you want to talk about?" asked Bryen, a touch

of worry running through him. He was just as happy to avoid the uncomfortable matter that hung between them as she was.

"The Protector's collar."

Bryen looked at her for a moment with a shrewd glint in his eye. "You want to remove it."

"I wanted to discuss with you removing it," she replied. "Because it's linked to me, I'm the only one who can remove it. Rafia was telling me what you had learned about the collar while you were at Haven. She explained to me how the collar could be detached and how I was the one who needed to do it."

"Did she explain the potential cost of doing so? What could happen to you? To both of us?"

"You know I did," answered Rafia.

Aislinn examined the scarred gladiator as she had so many times before to gauge his reaction to her suggestion. She had spent so much time with him that she felt a closeness to Bryen that she had never experienced with anyone else. Yet it was only now that she was seeing the very faint, thin black scorch mark that had joined the scars on his neck and cheek. A sand cat right here in the Pit, he had said. This new mark definitely did not come from a sand cat. She'd have to ask him about it at the right time, because she had a feeling as to how he had gotten it.

"Why do you hesitate now?" asked Rafia. "You were quite intent on having the collar removed when you first appeared on my dock."

"Circumstances were different then," he replied. "We didn't know the risk involved when attempting to take it off. I don't want to put Lady Winborne in any unnecessary danger." The brooding gladiator shook his head in frustration. "You said that removing the collar has only been attempted twice, and that each time the Protector and the person they were charged with guarding died."

"Yes, but that doesn't mean it can't be done," interrupted Sirius. "Two examples don't prove a possibility."

"You're right," agreed Bryen. "But that doesn't mean it should be done. It doesn't mean that the risk is worth it."

"Still a Protector, I see," murmured Rafia. Her words were quiet, so that only Aislinn could hear. "I wonder if his fear for you has gone well beyond the requirements of the collar."

Rafia's private observation made the words that Aislinn was about to offer catch in her throat.

"I couldn't agree with you more, lad," said Sirius. "There's no reason to take the risk."

"Whose side are you on?" demanded Rafia, fixing her sharp gaze on Sirius.

"What do you mean?" replied the Magus, somewhat perplexed as to why Rafia's ire had sparked so suddenly.

"You're arguing both sides," said Rafia. "You're supporting Aislinn and then Bryen. That's not helping anything."

"I'm not supporting anyone. I'm simply agreeing when relevant and good points are made."

"There is every reason to take the risk," interrupted Aislinn, before Rafia could continue berating Sirius.

Bryen looked at his former charge, his face softening as he stared into her eyes. There was an emotion there that he was afraid to interpret.

"Aislinn, why are you so willing to take this risk? You've already reduced the power of the collar to something that is easily manageable. Why risk death to remove it completely?"

"It's worth the risk," Aislinn replied.

"That's not an answer."

For a moment her thoughts were all a jumble in her head, then she provided an explanation that she didn't think that she would ever share.

"Because every time I think of the collar, every time I see the collar, it's a reminder of what my father did to you for my benefit. For me. He did it for me. He enslaved you for me."

He nodded. He understood. "You feel as if you owe me."

Aislinn nodded, staring at the white sand, afraid to raise her gaze to his. Then she forced herself to do so, and she saw the spark in her Protector's grey eyes and the crinkle of a smile on his lips.

"I want to do this for you," she agreed. "And also for me."

"You want to be free from me entirely," Bryen said. His smile was still there, although his gaze was questioning, almost sad.

"No, not free from you," she replied, this time her gaze strong and never leaving his. "Free with you."

"So you really want to do this?" asked Bryen, his usually hard eyes carrying a flicker of warmth. "Again, are you certain that you want to take the risk?"

"Yes, it's the right thing to do."

Bryen couldn't stop himself from grinning. She was using his own words against him. He had said the same thing when she had asked Bryen why he had healed her father.

"We will be here the entire time," said Rafia. "We will help guide Aislinn. And if the process becomes too dangerous, we will step in before anyone is hurt."

Bryen continued to stare at Aislinn, reading her expression with ease. She was frightened. Not of what she proposed doing. Rather, she was frightened that he wouldn't accept her offer. She was also determined. Stubbornly so. He had seen her like this many times before. She believed that this was something that she needed to do. When she got like this there was rarely any good way to change her mind.

Bryen offered a curse under his breath that made Rafia smile, then he nodded. "Let's try it. But if it's not working, you must promise me that you will do all that you can to ensure that Aislinn is protected."

Both Sirius and Rafia nodded, a knowing smile curling Rafia's lip. She had guessed that Bryen, normally just as stubborn as Aislinn, would go along with the proposal. She could tell by how he looked at the Lady of the Southern Marches that there was something more to their relationship than just the collar, even if neither of them was ready to admit it to the other.

"Then let's begin," said Aislinn, who wanted to get started before anyone could change their minds.

"You know what to do, child," said Rafia. "We'll be here with you in case you need us."

Aislinn nodded, then stepped closer to Bryen, so close that he could feel her breath on his cheek.

"Ready?" asked Aislinn. "I'll try to be gentle."

Bryen chuckled at that. "A joke from the Lady Winborne at a time like this. I never would have guessed it."

"Maybe it wasn't a joke," she replied with an unexpected sparkle in her eyes.

Before Bryen could consider her full meaning, she placed a hand on the Protector's collar, the silver cool to her touch. She could feel the power that remained within it, just as she had when she had weakened its hold on Bryen what seemed like an age ago.

"Carefully, child," urged Rafia. "Remember what we

talked about. Patience and skill are essential now."

Aislinn nodded, not bothering to respond, having already taken control of the Talent. She started slowly, extending the Talent to the collar in the form of a thin stream of energy, running the power over the entire piece of metal, looking for what Rafia had told her was the key to accomplishing the task that she had set for herself.

It didn't take her long to find it. The very last link that had been crafted to form the chain. That was the point where the silver had first been infused with the magic that had transformed it into the Protector's collar. That's where Aislinn needed to concentrate her efforts.

"Well done, child," said Rafia quietly. "You know what to do next. Be careful."

Although Aislinn heard Rafia, her eyes were closed as she focused solely on the next step. She knew that she needed to be careful. Rafia and Sirius had both been very clear about that. More times than she could count.

So she approached the next part of the process with a delicate touch. Maintaining her concentration on that last piece of metal, where the collar connected and encircled Bryen's neck, she reached out with the Talent, grabbing hold of the magic that the collar still contained.

Her eyes still closed, Aislinn smiled. Sirius had said that this would be the most difficult aspect of the entire process, yet she had gotten it on the first try. Pleased with herself, she slowly, very slowly, began to evacuate the power that remained in the collar and disperse it in the natural world.

She stopped for a moment, surprised by what she discovered. She could feel the power within Bryen, just as she had expected that she would. The Talent and the Curse, comprehending the challenge that he faced in trying to maintain control over the Dark Magic since the Seventh

Stone had merged with him. Yet it was so strong that she struggled to keep her concentration.

"What's the matter, child?" asked Rafia, noting Aislinn's flash of concern.

Aislinn ignored Rafia's question. She was almost done. She understood the danger presented by the Seventh Stone, but she wasn't worried. She would be finished in seconds. Beginning the process once again, she pulled out more of the collar's magic, slowly, carefully. She was almost there.

As she worked to complete the task, she ignored the strange feeling of lethargy that began to work its way into her. It was as if her very essence was slipping away from her along with the magic of the collar. Her strength started to fade, and she could tell that much the same was happening to Bryen. Their weariness accelerating, they both leaned into one another in order to stay on their feet.

"Aislinn, stop. You need to stop!"

Rafia's words were lost on Aislinn as she faded toward unconsciousness, sagging into Bryen. Both Protector and charge crumpled to the sand, Bryen falling onto his back with Aislinn tumbling onto his chest in a tangle of limbs. Aislinn could sense what was happening and she didn't know how to combat it. She realized with a rising panic that soon it would be too late to stop it.

She had almost finished pulling the magic from the collar, but because she and Bryen were tied together so closely, their spirits were being wrested from their bodies, some small speck of the power of the collar refusing to release them. That's what Rafia had warned her about, and now that they had been caught, she didn't know what to do. She never thought that this would become a problem if she exercised the Talent in the way that Rafia and Sirius had instructed, yet something had gone wrong.

Rafia and Sirius both watched helplessly as Aislinn and Bryen collapsed to the sand.

"We need to do something!" declared Sirius.

"I'm trying," replied Rafia through gritted teeth, ignoring the aggravation that rose within her that was caused by Sirius' very unhelpful comment.

The connection was the key. That's where Rafia needed to focus her efforts. That's where she needed to snap the link. So she used the Talent to try to fracture the connection that Aislinn had formed with the collar. Break the bond and the magic of the collar could no longer pull on the spirits of the Protector and his charge.

She cursed as her frustration mounted. She couldn't do it. First, she tried to cut the tie with Aislinn's Talent as you would a thread with scissors. She failed. The link was too strong. The magic of the collar resisted her efforts, and as it did that, it also continued to tug on Bryen and Aislinn, their spirits slowly being drawn from their bodies, their deaths becoming more certain.

Then, she tried to seize control of the connection herself, thinking that if she could do that, she could stop the pull. That didn't work either, and her increasing worry shifted into an almost paralyzing fear.

"It's not working, Sirius," Rafia said in a whisper as she fought desperately against the power that was killing Aislinn and Bryen. "Nothing that I've tried has worked and I'm out of ideas."

Hearing Rafia admit defeat, seeing Bryen lying unconscious on the white sand, and not knowing what else to do if Rafia couldn't break the bond, Sirius did the only thing that came to mind. It had worked the first time he had tried it. Why not now as well?

Placing a hand on Bryen's forehead, the gladiator barely

breathing as his spirit slowly drifted away, Sirius shot a tiny blast of the Talent straight into Bryen's brain, much like a magic-infused slap, hoping that it would awaken the Talent and the Seventh Stone within the Protector so that the power would heal him as it had done so many times before. If he could get that process going, then perhaps Bryen could save himself and then Aislinn.

Sirius got more of a response than he expected.

The reaction was immediate, Bryen's body shaking uncontrollably for several seconds, Aislinn flopping about on his chest. Then the Protector's eyes popped open.

Rafia stepped back, as did Sirius, worry and fear marring their features.

"What did you do?" asked Rafia.

"Gave Bryen a little help, I hope. And if not ..." He left the rest unsaid, because they had no other options for preventing their deaths.

For what seemed like an eternity, Bryen had drifted in a grey mist, unable to find his way out. Unable to help Aislinn. Unable to help himself.

Then a bright bolt of the Talent shot through the billowing fog, burning it away. He could see the sun again, shining down brightly, and he could feel the feathery sand beneath him.

Too weak to do what needed to be done on his own, Bryen allowed the Seventh Stone within him to do the work for him. But he was cautious, very cautious, because he could feel the Dark Magic within him sensing an opportunity in his weakened state.

The Curse pulsing behind the barrier that he had

constructed within himself that prevented the tainted power from corrupting him pushed against it, trying to free itself. The shield held, flexing in a few places, never breaking, never permitting the Curse to join with the power of the Seventh Stone as it surged within Bryen.

Bryen knew what was going on within him and Aislinn, and he didn't care that he had given such freedom to the Seventh Stone. He began to feel better, to feel stronger, as the power flooding through him took control of the connection between Aislinn and the Protector's collar, draining the last of the power from the silver and then slicing through the link completely. That brought a shuddering gasp of breath from Aislinn, who had barely been breathing as she lay across his chest.

The Seventh Stone wasn't done, instantly filling both Bryen and Aislinn with an energy meant to replace what had been stolen from them. Feeling more like himself again and certain that Aislinn was all right, Bryen released his hold on the Talent.

For the first time since he and the Seventh Stone had become one, he was grateful that the artifact had chosen to join with him, viewing the fact that he battled the Curse every second of the day as a minor inconvenience compared to what he had just been through.

Both he and Aislinn had been seconds away from their deaths. He had felt himself beginning to slide over the edge into the abyss. The power contained within the Seventh Stone had saved them both, consuming the last of the magic and preventing the Protector's collar from draining their spirits as it had tried to take advantage of the powerful bond between Bryen and Aislinn.

He shouldn't have been surprised by what had happened. He and Aislinn had connected closely during the time that the magic of the Protector's collar was in play, so it had made sense that releasing him from the silver torque would be difficult. However, he doubted that Rafia or Sirius had ever considered just how much of a challenge it might be to break the hold of the collar.

Whether he wanted to admit it to himself or not, he had bonded with Aislinn and she with him in a way that was both rare and unexpected, as well as quite unsettling and appealing depending on how you looked at it. The power of the Protector's collar had brought them together, though clearly there was more keeping them together than just that. Much more.

Taking a deep breath, which he found difficult to do with Aislinn still draped across his chest, Bryen reached to his neck. With a click, the Protector's collar slipped off. For the first time in more than a year, he was free from the symbol of his servitude. Aislinn, with the help of the Seventh Stone, had broken the power of the collar. And for the first time in history, the Protector's collar had been removed and both the Protector and the charge had survived.

Now the torque was no more than a piece of metal. Yet, as he raised the chain higher in the air so that he could get a better look at it, the midday sun reflecting off the shining silver, he realized that this simple piece of metal held more meaning for him than he had thought possible.

"Was this part of the plan?" he asked in a soft voice, still exhausted from the experience. "As a way to get your hands on me?" He tried to laugh at his own joke, but it was still too much of a strain.

Too tired to raise her head from his chest, she offered a mumbled response. "You wish."

6

TRUE CALLING

"You can find your quarters on the top floor," said the older man, his white hair cut short, glasses perched on the end of his nose as he read for the third time the message that the young man standing before him had just delivered. "Once you're settled, find Amanda. She will show you around, make sure you know where everything is."

"Thank you," replied the young man, his clothes stained with the grime of the road, the recent graduate of the Royal Medical School having just arrived from Murcia. This was his first assignment in the Kingdom, so he didn't know what to expect from the older physick who sat hunched over his desk, his eyes never leaving the piece of paper that he held tightly in his hands.

"If you have any questions, Amanda can answer them. She knows the happenings of this place better than I do. And I would ask that as you work with her you make sure that you continue her training. She has a knack for healing. I would see her education continue. Amanda should go to the Royal Medical School when you deem the time right."

The younger man stared at the physick in some surprise.

He had assumed that he had been sent to Burnt Meadows, a good sized village in the lowlands that bordered the southern edge of the Shattered Peaks, to continue his training under the physick who had worked here for decades, serving the farmers and miners who had made this way-stop into the mountains their home.

"I'm sorry, but it sounds like you're going somewhere."

"I am," replied the older physick, who pushed himself up from his chair in a rush and offered his hand to the young man, who shook it automatically, not really understanding what was going on. "Chrisia Teleride says here that you are not only well trained but quite skilled in healing. I have no doubt that you will do well here so long as you remember what you learned, follow your instincts, and, most important of all, listen to what Amanda has to say. She'll make sure that you get used to life in Burnt Meadows quickly."

"Do you have any idea when you will be returning?" asked the young man.

The older physick caught the look of fear that crossed his replacement's face, ignoring it. There was nothing that the older physick could do about that. The young man had his path and he had his own, and that path required that he travel to the east with all possible haste.

"I do not," replied the older physick, who decided to leave out the thought that had passed through his mind that he might not be returning at all. "Now off with you. Get settled upstairs and then find Amanda."

The young physick nodded, confused and somewhat numb because everything was happening so fast. Picking up his bags, he stumbled out of the older man's office, looking for the stairs that would take him to the higher floors of the small hospital and his new room.

Once the young physick had left, the older man remained standing behind his desk. He had been living in Burnt Meadows for longer than he could remember. The village had become his home and in many respects a refuge. He had started this small hospital when he had first arrived here, and it had expanded to become an important part of the larger community.

When he was younger, he had moved around a lot. But here, here with the mountains rising just to the north and the grasslands of the Breakwater Plateau stretching off to the south, he believed that he had finally found his place in the world. Apparently, though, it was not to be.

He read the note from the Duchess of Murcia twice more, just to make sure he got it right. It offered information about the young physick who would be taking his place, hopefully just for a time. It also contained much more than just that.

He had hoped that he had read it incorrectly the first few times. He hadn't, and that confirmation sent a shiver of fear down his spine.

The older physick shook his head in amused disbelief. There was nothing for it. The world was changing, and he had to change with it.

"Are you all right, Benjin," asked the young woman who stood in his doorway. "You seem distracted."

"Not distracted, just thinking, Amanda," he replied with a smile. "And that could be a dangerous thing. As a good friend of mine likes to say, thinking never hurt until you thought too much."

"More words of wisdom," joked Amanda.

"Whenever I can," Benjin replied. He had hoped that he could continue training his assistant in the healing arts before she went to the Royal Medical School, but their time together had come to an unexpected end. Amanda had been working with him for more than a year now, having replaced Samantha, a skilled physick who had passed away after assisting him for thirty years. Amanda had a great deal of potential as a healer. Once she had a bit more seasoning, she'd be ready for the training that was available in Murcia. "Keep an eye on the young one. He'll need your help."

"I'll do as you asked, Benjin. Don't worry."

"I know, Amanda. You always do. And I never worry when you're around." He hesitated before saying what had been playing through his mind, not wanting to alarm her. Still, better to be prepared than not. "One more thing, Amanda. Purchase more supplies for the stock room. Bandages. Medicines. Whatever you can acquire and as much as you can."

"Are you sure, Benjin? We already have all that we need for what we would expect to have to deal with for the next six months. It almost sounds like you're preparing for a war."

Benjin didn't bother to respond, his gaze hardening, suggesting to Amanda that he was asking her to do this for a very good reason. She gulped and nodded. "I'll get started on that immediately."

"Thank you, Amanda." He stepped around the desk and gave her a brief hug. "Now off with you. I'll be back as soon as I can."

Amanda nodded and then left the room to find the new physick. She had the terrible feeling that she might never see Benjin again.

Realizing that time was short, Benjin grabbed his traveling bag that he always kept packed and his walking stick, exiting the hospital with a quick step, wanting to leave the town as night fell, thereby avoiding any awkward questions from the residents as to where he was going.

He reached the lower hills to the north in less than an hour, the quiet and solitude of the darkness appealing to him as morose thoughts danced through his mind. Taking hold of the Talent, he extended his senses for leagues around to confirm that no threat lurked nearby.

Nothing he discovered set him worrying until he had pushed the Talent into the Shattered Peaks. Ten leagues away a cloud of darkness contaminated his senses. That could mean only one thing. He would need to be careful. The creatures that moved within that evil murk were fast. They could close the distance to him in a few hours if they caught his scent.

So he would need to remain wary as he made his way to the east along the base of the mountains to the meeting place that he hadn't visited since he had taken up residence in Burnt Meadows. Some of the others likely would arrive before him, and then from there they would all make their way to the Winter Pass. He just hoped that they would get there in time.

He was a healer, but he was a Magus as well. And it was time for the Magii to reclaim their place in the world and stand up to the evil that had hounded them since the First Ghoule War.

Because if the note that he had received was correct, war was coming. The Ghoules were coming. And the members of the Order of the Magii were the only ones who could combat the deadly power of the Elders.

7

OUT OF THE DARKNESS

The calm that eluded Bryen during the conversation that he had just engaged in with Sirius and Rafia finally settled over him as the dark of night fell over the city, the air carrying a sharp bite with the summer beginning to give way to autumn.

He had known this discussion was coming. The two Magii wouldn't leave it for long. Still, it didn't make it any easier. It had been much like his combats on the white sand, or at least it had felt that way to him as Rafia and Sirius tried to convince him to do what they believed was right, and he sought to avoid making a commitment for a little while longer.

By showing a deft touch with the Talent, Bryen had confirmed for the two Magii that he was ready to go to the Sanctuary. In their minds, he was capable of reconstructing the Weir, even though neither Magus had any idea how he was supposed to accomplish the challenge of fixing the weakening magical barrier.

Yet even as he stared out at the lights of Tintagel he struggled to turn his thoughts in another direction, the frustrating conversation continuing to play through his mind on a constant, tiresome loop.

"It's exactly as I explained," Sirius had said. "You have the power to do this, more power than almost any other Magus in the Kingdom."

"Not almost any other," corrected Rafia. "With the Seventh Stone having decided to merge with him, Bryen is the strongest Magus in the Kingdom."

"The issue was with your precision," continued Sirius, giving Rafia a scowl and doing his best to ignore her.

"You demonstrated that with great skill when you pulled the Dark Magic from Duke Winborne and healed him," said Rafia, patting him on the shoulder. "A deft touch, indeed. Something that neither I nor Duchess Stelekel could ever achieve. You should be proud of yourself."

"You've shown what you can do, lad," said Sirius, a gleam of pride in his eyes, as if the Protector's success somehow reflected positively on the old Magus. "It's time to apply the skills that you've mastered to more important matters. Matters that will determine if Caledonia stands or falls."

"I know what you both want. Why don't you just get to the point instead of dragging this out?"

"Sirius can't help himself," replied Rafia. "It's in his nature to belabor everything and beat around the bush. He thinks that he can get what he wants by trying to wear you down."

"Actually, it's just irritating," replied Bryen.

"Rafia, you're not helping," growled Sirius. The look he gave her made Rafia raise her hands in surrender. "And I do not belabor anything." Sirius shook his head in annoyance before turning his gaze back to the gladiator. "What do we want, lad?"

"To risk my life for a Kingdom that hasn't given a damn about me. That made me a slave and let me bleed in the Pit."

"That's certainly a blunt way of putting it," said Rafia, "though I can't argue the point. It's startlingly accurate."

"You're the only one who can do it, lad," said Sirius. "The Seventh Stone selected you. Whether you like it or not, the Kingdom is depending on you."

"You selected me when you used the Seventh Stone to heal me," countered Bryen. "Whether the Seventh Stone has the sentience to choose a host remains a question up for debate. Besides, you don't even know if I can do it. Just because I am the Seventh Stone doesn't mean I have any clue as to how to use the power contained within the artifact."

"That's beside the point, lad," countered Sirius. "Even if you can't do it -- at least not yet -- you're the only one who could. And that's the key consideration. You're the only one able to facilitate the power of the Seventh Stone."

"So you want me to go to the Sanctuary in the Trench, a place infested with black dragons and who knows what other monsters, not to mention the fact that as I make my way there I'll need to avoid the many Ghoules in Caledonia already searching for me, and then somehow reactivate the Weir even though I don't know how to do it."

"Yes," confirmed Sirius, grinning as if finally he had won his argument. "That sums it up perfectly."

"You wouldn't be going alone, Bryen," said Rafia, her usually flinty eyes soft, demonstrating her sympathy for his plight. To say that he had led a difficult life during his few years was putting it mildly, and she and Sirius were seeking to make it harder. "We would be with you every step of the way, as well as a few others I suspect."

Bryen raised his eyebrows at Rafia's comment, thanking her for that with a nod, though it still didn't solve his primary problem, a problem that had plagued him ever since he had toppled Marden Beleron from his throne. Forgetting for just a moment that the Ghoule Overlord had sent dozens upon dozens of Ghoule packs south of the Weir so that he could acquire the Seventh Stone, acquire him essentially, he had fought a black dragon in the Pit.

That was an experience that he would never forget. It had been one of his most challenging combats, and the thought of entering the territory where he assumed more than one of those beasts had made their nests didn't appeal to him, regardless of who might be accompanying him. Any way he looked at it, it appeared to be no more than a suicide mission.

"Even so, because I don't know how to fix the Weir," continued Bryen, "I'm more likely to die or become corrupted with Dark Magic rather than succeed, which puts you and anyone else going with me at greater risk."

"Yes, that's about right," agreed Rafia before Sirius could try to sugarcoat what they were asking him to do. "However, we are willing to take that risk."

There was no point in Sirius trying to make it seem as if the expected challenges wouldn't be challenging as they all knew they would be. Rafia completely understood why Bryen felt so little loyalty to the Kingdom that had enslaved him and his friends. Why should he risk his life for those who had treated him as less than human?

Rafia believed that the only way to convince the Protector to take part in what she had to admit would likely lead to his death and the deaths of anyone foolish enough to go with him was to appeal to the greater good and his better nature. For though Caledonia had treated him poorly, he still cared for certain people in Caledonia, even if he hadn't admitted that to himself or them.

Bryen sighed in frustration, not wanting to waste time determining whether Rafia's comment about risk applied to him, to them, or to both. "You know what you're asking me to do? You know the most likely result? Yet you still want me to take this risk."

"We do," said Rafia. "We regret having to ask you. We're sorry, truly, to put you in this position. Nevertheless, we must. We must think of all the people of Caledonia and what they risk with the Ghoule Overlord planning to invade once again. We must pursue the only option that would allow us to save the people of Caledonia. If we don't, then all is lost no matter how well the various Guards of the Kingdom fight against the Ghoule Legions. If the Ghoules make it past the Weir, then the fate of the Kingdom is sealed."

"Now you sound just like Sirius," said Bryen, shaking his head in vexation. "Very dramatic."

"I'm just speaking honestly," replied Rafia. If anyone else had said such a thing to her, she probably would have been insulted. Not so with the Protector. She had developed a soft spot for him, and not just because he was the son of two of her former students.

"There is no other way around it? No other course that we can follow? No other person who can do this?"

"As I said, this is the only way. You are the only one who can do it," replied Sirius, his escalating aggravation threatening to emerge. Clearly, he was growing tired of the effort to convince Bryen.

Most of the time, he came across as a somewhat befuddled teacher, yet that was only one aspect of his very complex personality, and certainly not the dominant part.

He had adopted that persona because it had proven useful in the Southern Marches.

As the Master of the Magii, he was far more comfortable giving orders rather than trying to persuade someone to do something that he needed to do regardless of what the consequences might be.

Before his temper could get in the way of the goal that he was trying to achieve, Rafia cut in again, sensing the change in the old Magus' demeanor.

"Sirius is right. We know you, Bryen. Despite everything that you've had to deal with in your life, you still put other people first. You are not a selfish person. You demonstrated that quality so many times in the last few weeks, I can't even keep count. You could have gone anywhere you wanted. You could have left Caledonia and never looked back when Aislinn freed you from the demands of the Protector's collar. Instead, you put in place the plan to topple the Beleron dynasty, free the gladiators, and save Duke Winborne and Aislinn. And then you went a bit farther than you needed to by aiding Duke Winborne and saving him from the Dark Magic locked within his collar."

"Lad, you are probably the toughest person I've ever met," added Sirius, his voice calm and strong, his eyes blazing with purpose and power. This was the real Sirius and not the role that he had played for much of the last decade. "You're a fighter. You've proven that time and time again. As a gladiator. As a Protector. You're a Magus as well, and from what we've discovered, you're also a healer. You would think that would be enough. But it's strange how the world works, as it seems that you're something else in addition to all that. You're a young man who despite all that the world has thrown at you still seeks to do the right thing, even if the right thing comes at great cost to yourself. It's who you are, lad. It's the mix of warrior and healer within you. No matter how much you might try, you can't escape it. You can't escape who you truly are."

"We're asking a lot of you," concluded Rafia. "We know that. But if you don't do this, the Weir falls without a fight and so does Caledonia. And if there's one thing I know about you, though admittedly we haven't known each other for very long, it's that you never shy away from a fight. No matter the odds. Just like one of those sayings Declan taught you."

"Stand fast, stand strong, stand free," Bryen whispered, primarily to himself though the two Magii both heard him.

"Yes, that's the one," murmured Rafia. "Do you think you can spare a few minutes after this for a better introduction to Declan. I'd really like to speak with him."

"Rafia!" protested Sirius. "Now is not the time."

"I was just making a simple request, Sirius. No reason to get your robes in a knot."

Rafia's attempt at humor broke the tension that had been building within the conversation and put a smile on Bryen's face.

Of course, he wasn't smiling now as he strolled along the parapet, trying to push that dialogue out of his mind, the frequency of the loop becoming burdensome.

Why Bryen had even engaged in the conversation with Sirius and Rafia he didn't know. Maybe he just wanted to be difficult. Maybe he just wanted to make the two Magii work for it. He had made his decision long ago. There was really never any doubt regarding what he needed to do or what he would do.

Because they were right. No matter how much he didn't like it, no matter how much he worried that he didn't understand how to use the Seventh Stone to fix the Weir and that he never would understand, he would at least try. He had no choice. He was the only option. The only chance for success, slim though it might be.

Deep down in his heart, though he had argued against Sirius' claim -- in part just to irritate the old Magus, because he couldn't resist any chance to get under his skin -- he did believe that the Seventh Stone had chosen him. Why, he couldn't say for sure. Perhaps it was for this, and if so there was only one way to confirm that belief.

His decision made, there was really no point in continuing to allow his fears and worries to fester in his mind. Leaving his solitary post on the eastern wall, he turned at the tower and began walking to the west along the northern wall.

With the night having descended over Tintagel, Bryen enjoyed wandering the walls of the Palace as he glimpsed the play of the city lights in the darkness. He walked in the direction of his former home, the Colosseum far off in the distance. At first the massive arena appeared to be just a dark shadow in the murk. As he drew closer, the white stone of the structure slowly gained greater clarity, glowing dimly thanks to the full moon that served as a guide for his eyes.

Every time he looked upon the enormous stadium, memories flooded back to him. The Colosseum and the gladiators' compound behind it had been his home for a decade. He had fought and survived on the white sand for longer than any other gladiator except for Declan. They were the only two gladiators to escape the Pit without being dragged across the sand and then buried unceremoniously in a potter's field.

And now he was here. The last time that he had been in the Palace was six years before. King Corinthus Beleron had summoned him so that he could be put on display before his combat against Stil Sheldgard, Champion of Sharston.

Strange, yes, and a bit discomfiting to have returned in the way that he had, but he had to admit that it was a nice change to be free of the gladiators' quarters. At least here he didn't have to worry about getting soaked by the rain because of a leaky roof or feeling the chill of the wind blasting through the building thanks to the many holes in the walls that so desperately needed to be repaired.

It still felt odd for him to actually be walking the Palace wall and grounds, much less having a room in the barracks of the Royal Guard that was larger than a closet. His new quarters gave him more space than he knew what to do with, and at first he had balked at taking the room. The Blademaster had told him that he had no choice. He had to accept it. It was a privilege that came with his new rank.

He was still coming to grips with that last adjustment. For their service during the uprising, the Dukes and Duchess Stelekel had declared the Blood Company a free company, beholden to no one but themselves, under the command of Captain Bryen Keldragan. Declan had assumed the role of Sergeant.

It still didn't sit right with Bryen. He believed that because of his more than a decade of experience gained during his time in the Royal Guard, Declan should be in command. Declan had said that he could do more for Bryen and the Company of Blood as a Sergeant, and once the grumpy gladiator made up his mind, Bryen knew from his time with him that there was no way to budge him.

"Captain Keldragan, I thought that I might find you here," said a quiet voice coming toward him from the other direction on the balustrade.

Aislinn Winborne stepped out of the darkness, a smile

on her face, knowing full well that her addressing Bryen by his new rank would make him uncomfortable, which was her objective. Her Protector was always in control, of himself and everything around him, so she enjoyed any opportunity that she could find to fluster him. Seeing the slight blush that appeared on Bryen's cheeks thanks to the torches lining the wall, she was pleased that she had succeeded so easily.

"Have your fun while you can," said Bryen. "I didn't choose any of this."

"No, you didn't," said Aislinn. "And I will have fun with it. Thank you for your permission."

"You really can be insufferable, you know that?" he said, not missing her sarcasm.

"I try my best," Aislinn replied with a laugh. "Really only with you, though. With you I can be myself."

"And no one else?"

"Everyone else has expectations as to how I should act. To them, I am the Lady of the Southern Marches. To them, I have to be the person they want me to be. With you, I can be me."

"You don't think I see you that way?" asked Bryen, offering her a challenge with a lift of his eyebrows.

"I know you don't," replied Aislinn with half a smile. She paused for a moment, stunned. Bryen had returned the Protector's collar, though no longer charged with the ancient magic with which it had been made, to his neck. She wasn't sure what to make of that. "You've seen me at my worst. Many times. So I expect that you have no illusions about who I really am."

"You're right about that," Bryen said with a mirroring grin and a nod. "The stories that I could tell."

"You won't do that."

"How do you know that? I'm sure there are many people

here in the Palace who would love to be regaled with tales of Aislinn Winborne, not only Lady of the Southern Marches, but also Magus and killer of Ghoules and Elders. I could weave many a colorful yarn."

"Because I know you," she said quietly.

The experience of releasing Bryen completely from the Protector's collar had frightened her, and not just because they had both almost died. No, what had troubled her even more was the fact that even though they had succeeded in breaking the magic of the silver that had connected her to Bryen, she felt as if the link that they had built during the time that he had served as her Protector remained just as strong as ever. Magic or no, she still believed that she knew him better than she knew herself, and she could sense where he was without having to give it any thought.

It was a connection that was more personal and intimate than she had ever expected or experienced before, and she didn't think that it could be severed. If she truly was honest with herself, she didn't want it to be. So perhaps her greatest fear was whether he felt the same way that she did. The fact that he had decided to keep the Protector's collar around his neck gave her hope that he did, indeed, feel the same way.

"Was the discussion with Sirius and Rafia as you thought it would be?"

"To the letter."

"What will you do?"

When they were both regaining their strength after removing the ancient power from the collar, Bryen had told her what he thought the two Magii would be asking him to do. She had been shocked by the audacity of the request even though it was what she had expected. When Sirius had used the Seventh Stone to heal Bryen at the Aeyrie after he had been wounded by the Elder Ghoule, she had spent just as much time researching the artifact and how it was used with respect to the Weir as she did how to release a Protector from the collar.

She had discovered that the latter was easier than the former so she worried what would happen when Bryen assumed responsibility for this enormous task, because she knew that he would. She knew him. And she knew that he had decided what he would do before Sirius and Rafia approached him. Still, she didn't want to push him and make it seem like she had taken his agency from him.

"You must do what you must do," Bryen said, interrupting her thoughts.

"Another of Declan's sayings?"

"Yes, and particularly appropriate for this situation."

Aislinn nodded. "So when will you be leaving?"

"I'm not sure yet. Rafia and Sirius said that a few things need to be worked out first. So I assume in the next few days. Their fears about the Weir weakening seem to be growing by the day."

"You'll need help, even with Rafia and Sirius going with you."

"That I will."

Aislinn's eyes narrowed. She had wanted Bryen to ask her to accompany him. Her abilities with a blade and her strength in the Talent would be of use on the journey. Instead, he just stared at her, his grin turning into a broad smile. She frowned. In her opinion, he was enjoying this way too much.

"You're going to make me ask?" The tone of Aislinn's voice hardened. Clearly, she wasn't happy. "Really? After everything that we've been through together, you're going to make me ask?"

"Well, I ..."

Aislinn didn't give Bryen a chance to finish what he was saying, pulling him behind her at the same time that she reached for the Talent, crafting a shield of white energy that blazed brightly in the night.

Just in time, too. The sharpened point of a Ghoule's blackened spear slammed uselessly against the barrier, a few sparks shimmering in the darkness where the steel met the unyielding power of the Talent.

She had noticed the change behind Bryen as soon as it began. At first, she didn't know what it could be. It was a black darker than the night, misty, almost ethereal, and it had begun to spin faster and faster until a portal of reflective burnt cinder had appeared right behind her Protector.

She realized what was happening when she saw the blur. It was the same Dark Magic that the Ghoule Overlord had used to escape Bryen while they fought in the Pit.

The Ghoule Overlord wanted Bryen dead, and he had sent assassins to complete the job.

Then she felt a tingle all across her body as Bryen took hold of the Talent, crafting a similar shield to protect them from the other side, another portal having opened behind her with two more Ghoules running through, spears at the ready.

They were trapped.

THE GHOULES STEPPED BACK after several ineffective thrusts and stabs with their spears to test the magical barriers that Bryen and Aislinn had created. The steel weapons couldn't penetrate the blazing power, doing nothing more than causing a trail of sparks to appear every time they struck the shields.

It was then that the Elders stepped forward, shouldering the Ghoules out of the way. This was a task that the servants of the Ghoule Overlord relished. Their prey stood before them, and all they needed to do to get him was break through the feeble magic of the humans. A simple task in their minds. Then they could take the Seventh Stone and feast on the girl.

The two Elders started in a similar fashion, sending shards of Dark Magic toward Bryen and Aislinn, believing that the power of their blows would shatter the humans' defenses on the first strike. No such luck. The shields held, blazing a bright white in the night in defiance of the evil sent against them.

When their first attempt didn't work, the Elders decided to work together, using the Curse to send a probing mist toward the barricades, seeking a weakness in the protective energy. That, too, got the beasts nowhere closer to the victory that they craved. The shields were stronger than the beasts assumed they would be with no obvious weaknesses to exploit.

Both Elders growled in frustration, then issued several sharp commands to the Ghoules standing behind them. The Ghoules stepped back a bit farther. The two Elders then spent several minutes attacking the humans, calling on more and more of the Dark Magic that was accessible to them through their twisted staffs of black ash. Their irritation mushroomed. Every attempt to shatter the shields failed.

For quite some time, Bryen and Aislinn were covered by a swirling mass of corrupted darkness, unable to see the stars or the lights of the city, protected from the Curse only by a thin layer of glowing energy. But they weren't concerned. They were confident in themselves and each other.

Every time the blackness that was darker than the night cleared, if only for a second, they peered through their shields. It was hard for either of them not to smile. The Elders clearly were becoming more frustrated. Nothing that the beasts tried gave them the breakthrough that they struggled to attain. The shields taunting them were simply too strong.

When the fight began, Aislinn was pleased with herself. She was more than holding her own against the Elder opposing her. As the combat progressed, she considered whether she should take the initiative instead of allowing the Elder to dictate the tempo of the combat. Yet she worried about what would happen if she did so.

Not because she didn't feel as if she could challenge the Elder on her own. Rather, she wasn't certain that she could battle an Elder and two Ghoules at the same time, as she had no doubt that as soon as she dropped her shield, the Elder would order the two Ghoules to join the fight.

Glancing behind her, Bryen appeared to be quite content to stay on the defensive, easily maintaining his shield against whatever attack the Elder opposing him threw at him. So perhaps she should control her natural aggressiveness a bit longer, even though she was finding it harder and harder to do that.

"This is getting tedious," said Aislinn, her patience running out after several more minutes of keeping her Elder at bay, the two Ghoules behind him clearly just as impatient as she was. The beasts wanted to attack, but they had no way to accomplish the task because of her skillful use of the Talent.

"Agreed," said Bryen without turning toward her, his

gaze locked on the Elder standing across from him, the two combatants separated by no more than a dozen feet. "Just give it a few seconds more. Let them wear themselves out. We'll have our chance soon. Be ready."

"What do you mean by that?"

"I reached out for some help. They're on their way."

Then she heard the roar that intensified behind the Ghoules. Declan sprinted down the battlements with a dozen of the Blood Company on one side, Jerad came from the other direction with a dozen of the Battersea Guard. The trap the Ghoules had set had been sprung a second time, now on them.

The two Ghoules on each side who stood behind the Elders didn't stand a chance. The beasts tried their best to fight against the soldiers who crashed into them, all to no avail. The tight confines of the parapet limited their movements and their options. Within seconds the gladiators and soldiers killed the Ghoules with long spears, the beasts stabbed multiple times before they collapsed to the stone.

Yet before the fighters of the Blood Company and the Battersea Guard could drive their steel into the backs of the two Elder Ghoules, the creatures placed shields of Dark Magic behind them, the billowing mist of black solidifying with no time to spare, several steel spikes slamming into the barrier rather than their mottled green flesh.

That was the opportunity that both Bryen and Aislinn had been waiting for, and they took full advantage. Distracted by Declan and Jerad, neither Elder had the strength to maintain their shield and fight a Magus at the same time, and they paid a price for their weakness.

Aislinn dropped her shield and sent a stream of the Talent toward the Elder standing opposite her, the Ghoule deflecting the attack with his black staff. He had expected to fight this Magus solely with the Dark Magic that the Ghoule Overlord had gifted him. He had not anticipated that less than a second after their duel had begun that the female human would be standing in front of him no more than a foot away.

He certainly hadn't thought that she would drive a painfully sharp steel dagger into his gut, twisting as she did so, and then slicing down to his groin. With an agonizing groan, the Elder Ghoule fell to the stone parapet, his guts spilling out along with his life.

Turning, Aislinn saw that Bryen was fighting the other Elder Ghoule with both the Talent and the dagger that was always on his belt. The Elder was holding his own, blocking Bryen's lightning-fast strikes with his dagger as well as the bolts of energy that he threw at the creature when they separated every few seconds.

The Elder Ghoule seemed confident that he could manage the prey that he had been sent to take, the beast's shield still holding behind him and preventing the other humans from stabbing him in the back. Unfortunately, the beast had never considered that maybe the human he was fighting was actually just biding his time and keeping him in place so that a threat that he had never considered could come into play.

That possibility didn't occur to him until the Ghoule felt the white-hot power of the Talent blast into his chest, the energy ripping through him, the heat burning through his flesh and into his organs, leaving his core a smoking husk. The Elder Ghoule remained standing for just a few breaths more, the reality of what had just happened to him dawning in his glazing eyes, before he collapsed onto his back, joining his dead brethren.

"Thank you," said Bryen, nodding to Aislinn. "That was quite impressive and quite timely."

Aislinn smiled at her Protector's compliment, but her pleasure was quickly replaced by shock. A spinning mist of black had appeared right behind Bryen. Aislinn reached for the Talent, ready to continue the fight as she assumed that more Ghoules would be rushing through the forming portal.

But before she could do anything, the Dark Magic did something that she hadn't anticipated, shrouding Bryen in a cloak of darkness, only the vague shape of his body visible within the swirling black.

"Bryen!" Aislinn screamed, not knowing what to do to help him.

The black mist swirled faster and faster, becoming as strong as a whirlwind, the power of the gale forcing Aislinn and the others on the parapet to crouch so that they weren't swept off the wall. Then with a flash of black that left spots dancing before her eyes, she realized that there was nothing that she could do.

It was too late.

The Dark Magic had vanished and with it Bryen.

He knew this place. He had been here before. The Sanctuary. The bowl-shaped depression that had been cut from the top of the tallest spire in the Trench was the resting place for six of the Seven Stones. Running around the edge of the hollow were the ten finely carved columns that identified the Ten Magii who had given their lives to protect the Kingdom from the evil of the Ghoule Overlord.

The last time that he had been here, he had thought that

it was just a dream. He had discovered that it had been more than that. Much more. Then, he had stood opposite the Ghoule Overlord, the massive beast grinning at him with a hungry look. He had left the Sanctuary with a thin, new scar marking his cheek and a memory of a foe who continued to haunt his dreams.

He had realized that experience had been more than just a dream, just as it was now. Because he knew without a doubt that the Dark Magic used against him had brought him to this quiet, lonely place and that the massive Ghoule towering above him, staff of black ash with the black diamond affixed to its top, was not a memory. He was all too real.

"Why do you still fight it, Protector?" The Ghoule Overlord stepped toward Bryen, seeking to close the distance between them. Bryen wouldn't allow it, gliding back through the Sanctuary, moving around the pedestals upon which six of the Seven Stones pulsed brightly, the energy contained within the artifacts forming the magical barrier that separated the Kingdom from the Lost Land. "The outcome has already been determined. Better to end this now. It will save you the pain and anguish that will become yours if you continue in your efforts to thwart the conclusion that is inevitable."

"I've never backed down from a fight."

"Even a fight you can't win?"

"Especially those."

"Brave words," murmured the Ghoule Overlord. "Will you be saying much the same when my claws rip your heart from your chest and my Ghoules feast upon you? When you lie dead at my feet, I will take what is mine. I will take what was stolen from me a thousand years ago."

"I won't just surrender it to you," said Bryen with a

bravado that didn't really mesh with the uncertainty swirling within him. "If you want the Seventh Stone, you'll have to fight me for it."

"As you wish, Protector," the Ghoule Overlord said, his satisfaction genuine. "I will take great pleasure in removing the Seventh Stone from your broken body."

"Do you really think that you can defeat me?" asked Bryen with an unnatural swagger, still dodging around the pedestals holding the Stones in response to the movement of the Ghoule Overlord until the beast finally stopped. Bryen realized that they were both now in the center of the pit that had been carved out to form the Sanctuary.

"You did well against the Elders and Ghoules I sent against you, Protector," said the Ghoule Overlord through a combination of the hisses, growls, and grunts that formed the Ghoule language. "I expected that you would. I know you now. I know what you can do. I know what you are."

Bryen considered what the Ghoule Overlord had said, realizing again that he could understand the Ghoule language and also speak it. A gift from the Dark Magic residing within him thanks to the Seventh Stone.

"You didn't send your Ghoules to kill me."

"Skilled and intelligent," said the Ghoule Overlord with a sharp bark that Bryen assumed was a laugh. "It's a pity that I will have to kill you. But you're right."

"You sent them to take me. You need me. It's the only way for you to gain control of the Seventh Stone. If they kill me, you don't know what will happen to the Seventh Stone. You need to be the one to kill me. Or you need to be there when I die if you're to have any chance of recovering the Seventh Stone."

"Well done, boy. Well done, indeed." The Overlord nodded his very large head, seemingly pleased that Bryen had reached the conclusion that he had. "Of course, I expected no less from you. Yes, you defeated my Ghoules and my Elders. Still, you are here. You are exactly where I want you to be. So again, why bother to fight? There is nothing to gain by resisting other than pain and sorrow. Why not just surrender yourself to your fate. You are alone here. There is no one to help you."

"That's never been a problem for me in the past."

"Maybe not, Protector. But it is a problem for you now. I know your history in the Pit. What you used to be. Obviously, you have some skill or you would not still be alive. Even so, nothing that you fought on the white sand compares to me. Nothing that you have done in the past has prepared you for fighting me."

"We've done this before," countered Bryen with a cocky grin. "I escaped you then. Why do you believe that I can't escape you now?"

"You escaped me because I permitted it, Protector. You were lucky. I did not know the full extent of your strength then. I did not know what you had become. But I know what you are now and what you can do. This time there will be no escape."

"So you say," said Bryen.

He wasn't certain what he could do to extricate himself from what he believed was the most dangerous situation that he had faced so far. As he had explained to Sirius, he had the ability to sense the power in someone who could employ the Talent or the Curse. Every time that he had done it before, the person who he had studied always had a limit. There was only so much power that the individual could manipulate before they burned themselves out.

What terrified him was the fact that when he examined the Ghoule Overlord, there seemed to be no end to the Dark

Magic that the beast could control. He appeared to have a limitless supply, as if the Ghoule Overlord himself was the very source of the Curse. So Bryen decided to bide his time and try to extend the conversation, hoping that an idea on how to disentangle himself from his rapidly deteriorating circumstances would come to mind in the interim.

"How can you even be here? I thought that the Sanctuary was protected. That you and your Ghoules can't be here."

The Ghoule Overlord barked, Bryen again interpreting the noise as a laugh, although the sound sent a shiver down Bryen's spine.

"The Sanctuary is protected. You are correct. My Ghoules cannot yet enter this place," said the Ghoule Overlord, extending his staff to the side to encompass the space that represented his greatest failure and what could become his greatest victory. "No one who has given themselves to the Curse can enter the Sanctuary. Except for me. There are no boundaries that I can't cross, no barriers that I cannot destroy. The Weir is weakening. It will continue to weaken. My Curse, as you humans call it, is now too strong for the protections that had once kept me from coming here. Your power dies, Protector, and mine ascends."

"Yet even with that you can't touch the Stones," said Bryen. He had been thinking about this since he had arrived in the Sanctuary. The Ghoule Overlord wanted to destroy the Weir, which relied on the power of the Seven Stones for its existence. Yet, the creature had made no move to destroy or simply take one of the Seven Stones that was sitting in plain sight. "You can stand right next to the Stones, but you can't touch them, can you? You can be here, but the power of the Weir is still strong enough to prevent you from disrupting it."

"What is your point, Protector?"

"That is my point. Wouldn't it be easier for you just to remove one of the Stones from the pedestal on which it sits? That would upset the flow of power into the Weir and the barrier that has kept you and your Ghoules to the north would dissolve. A simple solution. But you can't, can you? You can't touch the Stones."

"It is only a matter of time before my ..."

"You can't," nodded Bryen, laughing at the conclusion that he had just reached and enjoying how the Ghoule Overlord's expression had begun to change as a result from one of confidence to one of fury. Because that was his goal. He understood that a combat with the Ghoule Overlord was inevitable, and he would need every advantage that he could get if he wanted to survive such a fight.

"It is only a matter of time before ..."

"Yes, yes, I get it. It's only a matter of time before you can do whatever you want. You can stand here now. But you can't touch one of the Stones, which would be a lot easier than trying to catch me so you can take the Seventh Stone for yourself. Remove one of the Stones from its pedestal and you eliminate the Weir. You break the link between all the Stones. Simple. Easy. You're standing right next to one, in fact. It's less than a foot away. But you can't touch it. You, the Ghoule Overlord. You, who purport to be the very source of Dark Magic on this continent, can stand within a foot of one of the Stones, but you can't do anything about it. That doesn't suggest strength to me. That suggests weakness. That suggests to me that you can be conquered."

The Ghoule Overlord growled in anger, gripping his staff more tightly with his claw as he struggled to control his rising temper.

"You may be right, Protector," the Ghoule Overlord

admitted reluctantly. "The Stones are still protected. But you make a serious mistake by goading me. You will pay for that."

"How could that be?" asked Bryen, ignoring what his adversary had just said. "You're the source of Dark Magic in the Lost Land, are you not? Are you saying that the Ten Magii, even after a thousand years have passed, remain stronger than you? That their power dwarfs your own? Again, that suggests to me that you are not who you say you are. It suggests to me that you are nothing compared to the Magii."

Bryen could tell that he was succeeding at the task that he had set for himself. If he was to fight this beast, he wanted the Ghoule Overlord's rage guiding him, his emotions taking charge rather than calculated decisions. Better that the beast's fury clouds his thinking, and clearly Bryen's repeated barbs were having their intended effect.

"The power of ten Magii cannot stand against me. My power cannot be challenged!" the Ghoule Overlord roared. "The Curse is me and I am the Curse. The Dark Magic of the Lost Land comes from me."

"And yet the Ten Magii have stood against you," Bryen replied calmly. "And for ten centuries they have won. Every second that the Weir has remained in place, they have won and you have lost."

"Why do you seek to anger me, Protector? Do you understand who you are speaking to? I am the Overlord of the Lost Land. I control a power that no one else can."

"Except for me," said Bryen quietly, a smirk twisting his lips. Then he knew beyond a doubt that he had hit his mark. Not only had Bryen sought to anger the Ghoule Overlord, but he also wanted to push his adversary toward a rash attack. And he could see that it was coming by how the

Ghoule Overlord tensed, his knees bending, his claws digging into the dirt, his eyes narrowing.

Bryen only had a dagger in his hand, which he slid quickly into the sheath on his belt. He wished that he had the Spear of the Magii, believing that the weapon crafted by the Giants of the Rime would aid him in this fight. Foolishly, he had left the Spear in the barracks at the Palace, never thinking that he would need it with him while walking the battlements. Even so, a similar solution for fighting the Ghoule Overlord came to mind.

Just as the Ghoule Overlord leaped toward him, his long black staff raised above his head, the beast preparing to swing it down and crush his skull, Bryen reached for the Talent, crafting a blazing staff of energy that he held with both hands to block the blow. The power of the Ghoule Overlord's strike forced Bryen to one knee, the immense strength of the beast sending a jolt through his entire body.

For several seconds Bryen remained where he was, the Ghoule Overlord bringing his greater weight and strength to bear as he pushed down on the Protector's blazing staff. Bryen realized immediately that continuing to allow the Overlord to maintain the initiative was a losing proposition, so with a dip of his shoulder, he rolled to his right, swinging his staff behind him and hoping to catch the Ghoule Overlord across the beast's shins. No such luck as the Ghoule Overlord easily jumped over the swipe, although the maneuver did give Bryen the few seconds that he needed to regain his feet and put some space between them.

"Clever," grumbled the Ghoule Overlord. "Although not clever enough, Protector."

The huge creature charged forward, his clawed feet leaving furrows in the dirt. Bryen ducked to the side, blocking a swing from the Overlord's staff and then trying to catch the beast across the back of his head. Unfortunately, the Overlord had already moved and at the same time flung a shard of Dark Magic toward Bryen's gut. Not having the time to craft a shield, the Protector knocked away the bolt with his staff.

Before the Ghoule Overlord could attack again, Bryen seized the initiative. Calling on the Talent, Bryen threw a handful of fiery darts at his adversary. The Ghoule Overlord blocked them with ease.

That didn't bother Bryen in the least. The attack had served another purpose, giving Bryen the few seconds that he needed to close with the beast, swinging with his staff for the Ghoule Overlord's ribs.

He guessed that this attempt would be parried as well, and the beast was moving quickly to do just that, so Bryen twisted his grip on the blazing staff midstrike and slammed the stave into the side of the Overlord's head. It was a blow that should have sent the creature to his knees or even knocked him out.

It didn't, the strike pushing the Overlord back a few steps, and that was it. The Ghoule Overlord raised his head once more, cracked his neck, and then grinned at him.

Bryen cursed silently. With a hit like that against anyone else the combat would have been over. Even worse, he had yet to find a solution to his dilemma.

"You are doing well, Protector," said the Overlord, his wide grin revealing the sharp teeth lining his maw. "Better than the last time that we fought. But you still aren't good enough to best me. You're still not good enough to defeat me, even with the Seventh Stone."

Bryen danced back as the Ghoule Overlord swung down with his massive black staff, the black diamond on its head pulsing darker than the night. The blow missed, leaving a hole in the dirt that was more than a foot deep. Bryen didn't have time to think more on it, backtracking among the pedestals, his blazing staff a blur in front of him as he met the Ghoule Overlord's repeated attacks blow for blow. For the next few minutes, Bryen could do nothing but focus on defending himself and staying clear of the towering beast who sought to kill him and claim the Seventh Stone for his own.

It proved to be a huge challenge. Bryen stumbled, his knee catching one of the pedestals as he tried to evade another powerful swing by the Ghoule Overlord. For a moment he thought that he was going to drop his staff. Thankfully, he didn't, but a searing pain struck his right side.

The Ghoule Overlord, though blocked by Bryen's quick reaction to his most recent slash, succeeded in sliding his staff across Bryen's and cutting across the flesh along his ribs with the tip of the black diamond. Although the pain was almost unbearable, Bryen did his best to ignore it, pushing himself back to his feet and bringing his staff up to defend against what he expected would be the Ghoule Overlord's next and perhaps final attack.

"This has been a fun exercise, Protector, but I will take the Seventh Stone now," said the Ghoule Overlord, who had stopped his assault for the time being, believing that the injury that he had caused would disable his opponent. He stood now no more than a few feet away, his black staff planted in the dirt as he leaned on it, a black mist beginning to form above the black diamond, spinning faster and faster with each passing second. "I hope that you've enjoyed your life. I'll be taking that as well."

Bryen was more resigned than angry as he stared across at his huge opponent. As the combat had progressed, he had realized that he was not strong enough, not knowledgeable enough, to take on the Ghoule Overlord and have any real hope of surviving. At least not yet.

He had realized something else as well as he had fought the commander of the Ghoule Legions. Thanks to the Seventh Stone and the power that flowed within him, he knew what he could do to escape the Sanctuary. To give him a chance to fight another day.

"You'll have to wait a while longer," said Bryen. Then in a swirl of white mist that burst into the air and surged around him, Bryen disappeared. Even so, the Overlord's last words followed him.

"Our duel is not done yet, Protector!" roared the Ghoule Overlord. "The next time that we face one another, you will not escape. I will make you mine! I will make the Seventh Stone mine!"

"WHERE DID YOU GO?" demanded Aislinn.

She knelt at his side, examining the long streak of charred flesh that ran across his ribs.

She wanted to help him, though she wasn't sure what to do as she probed the injury with the Talent. She feared that it would fester like the last time that he had been struck with a shard of Dark Magic, that one courtesy of an Elder Ghoule in the forest surrounding the Aeyrie. Thankfully, she didn't sense the putrescence forming that she had seen with that wound, and the web of black had not yet appeared on her Protector's flesh.

"The Sanctuary," Bryen gasped out, the pain sizzling through him worsening. "The Ghoule Overlord was there. We fought."

"How did you get back?" asked Aislinn, who sent a small stream of the Talent into the injury, seeking to ease the pain. It would help for a little while, at least until someone with greater skill in healing could help Bryen with his latest wound.

As he lay against the cold stone of the battlements, Aislinn hovering over him, he analyzed how he had escaped the Ghoule Overlord, twisting how the beast had used the Curse to get him there for his own purposes, making sure to only use the Talent in its stead. It had to be the Seventh Stone that had helped him. Somehow, he had simply needed to watch the Ghoule Overlord form a portal as he had done in the Pit, and Bryen had been able to do the same himself.

It was as if watching was enough for this new ability to become ingrained within him. He knew as well that he could do it again without even thinking, simply needing to bring to mind wherever he wanted to go. He could form a gate in an instant, and then step through to where he needed to be. A new tool that could prove incredibly useful, so long as he didn't touch the Curse.

Still, there was a larger problem that he needed to deal with, two in fact. Not only must he learn how to rebuild the Weir, but first he must discover how to kill the Ghoule Overlord. Because Bryen was certain that before he had a chance to fix the Weir, if he didn't kill the Ghoule Overlord, the Ghoule Overlord would kill him. And then all of Caledonia would become a Ghoule hunting ground.

"Later, Lady Winborne," said Declan, who had rushed up on Bryen's other side when he had reappeared. "We need to get him help now."

"Dorlan! Kollea!" Declan's voice ripped through the quiet of the night.

The two gladiators, and now squad leaders of the Blood Company, ran down the parapet, avoiding or jumping over the bodies of the Ghoules who had fallen.

"Find the Duchess Stelekel and get her here as fast as you can."

Without another word the two sped off, never having seen the Sergeant of the Blood Company so worried before.

"Don't worry, Lady Winborne," said Declan. "Bryen will be all right. He's tougher than he looks."

Aislinn nodded, then gave the Master of the Gladiators a slight smile. She knew that his words were more for himself than for her.

"Uglier too," said Jerad, who poked his head over Declan's shoulder to look down at Bryen with a smile. "But we can talk about that when you're feeling better."

8

DIFFERENT KIND OF CONTEST

The week following the overthrow of Marden Beleron had been a blur for the Crimson Devil. After Duchess Stelekel declared the Blood Company a free company, Lycia found herself moving from the Colosseum to the barracks of the Royal Guard in the Palace. She was fitted for new clothes and armor. Food became less of a concern. She and the other gladiators were given time to heal. And perhaps most surprising, the Royal Guard bore them no ill will, or at least not at the level she expected, as there was little love lost for the deceased King and little desire for more bloodshed with the larger threat coming their way.

For Lycia, however, not having to prepare herself for her next combat was probably the hardest change of them all. Because when she was in the Pit, there was always another combat. It was the only given in her life. She liked that. Order. Precision. Certainty.

Before the rebellion, she and the other gladiators had to prepare themselves mentally and physically to fight in the Colosseum two times a week. She was used to maintaining a specific frame of mind that allowed her to walk onto the white sand with the confidence that she would walk back out. So she, like many of the gladiators, was used to being constantly on edge, never really coming down from the adrenaline that rushed through her upon surviving one combat and then instantly having to get ready for the next fight.

With the Dukes and Duchess outlawing the gladiatorial games, she no longer had to worry about that. Still, she found it difficult to break free from that mind set. She wanted to relax, she wanted to let it all go, yet she had lived for so long balanced on the sharp steel of a sword that she didn't know any other way to be.

She found herself with free time rather than spending all her waking hours in the practice yard, and she had no idea what to do with it.

In fact, even with all that time she now had on her hands, she had yet to do the one thing that was most important to her. Spend time with Bryen. She wanted to speak with him privately. Particularly after she learned about the assassination attempt, Elders and Ghoules suddenly appearing out of the dark on the Palace battlements. She had heard only bits and pieces, Declan reticent as always about what had happened, not giving her all the details that she wanted and only making matters worse when she discovered that Bryen had been wounded during the fight.

Having walked from the barracks on the northern side of the immense complex to the massive hall that served as the main entrance to the Corinthian Palace, she still found the experience surreal, shocked by what she saw. Gleaming crystal chandeliers lining the ceiling. Gold inlaid into the crown molding. Silk wallpaper. Paintings and tapestries hundreds of years old. Elegantly carved furniture worth more than a small cottage. Gleaming granite tiles set into the floor. Gardens blooming with flowers that shouldn't be growing this time of year.

Wherever she turned her eyes, it was almost numbing. The wealth and extravagance overwhelmed her senses as she compared it to how she and her brother had lived as orphans on the streets of Tintagel. The coldness and callousness that made up the ambiance of the Corinthian Palace thanks to the riches surrounding her helped her understand why the people had turned against the Crown so quickly.

Marden Beleron had no idea about the problems the citizens of Caledonia faced, nor had he cared. The people of Tintagel lived in a world of hunger, suffering, and other arduous challenges that resulted in large part because of his decisions, all of which were designed to perpetuate the fantasy world that he had created for himself that allowed him to see what he wanted to see and do what he wanted to do without any real consequences ... at least until just recently. When the two worlds finally clashed, thanks to the Volkun, reality had destroyed his fantasy.

Lycia looked away from the gleaming gold sconces that extended along the walls and into the distance, instead gazing down the several ridiculously long hallways that led away from the Corinthian Palace's western entrance. She had not been in this part of the expansive citadel yet. Composed of dozens of different buildings constructed at different times by different monarchs who all had a different perspective on royal architecture that left in place an eclectic and sometimes disconcerting aura that could be a bit jarring when you walked from one section of the Palace to another, she was struggling to find her way through the mishmash of styles.

Immediately after the rebellion, Bryen had taken a small

room in the barracks with the rest of the gladiators. After his injury the night before, Duchess Stelekel had insisted that he take more comfortable quarters at least until he was healthy once again. From what Davin had told her, Bryen hadn't been in a position to argue, though he had tried when Dorlan, Kollea, and the other gladiators were helping him from the parapet. So somehow she had to locate him within this monstrosity that housed thousands of rooms and stretched more than a half mile from west to east.

"It's a bit much, don't you think?" asked a strong, confident voice from one of the hidden alcoves that lined the walkway that Lycia had selected. "A testament to a man and his family who had no clue what the demands and requirements of being a King really meant. More focused on himself than on meeting the needs of others."

"I couldn't agree with you more," replied Lycia as a tall young woman wearing the leathers common to the practice yard approached from out of the gloom. A jolt of recognition ran through her. She knew this woman, Lycia's eyes crinkling in irritation. Since she had first met her in the Colosseum, her opinion of the beautiful Lady of the Southern Marches hadn't improved. In fact, it had soured. To hide her burgeoning dislike, the gladiator shifted her long braid of red hair from one shoulder to the other, gripping it tightly, her hands needing something to do.

"I remember you from the Pit," said Aislinn. "You were quite intent on taking your brother's place during our combat. You didn't have a very good opinion of me then."

"What makes you think that my opinion of you has changed since?" growled Lycia.

For just an instant, the recently freed gladiator thought to challenge the daughter of Kevan Winborne to another combat to show her the difference between a real fighter and one who played at it. With a grumble of annoyance, she realized that she couldn't do that now. Bryen likely wouldn't be pleased.

"I never assumed that it had changed," said Aislinn with a smile. This conversation hadn't gotten off to the start that she wanted, so she tried a different tack. She knew she couldn't please everyone, still she hoped to reduce, at least somewhat, Lycia's open antipathy toward her. "I can understand why you're angry with me."

Lycia stared at Aislinn, taken aback by what she had just heard. She had never expected this Lady of privilege to be so direct. "I'm sorry, what did you say?"

Aislinn smiled, pleased that her initial comment did as she intended. Defuse some of the tension between them, which she believed was only natural.

"I said that I know why you're angry with me."

Lycia's look of surprise transformed into one of shrewdness. "Why do you believe that I'm angry with you?"

"Because my father enslaved Bryen. He took him from the Pit and put the Protector's collar around his neck. I'm sorry for that. I know he's important to you."

Aislinn decided to leave out her belief that there might be more to Lycia's antipathy than just that. She had heard whispers that Lycia and Bryen had enjoyed a very close relationship during their time together in the Pit. She was unwilling to explore that road for a variety of reasons, not least of which was the fact that she wasn't certain she was ready to deal with the possibility that those rumors might actually be true.

"I would think that gives me plenty of cause to be angry with you."

"It does," answered Aislinn. "All I can do is apologize for my father's actions. If I had known what my father had planned when he was last here in Tintagel, I would have refused Bryen as a Protector. But I didn't learn of what he had done until he had returned to Battersea and had already affixed the collar around Bryen's neck. By then, it was too late. So again, for myself and my father, I'm sorry for what was done to Bryen. I didn't mean for it to happen. Bryen's a good person. He deserves better than what he's gotten."

Lycia didn't say a word for several seconds, simply staring at Aislinn. She had little experience with the lords and ladies of the land, so she couldn't tell if the woman who stood in front of her so confidently was being honest with her or she was trying to play her. If the latter, for what purpose she couldn't determine.

"You're the Lady of the Southern Marches. You're used to this finery. Of having your way in the world. I'm just a gladiator. Why should I believe that you feel any remorse at all?"

Aislinn's eyes narrowed as she thought carefully about how to respond. She wanted to be respectful to Bryen's friend. She also didn't want to appear uncertain or disingenuous, knowing that Lycia would detect both quite easily and pounce on either weakness.

"Why shouldn't you believe me?" she challenged the gladiator known as the Crimson Devil, supposedly a warrior almost as fast and deadly as Bryen when fighting in the Pit.

"You know, my first instinct upon seeing you just now was to stab you with my dagger. Thinking about that after your apology, I see that probably wasn't the most rational response. So I'll keep my dagger sheathed. For now. Until you give me cause to use it."

"My thanks for your temporary confidence in me," replied Aislinn with a quirk of her lips, not caring if Lycia was joking or being serious.

"Besides, I learned what you did for him with respect to the collar."

"It was the right thing to do."

"It was," Lycia replied. "It was also a brave thing to do. You didn't have to do it knowing the risk that it involved." The gladiator gritted her teeth, then said something to the Lady of the Southern Marches that she never thought that she would. "Thank you for that."

Aislinn nodded, slightly surprised herself. "You're welcome."

That part of the conversation concluded, the two women stared at one another for more than a minute, both knowing that their discussion was far from complete, yet neither sure how to continue.

"He's gone through more than you can possibly imagine," began Lycia.

"I know."

"And yet you're about to ask even more from him."

"How did you know about that?" asked Aislinn.

"Rumors travel faster within this Palace than facts," Lycia shrugged, "and Sirius probably revealed more than he should have when he was speaking with Declan a few nights ago. Magii don't impress Declan, so I have no doubt that he pressed Sirius until he got what he wanted. He's like a dog with a bone when it involves someone who's important to him."

Aislinn nodded again, not surprised that Lycia had picked up on the larger challenge facing the Kingdom now that the issue of succession was no longer relevant. Clearly, the Crimson Devil had a vested interest in her Protector.

"I do ask more of him," Aislinn admitted. "As do others. He's the key. He's the only one who can keep the Weir in place and the Ghoules from overrunning the Kingdom."

"It's not really fair you know. Removing Marden from the throne should have been enough."

"You're right," agreed Aislinn. "Unfortunately more often is expected from certain individuals when they have the strength to give."

"And he has the strength."

"He does."

"You must do what you must do," Lycia whispered, a slight grin seeming to want to replace her scowl, though she fought it.

"I'm sorry?" asked Aislinn, not sure that she heard correctly.

"You must do what you must do," Lycia repeated in a louder voice. "It's another of Declan's sayings."

"From what I've gathered, quite a popular one. How do you keep track of them all?" asked Aislinn with a broader smile, pleased to see that her question actually cracked the wall around Lycia's emotions and elicited a small smile as well from the hardened gladiator.

"That's a good question," answered Lycia. "Declan does have a lot of them."

The red-haired gladiator took a deep breath as she used to do when she was about to walk out into the Pit, trying to relieve some of the emotion that inevitably flowed within her and threatened to shatter her concentration. Now wasn't the time to let down her guard, talking with the Lady of the Southern Marches, as the conversation strangely had the feel of a combat to it.

"You must do what you must do," she repeated. "It applies to what we've been talking about. Bryen knows what's at stake. He knows what's required of him. He knows what needs to be done. You must do what you must do. He might hedge. He might not commit. Not yet anyway. But he's already decided what he's going to do. He does what needs to be done. Every single time. No matter what. He always puts the interests of others before his own."

"Some would say that's an admirable trait," countered Aislinn, catching the hint of disappointment in Lycia's tone.

"And I would agree with them. Still I fear that eventually his incessant desire to do what he believes is right will come back and bite him in the ass."

"Then we're of the same mind on that," said Aislinn. Not sure of what else to say, she began walking down the covered walkway in the center of the main entrance, the gardens on both sides blooming brightly with a kaleidoscope of color. "Come with me and I'll take you to Bryen. I know where his room is located. From what I understand, he's been demanding to be taken back to the barracks, arguing that the room Duchess Stelekel put him in was too luxurious and didn't fit his personality."

"Stubborn as ever," murmured Lycia. "I'm not surprised."

"Yes, he is, isn't he," agreed Aislinn.

"And he's always taking risks he doesn't have to take," continued Lycia, "as if he's the only person who can complete a specific task."

"You're right about that," Aislinn chuckled.

For the next several minutes, Aislinn and Lycia compared notes on the one person that they both knew exceedingly well, Lycia releasing her animosity, Aislinn letting go of her trepidation. And with Aislinn serving as a guide, it wasn't long before they reached the door that led into the suite that Duchess Stelekel had set aside for the Captain of the Blood Company.

Lycia hesitated before walking in upon hearing several other voices behind the door, in particular the loud rumble of her brother, who was probably regaling Bryen with an unlikely tale from a fight in the Pit.

"Thank you for freeing Bryen," said Lycia quietly. "As I said, you didn't have to do that, yet you did. That's a credit to you."

Aislinn smiled gently. "You're welcome."

Lycia then pulled open the door, about to step inside, when she turned back to Aislinn. "Just so we're clear, I still don't like you, though I respect you for what you did for Bryen. Perhaps my brother was right to name you the Vedra. Not only wickedly fast, but also courageous."

Aislinn nodded again, not knowing what to do with the unexpected compliment.

"Just don't forget that I'll be watching you. I won't let you hurt Bryen. As I said, he deserves better than what he's been given."

"I agree.

Lycia nodded again, glad to see that they had reached an understanding, then she walked into the suite.

When the double doors closed, Aislinn allowed her smile to return, pleased that she and Lycia had come to an agreement of sorts. And with no bloodshed.

Would wonders never cease?

9

TAKING COMMAND

"We cannot wait," proclaimed Sirius, the old Magus standing in one of the dozens of gardens dotting the grounds of the Corinthian Palace.

This larger space offered the additional benefit of serving as a small amphitheater, finely carved stone benches curling around a small circular stage giving the several people who had been listening to him for the last half hour somewhere to sit. None of them had any desire to use the throne room, too many memories of Marden Beleron still fresh in their minds, so Jurgen Klines, once and still the Blademaster of Caledonia, and now the Captain of the Royal Guard as well, had suggested the open alcove, which Duchess Stelekel had accepted gratefully.

"We must move quickly," Sirius continued. "Just as we suspected, our ancient enemy moves forward with his plans. The Ghoules are pushing through the Weir."

Just a few years before, the Dukes meeting with Sirius, Rafia, and Noorsin might have scoffed at what the old Magus was saying, that an enemy that had been forced behind the Weir a thousand years before threatened the

Kingdom once again. Not now. Not after the reports that they had received. Not after what several of them had seen. Not after the duel that played out in the Pit.

Tetric battling Sirius, Dark Magic opposing the Talent, was shocking enough. Watching the King's Advisor transform into the Ghoule Overlord had frightened them in a way that nothing else ever had or could.

They understood that they needed to act fast. Even so, they were worried. They feared that despite anything they might try, it still wouldn't be enough to protect Caledonia from the coming onslaught. It would take too much time to marshal all the forces of the Kingdom, and even then they doubted that all of the Duchies would heed their call.

"You have confirmation of this?" asked Wencel Roosarian, Duke of Roo's Nest.

He wasn't challenging the old Magus' statement. He simply preferred to have all the necessary information with some understanding of where that information came from before making a decision. Facts drove him. Not guesses or supposition. His one weakness being that sometimes he waited too long for the facts that he craved to make a decision, and by then the situation had changed. The facts that he had pieced together no longer applied to the new circumstances that still required fast action.

"We do," answered Noorsin Stelekel, Duchess of Murcia. Rafia nodded her agreement. "A Magus scouted the peaks along the western flank of the Winter Pass. She was able to watch for a time without being detected. She then moved farther south when the Ghoule packs started coming in her direction. The Ghoule Overlord has his Elders forcing the beasts through the Weir. For now, it appears that they have not yet emerged onto the Breakwater Plateau."

"He was doing that already," said Cornelius Stennivere,

Duke of the Three Rivers. "Kevan confirmed that for us with all the Ghoule packs the Battersea Guard eliminated before coming here."

"Yes, that's correct," said Rafia, "yet incomplete. Based on the number of Ghoules that the Magus saw already having crossed through the Weir and the even larger group still on the north side waiting to risk the barrier, we're not talking about packs anymore."

"Legions," said Kevan Winborne, Duke of the Southern Marches, in a somber tone.

"Legions," confirmed Rafia.

An uncomfortable silence settled over those assembled in the garden. They had hoped that they would have more time to prepare their defenses. Apparently not. They had always known that the Ghoules would come again, and not just because of Sirius' constant warnings, though they had hoped that it wouldn't be for several more centuries.

It had taken the events in the Southern Marches to jolt them into accepting the reality of what they faced now. Even so, it was difficult for them to wrap their minds around such a dire menace, a danger that threatened the very existence of Caledonia and its people.

"Are they moving down the Winter Pass?" asked Tarin Tentillin, Captain of the Battersea Guard, one of the few people in the small amphitheater who had experience actually fighting Ghoules.

"Thankfully, not yet," replied Noorsin. "But our scout doesn't believe that they'll wait for long."

"The weather," nodded Tarin.

"Yes, the weather," confirmed Rafia. "The Winter Pass is as clear as it will ever be, though only for the next few months. Our scout believes that the Ghoules are preparing for a long stay and are wary of an attack. Once they have a few more Legions through the Weir, the Ghoules will start moving south toward the Breakwater Plateau."

"Can they get enough Ghoules through the Weir in the next two months to threaten us?" asked Cornelius. "We've managed well enough against Ghoule packs. Legions are a different matter entirely."

Sirius thought about the question for a moment, nodding his head as he considered the issue. "It's hard to say," he finally replied. "With the Weir weakening, we just don't know."

"Best guess?" asked Kevan.

"Best guess," said Sirius, considering. "A dozen Legions, one or two more maybe."

Silence fell on the gathering once again. Twelve Legions. Twelve thousand Ghoules. If Sirius' estimate was accurate, even with the combined forces of the Southern Marches, Roo's Nest, the Three Rivers, Murcia, as well as the Royal Guard making the long journey as quickly as possible to where the Winter Pass broke through the Shattered Peaks, they would still face a battle that could only be described as desperate when they matched their troops against twelve Ghoule Legions and potentially one with a foregone conclusion, the thought of that conclusion sending a chill down into their bones.

"We need to move our forces northwest toward the Winter Pass," said Wencel, surprising his companions with the speed of his decision. "As swiftly as possible."

"Companies of the Royal Guard are already moving in that direction," said Jurgen Klines. "The bulk of the Guard will be underway the day after tomorrow."

"I'll get my Guard moving by then as well," said Cornelius. "It won't take them long."

"As will I," said Wencel. "We'll travel together."

"Good," said Kevan. "Tarin, when can you have the Battersea Guard moving?"

"By tonight, Duke Winborne. Preparations to break camp began last night."

"Why am I not surprised," said Kevan, who turned his focus to his fellow rulers. "The Battersea Guard will be with you."

"As will the Murcian Guard," added Noorsin. "They began preparing to move last night as well."

"We will still be at a distinct disadvantage," said Wencel. "Although we will have good numbers, we will not have the strength to fight twelve thousand Ghoules for very long. I'm sorry to say it, but it must be said. A single Ghoule is worth three or four of our soldiers."

"You're correct, Wencel, we will be at a distinct disadvantage," agreed Noorsin. "So with that in mind I have sent messages to the other Duchies explaining the danger that Caledonia faces and what's required of them."

"Do you think that they'll respond?" asked Wencel, his nervousness leaking into his shaky voice. He was not a man who liked uncertainty, particularly in a time such as this. "We can certainly use their assistance."

"We can only hope," replied Noorsin. "Some of the Duchies will come, I believe. Some ..."

She left the rest unsaid. They knew that some of the lords and ladies of the land would see the removal of Marden from the throne and the impending Ghoule invasion as an opportunity, something to be used to their advantage, as they were not above putting their own interests before those of the entire Kingdom. Everyone in the amphitheater understood the politics of Caledonia and the other personalities who would be making those decisions better than anyone.

"There is another option that we need to consider," said Rafia. "One that gives us a bit more hope."

"Yes," said Sirius. "Preparing to fight the Ghoule Legions is essential. But there is another parallel path that we can and must take."

"What would that be?" asked Cornelius. "I'm open to anything that gives us a better chance at success."

"The Weir is weakening," said Sirius.

Cornelius shook his head in irritation. "We know that, Sirius. What's your point?"

"The Weir is weakening, which of course allows the Overlord to send his Ghoules through the barrier," explained Rafia. "We believe that we have a way to reconstruct it. Rebuild the Weir, and we stop the Ghoule Overlord in his tracks."

Rafia's comment elicited several gasps from those assembled. For Aislinn, who had been sitting quietly next to her father, it brought a silent groan. She knew that inevitably the conversation would move in this direction. Even so, she didn't like it. She had been trying to prepare herself for it, the thought of what was going to be asked of Bryen still troubling her.

"How could the Weir be rebuilt?" asked Wencel. "Ten Magii died to construct the Weir, and from what you've been telling us for years, Sirius, even if we gathered together the ten strongest Magii of this age, they couldn't do what the Ten Magii did a thousand years ago. Twenty Magii couldn't do it. A hundred. So how could we possibly believe that rebuilding the Weir is no more than a fanciful dream?"

"We would not present this option unless we thought that it was legitimate," replied Sirius, his pedantic nature replaced by the fiery stare that signified his shifting to his role as Master of the Magii. "Besides, there is no good reason not to pursue it. This additional path will not prevent us from offering the defense that has already been agreed upon. A defense, I must say, that is absolutely critical. But as we all know that defense will not be enough. It can only buy us time. And how much time we just don't know. Rebuilding the Weir is the best way that we can achieve any form of real victory."

"The only way to stop the Ghoule invasion is to reconstruct the Weir," confirmed Rafia, jumping in before any other questions could be asked. Better to give the full explanation first and take questions later. "If the Weir falls, and it will fall, then Caledonia is lost."

"How are we supposed to ..." began Wencel, trying to interrupt.

Rafia cut him off before he could continue. "What I am about to tell you is not the complete story. It is only enough for you to understand why we believe that what we propose might actually work."

The Keeper of Haven then spent the next several minutes explaining the history of the Seven Stones and in particular the importance of the Seventh Stone. Most of those listening to her explanation already knew at least some of what she was laying out before them, so it was really more lecture than conversation. It was when she touched on Bryen's ability to manipulate the Seventh Stone that murmurs of surprise rumbled through the alcove.

"You're saying that this young man, the Volkun, who was no more than a gladiator just a year ago, can make use of the Seventh Stone just as the Ten Magii did?" asked Wencel.

"I wouldn't say it if it wasn't true," said Rafia.

"How is that even possible?" asked Cornelius. "He's only been free of the Pit for a year."

"A lot can happen in just a year," replied Sirius. "We

don't know why it happened. We don't know exactly how it happened. We do know that Bryen can manage the power contained within the Seventh Stone. He has already demonstrated this skill to me, Rafia, and Noorsin multiple times. Bryen's connection to the Seventh Stone gives us a chance that we wouldn't have otherwise."

"So you're saying that the Volkun working with the Seventh Stone could control enough of the energy required to rebuild the Weir?" asked Wencel. "And if he does, in a timely manner of course, then his actions will limit the number of Ghoule Legions that we must fight, increasing our chances of actually surviving the battle that we have no choice but to fight?"

"Yes, that's exactly what we're saying," confirmed Sirius.

"Then it's not a difficult decision at all," murmured Wencel.

"And what of Aislinn's Protector?" asked Kevan. The fact that her father asked this question surprised his daughter and also pleased her. "If he attempts this, does he face the same fate as the Ten Magii?"

"We hope not," replied Rafia, shrugging her shoulders, not in disinterest, rather because she simply didn't know what would happen, and she didn't deal in possibilities.

"But you don't know," confirmed Kevan.

"We don't know," said Sirius, nodding his head gravely.

"It is a massive risk for Bryen," said Tarin.

When the Captain of the Battersea Guard had first met the Volkun in the shadow of the Colosseum, Duke Winborne intent on purchasing him as a Protector for his daughter, he had disliked the gladiator at first sight, believing that someone accustomed to battling in the Pit didn't have the quality or skill to fight a true soldier. Bryen had proven him wrong time and time again and, as a result, his opinion of the Volkun had changed.

Tarin still found Bryen to be a bit irritating at times. However, he understood that the Protector did it just to see if he could get under Tarin's skin. Tarin, himself, was guilty of returning the favor. And after they had reached a truce of sorts in how they interacted with one another, their relationship had shifted toward friendship, though grudgingly at first on both their parts.

"It is," agreed Rafia. "We have already spoken to him about it. Several times, in fact."

"Look at what he's done for us," interrupted Aislinn, no longer able to contain herself. "For all of us. We would not be here now without him. We would not be free of Marden or Tetric without him and the assistance provided by his gladiators, many of whom died on our behalf. How could we ask him to do more?"

"Because no one else can do it," her father replied sadly, understanding how much his words pained his daughter, yet still feeling the need to say them. "If what Sirius and Rafia say is true, he's the only one who could do it. The only one who could have any hope of preventing the Ghoules from conquering the Kingdom, and that's a chance that I simply can't let slip by."

"Do you think he will do it?" asked Sirius, ignoring the emotion playing across Aislinn's face. He sympathized with her plight. Still, her mental state was of little importance to him in this particular moment. The broader picture had to come first. "He was your Protector. You achieved a closeness with him that cannot be gained in any other way. You know him best."

Sirius' question stopped her next protest, which was on the tip of her tongue. She did know Bryen, and she liked to think that she knew him better than anyone else after all the time that they had spent linked together. Although after her recent conversation with Lycia, she wasn't so certain of that. Even so, it was also that conversation with the slightly intimidating gladiator that confirmed her answer.

"You must do what you must do," Lycia had said. She was right. Bryen would do what he needed to do, despite the cost to himself. He had already proven it. Time and again. Rather than leaving Caledonia for good when he had the chance, he had chosen to come here and start a revolt that had little chance of success, in large part to help her and her father. He would do what he must do. Even if it meant his death. She had no doubt of that.

"Yes, I believe he will."

"Do you think that he can do it?" asked Wencel. Seeing the angry look that Aislinn shot him, he quickly clarified. "Not because he's lacking in any way. Rather because this is a huge challenge. It's almost too much to expect that one person can achieve it. It took Ten Magii to construct the Weir. We're putting a huge burden on the shoulders of just one young man."

"He can do it," cut in Tarin, feeling confident in his response. He had spent enough time with the Protector to know that he would do all that he could to succeed ... or die trying. "Have no doubt of that."

Rafia and Sirius nodded their agreement, although they didn't explain why they agreed with the Captain of the Battersea Guard. They had no desire to reveal the true and full extent of the power that Bryen could harness through the Seventh Stone. Doing that could lead the entire conversation down a rabbit hole from which they might never emerge.

"He has the skill and he has the strength to do it," said

Noorsin, having stayed silent for most of the discussion. She already knew what needed to be done and didn't need convincing like some of the others.

Noorsin gave those assembled in the amphitheater a few seconds more to ask questions. No one did, those sitting on the benches keeping their thoughts and fears to themselves. So she moved the proceedings along. With the Ghoule Overlord seeking to force as many Legions through the Weir as he could in the next few weeks, time was not on their side.

"Then that's settled," she declared. "We'll decide later who will ask Bryen, or rather I should say the Captain of the Blood Company, to take on this task."

Clearly, the Dukes were uneasy with what had to be done, not necessarily because of what would be asked of the Volkun, instead because so much depended on him. It was a sobering thought to think that the fate of the entire Kingdom rested on one young man. Still, they had no choice but to place their bets on his success. As Rafia and Sirius had explained, they had no other options.

That part of the discussion complete, Sirius and Rafia returned to their seats, and it was then that Kevan rose from where he was sitting next to Aislinn.

"Before we disperse, one other topic if I may?" asked the Duke of the Southern Marches. Seeing everyone nod, he continued. "With the King dead, if we are going to mount an organized defense against the increasing number of Ghoules coming into the Winter Pass, we need someone to take charge of the Royal Guard and the Duchy Guards. We must fight as a single, cohesive Army of Caledonia if we are to have any chance of holding back the Ghoule Legions."

"We need a general," said Jurgen Klines.

"We need a general," confirmed Kevan. "And before we

enter into another long discussion, I'd like to make a proposal."

"That you serve as General of the Caledonian Army?" asked Cornelius. It seemed like the most logical solution to him. Kevan was eminently qualified, and the Battersea Guard already had acquired a great deal of knowledge and experience fighting the Ghoules.

"Actually," replied Kevan, "no."

"What do you mean no?" demanded Noorsin. She, too, thought that he was the most qualified candidate to assume such a role.

"Thank you for your confidence in me, Noorsin, but I believe that there is a better candidate among us. One who has already demonstrated all the necessary qualities of a thoughtful, strategic, and strong leader."

"Who?"

"You."

"Me?" replied Noorsin, knocked off balance by the suggestion.

"Yes, you." Kevan knelt down in front of her, holding her hand in his own. "There are many reasons why you are most qualified to take on this role. You're intelligent. You see the bigger picture. You have your eyes and ears who can provide you with the information that we will need to make the best informed decisions possible."

"My eyes and ears can give us this information whether I am general or not."

"True," Kevan admitted, though he continued with his argument. "Keep in mind as well that while I was here in Tintagel, a prisoner of the King and his Advisor, you were working with my daughter to bring together as many of the Duchies as you could in a very short period of time and getting them here to aid in the overthrow of the Crown."

"You're forgetting the role that the Volkun played. Without him, none of this would have been possible, just as Aislinn said."

"Agreed," said Kevan. "We owe a huge debt to Aislinn's Protector."

"Bryen," corrected Aislinn, wanting her father to acknowledge him in a more personal way.

"Bryen," sighed Kevan, impressed by his daughter's boldness and irritated by it at the very same time. "Nevertheless, we owe a great deal to you as well, Noorsin. You brought us together. And you continue to keep us together. You should be the General of the Caledonian Army."

"Hear, hear," said Cornelius, Wencel and Jurgen Klines nodding their heads in agreement.

Recognizing that the decision had been made, Noorsin realized that the many objections running through her mind in that moment would be useless. So she took a deep breath and nodded herself. Then, with Kevan still holding her hand, she pushed herself up from her seat.

"I hope that you all know what you're in for," she said, attempting to inject some humor into a very serious situation.

"We do, indeed," said Kevan. "And I expect the Ghoules will have no idea what's in store for them with you in the lead."

"All right then," said Noorsin. "Let's get to work. We already have the Royal Guard moving toward the Winter Pass and the Duchy Guards preparing to follow. We know the Ghoule Overlord is pushing as many Legions through the Weir as he can. Let's discuss a possible strategy for making sure the Ghoules can't make it onto the Breakwater Plateau."

"Did you have something in mind?" asked Rafia,

catching the glint in Noorsin's eye. She knew her former student and assumed that she had already begun thinking about this dilemma.

"I did, in fact."

"I'm not surprised," the Magus replied. "What have you already mapped out, General Stelekel?"

10

THE HUNT BEGINS

For most of the afternoon, the Ghoule Overlord stood atop the promontory that gave him a good view of his Elders creating portals through the Weir, which allowed his Ghoules to risk a crossing. Risk was the key word, because nothing was ever guaranteed when attempting to pass into the lands to the south of the magical barrier.

The ground was covered in snow, six inches deep at least, with more still coming down. The light flakes that could so quickly bog down a marching army elicited a grimace of distaste from the commander of the Ghoule Legions as they settled on his broad shoulders. If this weather continued, and judging from the clouds he expected that it would, then it would hamper his Legions' efforts to push farther south once they entered the humans' lands.

Speed was all important. His Legions needed to get to the tip of the Winter Pass as rapidly as possible. Yet two realities constrained his desires. His Elders could complete their task only so fast and even when they applied the Curse cautiously the work was fraught with danger.

The Ghoule Overlord watched intently as one of his Elders called on the Dark Magic he had gifted to him, the Curse spinning out of the top of the Elder's staff in a silky mist. Once the Elder had enough of the power under his control, he turned his focus to the Weir. Using the Dark Magic that swirled around the palm of his claw, the beast began crafting a portal, essentially a makeshift tunnel just large enough for one of the Ghoules waiting behind him to traverse if the Ghoule moved quickly enough, because the passageway wouldn't last long. The Elder had no ability to hold back the Talent that, in addition to the Curse, had been used to craft the Weir.

If the Elder wasn't careful and he didn't pick the right time -- when the section of the Weir that he selected flashed black, which signified that there was only Dark Magic to his front -- then any Ghoule in the portal would be caught, the Talent burning into his body, leaving nothing but ashes where the Ghoule had once stood. And if the Elder didn't release the Dark Magic fast enough when the Weir shifted back to its original form, then he would be caught as well, pulled into the barricade or obliterated by the power contained within it.

A shriek of agony pulled the Ghoule Overlord's pitch-black eyes to the left. Another Elder had crafted a shaft through the Weir, taking advantage of the flashing black in front of him. Three Ghoules had made it across to the human lands, sprinting through the barrier. Three Ghoules had not been so lucky, nor had the Elder.

The three Ghoules captured by the Talent woven within the Weir had already started to burn, their faces contorted by their screams of agony as their flesh began to char and flake away from their bodies. It was a long, tortuous process. Thankfully, none of the other Ghoules waiting to make their way through the Weir could hear their cries as the beasts died in silent torment.

The Elder suffered the same fate, though faster. When the Dark Magic in the Weir transitioned back to grey, signaling that the Curse and the Talent were once again woven together as they should be, a bolt of sizzling energy blasted back into the Elder through the Dark Magic that he had used to connect to the Weir. The power destroyed the beast in an instant, the ashes of his body billowing in the breeze, heavily falling snow already working to remove any hint of the Elder's previous existence. A terrible way to die, but a better fate than the one suffered by the Ghoules trapped in the Weir.

The Ghoule Overlord shook his head angrily, a low snarl of fury rising in the back of his throat. One Ghoule lost for every Ghoule who made it across, and for every twenty Ghoules who made it into the Winter Pass, an Elder died. Those were not good numbers, and they suggested that his Elders would not be able to push ten Legions into the human lands within a month.

He thought about his dilemma for a moment, searching for some solution. Finally, he concluded that there was little that he could do. His Elders would simply have to work faster.

He didn't care if they died. He could create more Elders as he needed. He couldn't risk losing this opportunity to move his plans forward faster than he had anticipated.

He knew where the Seventh Stone was now.

He knew who the Seventh Stone was.

Once he had the Seventh Stone, he could destroy the Weir once and for all and push forward all his other plans that were dependent on that task being completed.

Two times now he had faced the Protector in the Sanctuary. Two times now the Protector had escaped. The first time the Ghoule Overlord had chalked it up to luck. The second time, a seed of worry had begun to grow in the back of his mind.

How had the Protector learned how to use the Seventh Stone to create a portal and escape him?

The human shouldn't have been able to, not without destroying himself in the process. No Magus since the ten who crafted the cursed Weir could create a portal on their own. No one Magus could control the Seventh Stone.

Yet the Protector had done it. The Ghoule Overlord was angry at the pace at which his Elders were working. Even more so, he was angry with himself for failing to kill the Protector when he had the chance. He promised himself that the next time that he encountered the Protector, he would not allow him to get away. Too much rode on the Protector. His death was a necessary part of the Ghoule Overlord's plans.

He was angry with himself as well for believing that the King's Advisor could achieve the goal that he had set for him. It had proven very easy to corrupt and then make use of Tetric, playing off his unquenchable and very obvious desire for more power. He had identified the Magus himself, learning of his connection to the Master of the Magii, knowing what was truly in his heart.

When he sought to turn a human, it often was a difficult exercise. There always seemed to be a natural resistance within the human that needed to be broken first, the person often recoiling at what it truly meant to be reshaped by the Curse.

Such was not the case with Tetric. All that it had required to make the former Magus his slave was a single demonstration of the power that the Ghoule Overlord offered. After that the Magus was his.

Tetric's greed was so great that he never considered and never cared about the cost of accepting the gift given to him. Within seconds of feeling the new power surging within him, the Curse immediately began to corrupt Tetric. After several years, the human within Tetric had withered away to the point where he was no more than a shell of himself, which had permitted the Overlord to take his skin for his own so easily.

So many promises, thought the Ghoule Overlord, so little gained. Yes, Tetric had done what was needed by influencing the now dead King of Caledonia, thereby weakening the Kingdom so that the humans would find it harder to resist his Legions. However, more had been required of him. More that was crucial to his plans. More that had never been fulfilled.

"I don't expect much from you," he had told the Magus when the Ghoule Overlord first had turned Tetric to the Curse. "You will not get what you desire if you fail to give me what I want."

"I will not fail you," the Magus had replied. "I promise you that."

"Promises mean nothing to me, Tetric. I only care about results. Do we understand each other?"

"We do. You have nothing to fear. I promise that I will fulfill my end of the bargain."

Tetric's overarching confidence and lack of fear while standing across from him, which suggested that he didn't fully understand the consequences of the decisions that he was making, had been the first sign that the Magus was different from the others. The Ghoule Overlord had ignored the subtle warning, allowing himself to believe otherwise.

He needed to believe otherwise. Because he had few chances like this. He had never had the opportunity to turn a Magus to his purposes since he had stolen the Seventh Stone so many centuries before.

"Then I will give you a taste of my Dark Magic," the Ghoule Overlord had said.

Pulling the Curse out of the black diamond that rested on the top of his staff of twisted black ash, the mist had spun a few times around the jewel, then shot like an arrow straight into Tetric, flowing into his mouth and his nostrils, his body spasming uncontrollably in response to the Curse. It was over in seconds, the Dark Magic receding, though the human continued to shudder violently for almost a full minute before he collapsed in a heap at the clawed feet of the Ghoule Overlord.

For several minutes more the human had shivered uncontrollably on the ground as the Curse worked its way into every cell of his body. The Ghoule Overlord sensed when that process was complete. He knew that the Magus was his, body and soul.

What happened next, though, had surprised him. The human had pushed himself to his feet immediately, his eyes revealing a flashing black spark in the back of his pupils, confirming that the Dark Magic flowed within him. Usually, it took much longer for a human to do that, their bodies needing more time to grow accustomed to the power now surging within their veins. Except for the Magus, who appeared energized and transformed by the Curse.

Perhaps he had been wrong to worry about Tetric's greed and lack of fear. But no, looking back, he had been right. The Magus simply had enjoyed the benefit of the additional strength provided to him by the Talent.

The Ghoule Overlord should have listened to his

instincts then, because he was paying for his failure to do so now. Just like all the humans he had corrupted over the centuries, this King's Advisor had proven to be no different than any of the others. Full of promises. Only promises, in fact.

Tetric would say anything to gain what he wanted. Agree to anything. And he failed to do what needed to be done to achieve what the Ghoule Overlord demanded. Just like all the rest, those promises proved to be no more than that. Words in the wind.

When the Ghoule Overlord had reached that conclusion, he realized that a new approach was necessary when he learned that the Seventh Stone was free of the Aeyrie for the first time since the construction of the Weir. He could not trust a weak Magus to acquire it, which was why the Ghoule Overlord had decided to play a larger role, taking Tetric's form so that he could track the Seventh Stone in the open.

He had achieved his goal. He had identified the Seventh Stone. Yet he had not taken it. He had been so close in the Pit, just a few feet away. Then again in the Sanctuary. Shockingly, he had failed both times. And it was these failures that galled him the most.

The massive Ghoule growled in anger as his mind continued to work its way along the same path that he had trod for the last thousand years. The Seventh Stone was the Key. Only with the Seventh Stone could he destroy the Weir. Only with the Seventh Stone could he conquer the human lands to the south. Only with the Seventh Stone could he then take his Legions into the Wyld.

That would be just the beginning. With the Seventh Stone, all the lands of men would come to fear his Ghoules. His Legions could not be stopped. The Ghoules were growing. They needed space. They needed to hunt. They needed food. They would find both in Caledonia and beyond.

He couldn't forget about his burning desire for revenge either. It was there. Always. Within him. Driving him forward. Marking him. Coloring his decisions.

Ten Magii had gained the Seventh Stone, which was already infused with Dark Magic, by stealing it from him. He had never forgotten that. His failing to protect the Seventh Stone and the black diamond had led to the construction of the Weir and the pain and frustration his people had experienced since their first failed invasion.

When he finally destroyed the Weir -- and he would destroy the Weir -- he would have his ultimate revenge. He would inflict upon the people of Caledonia even more pain and anguish than his Ghoules had suffered through the centuries because of his own failure.

Another Elder stepped up to the Weir, taking the place of the one who had just been killed by the Talent lurking within it, the action interrupting the Overlord's thoughts. This Elder waited, the barrier in front of him flashing black and white so fast that you couldn't track it with the eye.

This Elder was smarter than the one who had just died. More patient too. When the color shifted to black, he waited a few seconds more to confirm that the change had occurred. Then he began to weave the portal. Yes, this one would have better luck than the Elder who preceded him.

"Is my pack of Ghoules ready, Nibli?" asked the Ghoule Overlord.

"They are, Master," replied his second in command, who trudged up the slope through the ever-deepening snow. "They wait for you just below."

"I will take them with me now," nodded the Ghoule

Overlord. "Bring them forward. We have a long way to go and not much time."

"Yes, Master. We will take the Winter Pass while you are gone. Then we will move south. We will be ready to take the humans' lands."

"Good. But first, I will claim the Seventh Stone."

11

LIKE OLD TIMES

It was early morning, a faint glimmer of light just now peeking over the eastern parapet of the Colosseum. The Master of the Gladiators savored this time of the day.

The quiet. The calm. The hint of things to come.

Declan sat in the first row of the stands, leaning his elbows on the stone and looking down at the white sand. He still marveled at how Bryen had collapsed the tunnels except for the one that led away from the Pit, thereby forcing the Royal Guard to attack through a single entrance during the revolt.

That tactic had given the gladiators a fighting chance against overwhelming odds, and they had certainly made the most of it. Who knew two hundred slaves, men and women consigned to the white sand for various offenses, some real, others imagined, could serve as the catalyst for the overthrow of the Crown?

His thoughts continued to drift as the sun finally touched the Pit, memories of the last few weeks flooding through him. He had never believed that his life could change so drastically so quickly. But it had. And all for the good, he admitted. He just found it a bit disorienting as he gradually got used to certain aspects of his new existence.

Bryen's ability with the Talent, which had been a huge shock, though his new skill had proven its utility instantly, the rubble within the Colosseum attesting to its value. The formation of the Blood Company with him taking on the rank of Sergeant. Bryen had protested, arguing that with Declan's experience in the Royal Guard he deserved to be Captain. Declan had refused. He knew where his skills and knowledge should be put to use. Guiding Bryen as his Sergeant was the best way to do that.

Surprisingly, all of the surviving gladiators had decided to join the Company. He had not expected that. He had assumed that at least a few would leave the city, start a new life, try to escape the memories of their time on the white sand. Either they weren't ready for that or they felt that they had some unfinished business, just like he did. Staying with the Company and the Volkun, who had risked more than just his life for them, apparently was the only way to eliminate that niggling feeling from the back of their brains that a debt was owed still.

After twenty years in the Colosseum, ten as a fighter, ten as the Master of the Gladiators, Declan was used to the rhythm of life here and didn't look kindly on anything or anyone that sought to adjust his established routine. He had to admit, however, that the changes made since the overthrow of Marden Beleron had given him an energy and exhilaration that he thought he would never attain again. It was almost as if he was looking at the world through a different set of eyes, and he liked what he saw.

Although there was one aspect to his new life that he found a bit perplexing, and he wasn't sure what to do about it. Three times now, twice in the Palace and once in the gladiators' compound, all while he was training fighters, either the Blood Company or the Royal Guard at the request of Jurgen Klines, the Magus had appeared, standing where he could clearly see her, her dark, enigmatic eyes watching carefully, taking everything in.

Studying him, he was certain. Why, he didn't know. And though he did want to know, he had not yet found the opportunity to ask her, the Magus striding off with purpose when each session concluded before he could corner her.

Each time she appeared, he did his best to ignore her, though it was a difficult thing to do, not least because he could sense the power emanating from her.

She was a beautiful woman. Her curly hair, evidently having a mind of its own, drew his gaze more frequently than he cared to acknowledge. More intriguing, she radiated a confidence and an energy that he found peculiarly alluring. He hadn't experienced such a feeling in a long time.

Yet, she had not introduced herself. She had simply observed. Strange, but who was he to judge?

If she wanted to watch him, she could do so. If she wanted to speak with him rather than simply staring at his every move as if she were measuring him, she could do so. He would wait. He decided then that he wouldn't go after her.

The clash of steel brought the Master of the Gladiators' eyes and focus back to the white sand. Davin, Lycia, and Bryen had been running through a series of forms to warm up for their training session, and the real fun had just begun.

Bryen had taken a position in the center of the Pit, twirling in front of him with comfortable skill the double-bladed spear that he had acquired at the Aeyrie. Davin and

Lycia circled him, Davin with his preferred spear, Lycia with a curved sword in each hand.

It reminded him of what it was like before Duke Winborne took Bryen from the Colosseum. These three had always trained together. So just as he had done so many times before, his critical eye began to note ways that they could improve their performance as Davin lunged with his spear, Bryen spinning away, knocking the tip of his friend's weapon to the side, then in the same motion raising the blade on the other end of his spear to parry first a slash and then a powerful cut by Lycia, who sought to use her brother's attack to her advantage. As Declan expected, it didn't work as the twins hoped that it would.

Bryen had dealt with their first assault easily, but this was just the beginning. During the next few minutes, Declan watched with increasing pleasure as the three gladiators glided across the sand, sword striking spear, spear striking spear, demonstrating a skill that few could ever hope to achieve. Best of all, in this moment they were not preparing to fight for their lives on the white sand. That added a measure of enjoyment to his observing and critiquing that he had never experienced before.

Declan understood why Bryen wanted to do this, and it wasn't just so that he could spend time with his friends. It was only yesterday that he had gained Duchess Stelekel's permission to leave the rooms she had assigned to him in the Corinthian Palace, the Magus satisfied that he had healed enough from the wound that he had suffered while dueling with the Ghoule Overlord to begin his regular activities again. Just as Declan had ingrained within him, Bryen wanted to get out onto the sand as quickly as he could so that he could test his strength and determine what else might be required for him to make a full recovery.

How that entire episode had occurred, Bryen disappearing from the battlements of the Corinthian Palace within a black mist and then returning in a white mist that appeared out of nowhere, filled him with a sense of dread. But that was the way of the world now, wasn't it? Bryen had new responsibilities and new abilities that would terrify most sane people. And Declan was willing to admit, at least to himself, that what Bryen could do made him uncomfortable.

It always had, Declan having some experience with Magii from his time in the Royal Guard. Which begged the question, why were his eyes always drawn to the curly haired, intimidating Magus when she was around? He grumbled with displeasure. That thought was neither here nor there. So he returned to the here and now.

He refused to allow his unease with Bryen's new ability to get in the way of doing whatever he could to help the young man whom he viewed as his son. Unlike his time in the Colosseum, where routine was preferred and a welcome part of life, change was a constant now. He could do nothing about it and trying to fight it was wasted time and effort. Because though change wasn't always good, it wasn't always bad either. It just was. So better just to adjust.

Bryen caught Declan's eyes as he stalked around the Pit much like the wolf he had been named for. He smiled, though only briefly, his eyes on a swivel as he tracked Davin and Lycia, the brother and sister keeping him between them. The twins seemed to know what the other was going to do before he or she did it, which exponentially increased the difficulty that Bryen faced.

Despite that, Bryen relished the challenge. When he turned slightly toward Lycia, Davin jabbed with his spear, aiming the blow for Bryen's calf. He had expected that, Lycia having stepped gracefully away from him while Davin left himself slightly exposed. Bryen used that slight opening to break the noose they had set over him, giving Lycia a nudge in the hip with the haft of his spear so that she stumbled toward her brother.

That gave Bryen the relief that he had sought. Now Bryen had both Davin and Lycia to his front, no longer needing to protect his back. He took full advantage. Feinting toward Lycia, who was still regaining her balance, she had no choice but to scuttle away from him. Then Bryen swung toward Davin's thigh. When the gladiator brought the haft of his spear down to block the blow, Bryen immediately pivoted on his heel, stabbing backward with his spear to keep Davin wary and put some distance between them so that Bryen could attack Lycia with a series of slashes and lunges that forced her to scramble around the Pit.

As the practice combat continued, Bryen felt more and more like himself. The wound from the Ghoule Overlord had not acted like the others he had received when struck with the Curse. This appeared to be no more than a burn across his side caused by one of the facets of the black diamond, although it was taking longer to heal when compared to some of the other injuries he had suffered during his time as a gladiator. Even his application of the Talent hadn't helped as much as he hoped it would.

Nevertheless, after his previous two bouts with Dark Magic, both of which had almost killed him, Duchess Stelekel had wanted to make certain that he was all right. That had translated to several more days stuck in a bed with Aislinn keeping an eye on him as much as she could.

Not a fun experience, not like right now as he skimmed across the sand like a cutter through the Silent Sea, giving just as good as he was getting. He had been away for more than a year, but it didn't seem like he'd ever left the Colosseum.

He was still a bit tired, though that was normal as his body continued to heal. The burn was slowly becoming another scar to go with the many others he had acquired already, the wound now offering him little more than a sting as he challenged his friends.

He felt good. Strong. Besides, he needed to keep his skills sharp for what would be required of him. For what he needed to do next. Whether he wanted to or not. So what better way to prepare than to practice with his two best friends, both of whom happened to be two of the best gladiators in Caledonia.

As Bryen moved her around the Pit, despite the fact that he was getting the better of her by controlling the pace of the fight -- something that usually set her temper flaring -- Lycia couldn't stop smiling. It had been too long since she had tested herself against Bryen, and she relished the opportunity to do so again. Even more so, the chance to finally get some time with him, although she would have preferred that Davin make himself scarce so that she could be alone with him.

At least she didn't have to deal with the Lady of the Southern Marches. Lycia still hadn't decided what she thought of Aislinn Winborne, her opinion shifting every time she interacted with the woman. However, she had made her mind up regarding the Duchess of Murcia, concluding that she was a woman of steel wrapped in a velvet gown. She had also concluded that the two women and the Dukes were little different from one another, all of them wanting to get their hooks into Bryen, each one for different reasons.

She pushed away her concerns, not wanting to deal with

that burden as she enjoyed her time in the Pit. This practice session against Bryen brought to mind the first time that she had trained here. Declan had put her and Davin on the white sand to test their skills against Bryen, his best gladiator. Her brother had been overly confident right from the start, thinking himself a better fighter than most after their many melees on the streets of Tintagel before they had been thrown into the Colosseum.

When their parents died, Lycia and Davin had nowhere to go. Their uncle had taken their house and thrown them out, not wanting to deal with children. That wasn't entirely correct, actually. Her uncle had offered to allow them to stay in their own home so long as Lycia was willing to perform certain services for him.

Before Lycia could knife him, Davin had, and from then on they had struggled to scratch out a meager living in the capital, avoiding whenever they could the many miscreants who sought to take advantage of or profit from them. And when they couldn't, their knives came into play.

They had survived for more than a year, begging when absolutely necessary, usually stealing. It was a rough life. An uncertain life. A treacherous one, as well. Whenever danger threatened, a frequent occurrence usually in the form of another thief trying to take the food that they had acquired or, on occasion, some lord or merchant thinking that they could have their way with either of the street rats, blood tended to be shed.

But never theirs. No, never theirs. Because the twins knew how to fight. Their father, a former soldier, had taught them what he could before he died. What they had learned had helped them survive that ordeal, and it gave them a fighting chance when they entered the Pit. Still, it hadn't prepared them for coming face to face with the Volkun.

When they first stepped into the Pit, they had studied their opponent just as they had done on the streets. Identifying strengths. Looking for weaknesses.

Bryen was tall and lean, not an ounce of fat on him. Because of that, Davin had assumed that he could use his several additional stones of muscle to take down the Volkun just as he had so often done in the alleys of Tintagel. Lycia had been less certain and more circumspect when she had seen Bryen for the first time. Davin tended to be impulsive. He'd jump into things and if it wasn't working out, he would find some way to extricate himself and move on. A risky approach at times though one that worked for him.

Lycia preferred to observe and learn, thinking before she made any decisions. And it was because of her thoughtfulness that she understood that Declan wouldn't have pitted her or her brother against Bryen when the two first arrived in the Colosseum if there wasn't a reason for it. It wasn't just to test their skills. It was also to make a point to them, to show them the level they needed to aspire to if they hoped to live for any length of time in the Pit.

In fact, she remembered that experience, half a decade in the past, as if it were yesterday.

"That's it. Never square. Always one foot in front of the other," Bryen had said.

Lycia had turned her body as Bryen circled around her, always keeping her eyes on his as she soaked in his instructions. "Stay on your toes for balance," he had urged.

Bryen had feinted a quick jab toward her, and she had scuttled back a few feet, always keeping her right foot forward and her sword in front of her, just as her father had taught her.

"Good," Bryen had complimented her. "Well done.

Remember, always on your toes. If you're caught on flat feet, you're dead."

Davin had tried his luck against the Volkun before she did, thinking that it would be an easy lesson, one that he would administer, actually. It hadn't been. It had been a humbling encounter and one that had stayed with her brother for weeks afterwards.

Once Bryen had put Davin in his place, Lycia's brother had found a spot along the wall of the Pit where there was just a hint of shade, attempting to get out of the hot sun and cool off, though his temper had continued to simmer even after Lycia had tried to talk some sense into him.

"You can't expect to come here and win right at the start," Lycia had told Davin.

"Why not?" he had demanded, his ire still up, not used to getting beaten. "It worked on the street."

"It's not going to work here," she had said with some fire, trying to smother his anger and capture his attention. "We are not fighting thieves. We are not fighting people seeking to use us. We are fighting people whose only desire is to kill us."

"That still shouldn't ..."

Davin had tried to continue his argument. Lycia had refused to allow him to waste her time.

"We are fighting people who know how to fight. Who know how to fight better than we do. You've heard the whispers about the Volkun in the streets. They wouldn't say those things if there wasn't some truth in them."

"Yes, but I just thought that those were rumors. They seemed too fanciful to believe."

"Clearly they are not," Lycia had clarified for him.

Though neither of them had ever visited the gladiatorial

games, they had heard of the Volkun. Fast. Relentless. Deadly. The best gladiator in the Kingdom.

They hadn't cared. Their concerns were more mundane. Food. Shelter. Safety. Until now. Now they needed to add survival to the mix.

And Davin needed to realize that you couldn't judge a book by its cover. Bryen didn't appear all that imposing. That was likely part of the reason why he was so successful in the Pit, surprising some of the more overconfident gladiators.

Lycia had understood. Davin had only tested himself for thirty minutes against the boy who was no older than he was and who had introduced himself as Bryen, her brother having ignored Lycia's attempts to explain to him who his adversary really was. Because he was a bit taller than Bryen and obviously more muscular, Davin had thought that he would do well against his smiling adversary.

He hadn't, spending more time picking himself up from the sand than actually fighting. Bryen was faster and demonstrated greater skill than Davin had anticipated, though that didn't prove to be Lycia's experience. She had known what was going to happen, and after her brother had decided to ignore her warnings, she had let him go. Sometimes there was only one way to learn. The hard way.

"Instead of staying angry," Lycia had said. "Get smart. Watch. Learn. Then apply. That's our only chance here. The Volkun wasn't trying to make a fool out of you. He was trying to teach you. You were so wrapped up in yourself that you ignored the tutorial."

With that, Lycia had left Davin along the wall of the Pit, walking as confidently as she could toward an opponent who she knew she couldn't beat. It had been frightening, but she had refused to allow her fears to show.

Instead, she had taken all that she had learned from watching her brother and used it during her own session with the Volkun. Lycia had lasted a bit longer than Davin had against Bryen, in large part because she hadn't approached the session with a host of misplaced assumptions as her brother had, and she had absorbed the stream of advice that Bryen offered, grateful to receive it, putting everything he advised to use as soon as she heard it.

Still, even as Lycia continued to take in everything that Bryen had to say, questions had run rampant through her mind. How long had the Wolf lasted as a gladiator? The scars lining his arms certainly attested to his skill. How had he acquired the scars on his cheek and neck? They appeared to be newly healed. And why was his hair turning grey prematurely? No, not grey. White. Was it the stress of fighting in the Pit? Something else?

"Lycia, focus!" Bryen had shouted at her. "If you lose your concentration on the white sand, you die."

Lycia immediately had pushed all her questions to the back of her mind and brought her sword up again quickly, catching Bryen's blade as it swept toward her neck. She then had danced back and put some space between them, thankful that he was just trying to wake her up and hadn't continued his attack. It hadn't taken her long to figure out why the crowd had given Bryen his name. He did move like a wolf as he glided across the white sand.

Lycia forced herself back to the present, understanding that if she continued to allow her memories to cloud her focus, Bryen would knock her on her ass again in an instant, the only reason he hadn't yet being the fact that he had been focusing most of his attention on Davin.

To ensure that Bryen didn't gain the upper hand on her, Lycia feinted a lunge with one sword, then swung for Bryen's head with the other blade. She hadn't expected her strike to hit, and it didn't. Her attack served another purpose. It allowed her to get behind Bryen once more, the twins circling him again, waiting for the perfect chance.

Bryen smiled, impressed by how swiftly Lycia placed the noose back around his neck. Either Davin and Lycia had improved their skills since he had last practiced with them or he was still feeling the effects of his latest wound. He was going to give himself the benefit of the doubt, telling himself that it was probably both as his side began to ache. He might have overdone it, he had to admit. Still, he refused to stop the combat. That wasn't his way.

Besides, he had a feeling that the combat was coming to an end. Lycia had performed a very nice maneuver to divide his attention between them, just as she and Davin had done much the same so many times before. It was what they specialized in and had brought them so much success during their combats in the Pit. So he decided to try one more attack, just to see if he could get lucky, even though he assumed that against his two friends it was a fool's errand.

Unfortunately, it didn't take long for Davin and Lycia to prove him right. Bryen launched himself at Lycia, swinging low with his spear, then coming right back around with a blow aimed for his friend's head. Lycia blocked both strikes, though she was slow to stop the second, which forced her off balance.

Bryen was about to exploit that weakness when he felt himself falling through the air, Davin having swept his feet out from under him with his spear. He landed heavily in the feathery sand of the Pit, a small grin breaking out on his face.

Peering up from where he lay, his vision narrowed to the point of Lycia's sword, which was just above his right eye.

She stood behind him so that she appeared to be upside down when he was looking at her.

"Better to go for the throat," Bryen said. "I can't turn my throat. But if I turn my head when you go for my eye, the steel might just slide off the bone. I might be able to get back up or perhaps even use a dagger against you."

Mention of the dagger made Lycia look down. Bryen held his foot-long blade poised just to the side of her knee. She calculated quickly what could happen if Bryen was correct about her missing his eye, concluding that he was right. He would be wounded, badly, but he could still fight through the pain. Knowing him, he still would. If he stabbed her in the knee, she would lose her mobility. Not a fair trade.

"Why are you always teaching a lesson?" asked Lycia. "Why can't you just yield like everyone else?"

"Habit," Bryen replied with a smile. "Too much time spent with Declan."

"I heard that," came a gruff voice from just above them.

For just a moment, Lycia stared down at Bryen, studying him. He really hadn't changed much since he had been gone, except for that damned collar that he still wore around his neck. Then she gave him a grin, the mischievous look in her eye bringing Bryen back to when he and Lycia used to spend time together in the gladiators' compound.

"The famous Wolf on his back in the Pit," said Davin. "I never thought that I'd see the day."

"There's a first time for everything," Bryen replied.

Finally, Lycia removed the tip of her sword from just above his eye, then she knelt down on one knee, leaning in close to Bryen so that he could only see her face and nothing else, their noses, their lips, almost touching.

"What will you give me if I let you up?" asked Lycia, her

voice taking on a tone that he had not heard since he had left the Pit.

"What do you want?"

"I'll let you know when the time is right," she said. "Just be ready for when I decide to collect."

Lycia then offered her hand to Bryen and helped him to his feet. Before he could brush the white sand from his clothes, Lycia pulled Bryen in close to her.

"And you can be certain that when I do collect, you will enjoy it," whispered Lycia.

Then she kissed Bryen lightly on the lips. With a grin, Lycia sheathed her twin swords and walked away, making for the tunnel that led to the gladiators' compound.

Bryen's gaze followed Lycia as she left the Pit. Davin picked that moment to sneak up next to him.

"What was that about?" asked Bryen.

"I could guess," replied Davin, patting Bryen's shoulder in a comforting way. "But I really don't want to."

"That's probably a good idea."

"I know it's a good idea. Just remember."

"Remember what?"

"The golden rule for surviving in the Pit."

Bryen chuckled at that. He and Davin had engaged in this conversation many times. "Don't make Lycia angry."

"Correct," replied Davin. "I'm glad you haven't forgotten despite all your time away from the white sand. You know Lycia. Very mysterious. Also very dangerous."

"That's what I'm worried about," grumbled Bryen.

"Nothing to do but see what happens," offered Davin unhelpfully. "You'll find out one way or the other."

"That's not very comforting."

"It wasn't meant to be."

12

SOME NEEDED PERSUASION

"I always found in a situation like that, your opponent trying to come in tight on you, that turning the blade just so," said Declan, who twisted the sword in his hand to a forty five degree angle and held it in that manner, "gave you a better chance of knocking away the spear or at least sliding across it with your blade. Then you should be in a position to slash backward for the leg, and you won't have to turn the blade again. You'll find the quadricep or the hamstring every time, depending on how much your adversary has overreached when he or she slides past you."

"Yes, I agree," said Tarin Tentillin. He and Jerad had joined Davin, Lycia, Declan, and Bryen in the Pit after their early morning training session. Bryen had suggested that his two friends from the Battersea Guard join the gladiators to test their skills. They had arrived later than they had wanted because of the need to help Duke Winborne prepare the soldiers of the Southern Marches for the journey to the Winter Pass.

"You can also change your grip if necessary," continued Tarin. "It's harder to do, but it's less wear on your wrist."

"I've tried that," said Jerad. He rotated his grip on the hilt of his sword so that when he extended his arm fully the blade didn't line up perfectly straight with his wrist as it normally would. "I see your point, but it feels strange. Almost unnatural."

"Try it a few times," suggested Tarin. "And definitely if you take on Lycia again. The grip that Declan is suggesting would have helped you when she cut across your side. Of course not entirely because she's so fast, but you may have been able to catch her if you didn't need to take the extra half-second to get your sword at the appropriate angle to meet her attack. After that, you can make a better judgment. "

The soldiers of the Battersea Guard and the gladiators had trained for several hours. That done, as was the wont of fighters, they were discussing how to improve on their performance in the Pit, while also trading stories. Bryen hoped that it was the beginnings of a loose camaraderie that would strengthen over time. With the challenges that he expected to come his way, he understood that building a stronger fellowship among the people who would be working with him was essential to his and their success.

As the others continued their discussion, Jerad found himself distracted after being the focus of the group's attention for a short time. Lycia stood across from him. She had shown during their combat why she had been named the Crimson Devil. She was fast. Very fast. Almost as fast as Bryen. And she was an excellent fighter, having learned every trick there was to survive on the white sand.

Jerad had held his own for most of the bout. It wasn't until the last minute that she caught him in a mistake, making a last-second attempt to knock her to the ground with a poorly timed charge, and thus the lengthy conversation about how to grip a sword when attempting such a maneuver so that you could more easily defend against the inevitable counterattack.

It was her fiery spirit that had caught his attention, which he had seen firsthand during their combat and the others that he had watched her fight that morning. She hadn't lost a single bout, her combat with her brother ending in a draw as the two gladiators both demonstrated why they had become favorites of the crowd. Unable to drag his eyes away from her, he realized that there was something about Lycia that pulled his attention toward her. It didn't take long for Lycia to notice.

"Is there a problem, Sergeant?" Lycia's strong gaze was challenging, her eyes harder than granite, just as they had been when they had competed in the Pit. Jerad was getting the feeling that Lycia viewed most interactions with other people as competitions, and she seemed aggravated by his unforeseen and perhaps unwanted attention.

"No," Jerad replied quickly with what he hoped was a disarming smile. "Why would you think that?"

"Because you've been staring at me for the last five minutes. I feel like there must be a sprig of parsley stuck between my teeth and you're afraid to tell me it's there."

"No, I assure you. It's nothing like that."

"Then what is it?" asked Lycia with raised eyebrows, not backing down.

Her tone remained a challenge. Jerad wasn't worried. He was used to relying on his charm to win over people, especially the ladies.

"I just like looking at you," he replied casually with his characteristic grin, throwing in a little sheepishness when he saw that she still wasn't smiling. "There's something about you ... I just can't put my finger on it."

Lycia studied him for a time, considering, then she nodded her head. "Good to know. Stop it. Now."

"You don't want me to look at you?" Jerad asked, realizing that he might need a different approach than had worked with other women.

"Not the way you're looking at me now."

Jerad didn't know if he should try to intensify his charm or just give up. So he decided to pursue the conversation because he was curious about her reaction. "Why not?"

"I've heard quite a bit about you," Lycia said.

"Only good things, I hope," Jerad said, keeping his grin, which had been in danger of slipping. Lycia finally smiled at something that he had said, though that smile held little warmth.

"Not entirely," Lycia replied, crossing her arms. "Bryen says you're a good fighter and a good friend." That comment helped to revive Jerad's confidence, which immediately deflated after what Lycia said next. "But the soldier I was speaking with said that your eye tended to wander. She says that's because you are afraid to commit to a relationship. She mentioned that several times, in fact. Your inability to commit."

"Ah, well, I can assure you ..." Jerad said as he started to defend himself.

Lycia cut him off. "She also said that because of your inability to commit, you couldn't stay focused on any one woman for more than a few days. Looking at you now and how you're reacting to my words, I'd have to say that I agree with her."

"That's a very specific evaluation, one that I would challenge. Who told you all this?" Jerad's heart was in his throat, a slight sheen of sweat appearing on his forehead, which made Lycia smile again, although the smile never reached her eyes.

"She said that she was your Corporal," Lycia replied. "A very intense soldier from the Battersea Guard. I liked that about her, her intensity. She didn't seem to be the type of person who you wanted to anger very frequently."

"Dani?" Jerad whispered.

"Yes, Dani," said Lycia. "That is her name, correct?"

"Yes, that's right," Jerad confirmed, though he could barely get the words out, his mind a jumble of disparate thoughts.

"A bit of advice, Sergeant," said Lycia.

He could only nod in response, trying to puzzle out why Dani was talking about him and why what she had said hit so close to the truth.

"If you keep looking for something better, or something different, then you're going to miss out on what's already right in front of you. And often what's right in front of you is much, much better than what you think might be of interest to you."

Jerad nodded again, only half listening. He thought that his constant banter with Dani was fun and harmless. He flirted with everyone. Obviously, he was missing something or perhaps willfully ignoring it.

"And one other piece of advice, Sergeant. Your Corporal clearly has a great deal of skill with the blade. I wouldn't make her angry. Be safe by being smart."

Jerad smiled and nodded a third time. He really needed to rethink his approach to women. Perhaps he should speak with Dani. Apparently, there were some issues that they needed to discuss. He liked his interactions with Dani. They were flirtatious and fun. It was also easy to converse with her. Jerad didn't want to change that. He didn't want to make that mistake. Then again, perhaps his mistake had been not making his feelings known to her and then hiding his emotions behind his flirtatious behavior.

Tarin's commanding voice brought Jerad's eyes back to the larger group.

"You all right, Sergeant?" asked Tarin, who was worried. His second in command had turned remarkably pale.

"Yes, Captain."

Tarin looked at Jerad a bit longer, then nodded, apparently satisfied with his response. He then turned back toward Declan. The Master of the Gladiators was a font of knowledge. So he decided to pick his brain.

"So tell me, Declan. Bryen shared quite a few of your sayings when he was with us in the Southern Marches. I've found that with some of our younger soldiers," Tarin pointedly shifting his gaze toward Jared as if to emphasize his point, "that they sometimes lose concentration."

"Lose your concentration ..." began Declan.

"And you lose your life," finished Bryen, Lycia, and Davin in perfect unison.

"Rightly so," nodded Declan, pleased that the three gladiators recalled his advice so readily.

"I couldn't agree more," said Tarin. "Bryen started as a gladiator at a very young age. Young minds tend to wander. How did you get him to concentrate?"

"Do you remember what I used to tell you, lad, before each of your fights?" asked Declan.

"It's hard to forget," replied Bryen. "I'll see you on the other side, because I doubt that you'll be walking out from those gates again."

"Not very encouraging," said Davin. "I'm starting to see where Bryen gets his approach to helping people about to risk their lives."

"No, not very encouraging," replied Bryen. "It was very motivating."

"If you hadn't noticed, our somewhat intimidating friend here finds it difficult not accepting a challenge," said Declan. "So I challenged him before every combat indirectly. And each time I did, he came back through those gates, so I kept doing it until I didn't feel the need to worry about him anymore."

"How long did that take?" asked Lycia.

"Several years," said Declan. "By then I realized that the only person who could beat Bryen in the Pit was me, so I felt like his chances of walking off the white sand were fairly strong."

"Yes, he does have a knack for surviving situations he shouldn't," said Tarin. "When I first met Bryen, I thought very little of him."

"The feeling was mutual," confirmed Bryen with a sardonic grin.

"Rightfully so," said Tarin. "I never thought that a gladiator could best a soldier of the Battersea Guard."

"Hold on," said Davin. "You didn't think that a gladiator ..."

"I was wrong, of course," clarified Tarin immediately, not wanting to give offense where none was intended. "When he killed four assassins in a matter of minutes, my doubts about him disappeared, although I took my time before telling him. Didn't want it to go to his head."

"Smart move," agreed Declan. "His ego, though not readily revealed, is big enough as it is."

"He did what?" asked Lycia. Her hard gaze suggested that she wasn't thrilled that he had taken such a risk. "What fool would fight four assassins on his own?"

"I had no choice," said Bryen, trying to mitigate Lycia's

anger before it really started burning. "The magic of the collar required it. I had no choice as a Protector because Aislinn's life was in danger."

"Aislinn?" replied Lycia, not at all impressed with the reason he had to risk his own life and not pleased that he had become so familiar with his charge that he used her first name.

"Lady Winborne at the time," corrected Bryen.

"What else were you required to do for Lady Winborne?" asked Lycia, ice crystallizing around her words.

Before Bryen could respond, not expecting the flash of anger behind Lycia's eyes, Tarin chose that moment to interrupt, shifting his gaze to Jerad.

"Remember when he stood on his horse and took on that Elder Ghoule?" asked Tarin. "Talk about reckless."

"He did what?" asked Lycia, her voice now dangerously quiet.

Jerad was more than happy to fill her in, missing the implications of her tone and pleased that he was no longer the focus of her attention. "I won't bore you with the details, but it was at the pivotal moment in the battle. Our company had put up a good fight against several dozen Ghoules, but the Elder Ghoule had massed his fighters, sending them all against us at once and the pressure was becoming too much for us. Several of our soldiers had fallen. Lady Winborne kept the Elder busy so that he couldn't direct his Dark Magic toward us. Despite that, we were close to being overwhelmed by the sheer number of Ghoules. Then out of nowhere Bryen shot from the tip of our wedge formation, riding his horse directly toward the Elder Ghoule."

"Why am I not surprised," muttered Declan. Bryen had always been brave, almost to the point of imprudence. "I hasten to note that there's often little to separate foolishness from bravery."

"Three Ghoules stepped in front of his horse, seeking to protect the Elder," continued Jerad, caught in the grips of his own story. "Rather than turning away as most sane people would do, Bryen pushed himself up onto the back of his mount, holding the reins in one hand and his sword in the other. Right before he slammed into the Ghoules, who were ready to stab his horse in the chest with their spears, he pulled back sharply on the reins. His mount dug its front hooves into the dirt, and when its backside went up into the air, so did Bryen, flipping over the Ghoules to land right in front of the Elder Ghoule."

"The Dumerians?" asked Declan, remembering the horse riders from the plains who had taught Bryen quite a bit when they were in the Colosseum.

Bryen nodded. "I was sorry to see them go."

"As was I," murmured Declan. There was only one way to leave the Pit after all.

"You still haven't learned, have you?" asked Lycia, though she didn't expect an answer from Bryen. "Even though you left the Pit, you never really did, did you?"

Jerad was surprised by Lycia's comment, and with the angry glint that he saw in her eyes and the signal that Davin was giving to him to stop talking, he ended his story swiftly.

"Bryen then took on the Elder Ghoule, broke the beast's staff, broke his own sword in the process, and then stabbed the Elder in the heart with what was left of his steel ... though not before the Elder stabbed him in the side with his broken staff and Bryen almost died because of the Dark Magic that it contained," finished Jerad.

"You almost died?" Lycia's face had turned a bright red, and both Davin and Bryen wisely decided to take a few steps away from her. Before she could say anything else, the Captain of the Battersea Guard interjected with his take on what had happened.

"Quite foolhardy, in my opinion," said Tarin. "Nevertheless, I have to admit that what Bryen did worked, and despite the risk that he took, he saved us all. If he hadn't killed the Elder, I doubt that Lady Winborne would have been able to hold him off for much longer."

"Yes, foolhardy comes to mind," said Lycia, staring at Bryen with a sharp look. She hadn't heard that story, and she wasn't pleased that he had placed himself in such a dangerous situation. Then again, she wasn't surprised by his actions. He was who he was. He wasn't going to change. Still, her gaze promised Bryen that they would be having a conversation about this, particularly on the need to demonstrate greater caution in the future.

Getting the gist of what was to come from Lycia thanks to her icy stare, Bryen was thankful that Duke Winborne, Duchess Stelekel, Aislinn, Sirius, and Rafia chose that moment to walk out of the tunnel that led from the Pit to the gladiators' stockade. He knew why they were there, and he wasn't looking forward to the conversation to follow. But he also knew that if they hadn't arrived, then Lycia would have put her pointed thoughts to words. He wasn't in the mood to suffer through the lecture that she clearly planned to give him, the pain of the conversation that Rafia and Sirius wanted to have with him preferable to that.

"I TAKE it that you and the other lords and ladies of the land have been discussing the larger threat facing the Kingdom," said Tarin.

"Yes, we will need every fighter who we can muster at the Winter Pass," explained Sirius, his eyes seeking those of the gladiators and soldiers who had circled around him. "We need to buy time for Bryen to accomplish his mission. The Ghoules will come. Of that, have no doubt, and even if we tried to hold them back with all the Royal Guard and all the Duchy Guards, we would still be hard-pressed and fighting a losing battle. The key to our success, our only chance to keep the Ghoule Overlord and the bulk of his Legions out of Caledonia, is to rebuild the Weir."

Everyone standing around Sirius listened in rapt attention, finally getting the full story as the Magus outlined all that needed to be accomplished, the challenges involved, and, perhaps most unsettling, the very short timeline for seeking to prevent the coming Ghoule onslaught. Everyone except for two.

Bryen listened with half an ear, Rafia catching his eye and giving him a sad smile. They both had heard much the same from Sirius multiple times, the old Magus continuing to push Bryen toward the path that he thought was necessary. Bryen was the only one who had any chance to repair the Weir, even though he had absolutely no idea how to do it. The fact that his efforts might come to naught was irrelevant to Sirius.

If Bryen failed, so be it. Sirius didn't expect a miracle, but at least they would have done all that they could to protect the Kingdom. A Kingdom that until recently had little use for Bryen other than to see him bleed right here on the white sand of the Pit. Now, that same Kingdom for the sake of its survival required that he risk his life once more.

Ironic, wasn't it? The same Kingdom that had treated him and his friends as less than human required him to accept the possibility that he would need to make the ultimate sacrifice in order for that same Kingdom to persist in the face of the Ghoule threat.

Bryen understood that the necessity of his possible sacrifice was real. Sirius had belabored the point time and time again just as he was doing now, having just moved on to explaining how the Weir was created and that the Seven Stones, which provided the power that generated the magical barrier, were weakening, which meant that the Ten Magii's construction was degrading over time.

It was not unexpected. No magical application, no matter how powerful, could maintain its strength forever. The reality of the situation suggested that the fate of Caledonia was balanced on a razor's edge. No one knew when the Weir was going to fail. It could last one year. Maybe another decade. Two, perhaps. Maybe even a century.

Of course, all that didn't really matter if the Ghoule Overlord, even at great cost, could force his Legions into the Kingdom as he was doing now. The Ghoule Overlord's callousness toward his own creatures ensured that the razor would tip in only one direction, and one that did not favor the people of Caledonia.

"We all know that more and more Ghoules are breaking through the Weir," continued Sirius, the Magus giving Bryen a disapproving look to bring the Volkun back to the dialogue since he appeared to have been daydreaming. "That will only continue as the barrier degrades, until the Legions once again inundate the Breakwater Plateau and the lands below just as they did during the First Ghoule War. We have no choice. We must act now. We must risk all now. If we wait any longer, it won't matter. We will have ceded the initiative to the Ghoule Overlord, and we cannot permit that to happen. We must exercise what control we can, and that means moving forward on two fronts as I've proposed. It is our only option."

Bryen smiled again, this time shaking his head slightly, a movement that required Rafia to hold back a laugh. He was certain that the Keeper of Haven was thinking the same thing that he was. Sirius, Master of the Magii, clearly liked to hear the sound of his own voice.

As amusing and expected as that was, Bryen still needed to make a decision. Now. The same questions that had been passing through his mind during the last few days reared up within him once more.

Why didn't he leave Caledonia when he could have? Why didn't he take a ship to the Territories as he had wanted to for so long? Why did he still feel some responsibility to the people of the Kingdom who until now only cared if he put on a good show here in the Colosseum? Why did he always have to do what was expected of him despite the potential cost?

"You must do what you must do." Every time these and his many other questions looped through his mind, after each one he heard Declan's gravelly voice say, "You must do what you must do." At least he knew the answer to his last question.

Bryen glanced across at the Master of the Gladiators, who listened intently to all that Sirius had to say. Declan had played an important role in molding Bryen into the person whom he had become, his influence seen not only in Bryen's martial skill but also in his ability to evaluate a difficult situation by taking in all the relevant variables and making a good decision. And if the circumstances that made up that situation changed, such as during the Battle of the Horseshoe, he had the flexibility and creativity to adjust his strategy on the fly.

Bryen shook his head slightly again, reluctantly admitting the truth to himself. There was nothing for it. He was who he was. He couldn't change that, and in all honesty, he didn't want to. Declan was like a father to him.

The fact that he was where he was now, in a position where the fate of the Kingdom essentially rested on his shoulders, was because of all that Declan had done for him as he grew from a frightened child into the Volkun, the most dangerous gladiator in all of Caledonia, while also picking up a few other unique skills along the way that he was still learning to master.

"You must do what you must do." There really was no good way around it. And there really was no reason to try to fight it. That was wasted time and wasted effort, and he hated to do either.

Bryen knew what was required of him. He had known since Sirius and Rafia had first discussed the matter with him. Then, he hadn't felt the need to make it easy for them. Now, he just wanted to get started.

If he was going to do this, he wanted to do it, so that if he was successful he could move on, and if he wasn't, well ... it really didn't matter if he wasn't successful, because if Sirius and Rafia were correct, he and most of the people with him now would be dead.

"Sirius, I'll do ..."

Bryen didn't have the chance to finish what he was going to say because Sirius simply continued with his argument, ignoring everything else around him.

"As you know, you are needed, Bryen. You are the only one who has a chance at reconstructing the Weir. The way will be fraught with danger, I'm certain. So you will need all the assistance that you can get. And I have no doubt that many of these good folk with us now will be more than willing to help you. Have no fear of that."

"Sirius, enough." Bryen finally cut off the Magus, catching him while he was taking another deep breath before he rambled on. "I'll do it. You can stop trying to persuade me. Besides, you've made the same argument three times now. You've just flipped the words around. I'm sure that everyone here understands what's required. Can we move on to how we're going to make this happen? Time is short, just as you've been saying for the last fifteen minutes."

"I have not been repeating myself," declared Sirius, feeling somewhat slighted, but only just as he was more pleased that Bryen had agreed to do as he had asked.

"Actually, you have," confirmed Rafia, unwilling to let go of this opportunity to tease Sirius. "You've been droning on more than usual."

"I have not been droning on," protested Sirius. "Besides, you've barely been listening to me the entire time."

"I know what I'm talking about because I've heard it all before. And I have been listening. I've had no choice but to listen to you for the last ..."

Before the Keeper of Haven and the Master of the Magii could engage in the bickering that was so much a part of their relationship, Declan stepped forward.

"Clearly you two have issues to resolve. But we are not here to listen to you. If you wish to continue, take it elsewhere. We have more important matters to discuss."

Declan's words made Rafia stop short, her mouth open for just a moment as she tried to think of the last time that someone had dared to interrupt her in such a way. Then she closed her mouth abruptly, not wanting her surprise to continue to show. She was even more shocked when she interpreted the look that the Master of the Gladiators was giving her. He seemed to think that she was wasting his time, and he didn't care for that. Not in the least.

She had yet to speak with Declan in any depth, having watched a few training sessions and gathered some useful information about him from others. So far all that she had heard about him was true, because few had the courage to interrupt her, and no one had the courage to challenge her as he had just done. Even more surprising, and perhaps even more provocative, was the fact that Declan hadn't bothered to wait for her reply, instantly shifting the discussion to what was on his mind.

"Why must Bryen be the one to rebuild the Weir?" he asked, turning his unflinching gaze toward Sirius. "Why can't someone else do it? I'm not going to pretend that I know all that goes into what's required in terms of working with the Seven Stones. It just seems like this is delicate work and better left to someone with more experience. You? Lady Rafia? Duchess Noorsin? You all seem to have better qualifications for this than Bryen, who has only been a Magus for less than a year."

"She's not a lady," mumbled Sirius.

"Sirius, keep your mouth ..." Before Rafia could say what was on her mind, Declan silenced her and Sirius with a look, making her distinctly uncomfortable.

"Declan, I'm just as strong as the Magii you identified," replied Bryen. "I'm actually stronger than they are."

"That may be," replied Declan. "I'll take your word for it. But how could you be expected to do something that required the Ten Magii to accomplish? I don't care how strong you are. It just doesn't make sense. One Magus cannot be expected to do the work that originally required ten."

"There's more to it than that," answered Bryen.

"Then tell me. There are more Magii here. Why must it be you to repair the Weir? Why can't they do it?"

"Because I'm more than just a Magii," replied Bryen. "I'm also the Seventh Stone."

"You're what?" The looks of shock on the faces of Tarin, Jerad, Davin, and Lycia reflected Declan's disbelief. "What do you mean? How is that even possible?"

"I don't know how it's possible. I just know that it happened. I am the Seventh Stone. It's a part of me now, and that means that I can use the power that the Seventh Stone has gifted me to reconstruct the Weir."

"What did you do, Sirius?"

Declan's voice was unnervingly soft and cold, his expression frigid. Declan now stood across from the old Magus, having shifted his positioning, his meaning clear, the challenge obvious. The idea of fighting a Magus didn't appear to faze him.

"It wasn't intentional," Sirius answered finally, the Magus seeking to defuse the situation, even though he could count on his fingers the number of times that he had backed down from a challenge during his long life. "It was done to save Bryen's life. I had no choice. Aislinn was in the Aeyrie with me taking the Test to become a Magus. While we were doing that, Ghoules attacked. Bryen must have killed at least half a dozen of the beasts and three Elders before Aislinn and I made it back outside."

"That sounds like the Volkun," murmured Davin.

"Agreed," confirmed Tarin.

"When we exited the Aeyrie, we saw that Bryen had been injured by one of the Elders, a shard of Dark Magic striking him," continued Sirius. "Neither Aislinn nor I have much skill in healing. Ironically, Bryen has great skill in healing, something that I find quite fascinating when you consider how skilled Bryen is at ..."

"Sirius, please stick to the point," interrupted Rafia gently. She realized that the Magus was about to go off on one of his infamous tangents. With the current tension circulating among the people standing in the Pit beginning to build that wouldn't help the conversation.

"Oh, yes, right," said Sirius, catching himself with Rafia's aid. "My apologies. There was no way that he could heal himself with the wound that he had sustained. Recognizing the dire nature of Bryen's condition, I brought him into the Aeyrie. In the past Bryen had healed himself using the Talent, although he didn't know that he was doing it at the time."

Declan shifted his posture, relaxing a bit. He, too, had witnessed the wounds that Bryen had received while fighting in the Pit that should have killed him, but hadn't. Bryen had survived when anyone else would have died, a fact that Declan had wondered about on occasion. Until now.

Noticing the change in Declan, Sirius took it as permission to continue. "So I then sought to tap into Bryen's innate ability to heal himself. I hoped that by having Bryen go through the Test to become a Magus, the additional power used in the process would jolt Bryen's natural healing into action."

"Unfortunately it didn't," added Aislinn quietly.

"It didn't," confirmed Sirius. "Taking the Test didn't help. Bryen was dying. Not knowing what else to do, I placed the Seventh Stone on Bryen's chest, hoping that he could harness the power contained within the diamond and use that to heal himself."

"And it did," said Declan, beginning to understand.

Sirius nodded. "Somehow Bryen used the power contained within the Seventh Stone to heal himself. That's why he's standing before you today. And for some reason that I can't explain the Seventh Stone dissolved while Bryen was using it and the jewel merged with him, becoming a part of him. The Seventh Stone is Bryen and Bryen is the Seventh Stone. The two are now inseparable, or at least as inseparable as they can be."

"You have no idea how to remove the Seventh Stone?" asked Declan resignedly, having assumed that the Magus would have already considered the question.

"No," replied Sirius. "If I could, I would. But none of us -- me, Rafia, Noorsin -- know how to accomplish that task."

"Why didn't you tell me this?" demanded Lycia, the fire in her words startling several of the people gathered in the Pit, particularly Aislinn. She was beginning to get a better sense of the relationship between the red-haired gladiator and Bryen, and she understood the hurt and betrayal Lycia obviously was feeling.

"It wasn't top of mind when I came back to Tintagel," answered Bryen. "There were more immediate matters that needed to be dealt with at the time."

"More immediate matters than the fact that you had become a Magus and were now joined with this Seventh Stone, the most powerful magical artifact in Caledonia as Sirius just explained to us multiple times?" challenged Lycia, her comment clearly not a question.

Sirius was about to protest that he had not repeated himself as Lycia suggested that he had. Instead, seeing the fiery glint in the gladiator's eyes, wisely he kept his mouth shut. A rare occurrence.

"Well, when you put it like that ...," said Bryen with an

apologetic shrug, his attempt at disarming her anger having little effect.

The look that Lycia gave Bryen was like a dagger in his heart. He knew that he had hurt her. It was his fault. He'd been avoiding her because he didn't know what to tell her or how. So much had happened since he left the Pit. So he had avoided the issues between them by avoiding her. He acknowledged now, at least to himself, how poorly he had acted.

With the lull that had fallen over the conversation, Davin tried to break the tension that had been escalating steadily.

"You know it really shouldn't be too difficult," he said with a grin that suggested that he was looking forward to the challenge. "We simply need to sneak into the Shattered Peaks, locate the Sanctuary -- I assume that one of you knows where it is," looking at Sirius and Rafia, "and then Bryen figures out how to use the Seventh Stone to rebuild the Weir before the Ghoule Overlord sends his Legions into Caledonia to kill us all. A straight-forward task with little cause for concern."

"Yes, it sounds simple, doesn't it," grumbled Lycia. "Now what's the rest of it. You haven't told us everything because there is always a catch."

"The catch," said Rafia, before Sirius could respond, "is that we'll be traveling through an area infested with Ghoules. And assuming that we make it to the Trench where the Sanctuary is located, we face black dragons and perhaps something even more dangerous. So our chances of surviving the journey are questionable at best. Even so, as Sirius made clear multiple times, we must still try."

~

"It's settled then," said the Duke of the Southern Marches. "Duke Roosarian, Duke Stennivere, and I, and Duchess Stelekel, make for the Winter Pass while the rest head to the Sanctuary."

"Not quite," Bryen said, the Protector's hesitation filling Kevan with a feeling of trepidation. "I'll do it on one condition. Well, maybe more than one."

"One condition?" asked Kevan, taken aback. "You understand what we're dealing with here? This is a threat to all of Caledonia, and you want to negotiate? I would think that you would have at least some sense of loyalty to your Kingdom."

Kevan had expected something like this from the Protector. He didn't trust that Bryen would do as needed. Why would he risk his life?

Although he refused to admit it, if Kevan was in the Protector's position, after all that had been forced upon him he'd probably seek to make the most of his circumstances as well. Still, Bryen's request was his worst fear. The Kingdom had no other option, yet there was little incentive for the Protector to take on the responsibility that only he could accomplish unless he could get something out of it for himself.

Aislinn touched her father's arm, stopping him from saying more.

"What is your condition?" asked Aislinn.

"Every gladiator in Tintagel has been declared free because of their role in removing Marden Beleron from the throne. That's a good first step," began Bryen. "I would ask that every gladiator who is a part of the Blood Company be given a fair and generous stipend if they choose not to go with me to the Sanctuary and instead decide to leave the Company. They have given more to this Kingdom than should be required of anyone. For those of the Blood Company who choose to go with me, in addition to the stipend they be given six hundred golds as a benefit that they can use or their families can use in the event of their death. And, if we are successful, each surviving member of the Blood Company be granted twenty acres in the Territories, either in Fal Carrach, the Highlands, or Benewyn, so that they have something waiting for them if they want to leave Caledonia."

"That's what you want?" asked Kevan, slightly confused, having expected much worse.

Clearly, even after all this time Kevan didn't have a firm grasp on what drove the young man. The Protector could have asked for anything as the likelihood of actually reaching the Sanctuary was less than certain. Still, he had expected that the gladiator would want something for himself, not anticipating that his focus would be on others, the amount of six hundred golds not lost on him as this was the price he had paid for Bryen so that he could force the gladiator to become Aislinn's Protector.

"Nothing for yourself?" confirmed Aislinn, who really wasn't surprised. Unlike her father, she felt like she knew Bryen better than anyone, despite what Lycia might think.

"No, just that." Bryen nodded to Declan, Lycia, and Davin, who stood there silently, still trying to comprehend what he had just done for them, assuming, of course, they survived the dangers that inevitably they would face on the journey. "I believe that my request is more than fair."

"Done," said Kevan, going against his natural instincts to negotiate and recognizing a good deal when he heard one.

"I'll need that in writing and signed by you and the other Dukes and Duchess Stelekel before we can proceed."

"You walk a fine line, gladiator," grated Duke Winborne, recognizing an obvious insult.

"Words are like the wind, are they not, Duke Winborne? Better to have everything signed and sealed. Then there can be no mistakes. No misinterpretations. No misrememberings."

"You know, lad, you can be quite aggravating. I don't believe that I have ever ..."

"We know, Duke Winborne, we can all attest to that fact," interrupted Tarin, not wanting the conversation to take the wrong path. "Would you not agree that Bryen is taking the correct approach? For an arrangement such as this, and the risks that are entailed, this seems a more than fair offer. And if you were placed in the same position as he, you, too, I am certain, would request that the agreed-upon terms be set to paper. That way, knowing that some may not survive the struggles ahead, there will be no confusion, and there will be no attempts at renegotiation."

"I agree wholeheartedly, Captain Tentillin," added Aislinn. "The fighters of the Blood Company deserve no less."

Duke Winborne looked at Duchess Stelekel, who gave him a brief nod, before responding.

"We have a deal, Protector. All the appropriate documents will be completed later today. You have nothing to fear in that regard."

"Why?" asked Tarin quietly, his question only for Bryen. "You could have asked for anything or more. You could have asked for your own Duchy and they would have given it to you. They had no leverage. They still don't. Everything depends on you. You could be the next King if you wanted."

"These men and women bled for me. They didn't have to. It's the very least that I can do for them."

The perplexing look on Tarin's face did not disappear. He still couldn't quite fathom why Bryen refused to seek something for himself.

Now that his primary concern had been addressed to his satisfaction, Bryen turned away from Tarin and sought to shift the conversation.

"I take it that we're leaving for the Sanctuary in the next few days?"

"That's our objective, yes," replied Rafia.

"And you know how to get there?" asked Lycia.

"We do," confirmed Rafia. "Sirius and I will be with Bryen every step of the way."

"Once we get there," said Declan, clearly having already decided that he would be accompanying Bryen, "how does the Seventh Stone work with the other Stones that were used to craft the Weir?"

"And how exactly does Bryen use the Seventh Stone?" asked Lycia. "You said it was a part of him, but you never said how it worked."

"All good questions," said Rafia. "And believe me, we will have plenty of time to explain all that as we make our way to the Trench. First, though, we must deal with a more crucial issue."

"Who will be coming with us," said Bryen.

"Correct," said Rafia, nodding toward the Protector. "It's a dangerous mission and we need volunteers who have the skills we need to get Bryen to the Sanctuary and understand that our success with this endeavor is far from assured."

"Actually, it should be quite fun," interjected Davin. "Ghoules. Black dragons. Who knows what other dangers? What's not to like?"

13

TESTING THEIR SKILLS

"Anything we need to worry about, Benin?"

The broad Sergeant had just trotted his horse next to Jurgen Klines, who maintained a steady pace on his destrier as the long column of soldiers followed behind him. The Blademaster found it difficult not to smile when he looked at Benin, though he did succeed in suppressing the urge, only a slight twist of his lips visible.

The Sergeant was one of the best fighters that Klines had ever had the pleasure of training. The man was motivated and smart. He learned quickly, putting whatever he was taught immediately into practice, which benefited himself and the soldiers who fought for him.

He was also restless. Klines had seen it in his eyes the first time that he had faced off against the Sergeant in the practice yard. Despite the iron discipline that Benin demonstrated as a soldier, he still felt the need to be himself. To show that he could be an individual yet still conform to the regimen of military life. And he did that in a unique way.

Benin had a talent for braiding his long beard that was both wondrous and worrisome at the same time. When

Benin had first started what had become a calming exercise for him, helping to reduce the stresses of daily life, another soldier had made the mistake of laughing at the design that he had crafted.

If the Blademaster recalled correctly, somehow the Sergeant had twisted and plaited his whiskers, which unwoven stretched well beneath his belt, into three separate braids that he had then woven together to display what resembled the ancient symbol for luck. The soldier, unable to keep his opinion to himself, had said between chuckles that the design reminded him of something else of a more lascivious nature.

The fight that followed had been short and served as an excellent lesson. The soldier had lost three teeth and suffered a broken nose and serious concussion, Benin knocking him to the cobblestones with a single, powerful blow. Since then, no one had been foolish enough to make fun of the Sergeant's unique skills, and the soldiers who served with him now looked forward to each of his new creations, some even trying to emulate Benin, though none had as of yet demonstrated his adroitness.

"No, Blademaster," replied Benin. "The scouts report nothing out of the ordinary on the grassland, but they have stayed out of the Dark Forest as you ordered. That cursed place remains a mystery."

"Good," he replied, not surprised by Benin's opinion of the woodland they were riding toward. Many of the soldiers with them shared it. "We'll learn more about the Dark Forest from the Magus than our scouts ever could have discovered." Klines nodded toward the Sergeant's chest. "An interesting new design, Benin."

Benin smiled, sitting a bit straighter in his saddle as the dark green smudge of the imposing woodland to their front gained greater clarity with each step the horses took. "Thank you, Blademaster."

"It appears to be a double-bladed spear, Benin."

"In honor of the Volkun, Blademaster. He has done more for us than we had a right to expect," replied Benin with a nod.

"A worthy tribute," replied Klines with a nod of his own. "I'm sure that the Volkun would be impressed."

"That is kind of you to say, Blademaster. Thank you."

"I'm just speaking the truth, Benin." Klines kept his gaze focused on the Dark Forest, the massive line of green that extended for leagues to each side slowly transforming into soaring individual trees. As he expected, at the very edge of the wood a lone rider wearing colorful robes watched them approach, her curly hair held back by a tightly tied shawl, though the strong breeze forced her to tuck loose strands of hair behind her ears regularly. "I see that our guide waits for us."

"Yes, Blademaster. When I spoke with her, the Magus seemed to be chomping at the bit to get moving."

"Then let's not disappoint her," replied Klines, who urged his horse to a trot, Benin and the soldiers trailing behind him doing the same to keep pace.

Within just a few minutes, the three companies of Royal Guard -- three hundred soldiers in total -- accompanying the Blademaster reached the verge of the Dark Forest. Klines, who was also now the Captain of the Royal Guard thanks to the timely and much-appreciated demise of his predecessor, Killen Sourban, was still getting used to that new title, although assuming the responsibility that had gone with it had been a simple enough adjustment.

The few hundred soldiers who had been loyal to Sourban, and through him to the King's Advisor, had been removed from the service. The thousands who remained had been pleased by the change in leadership, unaffected by the fact that Klines was the one who had removed Sourban from his position of power ... permanently. In fact, they had applauded it.

Klines had ridden out from the capital with the three companies at the request of Duchess Stelekel, who in her position as General of the Caledonian Army had asked that he work with the Magus to investigate reports of Ghoule packs to the north of Tintagel. With the bulk of the Royal Guard and the Duchy Guards moving to the northeast and the Winter Pass, she wanted to eliminate as many of the beasts that might be roving around the city as possible. She was worried about what the Ghoules could do to harm their efforts to defend against the Legions coming from the north if any packs were given free rein to their rear. A very legitimate concern in Klines' opinion, and one that needed to be addressed.

"Did you prepare your soldiers as I asked, Blademaster?"

"I did, Magus Rafia," answered Klines.

There was a spark to the Magus' eyes that Klines found disconcerting. He understood that it had something to do with the power that she controlled with the Talent. Normally that wouldn't have bothered him as he had come in contact and worked with a few Magii over the years, all of whom had a unique ability to make other people feel uncomfortable, and some who often enjoyed doing so.

But with Magus Rafia it was something else. A wildness emanated from her -- the feeling that she might do anything -- that made him distinctly nervous. Then again, perhaps that was a good thing. Perhaps that wildness would prove useful when they entered the Dark Forest.

"Noise will be kept to a minimum," he confirmed. "We

will communicate with hand signals as much as possible and no louder than in a whisper when not possible. Movement will be avoided once we are in position. We've already wrapped all loose metal in cloth so that it doesn't clash together and announce our presence at the worst possible moment. Most important of all, once we enter the wood, you are in command."

"Thank you," replied Rafia, pleased that the Blademaster had been so thorough, although she had expected no less. Klines' competence was beyond question. "I appreciate your flexibility. Will that last be a problem for you, Blademaster? It has been for some others in the past."

"No, Magus Rafia. It will not. The soldiers have been told why and they understand."

"That's good to hear, Blademaster," replied Rafia, a smile curling her lips. "I appreciate your confidence in me. And as I told you before, there is no need for such formality. Just Rafia will do."

"Yes, Rafia," Klines replied, unable to acknowledge her kindness without offering her a nod of respect.

"Then let's begin," said Rafia, who dropped from her saddle and handed the reins to a soldier who had come forward, all of the men already well versed in the plan. "Leave the horses here as we discussed. They will only be a hindrance among the trees. Leave a few squads to watch over them until we return. We don't have far to go but time is short for us to get into position."

Benin quickly took charge of the situation. Within a matter of minutes, three companies of the Royal Guard marched into the Dark Forest, a skirmish line of scouts fifty yards to their front and on each flank.

The soldiers knew what to expect upon entering the massive grove, though many still found the experience discomfiting once they stepped just a few feet into the forest, the light shifting to shadow and the constant wind playing across the grassland dying down to an unnerving quiet. The massive trees grew so close together that in some places the underbrush was almost impenetrable. The large roots, many as thick as a broad-shouldered man, crisscrossed the forest floor and served as constant obstacles that required the soldiers to step out of formation, the once organized companies unavoidably breaking into smaller groups as they moved deeper into the wood.

Because the trees shot into the air for hundreds of feet, barely any of the bright midday sunlight reached the forest floor, requiring the soldiers to walk through a perpetual gloom. And despite the warmth of the day, several of the soldiers shivered unexpectedly, the temperature in the wood quite a bit colder than out on the sunny plain.

For some of the more superstitious Guards, it brought to mind the stories that the spirits of the dead, many of them soldiers who a thousand years before had fought in Arick Winborne's army to delay the Ghoule Overlord and his Legions, still roamed between the trees. Restless, thinking that their work was not complete even in death, still searching for more Ghoules to kill.

The three companies marched as best as they could through the hindering wood for what the Blademaster judged was no more than a mile before Rafia raised her hand, bringing the soldiers to a halt.

"We are close?" whispered the Blademaster.

"I believe so," replied Rafia. She took a quick look around, pleased that she had found the small glade that she had scouted earlier in the day. Shadow still draped itself over the clearing, making it difficult to see. However, the uncommon and appreciated space between the trees in this part of the forest would serve her purposes well. "Call back the skirmishers and form the soldiers into ranks. We will wait for the beasts here."

With a few quick hand signals, the Blademaster did just that, Benin and the other Sergeants ensuring that the soldiers moved into position rapidly and silently, the only breaks in their formation the towering trees that were an immovable part of the landscape. Still, Klines had to admit that the Magus had selected a good location to make their stand.

The dense trees and roots that ran off into the distance on both sides would function as a natural wall, making it difficult for the beasts they were about to fight to come at them from their flanks or from behind. And that was a key consideration. The Ghoules were deadly adversaries, so the necessity of limiting their avenues of attack.

As the soldiers moved swiftly to obey Benin and the other Sergeants, Rafia reached for the Talent, the energy of the natural world filling her with a power and clarity that never failed to bring a smile to her face. It only took her a few seconds to find what she was seeking.

The four Ghoule packs that she had been tracking since the break of day were less than a mile away and getting closer. Even so, she growled in irritation at her arrogance. She had believed that this had been the perfect spot to take on the beasts, but the Ghoules were proving difficult as they had changed their track somewhat.

She needed to remedy the situation. Rather than attempt to move three hundred soldiers who stood ready for a fight away from the place that gave them the best chance for surviving the coming encounter, she chose a different approach to ensure that the Ghoules came directly at them as she desired.

"The Ghoules are close and should be here in a matter of minutes," said Rafia in a rather loud voice, the sound traveling widely throughout the silent forest. "A good decision on the formation, Blademaster. It should work well."

"Magus Rafia ..."

"Just Rafia," the Magus replied automatically, her voice almost a shout now.

"Rafia," corrected Klines, giving her a slight nod as an apology, though his face betrayed his worry as the sound of her voice likely traveled a league or more through the wood. "I thought that we were to keep our voices down."

"You are correct, Blademaster. We were. However, the Ghoules shifted their position farther to the west than I thought they would. Our speaking now won't reveal what's here because of their distance from us. It will attract their interest and pull them in on the angle that we prefer. So for the moment, you and I are the bait."

Klines smiled devilishly, liking how the Magus thought. "Well done, Rafia."

"Thank you, Blademaster," she replied. "Now explain the formation you selected to battle the Ghoules."

"It was the formation that Declan used when holding out against the Royal Guard during the insurrection," he replied. "It's something that Arick Winborne perfected, what he called the testudo. It worked well in both situations and with the obstructions on our flanks I hope that it will serve us well here."

Rafia's eyes glanced behind them, her smile broadening. Shield bearers holding scuta, the rectangular, slightly curved steel shields that were as long as a man was tall, formed the front rank. The second row of soldiers stood ready to position long spears over the shoulders of the shield bearers. Next came the swords to fill any gaps that might occur during the fight, and behind them stood the archers as either a last defense or a potentially momentum-shifting offensive weapon if events played out in their favor.

"Yes, a very smart decision, Blademaster."

"In speaking with Declan and then Tarin Tentillin, we believed that the testudo would serve us well in circumstances such as this, the confined spaces created by the trees working to our advantage so long as the Ghoules are unable to break our line. Hopefully, that will prove to be the case."

Rafia nodded her head, considering, deep in thought for several heartbeats. She then used the Talent again to check the positioning of the Ghoules. The beasts had shifted their location as she desired. If the creatures continued on their current route, they would run right into the center of the Royal Guard, just as she and the Blademaster had planned.

"The Master of the Gladiators certainly is a surprising man," said Rafia. "He comes across as a man as strong as the steel he wields, yet he seems to be so much more than that."

"He is, indeed," agreed Klines, surprised that the Magus was interested in the former slave. "The only gladiator, other than the Volkun, to escape the white sand without being dragged across it."

"Have you known him long?"

"Twenty years."

"Twenty years," echoed Rafia, her shock evident in the tone of her voice. She had learned that most gladiators lasted less than a year in the Pit. "How is that possible?"

"When I first became Blademaster, around the time that Declan was forced into the Pit, I found that few in the Royal Guard at that time could offer me much of a challenge in the practice ring," explained Klines. "So I started looking for someone who could. I'm not trying to brag, simply stating a fact. The practice regimen then for the Royal Guard wasn't what it is today."

"Declan?"

"Yes, Rafia. I had come across Declan a few times when he served in the Royal Guard. An excellent soldier and one of the best fighters in the Guard. I had heard about what happened to him and why he had been sent to the Colosseum."

"What did happen?" asked Rafia, her interest piqued.

"Politics taking precedence over justice," replied Klines, shaking his head in disgust. "That is not my story to tell, although I'm sure Declan will tell you if you ask."

"Of course," replied Rafia.

Klines nodded, glad that the Magus had not pressed him. Then he returned to her original question.

"I watched one of his combats in the Pit, and I knew then that he was the only one who could match me, and he has ever since. We started sparring shortly after that combat and have done so for the last twenty years."

"From what I have seen, Declan is exceedingly skilled with a blade," offered Rafia.

"That he is," replied Klines. "He is an excellent fighter. Smart. Tenacious. Demanding. More important, he is a good man. Every gladiator who has ever fought for him, every gladiator still alive today, would likely say the same. He made sure that they learned how to fight and he taught them all that he could to ensure that they lived as long as they could on the white sand."

"I assume that only so much could be expected with respect to that."

"Yes," Klines agreed, nodding his head sadly. "Inevitably, for almost all the gladiators, the odds caught up to them. No matter how hard Declan tried to help them, fighting in the

Pit proved to be a numbers game for most. Eventually you would be dealt a losing hand."

"There are so few good men left," said Rafia. The Magus' posture straightened, her eyes sharpening. The Ghoules were getting closer, now no more than a few minutes away. They were taking their time just as she suspected that they would. The beasts would wonder why two humans had entered the Dark Forest on their own, thinking that it might be a trap. Still, it didn't worry her. She had a surprise waiting for the Ghoules that should make the beasts reckless and give the Royal Guard a needed advantage at the beginning of the fight. "The more I learn about him, the more I like him."

"That I can understand, Magus." Klines hesitated before offering what he thought to say next, then decided to take the risk as he had guessed why the Magus was so curious about his friend. "A word of advice, Rafia?"

For a moment, Rafia stared at the Blademaster with a gaze that had wilted Kings and Queens. It didn't have that effect on the Blademaster, who looked at her calmly. She was pleased by his response, or rather the lack of it. She nodded that he should go ahead.

"Don't allow Declan's crustiness to get in the way. He has a hard hide, and he's needed it, but if you're willing to put in the time to get beyond that, you'll like what you find."

"Thank you for the advice, Blademaster. I will keep it in mind."

Rafia shifted her focus to the trees to their front, which immediately caught Klines' attention. "They're coming, Blademaster. Less than a minute. Right at our center as we wanted."

KURZEN HELD his clawed fist up in the air, the four packs of Ghoules gliding around him halting immediately. None of the creatures made a noise as they waited expectantly. Initially, he had been certain about what he had heard. Perhaps he had been wrong. They had been farther away at the time. Then a faint murmur of noise maneuvered its way around the massive trees of the Dark Forest, teasing his ears once again.

He had been right. Human voices. Just up ahead. Only a few at most. That thought brought a smile to the Elder's face, as it did for many of the other Ghoules with him, the curling of their lips revealing their sharp, flesh-tearing teeth.

Kurzen had come to the lands of the humans before, having crossed through the Weir several times. He had already earned his bone knife. Many of the Ghoules with him had not, this being their first time through the magical barrier. So this might be a chance for a few of them to claim their prey and craft the highest symbol of a Ghoule's honor.

Still, he needed to make sure. He couldn't risk a large engagement with the Caledonian soldiers yet. Nibli had been clear about that.

Kurzen and his packs were to remain hidden within the Dark Forest. They were to wait until the soldiers left the city and traveled northeast toward the Winter Pass. Their Master had said that they would. The humans would have no choice. They would have to defend against the Legions entering the Winter Pass.

He had already seen thousands of soldiers doing exactly as Nibli said they would with several thousand more preparing to follow them. Moving northeast. Moving toward their doom when they faced the Ghoule Overlord and his Legions. Once all the soldiers had gone, he and his Ghoules would have their fun, slaughtering any humans they came across and creating havoc in the countryside, perhaps even in the city itself if circumstances permitted such boldness.

A thin black mist began to spin around the top of Kurzen's staff of black ash as he called upon the Curse. He then extended his senses to the east. It didn't take him long to find what he was looking for. They weren't very far away at all. His grin broadened maliciously. At least a few of his Ghoules would be carving their bone knives tonight and all of his fighters would be enjoying the delicacy of human flesh.

Two humans were no more than a quarter mile to their south. Why they would be here within this grove he didn't know, and he really didn't care. He had identified no threats for leagues around, just these two humans who had picked a particularly bad time to enter the Dark Forest, so he could do as he wished. Killing these humans would not affect his Master's larger strategy.

Bad for the humans. Good for him and his Ghoules.

In a guttural whisper Kurzen communicated with his Ghoules what waited just a little farther away in the wood, all of them eager to kill their prey. With a sharp nod of his head, Kurzen released the Ghoules from where they stood, the beasts sprinting forward, dodging around the massive trees with an unnatural and deadly grace, as they homed in on the unsuspecting humans.

It was a huge surprise for the Ghoules, then, when they reached where they thought they had last heard the human voices. It was an unexpectedly large space between the trees, and it was empty.

The Ghoules stopped in the center of the murky glade, looking around in confusion, the Elder standing at their back appearing to be just as perplexed. The two humans had been right here. He had checked just moments before.

Kurzen was about to reach for the Curse once again to see if he could locate the pair when a shimmering in the center of the clearing caught his eye. Several of the Ghoules saw it too as the glare intensified, flashing brightly on the southern side of the dell, so bright that several of the Ghoules had to turn away, their eyes accustomed to the gloom of the Dark Forest.

With a final flash and rumble that resembled thunder, the flickering disappeared. Kurzen blinked a few times, trying to clear the black spots that afflicted the Elder's lizard-like eyes. What he was finally able to make out to his front sent a rare tremor of unease down his spine.

Soldiers stood on the other side of the glade. Hundreds of them. Several Ghoules were already down on the soft loam, skewered by long spears, and the humans were advancing step by step, their formation appearing as a solid mass as they walked over the dead and lunged with their lances for his fighters.

~

He couldn't see them yet, though he knew that they were close. Jurgen Klines had fought in more skirmishes than he could remember, and that experience had helped him in an unexpected though very useful way. He had discovered that he had the unique ability to know when the enemy approached.

Sensing that the Ghoules were almost upon them, Klines quickly issued his final orders through a series of hand signals that traveled along the front line and then back through the ranks that were four deep. The soldiers stood there calmly, keeping their nerves under control as best as they could. They knew what was going to happen next, and they didn't want to do anything that might ruin the surprise.

After using the Talent to confirm the Ghoules' change in direction, Rafia had shifted her application of the natural magic of the world to form an illusion around the three companies of the Royal Guard that allowed them to blend in with the surrounding forest. A Ghoule could look directly at them and so long as no one moved, the beasts wouldn't suspect that their prey stood right in front of them.

It had been nerve-wracking when the Ghoules first appeared in the clearing. The soldiers had thought that the beasts would see through the reality that Magus Rafia had crafted. They had been pleasantly surprised when the Ghoules had failed to do so.

But as one second bled into the next, the soldiers had grown anxious. They were ready for the fight, and they wanted to get to it. So they did, driving their spears into the unsuspecting Ghoules closest to them. That action destroyed the illusion and allowed the Ghoules to see them. Still, the Caledonian soldiers removed half a dozen of the beasts from the battle before it really even began.

"Advance!" ordered Klines, his troops responding exactly as they had been trained.

In a measured step, the Blademaster's soldiers moved forward, walking over the dead Ghoules, keeping their formation intact as they did so. They engaged the second line of Ghoules before the beasts really understood what was going on.

The Ghoules' surprise and indecision played right into the Blademaster's hands as his troops enjoyed the benefit of avoiding a concerted attack by the creatures for a little while longer, his shield bearers seeking to get as close as possible so his spears could strike at the beasts.

Thankful that none of the Ghoules had attempted to skirt the natural barriers on his flanks, Klines decided to see how long he could control the momentum of the skirmish and make the best use of the small clearing.

"Archers, release!"

The steel-tipped shafts shot over the first three ranks of soldiers with devastating effect, puncturing another half-dozen creatures, the force of the handful of missiles that struck each beast slamming them backward to fall on the turf and curling tree roots. The soldiers in the first two ranks took full advantage, continuing their inexorable advance, the shields pushing back or knocking down the Ghoules, the spears in the second rank aiming for throats or hearts, and when the soldiers stepped over the dead or dying beasts, the swordfighters in the third rank drove their blades into the creatures just to make certain that they wouldn't rise again.

The Blademaster was impressed, his soldiers eliminating a pack of Ghoules in only a few minutes. He didn't allow that confidence to become arrogance. He knew that a harder fight was coming, not only because the remaining Ghoules finally were getting themselves organized, but also because of the black mist that he saw twisting up into the air at the back of the clearing.

"Rafia!" called Klines, gesturing toward the rapidly spreading darkness. "The Elder."

"Leave him to me, Blademaster," she replied, having stood next to Klines at the beginning of the fight, now moving away from him so that she would have a better angle for engaging the creature who could make use of the Curse. "Keep killing the Ghoules."

Peering across the clearing, Rafia saw that the Elder was focusing his attention on the Blademaster as the beast prepared to release his Dark Magic. That was something she couldn't permit. So she sent several bolts of blazing energy toward the Elder. She didn't think she'd be lucky enough to eliminate him with her first attack. She simply hoped to draw his attention away from the Blademaster and his soldiers, and in that she succeeded.

The Elder swung his black staff in the air, knocking away the bolts crafted from the Talent. He glared malevolently at the woman who stood across from him. He should have assumed as much. A Magus. That's why he had failed to identify the threat hidden within the wood. She would pay a heavy price for her temerity, for her believing that she could deceive him so easily and actually challenge him in a duel of power.

With a quick flick of his wrist, a shard of Dark Magic shot from the Elder's staff, streaking through the air toward the woman. When she failed to form a shield, he assumed that she would be an easy kill.

He was mistaken.

The Dark Magic slammed right into her glowing palm, where it had no visible effect upon her. Rather, the power that she controlled latched onto the Curse, forming a thin covering around the sable energy. Then, with a few twists of her other hand, the Magus crafted the energy into a blazing ball of white with a dim black center.

With a malicious smile, she flicked her wrist toward him and the ball shot right back at the Elder. For just a moment, the beast was too shocked by what the Magus had done, never having seen such skill before. His amazement and momentary paralysis almost cost him his life as the orb sped toward him in a blur.

Right before the sphere of energy struck him, the Elder raised his staff to knock the ball away. Even so, his delay came with a costly price, as a tiny portion of that energy skimmed across his side, burning through his robes, searing his flesh, and knocking him to the ground.

For just a few breaths, the Elder lay there, realizing much to his relief that he hadn't died. He was just wounded. The pain was excruciating, the Magus' power eating into his flesh, but he could live with that torment for a short while. He raised his head after a few seconds, his lips twisting because of the growl that emanated in the back of his throat. The human had gotten lucky. This Magus belonged to him. He would feast on her tonight.

The Elder was about to push himself up off the ground and rejoin the fight when his skin prickled. There was an electric charge in the air. He didn't know why and the sensation sent a prickle of fear through him. Then Kurzen looked up, realizing that he was about to pay the price for his overconfidence. The last thing that he saw was a streak of white energy that shot down from the sky and blasted into him.

"Was that satisfying?" asked Klines, having come to stand once more next to Rafia.

"Very," she replied, using her favorite weapon to kill the Elder, which left nothing but the faint impression of the Ghoule next to the thick root. The immense power that she employed had burned the beast's body to cinders in less than a second, those ashes lost within the shadows of the Dark Forest.

Klines nodded, reminding himself to never get on the Magus' bad side in the future. When he had first met her, she had come across as a bit volatile, the lightning bolt that she had just employed having confirmed his suspicion, and he had no wish to test her patience after seeing how easily she dealt with the Elder. That threat gone, he surveyed the compressed battlefield.

All of the Ghoules were down. With Rafia forcing the Elder to focus on her rather than commanding his packs, the Ghoules fought as individuals and never attacked in a coordinated fashion, which played right into Klines' hands. Because of that, his troops had killed every single Ghoule with a pleasing efficiency. He counted a handful of his soldiers among the dead and more than a dozen had been wounded. Still, he was thankful. It could have been worse. Much worse.

"A good fight, though still too close," remarked Klines. "My thanks to you for distracting the Elder."

"My pleasure," replied Rafia. "The only good Elder is a dead Elder."

"I couldn't agree with you more." He continued to scan the glade, watching as his soldiers provided aid to those in need, others preparing the dead for the march back to Tintagel. "This was only an Elder and four Ghoule packs. If the Elder had one more pack, or there was one more Elder, this could have ended differently. Their size and numbers are an advantage. A battle with a one to one ratio will not end well for us. To ensure our success, we need a handful of Magii to keep us in the fight, because the Ghoules are never without at least one Elder."

All the scenarios running through the Blademaster's mind regarding what would be needed to hold their own against, much less defeat, the Ghoules were sobering. Numbers were critical. The more soldiers he had, the better their chances of success. Yet even then, there were no guarantees, not with the Dark Magic exercised by the Elders. A grim thought, and one that could not be ignored.

Rafia nodded. "Yes, probably so. It's a good lesson for us all. Never underestimate the Ghoules. We do so at our own peril. But your tactics were sound, Blademaster. Be happy with that."

Klines grunted in response, offering the Magus a short nod. "At least now we have some in the Royal Guard bloodied against the Ghoules. They can share their experiences with the other companies, and we can take what we learned and apply it in the future."

"Yes, I expect we'll have more of these skirmishes," said Rafia. "We may have cleared the Southern Marches of Ghoules, but that won't help us now. Clearly the Overlord is sending some of his packs through the Weir and then to here and other places. I wouldn't be surprised if there were more Ghoules coming this way with the express purpose of creating confusion behind our lines."

"I expect you're right, Rafia. We'll need to take that into account. Anything the Ghoule Overlord can do to make it harder for us to fight him at the Winter Pass will benefit him. I have no doubt that this is just the beginning."

"We need to get back," said Rafia. "I need to head west with the Volkun in two days' time. By then we need to have our larger strategy in place to defend against the Ghoules. I agree with you that if there are four packs in the Dark Forest, then there will be more on the way. We will need to adjust our approach so that we can defend against these packs while still seeking to hold the Winter Pass. If we don't, we've sealed our own fate before the real fight even begins."

14

THANK YOU

The sun beat down on him mercilessly, reflecting off the white sand and the stone that formed the Pit. It didn't bother him in the least. His wound had healed, no longer impeding his movements -- even the sting while dueling Davin and Lycia the day before fading to almost nothing thanks to his use of the Talent -- and allowing him to achieve the level of prowess that Declan had instilled within him and he expected of himself.

Bryen grinned as he continued with his practice regimen, moving with a grace that few could achieve, the Spear of the Magii slashing, cutting, and slicing through the air. It felt good to sweat. It felt good to let his thoughts wander for a time. It felt good to allow the peace and quiet of the empty Colosseum to wash over him. It felt good to be back in a place that had become such a big part of who he was, that had actually made him what he was, without having to worry about who his next opponent would be.

Yes, the Pit was a place of blood, pain, and death. Bryen understood all too well the reality of what had occurred within these circular stone walls, having experienced it himself for ten years. During that time he had competed in more than five hundred combats against man, woman, and beast. He had survived them all, coming close to losing his life more times than he cared to remember, and they had all left an indelible impression upon him.

If he really tried, he could recall the faces of all his opponents, although he rarely attempted to do that. Those memories were better left in the past.

In addition to the sense of familiarity that he craved, his main purpose in returning to the Pit was to try to get his thoughts in order. Declan had trained him to narrow his focus until it was razor sharp, his mind needing to be just as keen as his blade. That training was rooted within him, and he put it to use now as he contemplated what he was going to say later in the day.

He had decided that he would go to the Sanctuary well before Sirius and Rafia had begun trying to convince him. There were many reasons to do it, as Sirius had explained to him repeatedly, unnecessarily, and irritatingly. Yes, he had to think about all the people who would suffer at the claws of these beasts if the Ghoule Overlord's Legions were permitted to cross into Caledonia. But there was one simple truth that he had not revealed that had guided his decision making in this matter.

The Ghoules had killed his parents. Locking the beasts behind the Weir was the best way to gain any semblance of revenge upon them. That and killing the Ghoule Overlord.

Yet he had delayed giving them a response because he didn't want to come across as malleable to the two Magii, understanding that if he acceded to their request too quickly, it wouldn't bode well for his future interactions with them. The two Magii were too accustomed to getting their way, either with brute force or subtle manipulation, using people as they needed for their many machinations.

He was done being used. So he had allowed them -- well, Sirius, really, since Rafia had taken a more subdued approach than her partner -- to make their argument, which Sirius had done so many times that Bryen could repeat it word for word. It was almost as if the Magus believed that if he offered his justifications frequently enough, he would wear down Bryen to the point where he had no choice but to agree with their request.

Bryen had concluded as soon as he had become the Seventh Stone that he would have to attempt to repair the Weir. He wasn't certain about how to actually accomplish the task. He could worry about that later. That was a problem to be worked out in the weeks to come.

As soon as the Seventh Stone had merged with him, he had experienced a feeling that he had yet to share with the two Magii. He had gained an awareness that at first had unsettled him but over time had become more comfortable.

He could sense the Seven Stones now. All of them. And, as a result, he could also sense the Weir. It was a low thrumming at the very back of his consciousness, beating in time to the flickering power contained within the gigantic shield, a feeling that he couldn't escape. It gave him the ability to measure the strength of that magical barrier, the tremendous power that was used to construct it. It also gave him something else that he believed would prove critical if he actually reached the Sanctuary.

He had discovered that the energy of the Weir contained another component that he had suspected would be there based on his conversations with Sirius and Rafia of which the two Magii appeared to be unaware. A power that he believed would prove essential to his completing the task.

Some part of the consciousnesses of the Ten Magii, that of his forbear Viktor Keldragan and the other nine Magii, had bonded with the Weir upon their deaths.

Bryen had decided not to tell Sirius and Rafia about this new development. It was bad enough dealing with all the concerned looks that they shot his way every time they saw him, worried about the Dark Magic contained within him. He had no doubt that they wondered regularly when they would need to kill him, not if, the two Magii suspecting that at some point in the future the Curse would break free from its bonds ... though he assumed they hoped that wouldn't happen until after they reached the Sanctuary.

Consequently he didn't feel the need to complicate an already complicated situation by telling them that he could now feel the essences of the Ten Magii within the Weir. That because of the Seventh Stone these spirits were a part of him now.

No, better to keep all that to himself. Life was hard enough as it was, and it would only get harder in the days ahead. There was no need for him to make it even more difficult, as telling Rafia and Sirius about the Ten Magii would mean that either one or both of them would be tied to him at the hip for however much longer he remained alive.

Besides, Declan had taught him to be a realist. He was absolutely certain that if he survived his attempt to fix the Weir, and Sirius and Rafia knew that he could connect with the essences of the Ten Magii, one or both of the Magii might try to kill him shortly afterward. They wouldn't want to risk allowing a Magus with so much power to live when that Magus faced the constant threat of becoming tainted by the Curse, potentially becoming something even worse than the Ghoule Overlord.

So he kept that new knowledge to himself for now, not feeling the need to share that information until there was greater certainty about what the future held. A foolish thought, he knew. Trying to obtain certainty in an uncertain world.

Still, he felt the need to try. And one way to help achieve that certainty was to succeed at what he was about to do in a few hours. Because if he was to have any chance at all of making it to the Sanctuary, he would need help, a lot of help, and he hoped that some in the Blood Company would be willing to share the risk with him.

Thoughts about how he should address the Blood Company ran through his mind as he practiced the forms that Declan had ingrained within him so assiduously. He relished the simplicity of his movements, his economy of motion, how the Spear of the Magii whipping through the still air brought him a faint touch of joy, and he realized that the only way to approach his comrades in arms was to do what he had done before the uprising. Speak simply. Speak directly. Speak from his heart. They were warriors one and all. They deserved nothing less than the whole truth.

As the Volkun enjoyed his time in the Pit, the Duke of the Southern Marches stayed where he was within the shadows of the tunnel that led out onto the white sand. He had been looking for the Protector for much of the morning. He should have assumed that he would find him here, the young man spending as little time in the Corinthian Palace as possible.

Rather than approach him as soon as he arrived, he had chosen to wait for a time and watch. He knew that the young man was a deadly fighter, having observed him frequently when he was in Battersea. Unbelievably, it appeared to Kevan that the gladiator had improved his martial skills in just the six months since he had last seen him in the Broken Palace's practice yard.

"Is there something that I can do for you, Duke Winborne?" asked Bryen as he glided across the white sand, his spear a steel blur. "Or were you going to simply stand there and watch?"

Kevan pushed himself off the white stone wall. He should have surmised that his daughter's Protector would realize he was there. The young man had a preternatural ability for knowing everything that was around him every second of the day. Kevan couldn't begrudge him that. The young man's skill in that regard had certainly proven useful when protecting Aislinn.

The Duke of the Southern Marches walked out of the shelter into the blazing sunlight of the Pit, shading his eyes for a few seconds to give his vision time to adjust. He stopped a few feet away from Bryen. He was just as tall as the Protector, as broad at the shoulder, but he carried an extra fifty pounds compared to the younger man, who was slim, wiry, and built of corded muscle.

"I was wondering if you'd have a few minutes to spar with me?" asked the Duke.

Bryen stared at the man who had collared him, trying to discern why the Duke had any desire to train with him. No good reason came to mind, though he had to admit that he was curious, and there was really only one way to find out why Aislinn's father would take such a risk. Deaths did happen on occasion during practice sessions, most often when there were scores to be settled.

"You realize that this doesn't work anymore, right?" asked Bryen, motioning to the silver collar circling his neck.

Kevan smiled at the Protector, then nodded. "I'm well aware, but thank you for pointing that out."

It was Bryen's turn to smile. "If you're not concerned by the fact that you'll be practicing against someone who still holds a grudge against you and will no longer be impeded by the magic of the Protector's collar, I'm game."

"Good. I've been wanting to test my skills against you for quite some time."

"Be careful what you wish for, Duke Winborne. Sometimes when you get what you want it isn't what you expect."

"I'll keep that in mind. Thank you for the warning."

Kevan pulled the sword from the scabbard on his hip, throwing the sheath against the far wall of the Pit so that it wouldn't obstruct him in any way during the duel, then nodded to signify that he was ready to begin.

For almost a minute the two men stared at one another, neither apparently wanting to make the first move. Then with a lightning-fast first step, Bryen lunged forward, the blade at the top of his spear whipping down toward Kevan's shoulder.

The Duke got his sword up just in time to block the strike. Even so, the speed of the cut caught him off guard and made him stumble backwards several feet. It took Kevan a few seconds to regain his balance. He brought his sword up again when he did, assuming that he would have to meet another attack by the Volkun. Surprisingly, the young man hadn't moved from where he had come to a stop after forcing Kevan to retreat.

Kevan examined Bryen with a critical eye, the young man holding his double-bladed spear comfortably in his hands. His eyes were hard, his gaze strong. He was balanced on his toes, knees slightly bent, and he breathed slowly and easily. He appeared to be ready for anything that Kevan might try against him. The Protector exuded nothing but confidence, not a drop of arrogance within the gladiator.

Kevan initiated the next round of the combat. Feinting a slash toward Bryen's left shoulder, the Duke spun on his heel, aiming a backward cut toward Bryen's other shoulder instead. Kevan growled in irritation when his steel met the haft of the Protector's spear. Even more aggravating was that it had taken very little effort on the young man's part to defend against his attack. The Protector hadn't even moved, simply raising his spear as if he had seen right through Kevan's bluff.

Kevan stepped back once again. He had thought that by doing this he'd have an opportunity to test the Protector. Instead, he felt like he was the one being examined.

Bryen had mixed feelings about sparring with Aislinn's father as he stood there calmly, staring at his opponent. On the one hand, it was an opportunity to make his displeasure known regarding his treatment by the man who had enslaved him. On the other hand, he worried about how Aislinn would take it if he injured or even killed -- accidentally, of course -- her father. So he decided to take it slow and not push the Duke too hard at first.

"Don't hold back!" shouted Kevan. "I can't improve if you don't press me."

With a sly grin, Bryen nodded, shoving his concern for Aislinn to the side. For several minutes Kevan didn't have a chance to think. All he could do was trust in his instincts, Aislinn's Protector on him in a flash and not letting up, the young man twisting and turning, gliding across the sand, forcing Kevan this way and that, seizing the momentum of the combat and refusing to let it go.

The Volkun had returned to the Pit.

Kevan counted at least a dozen times when the young man could have finished him if he had wanted to, but the Protector had refrained. Why, he didn't know. He mused briefly that it was to make a point, to show Kevan that he hadn't stood a chance as soon as he had asked to challenge him. As the combat continued, he guessed that there was likely more to it. The young man was a skilled fighter, yes, but he wasn't a cold-blooded killer, even when he had the opportunity to duel a man who he disliked so vehemently and for such good cause.

Then it was over. Kevan stood near the center of the Pit, Bryen's blade against his throat, his own sword several feet away, knocked from his hand.

"That was impressive," gasped Kevan as he tried to catch his breath, the heat of the young man's steel warmed by the hot sun reminding the Duke that it would only take a flick of the Protector's wrist for his blood to flow. "You could have killed me a dozen times."

"Sixteen, actually," replied Bryen, who after several long seconds, and what appeared to be a short fight with his conscience, reluctantly removed the blade from the Duke's neck and stepped back.

Kevan couldn't stop himself from chuckling. "My thanks that you decided not to carry through when you had all those opportunities."

Bryen nodded, and then turned to walk away. The Duke's unanticipated request made him turn back.

"Could you show me that last move that you used to take my blade?"

Bryen hesitated at first, then nodded again. He walked a few steps, picked up Kevan's sword and handed it to him hilt first. Then he spent the next few minutes showing the Duke how he had twisted his wrist in such a way as to catch the sword hilt on the haft of his spear so that Kevan had no choice but to drop his weapon. It was either that or suffer a broken wrist.

"That's clever," said Kevan. "Where did you learn to do that?"

"Declan," replied Bryen, not feeling the need to elucidate.

"The Master of the Gladiators," nodded Kevan. "A very smart man. I'll need to remember that."

The Duke was about to say something else, then hesitated. For several seconds, the two just stared at each other uncomfortably. Bryen could tell that the Duke hadn't visited him here just to fight in the Pit, that he wanted to talk to him about something else. Either he didn't know how to start or he wasn't ready. Against his better judgment, he decided to help the man who had chained him.

"Why did you really come here, Duke Winborne? It wasn't to test your skills against me. At least not entirely."

Kevan paused before responding, pleased by Bryen's directness. The young man treated a Duke just as he would a soldier of the lowest rank. That appealed to Kevan, though he was loath to admit it. He wouldn't have said such a thing when he first met Bryen, viewing him then as nothing more than a criminal and a tool to be used.

"I wanted to say thank you. For what you've done for my daughter. You've saved her life I don't know how many times."

"I didn't have much of a choice."

"Maybe so," agreed Kevan. "Nonetheless, she wouldn't be here if not for you. Also, she's grown because of you. For the better. Not only with the blade. In other ways as well. She was strong to begin with, and you've helped her to refine that strength. My thanks. Truly. She would not be who she is today without your influence."

"You're welcome," nodded Bryen. "You give me too much credit. She did the hard work, not me."

"Are you always so self-deprecating?" asked Kevan, never having interacted with someone who cared so little for praise or acknowledgment.

"I'm simply speaking the truth, Duke Winborne."

"Of that, I have no doubt." Kevan gazed at the young man for a moment more, then nodded as if he had decided something important. "I also wanted to thank you for saving my life. I know it wasn't easy, and no one would have begrudged you if you hadn't. After what I've done to you, you could have let me die, and no one would have blamed you."

"You're Aislinn's father," was all that Bryen said in way of an explanation.

Kevan gave Bryen a sharp, respectful nod. He hesitated just a few more seconds before he plowed forward, realizing that the longer he waited, the harder it would become for him to say what he wanted to say next.

"I also wanted to apologize."

Bryen stared at Kevan, no expression appearing on his face, not revealing the shock that shot through him. His eyes remained hard. Always hard. Bryen rarely revealed any emotion, and those flinty grey eyes refused to give any hint of what he might be feeling.

Not knowing what else to do, Kevan continued. "Taking you from the Pit and putting a collar on you was a mistake. I shouldn't have done that. I know it's not a good excuse, it's just that I was trying to protect my daughter. When I took you from the Pit, I could have freed you. Instead, I kept you as a slave. I shouldn't have done that. I can't do anything about the past, but if ever there is anything that you need, that you want, you need simply ask. If it's in my power to give it to you, it's yours. It will never make up for what I did to you, I just hope that you will accept my offer, which is made in good faith."

Bryen continued to stare at Kevan, the Duke's words appreciated. Although they still had no visible impact upon him. He should have felt some emotion. Yet in that moment he experienced only calculation, as Bryen tried to determine if Duke Winborne was being genuine or simply doing as Aislinn may have requested of him. He guessed the former and hoped that he was right. The Duke appeared to be sincere.

Bryen nodded, apparently accepting Kevan's apology.

"You don't make this easy."

"Would you?"

"No."

Bryen nodded a final time, then he began to walk away, heading for the tunnel that would take him back to the gladiators' compound and then the small room that had been his while he had lived beneath the shadow of the Colosseum for a decade.

"Bryen," Kevan called to him.

Bryen stopped abruptly, his head rising. He realized that this was the first time that Duke Winborne had ever used his given name. Every other time they had interacted the Duke had called him either "boy" or "Protector."

"I can never repay you for what you've done, but know that I am in your debt. I will always be in your debt."

15

STILL NOT FREE

"I'm not bothering you, am I? You seem deep in thought."

"Not at all," replied Bryen, who rose from where he had been sitting on the edge of the cot that had served as his bed for ten years.

"Are you hiding away?" Aislinn asked as she stepped into the small room that resembled a prison cell more than anything else.

Bryen had to press himself against the wall so that she could slip by him, her arm scraping across his stomach as she went past. When Aislinn perched herself on the small table at the other end of the tiny, rectangular room, Bryen remained standing where he was, leaning back against the crumbling wall.

In that moment, staring into her large eyes, Bryen realized that he missed her. He missed being able to talk to her, and he missed being with her. For a time, he thought that feeling just emanated from the collar. Yet with her standing so close, he didn't think the collar mattered anymore.

"I do my best thinking here," he replied.

"Are you sure that you don't mind me stopping by for a few minutes to speak with you? I don't want to interrupt. I know how hard it can be for you to think sometimes."

"No, not at all," said Bryen, smiling at her joke and gentle barb. "I'm honored. Visited first by the father and now the daughter, both in the same morning."

"My father was here?" asked Aislinn, unable to keep the shock from her voice.

"He was. He left less than an hour ago."

"What did he want?"

Bryen was going to make a joke himself, then decided against it, noticing the tension in Aislinn's posture.

"We sparred in the Pit for a time. He wanted to test himself against me."

"You can't be serious," Aislinn said disbelievingly.

"I am being serious."

"You didn't hurt him, did you?" she asked, a look of concern crossing her face. "Not that you don't have good cause after what he did to you, it's just that ..."

"Aislinn."

Bryen's soft voice broke her train of thought.

"I could have hurt him. I have no love for your father, and I won't say that I've never thought about taking my anger out on him, but I did not hurt him. He left here intact and with barely a scratch on him."

Aislinn nodded, relieved to hear that her father was no worse for wear. She wondered how Bryen had been able to control his temper, as she doubted that she could have if she had been placed in the same situation.

"He wanted to spar with you?" she asked. "Why would he want to do that? Why would he put himself in that situation?"

"I don't know," replied Bryen. "You'll have to ask your father. I can't answer for him."

"That's it?" she asked. "He just sparred with you?"

"He apologized and thanked me," said Bryen, a wry smile curling his lips, as if he didn't actually believe that it had happened. "I didn't expect it, and I didn't want it. He did so nonetheless."

"My father apologized to you?" asked Aislinn.

"Are you all right?" asked Bryen.

"Why do you ask?"

"You keep repeating what I'm saying," Bryen replied with an easy chuckle.

"You really can be difficult, you know that?" said Aislinn with a smile.

"So I've been told," replied Bryen. "Many times. With many more to come, I'm sure."

"What exactly did he apologize to you for?" asked Aislinn, still finding it hard to believe that her father ever would, even after all that he had done to Bryen.

"He apologized for making me your Protector."

"He did?"

"He did," confirmed Bryen with a nod. "Not because of the Ghoules and the other dangers that required me to risk my life on your behalf, but because of how difficult you can be. So very demanding. Obstinate to the point where a stone wall appears to be more flexible than you. Always thinking that you're right even when you're so obviously wrong. Definitely not good at following instructions."

As Bryen continued to explain, his smile grew wider. In response, Aislinn pushed herself off the table faster than Bryen expected and gave him a swift punch in the gut. Not too hard. Just hard enough to get him to stop.

"Are you done?" she asked, her voice firm and commanding, although her eyes sparkled with amusement.

"For now, yes," Bryen replied, rubbing his stomach where she had hit him. "He should have said aggressive as well. Unnecessarily so, at times."

Aislinn feinted another strike at Bryen, who protected his gut by turning his hip.

"Sorry," he replied. "I couldn't resist."

"I think I liked you better when you hated me," said Aislinn with a laugh. "You were much easier to deal with then."

"I like you better now," said Bryen. "Even though you seem to take particular pleasure in hitting me."

For just a moment, a strained silence settled within the room because of Bryen's comment. Aislinn took a step back and returned to a more comfortable topic.

"And my father thanked you? Are you sure he was my father? Not someone else? I don't think that I've ever heard him apologize for anything."

"Yes, he was definitely your father," said Bryen, grateful that Aislinn had let his remark go. "He's a hard man to forget. He seems to expect everyone to listen to him."

"That he does," agreed Aislinn with a smirk.

"He thanked me for keeping you safe."

"I can keep myself safe," Aislinn said hotly, a familiar fire popping into her eyes.

"I know. You don't have to get angry with me. Remember, we just talked about you being too aggressive." Bryen's smile helped Aislinn to release the irritation that had been building within her. She considered hitting him in the stomach again, then thought better of it. She didn't want to be too predictable. "I'm simply telling you what we discussed."

"It just bothers me," Aislinn sighed in resignation. "It's like he doesn't even know me. He doesn't want to acknowledge who I am and what I can do."

"He does know you, and he does know what you can do, though you are also his daughter," explained Bryen. "He's afraid for you. Or rather, he's afraid that he's going to lose you."

Aislinn let a few heartbeats pass before replying, her eyes taking in Bryen. He had changed so much since she had first met him. Bryen didn't do emotions when he first arrived in the Broken Citadel. Now, he was more open with her, and obviously he was more comfortable with her. Just as she was with him.

A conversation such as this would never have occurred when he was made her Protector. They had become closer as they spent more time together. Closer than either of them thought they would. Closer than either wanted. Even so, neither of them seemed to have the courage to trust the feeling that had grown between them.

"That's remarkably prescient on your part," suggested Aislinn as she forced herself back to their conversation. She was beginning to sweat a little bit from the warmth of the close quarters, her cheeks flushed.

"Thank you. I do have my moments," Bryen replied as he studied the Lady of the Southern Marches for several seconds. A rosy red had spread across her cheeks, making her even more beautiful. She was also fidgeting. Her fingers were wrapped in her skirts, twisting the material, which he knew after spending so much time with her was a sign that she was nervous. Clearly, there was more on her mind than just her father's visit. "Lady Winborne, you came here for a reason. You have not touched on that reason yet. Would you care to share?"

"Lady Winborne?" asked Aislinn as if he had just insulted her. She pulled her hands free from her skirts, noticing what she had been doing. She tried to smooth out some of the wrinkles, then realized that she was fighting a losing battle. "Since when am I Lady Winborne to you? We dealt with that long ago."

"You are Lady Winborne whenever I desire to irritate you or prod you into action," he replied with a grin and quick lift of his eyebrows.

Aislinn couldn't help but smile. "You know me too well."

"I agree," he said. "At times I believe that I know you better than you know yourself."

"Is that so?" asked Aislinn, taking Bryen's comment as a challenge. "Then what am I thinking right now?"

"That you miss having me around," said Bryen with a knowing grin.

Aislinn wanted to say that she did miss him, terribly at times, but she couldn't. She was nervous about what would happen if she did. "You're giving yourself too much credit, Protector. I have done just fine without you."

"Perhaps," agreed Bryen.

Aislinn nodded her head. "And what about you, Protector? We used to spend every second of the day together. Do you miss having me around? Do you miss having our training sessions? Our regular arguments? Do you miss how I could irritate you with just a look?"

"I do," replied Bryen solemnly, his eyes no longer laughing, instead serious.

"You do?" she asked, startled, never expecting such an honest reply.

"I do," he repeated, nodding. "I miss your stubbornness. I miss how you always believe that you're right, even when you know that you're wrong, because a Lady of the Southern

Marches can never be wrong. I miss how you wrinkle your nose, just as you are doing right now, when you disagree with what I have to say. I miss how you ..."

"That's all untrue and very unfair," protested Aislinn, who feinted another quick strike at Bryen's belly to get her Protector to stop. Bryen raised his hands in surrender.

"Some of it," he agreed with a laugh, pleased that Aislinn was smiling again, her dimples showing. "Now why are you really here?"

"Why are you here?" she asked, deflecting his question once again. "Why come back to this room? To this place after all this time?"

"It serves as a good reminder," he replied cryptically.

"A reminder of what?"

"Of where I came from. Of how I became the person who I am. With all that has happened, I worry sometimes that I will lose that, and I don't want to."

"I don't think you have anything to fear in that regard," Aislinn said, nodding, understanding. "Although you have become more annoying since I freed you from the collar."

It was Bryen's turn to fake a swipe at Aislinn in answer to her insult, his former charge leaning back on the small table and bringing her knees up, pretending to strike back, laughing as she did so.

"I guess I deserved that," Bryen admitted.

"You did," Aislinn agreed, glad that she could still do this with Bryen. Glad that she could still be herself. "You know that you're more than just what you learned here. You're more than just the Volkun."

"I know," said Bryen, his tone becoming more serious. "I'm also a Protector."

Bryen didn't say the last with the disgust that Aislinn

assumed that he would. "And a good one at that," she confirmed.

"Thank you," Bryen replied, nodding his appreciation. "I'm also the Captain of the Blood Company now. I'm a Magus. I'm the Seventh Stone. I understand what you're saying, and you're right." Bryen motioned with his arm to take in the cell that had been his room for so long. "But here, this place, it forms the core of who I am. It made me who I am. It gave me what I needed to do what I'm doing now."

"Yes, this place helped to make you who you are," said Aislinn. "I'd simply ask that you remember that you aren't just that person anymore. And with all that you've done in just the past year, clearly you can be whatever you want to be. The collar and this place don't hold you back any longer."

"Easy to say," he said with a twist of his head.

"But not easy to do. I know. One can dream."

As the Lady of the Southern Marches, she better than anyone understood how the expectations of the world, the demands made from the people around you, could keep you from following the path that called to you.

"We can dream, just not too much."

"Perhaps one day we can break away from our duty."

"One day," Bryen echoed. "Now why don't you tell me why you are really here."

For just a moment, Aislinn hesitated, then she explained why she had decided to visit.

"I wanted to tell you that I will be going with you to the Weir. My father still wants to protect me, to keep me from danger. After speaking with him last night though, he understands that this is something that he can't stop me from doing."

Bryen stared at her, the final puzzle piece falling into place as to why Duke Winborne decided to visit with him earlier that morning. Perhaps the Duke's offering of thanks and his apology were simply a way for him to try to get Bryen to continue to do as he had been doing since he had first arrived in Battersea and the collar had been placed around his neck. To protect Aislinn.

"And you're worried that I might try to stop you from going, which is why you're here."

"In part, yes. That thought had crossed my mind. So I wanted to get it out into the open now."

Bryen nodded. "I'm not going to try to stop you."

"You're not?" Aislinn's surprise was evident in her voice.

"No. It's your choice to make."

"I thought you'd fight me."

"Because it's dangerous?"

"Yes. I thought that you would agree with my father on this."

"You know it's dangerous, and you still want to go. You understand the risks. Why would you think that I'd try to keep you from going?" asked Bryen. "I know what you can do with a blade. I know what you can do with the Talent. Besides, you're probably more dangerous than anything we might come across along the way, and I see that as a positive. You can stand on your own, Aislinn Winborne. Don't ever let anyone else tell you otherwise."

Bryen noticed how her big eyes seemed to get even bigger as he said what he said, although her hesitation remained. She hadn't told him everything.

"What's the other part?" Bryen asked, breaking into her thoughts.

"What do you mean?"

"You said that you were here in part because you

thought that I'd try to stop you from going. What's the other reason for coming here?"

What was the other reason? Aislinn asked herself. She wasn't quite sure. She wasn't even certain if she was ready to admit it to herself. So she ignored Bryen's question and turned the conversation in another direction.

"Why do you still wear it?" Aislinn asked, pushing herself off the small table and coming to stand in front of Bryen, so close that he could feel her breath on his cheek as she ran her fingers across the cool silver of the collar.

Bryen took a moment before responding, Aislinn's proximity bringing a flush back to his cheeks, the warmth that he had experienced when she had first walked into his room rising within him once again.

"It doesn't feel right yet."

Her fingers, previously on the torque, moved up a bit higher to trace the scars on Bryen's neck, her soft touch following the mark left by the sand cat and then traveling to his cheek.

"The time doesn't seem right," he said again, not offering any useful details as to why he thought that was the case.

"You're free," said Aislinn, not understanding. "You're free of the collar. Free of me. You can go anywhere that you want."

Bryen brought his hand to the collar, touching the cool silver for just a second, then grasping Aislinn's fingers that had remained on his cheek with his own. Finally, he lowered his eyes, catching hers with his gaze.

"The collar does not hold me," Bryen said quietly. "But I'm still not free."

Aislinn stared into Bryen's eyes, recognizing the spark that she saw there, feeling the same within herself. Not wanting to think anymore, she decided to simply act.

She leaned against Bryen, planning to give him a kiss on the cheek. At the very last second, he turned his head so that their lips met. Both pulled back instantly, neither anticipating that that would happen.

Then both Aislinn and Bryen smiled, their lips touching again, their actions moving their thoughts in an unexpected but welcome direction.

16

AN EASY DECISION

Declan shrugged his shoulders, brought his elbows together, then flexed the muscles in his upper back by bringing his scapulas together. He was trying to adjust the new leather armor that he wore across his broad chest so that it fit more comfortably. He liked it. The armor had a good feel to it, supple and smooth though still strong, and he could tell from its quality that it would do its job.

Even so, there were several areas where it still chafed against his skin. In time, the discomfort would work itself out once he had a few more training sessions and loosened the leather a little bit more. At the moment, though, there was a spot right below his shoulder blade on his left side that itched fiercely, and there was little that he could do about it.

Despite the nagging irritation, Declan stood stock still, hands resting on his belt, a sword hilt visible above each shoulder. He was the Sergeant of the Blood Company now, and it wouldn't do for him to take the dagger on his hip and try to work the blade beneath his armor to get at the itch that was almost driving him to distraction. Very unprofessional on his part, and he didn't need to give the men and women under his command who were circled around him in the Pit fodder that could be used against him later.

Some of the fighters seemed to believe that because he was no longer the Master of the Gladiators, they could tease him in a way that they did their peers, thinking that he was one of them. He had quashed that mistaken assumption quickly and soundly.

They were all free men and women now and they could come and go from the Blood Company as they chose. When they were in the Company, however, he would treat them fairly and according to the rules that any similar military unit applied to function effectively, and they would be expected to treat him with the respect that he deserved as the second in command.

It hadn't taken long for the others to figure that out after he had made a quick example of Serla. He was a good fighter. Sometimes, he just didn't know when to stop. So when his jokes went over the line, Declan had shown him the error of his ways in the practice yard. It had been an exceedingly short though very comprehensive demonstration. Since then, discipline among the gladiators who were now soldiers had not been a problem.

To take his mind off his continuing discomfort, Declan's gaze shifted slowly from the right to the left, taking in the one hundred and seven gladiators who made up the Blood Company, declared by Duchess Stelekel a free fighting force led by Captain Bryen Keldragan. Because of the Duchess' sanction, the Company could accept applicants as it deemed appropriate. Perhaps not surprisingly, in the few days since the Blood Company had been formed, Declan had received several thousand requests from men and women wanting to serve, all most likely interested in joining because of the

Company's and their commanding officer's rapidly growing reputations.

All one hundred and seven of the founding members of the Company had fought with the Volkun during the rebellion, seeking their freedom and the overthrow of the King, two objectives that they achieved with stunning success. They were all that remained of the gladiators who had called the white sand their home, every single one choosing to continue their service to the Volkun.

All of them were proud of what they had achieved, and they were all hungry for more. For many, escaping the Colosseum, though certainly a wonderful result of their bravery, wasn't enough for them. They wanted something more from life. Having gotten used to the regimen and expectations that made up their existence in the gladiators' stockade, the Blood Company gave them what they needed as well as the chance to do more with themselves that just days before they had any right to imagine.

The soldiers stood around Declan, who was in the center of the Pit, in ever larger rings, seven in all. If it seemed strange for them to be there without the cheers and screams of fifty thousand spectators showering down on them as they fought for their lives, they certainly didn't show it.

Instead the often rambunctious group was strangely quiet. Expectant. Perhaps even eager, thought Declan. They knew why they were there, and they appeared to be looking forward to what was going to happen next.

When a ripple of motion cascaded through the rows of gladiators, Declan smiled. Only one person could have such an effect on these hardened fighters, and that meant that the show was about to begin.

The eyes of all those assembled on the white sand

turned to the tunnel that led into the Pit from the gladiators' compound. Bryen strode out of the darkness, the Spear of the Magii, shining brightly as it caught the sun, grasped comfortably in his hand.

Declan realized that the Lady of the Southern Marches followed him, though she smartly stopped at the end of the tunnel, not actually setting foot on the white sand, understanding that this wasn't her place. It was theirs.

As Bryen glided across the sand, his thoughts, once a jumble, swiftly attained some needed clarity. It was a common occurrence whenever he entered the Pit, a skill Declan spent a great deal of time honing within him.

Bryen was not comfortable in his new role as Captain of the Blood Company. He knew how it was all supposed to work, the discipline that was required to ensure that a company of soldiers worked together efficiently. If this were a battle, then there wouldn't be an issue. He and Declan would lead the gladiators, who would obey just as in any other company. It had happened before when these same fighters captured the Colosseum and then held back the Royal Guard long enough for Bryen to remove Marden Beleron from the throne.

Today, however, wasn't a battle. Today was something else. Because for many of the men and women standing on the white sand, what Bryen was about to ask of them would be a death sentence. So he wouldn't order these gladiators to join him on his quest. To take on an assignment that had little chance of success. No, he didn't believe that it would be right to make them do that.

He would ask them to join him. He would tell them the truth, of what he thought would happen, of why what he needed them to do was important. If they wanted to assume the risk, he would offer his heartfelt gratitude. And if not, he would thank them for considering his offer and let them be. It was the only right thing to do with his friends and peers who were still adjusting to their broken bonds.

The soldiers of the Blood Company stepped out of the way to give Bryen a path to the center of the Pit, all of the men and women nodding in respect as he passed. They appreciated what the Volkun had done for them, the risk that he had taken.

He had been free. Free of the Pit. Free of the Protector's collar as much as he could be. He could have gone anywhere that he wanted, somewhere far from the white sand. Somewhere safe. Somewhere where he could start a new life and leave the blood, sweat, and pain of the Pit behind.

He hadn't.

No, instead he had come back here. He had come back to them. To fight for them. To fight with them. And because of that decision, they were free.

They understood and respected the sacrifice that the Volkun, their Captain, had made for them. And they knew that after he killed the King of Caledonia, when the entire Kingdom was in his debt, when he could have asked the lords and ladies of Caledonia for anything at all, the Volkun had never asked for anything for himself. No, he had thought of them instead. What he had asked for, he had asked for them.

Declan already had told them of the deal that their Captain had arranged for them, giving them a few hints as well of what the Volkun would ask of them today. To say that it was generous was an understatement. Most had stood there in stunned disbelief when Declan had told them of the terms in his stentorian voice.

Before he had returned to them, they already had

respected the Volkun because of his skill in the Pit and how he treated them in the practice yard. This additional self-sacrifice and work on their behalf simply endeared the Wolf to them even more.

Bryen gave Declan a nod when he reached him, then he took some time to catch the eyes of every single gladiator standing in the Pit. Renata, who resembled a kindly grandmother but without a second thought would crush an enemy's skull with the morning stars that she preferred, the spiked metal affixed to the end of her two footlong clubs stuck in her belt deadly in her quick hands, nodding in respect and holding that position for several long seconds before finally looking him in the eyes once again.

Jenus, who was built like a barrel, actually several barrels, and understood how to use his size to his advantage, absorbing blows and then responding with a viciousness that was terrifying, followed Renata's lead.

Asaia, tall and thin, who had survived in the Pit for more than a year because of her unique skill with a barbed whip, her lips moving silently as she also offered her thanks to the man who had gained her freedom, did the same.

As did Nkia, who never spoke, her tongue having been cut out when she was a child. She allowed her ever-present jambiyas, the traditional curved daggers of her homeland, to do her talking for her.

And so it went. Each gladiator acknowledged their Captain as his eyes latched on to each one. Each gladiator, who had a history of demonstrating little respect for anyone, bowing his or her head to demonstrate their regard for the Volkun.

When that was done, Bryen bowed his head and closed his eyes, all the other gladiators following suit, as they remembered their friends and comrades who had died by their side during the uprising. More than one hundred in total when they fought to hold the Colosseum.

"Thank you for coming," Bryen said as soon as he lifted his head.

For just a moment the silence within the Pit combined with the expectant looks of his peers released a swarm of butterflies in his stomach. He'd much rather fight another black dragon than do what he was doing now. Yet what he wanted didn't matter.

His life and the lives of all those in the Kingdom depended on what these men and women, former criminals, former slaves, former gladiators, decided now. So not knowing what else to do, and not wanting his growing queasiness to cause him to expel his breakfast onto the white sand, he simply talked to them as he would if they were sitting down in the mess hall for dinner.

"Declan has already told you the terms that have been put in place for those of you who decide to accompany me on the journey that I must take. Let me explain what we'll be doing and then you can ask any questions that you might have. I and three other Magii will be attempting to reach the Sanctuary," Bryen said. All of the gladiators noticed how he had referred to himself, as they knew of his skill in the Talent, having seen it put to good use during the insurrection. "We require assistance in getting there."

"As many of you know, the Sanctuary is where the Ten Magii built the Weir, which keeps Caledonia free from the Ghoules of the Lost Land," Bryen continued. "Or rather as the Weir once did, because the Ghoules have returned, forcing their way through the magical barrier in greater and greater numbers. In fact, we have received word just this morning that several thousand Ghoules are now in the Winter Pass, having crossed through the Weir. And for those who believe these reports to be only rumors, I can assure you that they are more than that. They are the truth. The Ghoules have returned to Caledonia, and I have the scars to prove it."

That last comment gained a chuckle from several soldiers of the Blood Company, which brought a smile to Bryen's lips.

"The Sanctuary is located atop one of the towering stone spires in the Trench, far to the northwest. The black dragon that I fought here in the Pit came from there, and from what I understand that and other beasts, just as dangerous if not more so, have claimed that rugged landscape as their territory. Of course, there are also the Ghoules. The Ghoules are faster than anything that any of you may have fought in the Pit. They are smart. They are relentless. They are deadly. They are hungry."

A few of the gladiators shifted uncomfortably. All knew the proclivities of the Ghoules, and that if they ever came up against one, it would be better to die during the combat rather than be taken prisoner.

"To say nothing of the Elders, who have been gifted the Dark Magic of the Ghoule Overlord. We will leave the Elders to the Magii as much as we can. You can kill an Elder, just like you can a Ghoule, if you can avoid the power that they wield."

"No easy task," murmured Declan, many of the gladiators nodding in agreement.

"Assuming that we reach the Trench and then the Sanctuary -- certainly not a given because of the Ghoules, the Elders, the black dragons, and the host of other dangers we will face along the way -- the Magii and I will attempt to rebuild the Weir. If we can restore the power of the Weir, we can prevent the Ghoules from leaving the Lost Land. And if we can't, then the Ghoule Overlord will take advantage of the eroding Weir, bring his Legions through the Shattered Peaks, and ... well, you know how that will play out. We all remember the stories from the First Ghoule War."

"We all get eaten," said Majdi, a large man with an even larger laugh who was difficult to anger, but deadly once his rage took hold.

Bryen chuckled with everyone else in the Pit at the gladiator's remark that masqueraded as a joke, then nodded in agreement. "Yes, we get eaten."

"This is a dangerous mission," Bryen continued. "You could even say that it's probably suicidal. Though having fought in the Pit, we should all be used to that."

The gladiators laughed again, not necessarily because of the humor in Bryen's statement, but rather because of the truth that it contained.

"You have your freedom now," Bryen confirmed. "You will have a stipend to start a new life if you choose not to go with me. Yet I will ask anyway. I ask that you go with me to the Sanctuary. The Magii and I will do what is needed against the Elders. We will try to rebuild the Weir, although we can offer no assurances that we will succeed. Against the Ghoules, who I am certain will dog our every step, I would prefer to have those with me whom I can trust."

Several of the gladiators stood a bit straighter upon hearing that.

"What, you can't trust the Royal Guard?" asked Asaia. Her question brought another round of laughter in the Pit.

Bryen laughed with them. "I'd prefer to have fighters who aren't afraid of the sight of their own blood."

"We are the Company of Blood for a reason, Volkun," offered Dorlan. The very large, very muscular, and also very smart and patient man gave Bryen a knowing grin.

"That we are, Dorlan," agreed Bryen. "We are the Company of Blood. We excel at spilling the blood of others. But I warn you that if you choose to go with me, much of the blood we spill will be our own, just as was the case when we took down Marden Beleron."

Bryen took a moment before continuing, locking eyes with as many of the gladiators as he could.

"We are the best fighters in Caledonia. I do not say that out of arrogance or pride. I say it because it's the truth. I say again, as well, that if you join me on this journey, much of the blood spilled will be yours. The threats that we face are too many to think otherwise. So I ask that you think about that, think about what you could lose if you decide to accompany me, before making your decision. If you choose to accompany me, then I thank you. And if not, I understand your decision and do not hold it against you. You have already given more of your blood, more of yourself, to this Kingdom than the people of Caledonia deserve. If you choose to go your own way, then I wish you well. You deserve the freedom that you have earned and should be proud of what you have accomplished already."

Silence reigned in the Pit then, the unexpected quiet settling over the white sand for several long breaths. Then the sound of a sword hitting a shield echoed throughout the Colosseum. Followed by another. Next came the muted thud of a spear butt being pounded against the white sand. And so it went, the clang of steel on steel, the thump of hardened wood striking the sand. The clatter and noise intensified until it reverberated off the white stone of the massive stadium.

Bryen smiled then and nodded to the men and women surrounding him, thanking them. This was the traditional sign of respect for a gladiator about to enter the Pit, and

Bryen knew that it was a clear statement as to the decision all the soldiers of the Blood Company had just made. All one hundred and seven soldiers would be joining him on his dangerous expedition.

"Did you have anything to do with this, Declan?" Bryen asked, having to raise his voice to be heard over the almost deafening noise.

Declan looked at Bryen with a broad smile on his face. "This was all you, lad. It looks like you have the Company of Blood, heart and soul, whether you like it or not."

In that instant, Bryen felt the weight of responsibility drape itself across his shoulders, weighing him down.

Declan could see it in his eyes, so he gripped Bryen's shoulder tightly in commiseration and support. "This isn't something you can escape, lad. You need to understand that they joined the Blood Company to follow you. They're going to the Sanctuary, live or die, because of you. Because of what you did for them and what you continue to do for them. They want to repay you. And if it takes their blood to pay their debt to you, then they're willing to pay that price."

"Declan has the right of it," said Lycia, who came to stand next to Bryen, her brother as always in tow. "Besides, I've been looking after you for years. There's no reason to stop now." She then glanced pointedly at the Lady of the Southern Marches, who remained standing near the entrance to the Pit, the fact that her broad smile seemed to brighten the shadows around her aggravating Lycia even more than she wanted to admit. The Crimson Devil then pointed at Aislinn. "Also, I don't trust her. She's got shifty eyes."

"She does not," protested Bryen.

Lycia laughed, slapping Bryen on the back, just as she used to do when they were both consigned to the Pit.

"Stop looking at her eyes, Volkun. She's the Vedra. The Witch. Don't fall under her spell."

Lycia then released her hold on Bryen's shoulder and walked toward the tunnel, Bryen catching the mocking smile on her face.

As soon as Lycia turned away, her smile disappeared, replaced by a frown. As she walked past the Lady of the Southern Marches and into the gloom of the tunnel, she feared that Aislinn Winborne already had spun her spell over Bryen, and he didn't seem to mind one bit.

17

REACHING OUT

Sirius cleared his throat loudly to announce their presence.

"Should we come back at another time? When we're not disturbing you?"

"Yes, we really don't want to interrupt such an important conversation," added Rafia.

They had just walked into the office in the Corinthian Palace that had been set aside for Noorsin's use and stopped short in surprise, having discovered the Duchess of Stelekel wrapped in the arms of the Duke of the Southern Marches.

"I was offering my thanks to Noorsin for her helping me and Aislinn," said Kevan sheepishly, his face bright red at being caught in such a compromising position.

"Yes, well, the next time that I help someone, I hope that person offers their thanks in the same way," said Rafia lightly.

"The only person who will be helping you in the future will be me," the old Magus huffed.

"Don't get your robes in a bind," grumbled Rafia. She then turned her attention to the reason that they had come there. "Noorsin, Sirius and I were hoping to speak with you about connecting with the Magii."

"Yes, it seems that you and Kevan have the Caledonian Army well in hand," continued Sirius. "We need to ensure that the Magii are there as well if we're to have any hope of defending against the Elders at the Winter Pass."

"Of course," Noorsin replied, who reluctantly released her hold around Kevan's waist. Although Kevan clearly had been embarrassed by the interruption, she hadn't been. Rather, she was a bit miffed by the Magii's timing. "Kevan, you're welcome to stay and participate in the conversation."

"Thank you, Noorsin," the Duke of the Southern Marches replied, "but I think not. The last of the companies will be leaving for the Winter Pass tomorrow morning, and I need to speak with the Blademaster to ensure that everything that we just discussed is ready."

"It must have been quite a discussion," murmured Rafia, her eyebrows quirking suggestively.

Since he had no good response to the Magus' innuendo, Kevan released his hold on Noorsin. He had learned when he was much younger that if you had nothing useful to say, it was better to just stay quiet, so he nodded to the three Magii and then closed the door quietly behind him when he left the room.

"You didn't need to do that," said Noorsin, her voice sharper than usual.

"Do what?" asked Rafia innocently.

"Make Kevan uncomfortable. I know you have your issues with him after what he did to Bryen. But he is a Duke and he has to make difficult decisions. He is trying."

"We did no such thing," protested Sirius.

"We're not responsible for Kevan's discomfort, Noorsin," replied Rafia. "Everyone already knows about the relationship you two have been developing. Personally, I think that you could do better."

Noorsin shrugged. "I don't think your romantic history makes you the best person to provide an opinion as to where I display my affection."

"Point taken, but I must say that I think he's repressed," continued Rafia.

"He's not repressed, Rafia," sighed Sirius, although a part of him agreed with Rafia that Noorsin deserved better. He had known his former student a long time, and he only wanted the best for her. "He's just out of practice."

"Yes, that's it exactly," agreed Noorsin, who was surprised that her mentor had offered such an erudite and on-point comment regarding such a delicate manner. "It has been more than a decade since he lost his wife. He's still feeling his way. His fear of losing what he loves clouds his judgment. A difficult position for any leader."

"If you say so," said Rafia, still not convinced as to Kevan's character.

"Perhaps we could return to the reason that you're here," said Noorsin. "You mentioned wanting to talk to the Magii."

"Yes," said Sirius. "You know where all the surviving Magii are, correct?"

"More or less," replied Noorsin. "For obvious reasons, several of them tend to move around a lot, so I'm not entirely certain."

"Have you heard from many of the Magii?"

"A few," replied Noorsin, knowing that Sirius was referring to her efforts to get a message to all the members of the Order of the Magii through her many eyes and ears who existed because of her close connection to the Royal Medical School and the Royal Library. Her wording had been innocuous, in case any of her messengers were waylaid, but the Magii would translate the code easily enough. The Magii would know what was required of them and where they needed to go. "As you might suspect, it takes time to reach them in this manner, and there is no guarantee that we will reach all of them."

"That's why we're here," said Rafia. "Since Sirius and I will be going with Bryen to the Sanctuary, we must do this now if we are to have any hope of having all the Magii in Caledonia join you at the Winter Pass before it's too late."

"Do what, specifically?" asked Noorsin, her interest piqued.

"We will try to reach all the Magii now," said Rafia.

"With the Talent?"

"Of course with the Talent," confirmed Rafia, a touch of irritation sneaking into her tone because of the press of time. "How else would we do it?"

"It's too much for one Magus to do alone," continued Sirius. "That's why we will be linking our power and doing it together."

Noorsin nodded, pleased to be participating. "Show me how it's done."

"Take my hand," offered Rafia.

Noorsin gladly did as requested, grasping hands with both Rafia and Sirius, who then joined their free hands together to complete the connection, the three Magii standing in a small circle in the center of the room. She then reached for the Talent just as Sirius and Rafia did.

Rafia took the lead. Noorsin was surprised that Sirius would permit her to do so. Then again, once the Keeper of Haven had made up her mind, there was little point in getting in her way. It was much like stepping in front of a charging bull. You didn't make that mistake, because there was only one possible result.

Noorsin watched closely as Rafia tentatively reached out to her and Sirius, and then, with their permission, she linked the Talent accessible to them with her connection to the natural power of the world.

Using the huge reservoir of energy that was now open to her, Rafia searched as she would if she were seeking to locate a particular person or place. In this case, she focused her attention not only on a person, but on those people who also radiated the Talent just like the three of them did.

Rafia smiled as she visualized what she was doing. It appeared to her as if she were connecting to various points of light spread out across Caledonia. More than seventy in all.

Once she was satisfied that she had connected with every member of the Order of the Magii, she sent a short but precise message.

"The Ghoule Legions come. The Winter Pass. Ten days' time."

The communication dispatched, Rafia released her hold on the Talent and gently broke the connection.

"Will they come?" asked Noorsin.

"They will," Rafia said with absolute confidence. "Or they will die trying."

"But so few," said Sirius sadly. "Perhaps too few."

"We do what we can with what we have," Noorsin said. "We have no choice."

"Yes, and remember, we don't have to defeat the Ghoule Legions, we simply need to hold them in place," explained Rafia. "Right now, we're simply playing for time."

"We are also placing a lot of faith in Bryen," offered Noorsin, a touch of doubt evident in her voice. "I know from personal experience what that young man has done, what he can do. Do you really believe that he can rebuild the Weir?"

Sirius paused before responding. Rafia strangely remained silent.

"I don't know. I do know that if we are to rest the fate of the Kingdom on a single pair of shoulders, it would be on his. He will do all that he can, or he will die trying. You can ask for no more than that from anyone."

18

A NEW JOURNEY BEGINS

The stables of the Corinthian Palace were experiencing a level of controlled chaos not seen since the former King Beleron -- the father, not the son -- prepared to leave the capital on one of his annual pilgrimages around Caledonia during which he visited every Duchy and paid his respects to every Duke and Duchess in the land, something his son did only once during his rule and reluctantly at that. King Beleron initiated the practice at the beginning of his reign, and his effort in this regard had proven to be essential to his building strong ties to all the lords and ladies of the land, solidifying the connections between the Duchies and the Crown and confirming where royal responsibilities and commitments began and ended.

Although time consuming, as it often took several months for King Beleron to complete his roundabout journey, the time proved to be well spent. The Kingdom had enjoyed unprecedented peace and prosperity during his rule. Until, of course, Tetric had appeared and wormed his way into the Royal Court as the King's Advisor.

Thankfully, the danger presented by that disgraced

Magus was no more, due in large part to the young man who stood off to the side and along one of the walls of the courtyard, watching all that was going on with a bemused eye. He could have gone over to the Blood Company to check on their preparations -- he was their Captain after all -- but he saw little reason to do so. He was certain that Declan had everything well in hand, and he had no desire to become the target of the Master of the Gladiators' ire. Declan wanted things done just so, and if you got in the way of his efforts, even unintentionally, it was never a pleasant encounter.

Besides, he had little knowledge of how to prepare such a large group of soldiers for the journey that they were about to undertake. Best to leave it to those who did.

"You seem way too excited for a journey that could likely lead to our deaths," said Bryen. Aislinn, a huge grin on her face, leaned against the wall next to him, their shoulders touching companionably.

"I've been locked in this city for half a year," replied Aislinn, her smile revealing the dimples that Bryen had come to adore. "Dangerous or not, it's a relief to leave Tintagel. To finally be free of the gilded prison provided for me."

"That I can understand," he answered quietly. "You're not really living if you're not making your own decisions."

Aislinn and Bryen continued to watch the preparations, content with the new awareness between them. They had not spoken about what had happened between them in Bryen's cell. Neither had felt the need to do so. They had simply savored the fact that it had happened.

"And are you doing that now?" asked Aislinn. "Making your own decisions?"

Bryen took a moment to think before responding,

understanding why Aislinn was asking. For more than half his life he had been forced to obey the wishes of others, whether as a gladiator or as a Protector, having gained his freedom only recently thanks to the woman standing next to him. He knew that Aislinn feared that he had been pushed in this direction, that he was once again doing what others wanted of him rather than what he wanted to do for himself. In reality that wasn't the case.

He wanted to do this. Other people probably saw it as his overdeveloped sense of responsibility. He couldn't deny that didn't play a role in his decision making. Yet deep down he knew that it was more than that. There was a far less noble reason as to why he wanted to do this, a reason he kept locked within himself. He wanted to do this to gain revenge for his parents, and for the life the Ghoules had taken from him, during that dark, rainy night on a quiet Tintagel street.

"I am," replied Bryen with a smile and a playful nudge of his hip, making Aislinn blush just a bit. "This is the right thing to do, and not just for them."

Bryen nodded toward the two approaching Magii, Aislinn tracking his gaze.

RAFIA'S EYES missed nothing as she and Sirius approached the Protector and the Lady of the Southern Marches. Something had changed between the two of them. She understood the properties of the Protector's collar that Bryen still wore around his neck, about how the magic infused within the steel allowed the Protector and the person under his or her charge to feel what the other was feeling.

Although Aislinn had helped to break that and the other

bindings of the collar so that now it was no more than a silver chain, it seemed that Bryen and Aislinn had gained a closeness that exceeded even that of what was achieved through the collar. The glances and touches between the two were just some of the signals that Rafia couldn't fail to notice. Curious. Very curious, indeed. And certainly not a bad thing. In fact, potentially a very good thing.

Watching their easy engagement brought to mind a better time between her and Sirius.

"We never really finished that discussion, Sirius," reminded Rafia. "And we need to finish it."

"I have been doing the best that I can," protested the Magus.

"I know, Sirius," replied Rafia. "I appreciate that, and I don't fault you for where we stand. I've just been thinking that perhaps we both need something more now. We're different. We've grown in distinctly different ways since we were last together."

"That may be, but that doesn't mean that we can't continue as we have."

"Continuing as we have helps neither of us, Sirius. You know that. You agreed with me about that last night. It's just comfortable between us, which is fine." Rafia shrugged her shoulders helplessly. "I don't want fine. I want something more than fine."

The conversation was cut short because they had reached Bryen and Aislinn.

"Have you decided on the route that we will be taking?" Bryen asked, ignoring the tension that was so obvious between the two Magii, a tension that only seemed to have been exacerbated during the last few days.

"The less obvious route," declared Rafia, realizing that she and Sirius still had unresolved issues despite the lengthy conversation of the night before. Those would have to wait. "It might take us a bit longer, but that can't be avoided. We might even gain some needed breathing room, and that's more important."

"Why not follow the shoreline of the Bay of the Dead west toward Roo's Nest, then turn north there for the Trench?" Aislinn wondered. "I would think that the Ghoules will be after us right from the start, and that path would save us a good bit of time."

"We were discussing that just last night," explained Sirius. For a moment, both Aislinn and Bryen feared that the old Magus was going to dredge up more of what he and Rafia had spoken about the night before, none of which either of them had any interest in pursuing. Thankfully, rather than going off on a tangent as was so often the case with him, Sirius stayed on track. "It would be faster to follow the coast, even to take a ship. However, we believe that the most obvious routes will be watched most closely by the Ghoules. The path we're taking might give us a few days' head start."

"The Ghoule Overlord knows where we need to go," interrupted Rafia. "We both assume that he will try to catch us along the way, and if we take a ship he can simply wait for us to land and then take us with little trouble as there are few options for coming ashore near the Trench. If we can get ahead of him by just a few days that could mean the difference between success ..."

"And a bloody failure," offered Bryen, trying not to say it harshly, just truthfully. Their mission had little chance of successful completion to begin with, so better to be realistic about it. Besides, that fact would not stop them from trying to achieve their goal.

"You're trying to gain a few days on the Ghoule Overlord

by going through the Dark Forest after leaving Tintagel, then turning west once we reach the lower hills of the Shattered Peaks," said Aislinn.

"Correct," said Rafia with a nod. "We'll use the Dark Forest to shield our movements. We expect to be tracked right from the start."

"So when we are attacked, we can use the tight space of the wood against the Ghoules," continued Aislinn. "The open space along the shore of the Bay of the Dead or on the Breakwater Plateau favors the beasts. Knowing that they'll be behind us, we want to limit as many of the advantages the Ghoules have as possible."

"That's the plan, Aislinn," said Rafia. "We have few good choices, and I believe that this is the best one for now. If we need to change our strategy along the way, then we'll have a better chance to do that in the Dark Forest rather than on the Breakwater Plateau."

"I agree with that assessment," said Tarin Tentillin, the Captain of the Battersea Guard walking up behind the two Magii. With him came Jerad, his Sergeant, both carrying saddlebags across their shoulders and other supplies along with their weapons.

"Why are you so sure?" asked Sirius. "Rafia and I did not reach agreement on this approach until very early this morning after several hours of discussion."

"I was speaking with Jurgen Klines just a few days ago," explained Tarin. "Right after Magus Rafia and the Royal Guard eliminated those four Ghoule packs just within the Dark Forest. Quite efficiently, if I might add, from what Jurgen told me."

"Yes, that was a good fight, and that Elder got what he deserved," Rafia replied with a nod of satisfaction. "The Blademaster is quite competent."

"That he is, Magus Rafia."

"Just Rafia," the Magus corrected, now an automatic response as she hated the formality often bestowed upon her because of her position.

"Thank you, Rafia," said Tarin, giving the Magus a brief nod. "After talking with Jurgen we both agreed that there would be more Ghoule packs in the countryside and the Dark Forest. Whether to stop us from going to the Sanctuary or simply to create chaos behind our lines as the bulk of our forces move toward the Winter Pass, we couldn't say for sure. It really doesn't matter, does it? Better to stay concealed for as long as we can."

"No, it doesn't matter," agreed Bryen. "And you're right. The Ghoules will be a constant problem. No matter what route we take we won't be able to escape them. Our only hope is to stay in front of the beasts."

"Why can't you use the Talent as Rafia did before the Battle of the Horseshoe so that we can sneak by the Ghoules?" interjected Jerad.

"Bryen is the Seventh Stone," said Sirius, as if that was all the explanation that was needed. The blank look that followed pushed him to expand on his response. "The Ghoule Overlord wants the Seventh Stone, and because the Seventh Stone contains the Curse, and he is the source of the Curse in the Lost Land, he can find the Seventh Stone now that the artifact is no longer protected and shielded in the Aeyrie."

"So you're essentially a walking target," confirmed Tarin, clapping Bryen on the shoulder and offering a short bark of laughter. "Remind me not to get too close to you as we head to the Sanctuary."

"If you're worried, what are you two doing here?" asked

Bryen, unable to keep a smile from his face after Tarin's comment.

He knew the Captain of the Battersea Guard well, and he had no doubt that Tarin would be at his side all the way to the Trench, as he was never one to shy away from the hottest fighting. That still begged the question of what he was doing here as Bryen had assumed that Tarin and Jerad would be going with the Battersea Guard to the Winter Pass. Duke Winborne would be heading in that direction tomorrow.

"We're coming with you," replied Jerad, a grin breaking out on his handsome face that seemed to suggest that seeking the Sanctuary, despite all the dangers to be faced along the way, would be fun, an affliction that only appeared to affect him and Davin.

"Duke Winborne gave us permission," clarified Tarin. "He thought that you might need some adult supervision."

"He did or you did?" Bryen asked of Tarin.

Before Tarin could reply, a commanding voice sounded behind them.

"The same could be said for you, Sergeant Brexston. The need for adult supervision." Jerad sensed the person behind him step even closer, feeling her warm breath on the back of his neck. "A word, Sergeant?"

Jared visibly paled as he slowly turned around. Standing right behind him was a woman just as tall as he was, her long blonde hair tied in an intricate braid and knotted at the end by a leather strap. Strong and lithe, she wore the dark blue leather armor of the Southern Marches, which resembled one of the primary colors of the Silent Sea, that angry ocean slamming against the eastern coast of the province. Despite his best efforts, Jerad couldn't help but be attracted to her. Their banter was a constant between them. Beyond that he wasn't sure how to manage their relationship beyond their service in the Battersea Guard.

"Dani, what are you doing here?" Jerad asked, as he pulled her away from the group for a private conversation.

"Apparently seeing you off on a dangerous and potentially fatal assignment," she replied. "Did you really think that you could leave without seeing me first?"

"No. But I didn't think I needed to consult with you before I did this," said Jerad, somewhat confused.

Dani reached up and grasped the shoulder straps of Jerad's dark blue leather armor, pulling him close. "I understand why you want to do this. The Volkun is your friend, and he needs your support and assistance. I just want to make something perfectly clear with you."

Jerad didn't know how to respond, so all he could do was nod hesitantly.

"You will come back to me, Jerad. If you don't, I'll kill you myself. Do we understand one another?"

She kissed him then, softly at first, then with more passion, Jerad giving in to the warmth building within him. When she was done, she gave Jerad a nod, as if her action had just confirmed her words and that she now had the witnesses to prove it.

For just a moment, Jerad could only stare at Dani.

"We do," mumbled Jerad, his thoughts beginning to travel down a thoroughly unproductive but fun path.

"Good," said Dani, a huge smile breaking out on her pixielike face. Having achieved her objective, she turned. "Captain Tentillin, I will do my duty to the Battersea Guard in your absence."

"I would expect no less from you, Corporal," replied Tarin, not sure how to handle what he had just witnessed between his Corporal and Sergeant.

"Permission to speak plainly, sir?" asked Dani.

Tarin nodded, curious as to where this was going.

"I will hold you personally responsible, Captain, if anything should happen to Jerad while he is away."

"You have nothing to fear in that regard, Corporal," answered Tarin, unconcerned by the obvious threat. If Jerad didn't make it back from the Trench, then neither would he, so there was little to worry about. "I will return him just as you see him now."

"Excellent," said Dani with a grin. "As soon as you do, Jerad and I have a wedding to plan."

With that, she gave Jerad a final kiss, then strode through the confusion of the courtyard that seemed to part for her as she headed toward where the Battersea Guard had been billeted within the Corinthian Palace.

"You never said that you were engaged," chided Aislinn.

"I didn't know until just now," replied Jerad, a goofy smile still on his face after Dani's parting kiss, and it didn't look like it would be fading anytime soon.

"That woman is a force of nature," said Tarin.

"Indeed she is," agreed Jerad. "Why she picked me, I don't know. I'm just glad that she did."

"As we all are," said Bryen with a grin.

"Hear, hear," agreed Tarin. "You two deserve one another."

"Thank you?" said Jerad more as a question, not understanding the comment and not knowing whether or not he should be offended by it. Before he could pursue it further, Bryen turned the conversation back to the topic at hand.

"Adult supervision, you said," commented the Protector.

"Aye, lad," answered Tarin. "I don't have enough aggravation in my life, so I thought that I'd spend more time with you." The Captain of the Battersea Guard had a broad grin on his face, clearly enjoying his own humor. "Besides, it's a good opportunity to do some training."

"Training for whom?" asked Bryen.

"The Company of Blood," said Declan, stepping into the conversation and speaking loudly so the gladiators milling about could hear. "I've been out of the army for two decades. Captain Tentillin and the Sergeant said that they would help me with this pack of mongrels."

That comment brought smiles to the faces of the gladiators who were gathering supplies in the courtyard, even a few chuckles.

"Declan, is it?" asked Rafia.

"It is," he replied, turning his attention to Rafia. "But you already knew that, Magus."

Rafia's lips twisted into a mysterious smile. Apparently, her efforts to watch him surreptitiously in the practice yard had not gone unnoticed.

"Tell me, Declan, are you and your Company prepared for the dangers that we will be facing as we go to the Sanctuary?"

"Yes, Magus, we are well ..."

"Rafia," she interrupted. "No need for formalities."

Declan stared at Rafia for a moment. Despite all the people surrounding them, Declan felt as if they were the only two people there. Then, just as quickly, the feeling passed. She held his gaze just as strongly as he held hers.

"We are well prepared, Rafia," continued Declan. "Bryen has explained in great detail what we can expect from the Ghoules. We have all fought on the white sand against beasts like them. We're as ready for them as we can be."

"These are fearsome creatures, Declan. They are not easily defeated."

"Nor are we, Rafia," replied Declan. "We are named the Company of Blood for a good reason."

Before the verbal sparring between Rafia and Declan could continue, Noorsin and Kevan walked up to the group.

"Noorsin," said Sirius. "It was unnecessary but kind of you to see us off."

"It was the least that I could do," replied the Duchess of Murcia. "I see that you are almost ready. All the preparations have been made as you requested?"

"They have," Declan said. "Thank you, Duchess Stelekel. We appreciate all that you have done for us."

"It is nothing compared to what you and the Company of Blood have done and are doing for us," Noorsin replied smoothly. "How fortunate for me that everyone is gathered here. I would like to review some final details of our plan. If you could follow me, as I believe that Duke Winborne would like a few minutes to speak privately with Lady Aislinn."

The small group dispersed quickly as Duchess Stelekel requested, although Bryen took his time in doing so. Pushing himself off the wall, he looked squarely at Kevan. Aislinn studied them both as they faced one another. Neither said a word.

Then, the two men nodded, apparently having reached agreement on something important. Before Bryen walked away, he made a point of touching with his hand the small of Aislinn's back gently, protectively, the slight pressure sending a welcome spark up her spine, before he followed the others into the directed bedlam of the courtyard.

"What was that about?" Aislinn asked her father.

"Just a continuation of the conversation that we started in the Pit," he replied with a small smile. "Bryen is a good man."

"He is," she replied, not sure if the person she was speaking to was actually her father, as he never had called Bryen by his first name before without Aislinn requiring him to do so.

"He cares for you."

Kevan's comment caught Aislinn completely off guard. "You think so?"

"He cares for you," Kevan repeated with greater certainty. "It's quite obvious."

"Does that bother you?"

"No," Kevan answered immediately. "No, it doesn't."

"I'm surprised to hear you say that."

"I'm surprised myself," Kevan replied with a gentle chuckle. "Believe it or not, even I can adopt a different perspective when circumstances warrant it."

"What made you change your opinion regarding Bryen?" Aislinn asked, her curiosity piqued.

Now Kevan took a moment before responding. It wasn't the fact that the young man had returned to Tintagel when he had no cause for doing so, risking his own life for theirs. It wasn't because he had ended the rule of Marden Beleron, saving his daughter from a fate that he simply couldn't imagine. It wasn't because Bryen had saved Kevan's life when he could have just let him die and no one would have challenged his decision not to help. No, the reason for changing his mind was driven by something much simpler but in his opinion much more meaningful.

"The way that he looks at you."

Aislinn smiled at that, a slight blush coming to her cheeks. She wasn't embarrassed, however. Rather, she was actually quite pleased.

"You're not here to try to change my mind about joining Bryen on this mission, are you?" Aislinn asked her father, gratified by what he had said. That had been her initial thought when he had appeared with Noorsin, her father not coming here to see her off but rather to try one more time to convince her that accompanying Bryen and the others to the Sanctuary was too dangerous.

It was Kevan's turn to smile. That was exactly what had crossed his mind when he had agreed to go with Noorsin to the courtyard before the Company of Blood marched through the gates. He understood now that he couldn't do that, no matter how much he wanted to. He needed to give his remarkably capable daughter the opportunity to make her own choices, even when those choices frightened him.

"No, I just wanted to wish you well." Kevan then pulled Aislinn into his arms for a hug. "Stay safe."

"SHOULD I tell Duke Winborne that I'll keep an eye on the Lady Winborne," Lycia asked her brother as they watched the father and daughter engage in their private conversation. "He seems quite concerned about her, and I don't want him to worry."

"First, I don't think that the Lady of the Southern Marches wants you to keep an eye on her," Davin replied, adjusting the scabbarded swords across his back so that they rested more comfortably on his shoulders. "Second, based on what I've seen, I don't think the Vedra needs you to keep an eye on her. She appears to be quite competent all on her own. Actually, more competent than most."

"Why all the compliments?" scowled Lycia. "She's no more than a spoiled girl playing at something that she shouldn't."

"I'm not offering compliments," said Davin. "I'm simply

stating facts. You may see her as a spoiled girl, but she's also a Magus. That would worry most people and why it doesn't bother you I don't know. I can only assume that you were hit too many times in the head during your many combats. Also, though she may be a spoiled girl, she's still a better fighter than most of the members of the Blood Company."

Lycia made it a point to check the sharpness of her blades, running a finger along the steel of each one. She had spent several hours the night before making sure that her weapons were exactly as they should be. It was only a temporary distraction, however, from the thoughts that had plagued her since they had overthrown the Crown.

"I don't get it," Lycia tried to argue. "Why do you like her after everything she did to Bryen?"

Davin normally kept his temper in check. He knew from experience that taking such an approach had helped to ensure that he survived his time in the Pit. Still, he was losing patience with Lycia. He took a deep breath to calm himself, not wanting to create a spectacle in the courtyard knowing how quickly his sister was to anger when challenged on issues that struck a nerve. And clearly when it came to Bryen any attempt on his part to dispute her thinking struck a nerve.

"Bryen has come to terms with it. Therefore, so can I. Besides, what she did in the Pit was because of her skill and were not the actions of a spoiled girl. That's why I named her the Vedra. I'm treating her like I would anyone else. Whatever she is, she's earned it. Plain and simple. She deserves more of your respect."

Lycia growled an unintelligible response, clearly not wanting to hear what her brother had to say, the truth of his words working their way under her skin and only serving to magnify her aggravation.

Davin hesitated, then moved the conversation in a direction that he had avoided for quite a long time, not wanting to visit what was obviously a painful subject for his sister. He had a sense of what was going on with her. Still, he needed to ask.

"What's really bothering you, Lycia?"

She took a long time before responding, spending most of it staring at the steel of her swords, as if she was searching for some unseen imperfection, before finally answering.

"I'm just worried for Bryen. After all that's happened to him, he's now saddled with all of this. For some it would be a death sentence."

"For some, but not him," Davin replied with a nod, although he didn't believe that his sister was being entirely truthful with him. "He wouldn't have agreed to do this unless he believed that he could do it."

Lycia finally tore her gaze from her blades, suggesting with her look that her brother was being far too accepting, so Davin qualified his initial response.

"All right, yes, he probably would have agreed anyway. Why he has this desire to help others even at the risk of his own life, I don't know. I don't understand it. But it's a part of who he is."

"Neither do I," grumbled Lycia, "and that's why I worry about him."

"There's more to it than that."

"What do you mean?" asked Lycia, a touch of concern in her voice.

"What happened between you two in the Colosseum?"

Lycia hesitated before responding. She understood that her brother was not referring to her desire to keep an eye on Bryen, looking out for him in a way that she didn't for any of the other gladiators. What she had developed with Bryen in the Pit, and apparently had lost, was much too personal for her to share, even with her brother.

"Nothing," she replied, though she was unable to look Davin in the eyes when she did so. "Nothing at all."

Davin stared at her for several long moments, then he shook his head sadly. He wished that his sister would share more. It might help her. Even so, he knew that he couldn't force her to tell him something that she didn't want him to know.

"People change, Lycia. We've changed. After everything Bryen has been through it's only fair to assume that he has changed as well. I'd be worried if he hadn't."

"Maybe so," she replied quietly as she watched Bryen come to stand next to Aislinn once again now that her father had left. "But that doesn't mean I have to like it."

Davin was about to say something else, then decided against it as he watched the Blademaster walk up to the Volkun and the Vedra.

"Captain," said the Blademaster, nodding toward Bryen.

For a moment, Bryen didn't know who the Blademaster was addressing, a look of confusion crossing his face. A nudge from Aislinn helped him to figure it out.

"Captain," Bryen replied with a nod, slightly amused by the exchange in titles. "My thanks for all that you did for Lady Winborne. She was in a difficult position here, and I know that she greatly valued your friendship."

"She earned my friendship and my respect, young man, as well as that of my soldiers. Rightfully gained and freely given."

"You're being too kind, Blademaster," said Aislinn.

"I am only speaking the truth, Lady Winborne." Klines turned his gaze back to Bryen. "Lady Winborne is not very good at receiving compliments, is she?"

Bryen smiled. "Too true, Captain. She doesn't know what to do with them."

"And I take it that neither are you," said Klines. "You seem to care little for praise or commendation."

"There is little that can be done with either," replied Bryen. "Besides, I prefer not to focus on the past."

"You prefer to focus on the future, on what needs to be done," said Klines.

If the Blademaster thought that his sharp gaze would shatter Bryen's calm reserve, he was mistaken. Klines had nothing on Declan when it came to discomfiting stares.

"Yes, Captain. That's correct. I tend to focus on what comes next rather than on what's been achieved. You're only as good as your next challenge."

"That's rare in a place like this, young man. Many people here in the Palace or in any place of power prefer to focus on what they believe they've accomplished because often they have so little to rest their laurels upon."

Bryen smiled at that. He could understand why the Blademaster and Declan were such fast friends, having enjoyed watching their regular combats and learning a great deal from both when they dueled on the white sand.

"Rare, yes, but not unheard of. Some of us understand that we are judged based both on what we have done and on what we can do. It's a hard lesson, though a necessary one when you're consigned to the Pit."

"I imagine it is, young man," replied the Blademaster, giving the Captain of the Blood Company a warm smile. There was a great deal of Declan in the Volkun, and the

Protector was the better for it. "If you don't mind, Captain, may I have just a minute with the Lady Winborne?"

"Of course, Blademaster," replied Bryen, giving Klines another respectful nod. He then stepped away so that the two could have some privacy.

"Who told you, Blademaster?" asked Aislinn, wondering how he had learned that she would be going to the Sanctuary.

"No one. I just had a feeling. As I said before, you remind me of my daughter."

Aislinn didn't want to open an old, painful wound by asking about her, even though she was intensely curious, having gathered bits and pieces from the rumors flying through the Corinthian Palace that it had something to do with the now deceased Killen Sourban.

"Bryen is right, you know. I owe you a debt for all that you did for me."

"I did nothing, Lady Aislinn. You did it. I simply gave you the opportunity."

"Still, I am in your debt and will remain so."

"You're just like the Volkun," Klines said with a smile. "You've spent way too much time with him."

"Maybe so," she replied. "Of course, I had little choice."

"Excellent point." The Blademaster then revealed what he had been hiding behind his back. "Your Protector has an impressive weapon. I thought that you might have need of one as well as you make for the Sanctuary."

Klines then pulled on the gleaming steel hilt, drawing free from the leather scabbard a beautifully crafted and perfectly balanced sword, the Winborne sigil carved into the steel blade on both sides near the grip.

Aislinn reached for the hilt, hesitant at first, dazzled by the magnificent steel, obviously crafted by a master blacksmith. She tested the weight and the balance. The blade felt perfectly comfortable in her hand, as if it was meant to be there. Running a finger along the blade, she marveled at the sharpness of the steel.

"It's a beautiful sword, Captain Klines. I don't know how to thank you."

"No thanks are needed. It looks like it was made for your hand."

"It certainly feels that way."

"Good, I'm glad. The Vedra needs a weapon that is just as sharp as she is."

19

A DANGEROUS TOOL

It felt good to cross through the Weir and be back in the lands of the humans. The air seemed fresher here. More inviting and full of promise.

After his latest setback, that's all that the Ghoule Overlord could hope for, as there was little in the way of certainty now that the cursed Protector had revealed himself to be the Seventh Stone.

He still seethed at how his years of scheming had crashed down around him so quickly. He believed that he had taken the last step necessary to ensure the success of his plans by wearing Tetric's skin in order to scheme in the Caledonian capital and locate the artifact the thieving Magus had stolen from him.

Yet now Tetric was dead, and the Ghoule Overlord had been forced to reveal himself when fighting the Master of the Magii in the Pit.

To add to his shame, the Protector had prevented him from eliminating the Magus. For a split second, the Ghoule Overlord thought that he could accomplish his goal in one fell swoop, killing the Magus who had been a thorn in his side for a millennium and then taking the Seventh Stone.

But it was not to be. During the brief combat on the white sand, he sensed that the Protector was stronger than he had anticipated, probably as a result of his joining with the artifact, which meant that he would need to be more careful going forward with his efforts to acquire the Seventh Stone.

Then again, perhaps events would still play out in his favor. The damned Magii feared the weakening of the Weir, just as they should. The practitioners of the Talent would begin to feel the pain of their negligence, their failure to maintain the power of the Weir, as his Elders forced more of his Legions through the magical barrier and then down into the Winter Pass. Soon the humans would have no choice.

The Magii would need to repair the Weir, or at least attempt to do so, and there was little to suggest that they would be successful. More important, their efforts in this respect would give him another opportunity to kill the Protector, because the Protector was critical to that effort.

The Magii could only save the people of the Kingdom with the Seventh Stone, and that meant that the Protector would have to leave the safe confines of the capital. His Legions demanded the attention of the Caledonian Army, so the Seventh Stone would be lightly guarded at best. He would be vulnerable, and dangerously so, particularly during his journey to the Weir.

The only thing that mattered was the Seventh Stone, and to take the Seventh Stone he needed to kill its host.

The Ghoule packs that waited for him on the other side of the slope would help to ensure that happened. They had traveled hard the last few days west through the Shattered

Peaks until they had reached the knolls that bordered the Breakwater Plateau just north of the Dark Forest.

He and his Ghoules would pursue the Protector at all costs, but first he needed to discover the route that they would take, as there were several to choose from. And he worried that the Magii with the Protector might have a few tricks up their sleeves. He had no doubt that they would seek to deceive him, to enter the Trench in a way that he had yet to discover.

So the Ghoule Overlord wanted to hedge his bets and have more than one recourse in play. The Protector had proven time and again that he could stand against his Ghoules and his Elders. The power gifted to him by the Seventh Stone would only aid him in his endeavors.

With that in mind, the Ghoule Overlord called upon the Dark Magic that surged within his veins. The summoned energy spun faster and faster as more of the Curse burst forth. With each rotation the Dark Magic expanded until the portal that the Ghoule Overlord had been weaving became taller than he was.

Satisfied with his work, the Ghoule Overlord stepped through. Once again, he was in the Lost Land, the smell of decay and sulfur battling in the air. He had walked into a place that he had not visited for quite some time. There had been no need, until now.

The hallway was consumed by shadow, the row of barely visible, large, locked doors lining its length shrouded in darkness. He was beneath the Temple of the Ghoules, the very source of his power, the massive complex situated on top of the Cauldron far to the north in the Ghoule homeland.

The Curse was so pervasive within the Temple that the Dark Magic was almost made tangible here, the corrupted power calling to him. The Ghoule Overlord didn't have the time or the inclination to bathe in the wellspring of his very being, an energy that had sustained him for thousands of years. No, he had other, graver matters on his mind.

So he walked past the first three cell doors. There were no locks visible on any of them, but as he trailed his claw across the carved stone, runes that were almost invisible in the murk of the corridor flashed bright white.

As one, the three cell doors opened. For a moment, nothing but a musty smell seeped into the hallway followed by a bone-chilling cold. Then three shadows that blended into the gloom of the corridor glided out, the only sign of their passage the marks that their large, clawed feet left in the crumbling stone of the floor.

It took a moment for the Ghoule Overlord's eyes to settle on the beasts that stood before him, the creatures well over eight feet tall. Their armored skin appeared to be a hazy black and grey in an imperceptible pattern that allowed them to blend into the murk incredibly well. The only readily discernible feature was their blood-red eyes.

The Ghoule Overlord had not employed Slayers for centuries. There had been no need with him and his Ghoules locked on this side of the Weir. He was certain that the beasts would prove useful to him now. Strong and fast, the monsters could run standing up or on all fours, their powerful tails, which curled behind them and were as long as they were tall giving the beasts excellent balance and even some additional speed when necessary.

With a nod from their Master, the three Slayers followed the Ghoule Overlord through the portal of Dark Magic, stepping into the cold and crisp morning in the Shattered Peaks, the bright sun revealing every aspect of the assassins that he had called forth. Their muscled, armored skin had short spikes of bone sticking out of each creature's shoulders, thighs, and forearms, and those spikes extended all the way down the spine and tail. That and the razor-sharp claws, the four digits on each one longer than most daggers, made the creatures very efficient at what they did best.

The Ghoule Overlord had created these beasts for a very singular purpose. To hunt and then kill. They were so accomplished in their work that they even made his Ghoules nervous.

His Dark Magic still spinning across the top of the black diamond, with a flick of his claw, a thin mist drifted up from the Ghoule Overlord's staff, twisting and curling around the three Slayers in a random pattern before it broke into three strands, a tendril of the Curse entering the nostrils of each of the beasts. In unison, the Slayers raised their heads to the sky, their jaws opening to reveal serrated teeth and sharp fangs, two on the top jaw, two on the bottom jaw.

The Ghoule Overlord could barely sense the Protector now. He was too far away. But his Slayers would have no trouble tracking him because now they had the scent of the Seventh Stone. They would find the Protector quickly, and if they failed to acquire the Seventh Stone on their own and return it to him, then they would at least slow down the Protector and make it easier for his Ghoules to catch up. However, he doubted that would prove necessary.

The Slayers were the most efficient assassins that he had ever created.

His monsters never failed. Always killing their quarry. Even Magii.

He would regain the Seventh Stone, and then, once the Protector was dead, the Slayers and his Ghoules would feast, their victory over the humans guaranteed.

20

ALWAYS TRAINING

Jerad found the journey from Tintagel to the very edge of the Dark Forest boringly uneventful, the only thing impeding the Blood Company, besides the heavy rain that followed them out of the city, was the fact that a few of their number had little to no experience riding horses, several of the gladiators turned soldiers having spent their entire lives within the walls of Tintagel.

To address the issue, Declan paired the gladiators who required more experience riding their mounts with those among the Company who demonstrated great skill with horses, many of them having served in the Royal Guard before being sentenced to the Pit. The experienced riders then used the time it took them to reach the wood to train their pupils to the best of their ability.

It had gone surprisingly well ... for the most part.

As luck would have it, Jared was paired with Majdi, the unlucky gladiator who had slipped when his horse had jumped a small stone obstacle, his foot getting caught in the stirrup when he hit the ground on his back, the breath knocked out of him as he was dragged through the grass.

When Jerad had caught up to the large man and brought his horse to a stop, instead of the string of curses that he had expected, he had instead been greeted by a deep laugh that shook the gladiator's belly.

"Don't worry, Sergeant," Majdi had said once he had gotten his foot loose and pulled himself back into the saddle, none the worse for wear. "This animal got the better of me once, and more credit to him for doing so. It won't happen again. I promise you that."

And it hadn't. Majdi listened closely to every word of advice that Jerad offered, all the other gladiators doing the same with their own instructors. These men and women were trained killers, that could not be denied, but they were not fools. They understood the necessity and value of learning a new skill, and they approached acquiring this useful talent with a will.

The gladiators had discovered quickly in the Pit that if the Master of the Gladiators, and now the Sergeant of the Blood Company, wanted you to study something, you did. He was trying to keep you alive. Whatever you mastered likely would have a direct correlation to your odds of surviving in the Pit, and they had all taken that philosophy with them when they earned their freedom and joined the Blood Company.

Once they had established their camp for that night and the schedule for the sentries shared, Declan used the last few hours of light to practice the formations that he and Bryen had been teaching the Company, all with the thought that these alignments would give the gladiators the best chance against the Ghoules.

Declan had started the Company's training with the wedge, first two rows deep and then reforming on the move to four rows. From there, Declan had his soldiers shift into a square, again starting with two rows and then transitioning to a much more tightly compressed four rows.

Declan finished the exercise with the testudo, which had proven so effective against the Royal Guard and was now quite familiar to the soldiers of the Blood Company. The rectangular formation required four rows, shield bearers to the front on all sides locking their long, slightly curved steel scuta to one another, spears right behind that front rank, followed by the swords and then the archers. Declan was confident that this particular formation would prove useful when they finally met the beasts. And they were all certain that they would. In their minds, it was a given. It was just a question of when.

Tarin and Jerad watched the gladiators work with a sharp focus, neither offering a word of advice, understanding that it wasn't their place to insert themselves into the session until they were invited to do so. Tarin could understand Declan's concern that he had grown rusty and perhaps lost some of his military knowledge after having been forced from the Royal Guard twenty years before. Yet, after just a few minutes of observing, he had concluded that the Sergeant of the Blood Company's worry was completely groundless and resulted more from nerves rather than anything real.

In fact, Tarin and Jerad both had already picked up a few tactics that they planned to use when they returned to the Battersea Guard. They were impressed by the guidance given by Declan and the ease with which the gladiators immediately put that instruction to use.

They hadn't been aware of how many gladiators were former soldiers. Just as had happened with Declan, many of the fighters had been sent to the Colosseum rather than being hanged because they were liked and respected by their commanding officers or had been placed in an obvious situation where action needed to be taken but the sentence did not fit the crime, all of them obviously having benefited from the additional training Declan had given them with the hope that it would prolong their lives as they fought on the white sand.

"I may be a bit out of practice with all this," said Declan, having walked over to stand with Tarin and Jerad to gain a better perspective on his Company's conduct, "but they appear to be doing well."

"They are doing better than well," agreed Tarin. "I'd put this Company up against any company in the Battersea Guard. You know your work, Declan. Don't let anyone, including yourself, tell you different."

"You're being too kind, Tarin," Declan countered. "There are always opportunities for improvement."

"I'm just telling you what I see," replied Tarin, his eyes continuing to track the movements of the Company as they now marched at a steady pace, then moved to the right or left depending on the command that Declan shouted to them.

"Still, there is more work to be done with them. They must be ready. Fighting the Ghoules is not the same as fighting the Royal Guard."

"There always is, Declan," confirmed Tarin. "There always is. I can see where the Volkun gets it."

"Gets what?" asked Declan, after giving the Company a quick order to advance at a double time and then turn left.

"His humility," explained Tarin. "He cares little for praise, little for acknowledgment, little for being the center of attention. He simply wants to do his job and get things done."

"If that's the only thing he's learned from me, I'm pleased to hear it," grumbled Declan.

"I assure you, Declan, he has learned that and more," said Tarin. "And keep in mind that I say that from the perspective of someone who, strange as it may seem, genuinely likes the Captain of this Company yet at times also finds him to be quite irritating."

Declan chuckled upon hearing that. "Yes, Bryen does have a knack for getting under your skin."

"That he does," agreed Tarin. "A unique skill."

"Just remember that he only spends his time doing that to people whom he likes. Otherwise, he wouldn't waste his time on you."

"I figured that out," said Tarin, "and once I did, it made it much easier for me to work with him."

"Was that before or after he fought off those four assassins? Or was it the Ghoules on the coastal road?"

Bryen had been tight-lipped about his experiences in the Southern Marches; however, Aislinn had not held back on any of the details when Declan had asked her.

"Those two incidents certainly helped," admitted Tarin. "But it was something else that did it."

"What was it?"

"When he started training the Battersea Guard," Tarin replied. "After just a week of living in the Broken Citadel, any soldier who was not on duty started attending those practice sessions. I knew that if my soldiers respected Bryen, then I should as well. That's when my view of him began to change. That's when I began to see him as more than just a gladiator."

"And now, Tarin?" asked Declan. "Are the men and women here with us more than just gladiators?"

"They are, indeed, Declan," said Tarin, seeking to clarify

what could quickly become an unnecessary misunderstanding. "And please, I meant no offense with my last comment. The Blood Company is just as competent as any company in the Royal Guard, the Battersea Guard, or any of the other Guards, maybe even more so. They may have been gladiators, yet now they clearly are soldiers, thanks to your work with them. Besides, they've done something that no one thought was possible. They've taken down a dynasty and paid the price for that success in blood."

Tarin's comment appeared to placate Declan, who nodded his acceptance. Initially, Declan hadn't been sure of how to interpret the Captain's take on gladiators. It was then that Jerad decided to interject himself into the conversation after having spent the last few hours closely watching the Blood Company respond to their Sergeant's commands.

"Whatever rust you may have had, Declan, it appears to have worn off. I have just a couple suggestions, if I may?"

"Of course, Jerad," answered Declan.

"We should bring those soldiers on the left flank closer together," began Jerad, "otherwise the gaps between them could prove fatal. If an opponent slips through there and gets in among the swords, then the formation will break. And the archers in the back row need to be close to the swords. Not too close, of course, as they run the risk of getting caught by a backswing. Five steps back should do the trick."

For the next few minutes Jerad provided several other suggestions for discussion, Tarin and Declan enjoying the give and take among the three of them. When they were done, they spent the next half hour talking with the soldiers either as a group or individually, praising their performance and providing recommendations on how it could be improved.

"If you move your leg just so," Jerad said, nudging Lycia's forward-facing right leg with his foot to give her a slightly wider stance, and thereby ensuring that her hips were angled when she was holding her spear above the shoulders of the shield bearers, "you'll have better balance. If your spear gets stuck in the flesh or bone of a Ghoule and the beast falls, you won't fall with the spear if you're still holding on to it."

"I appreciate the advice, Sergeant," replied Lycia, who recognized the wisdom in his words, then added, unable to stop herself from teasing him, "still that's really quite forward of you, is it not? I always release the spear at the appropriate time."

Jerad stared at Lycia for a moment, not sure how to respond to her comment. He could feel his face beginning to warm with the first touch of a blush, which obviously had been her intention because a smile was beginning to break the straight face with which she had offered her remarks.

"My apologies," replied Jerad, unable to control his furious reddening and deciding that the best way to handle this situation was to do so delicately and with as much decorum as he could muster. "I didn't mean to offend you."

"I didn't say anything about you offending me," replied Lycia, laughing. "It seems that I should apologize to you. I was simply making a joke."

"I realize that now," said Jared. "Although you should know that apparently I'm engaged."

Jerad immediately regretted his words as soon as they left his mouth. They had a tone of desperation to them, probably revealing to Lycia that she was making him exceedingly uncomfortable. Which she was. He just didn't want his discomfort to be so obvious. Why was it that before he became involved with Dani he had no trouble at all speaking with women and now everything that came out of his mouth sounded like mush? It was as if the Corporal of the Battersea Guard had taken up permanent residence in the back of his mind.

"Apparently?" asked Lycia. "Either you are engaged or you're not, Sergeant."

"Well, Dani said as much the last time that we talked," clarified Jerad, "and I have no cause to disagree with her."

"And do you always agree with what a woman tells you, Sergeant? For some reason I find that hard to believe."

"No, I don't," replied Jerad, after giving the question more thought than Lycia had assumed that he would. "Yet when it comes to Dani, I rarely find a reason not to agree with her." He said the last with a warm smile that revealed to Lycia the Sergeant's true feelings for the woman whom she could only describe as a power unto herself.

Lycia stared at Jerad for several heartbeats, then she laughed for what seemed like the first time in a very long time. Jerad amused her. Even more so she was pleased that the Corporal of the Battersea Guard had gained what she wanted.

"Relax, Sergeant. I am simply playing with you. Congratulations on your engagement, although you don't seem as convinced about it as you should be."

Still laughing, Lycia walked back through the long grass to the camp that they had set up along the verge of the Dark Forest. For the first time in months, some of the tension that had afflicted her since Bryen had been taken from the Pit finally began to drain out of her, and all it had taken was a conversation with a man who had not yet gained the courage to admit to himself that he was in love with a woman.

"Sirius, we're having the same conversation that we've been having for the last few decades," argued Rafia, twisting a loose strand of her curly hair behind her ear, a habit that she didn't even notice, the action helping to calm her when she was feeling agitated. Sirius usually being the cause even when he wasn't trying to get a rise out of her. "This has got to stop. Rehashing the same argument time after time is not helping either of us."

"I know it's the same conversation, Rafia," retorted Sirius grumpily. "It will come to an end when you finally see reason. Then we can move on. Not before."

"What do you mean when I see reason?" challenged the dark-haired Magus. "Are you suggesting that you're right? That the reason we continue to have this same argument is solely because of me?"

What Rafia left unsaid was that if Sirius believed that he was right, then he also must believe that she was wrong, and that was something that she refused to accept.

"Of course I'm right, Rafia," Sirius replied, his indignation almost made tangible by his tenor and expression. "Why else do you think that I've been wasting my time and arguing with you about this for so long?"

"I'm wasting your time?" Rafia's eyes flashed dangerously.

"You know I'm right, Rafia." Ignoring her question, Sirius shook his head and grumbled some words that only he could hear, a habit that never failed to irritate Rafia, and it certainly did the trick then as her eyes narrowed even more in annoyance. "You're just arguing with me because you like to argue with me. You've always been like that."

"I'm arguing with you, Sirius," said Rafia, heat dripping

into her voice, having tried and failed to keep it free of any acidity, "because I don't agree with you. I happen to have a very different perspective from yours. Something that you refuse to acknowledge or accept."

"So you say."

"So I say?" challenged Rafia. She didn't know what was worse, the fact that Sirius refused to consider her argument because he disagreed with it or the fact that he refused to consider it simply because she was the one offering it. Which possibility it was, she couldn't tell for certain, and she wasn't sure that she wanted to find out. "I do say."

"Don't I know it," groused Sirius. "You say a lot. Then again you say very little at the same time. It's a unique and often exasperating skill."

"I'm sorry," whispered Rafia in a dangerously quiet voice that could slice into flesh just as well if not better than steel, "are you suggesting that there is no value in what I have to say?"

"I am not suggesting anything," replied Sirius. "I am saying it loud and clear. There is no substance to your argument. You are basing your suppositions on what you want rather than on what is real."

"And what do I want, Sirius?"

So caught up in his own opinion and his desire to make his point, the old Magus failed to catch the new tone in her voice, the hardness that had emerged. Rafia had never enjoyed and never put up with anyone ever explaining to her what she should want in her life or how she should view a particular issue, and she wasn't about to begin now.

"You want to live in a fantasy, Rafia. Not the real world. You seem to think that passion and love should remain despite the passage of time. That such a thing is even possible."

"And you don't believe that's possible?" she asked, already knowing what Sirius was going to say next, having heard much the same before in a variety of different ways.

"No, I don't believe that's possible. I just said that, and I've been saying that for longer than I should have to." Sirius closed his eyes for just a moment and took a deep breath, seeking to calm himself before he really lost his temper. If he allowed that to happen, then an already challenging evening would only become more laborious. In his opinion, even in the best of times Rafia was a difficult person to interact with. "I believe, I know, that with time, passion and love are no longer as important as they once were. In fact, they can only get in the way of the reality of life. With the passage of time, familiarity becomes more important than passion or love. Without familiarity we have nothing to build on as time passes. Familiarity is what ensures a lasting relationship."

"People come together for love, Sirius," countered Rafia. "They always have and they always will. Isn't that what happened to us so many decades ago? I will admit that familiarity can help in certain situations, that it's part of the equation, but love remains the key. Without love you have nothing."

"Ha! You just agreed with me!" shouted Sirius, his eyes sparkling with pleasure. Perhaps after all this time, and all the arguments, Rafia was finally being made to see reason.

Rafia stared at the old Magus for several heartbeats, fearing that he was about to push himself up from where he was sitting across the small fire from her and dance a jig because of what he viewed as a victory, a sharp retort on the tip of her tongue. She stopped herself, however, realizing that in her desire to win her argument with Sirius, she wasn't actually hearing what he was saying. And that's what made her pause.

If she was interpreting Sirius' argument correctly, then it became clear that he had asked her to marry him all those years ago because he believed that it was something that he should do. Because they were so familiar with one another, not because he wanted to, not because he loved her. That realization confirmed for her that she had done the right thing by telling him no, a decision that she had made based on a feeling rather than a reason.

For just a moment, a deep sadness filled her. She knew that she wasn't the easiest person to be with, and she had blamed herself – her own feelings, her barbed comments, her unwillingness to let anything go, her need to come out on top – for the failure of her relationship with Sirius. She realized now that she was partially to blame, not completely as she had believed for so long.

Rafia shook her head sadly. Sirius was right. She was wasting his time, just as he was wasting hers. They had different definitions of what a good relationship was. They were both right and they were both wrong. Why had it taken her so long to reach that conclusion?

For a few minutes, an uncomfortable silence settled between them, both seemingly lost in their own thoughts. They had picked a spot on the edge of the Blood Company's campsite. Declan was there as well, though he appeared to be less than interested in their conversation.

Tarin and Jerad had been with them during dinner, the two soldiers having left to make their rounds of the sentries. They had little concern that the soldiers of the Blood Company would not be taking their responsibilities seriously. Even so, better to make sure, because they both had no doubt that the men and women picketed a short distance within the wood that evening expected to be challenged by them, and they wanted to meet that expectation because it helped to ensure good discipline. As Declan liked to say, "If you know what to expect, then you know what to do." Another of the many sayings that the two leaders in the Battersea Guard had come to appreciate.

Rafia tried to refrain from letting out the curse that she really wanted to utter, knowing that it would only sour what was already a tedious and tense encounter. She also knew that there was no point in continuing this conversation. Unfortunately, she couldn't help herself, and that failing only served to irritate her even more.

"I am not agreeing with you, Sirius. I have never agreed with you. And to be honest with you, I don't believe that we'll ever agree." Rafia spoke in a quieter voice now, not wanting to escalate the situation as had happened so many times before. "I am simply saying that some familiarity in a relationship isn't a bad thing. It helps to grease the wheel of a romance when it gets thrown off kilter. That being said, in my opinion familiarity is not enough to create a lasting relationship. Love and passion are still required. Without those two critical ingredients, you have nothing to build upon. Familiarity is a good ingredient for a business relationship. When we were together, I wanted more than a business relationship."

"You're missing the point again, Rafia," groaned Sirius. "I don't understand why this is so hard. You just need to listen to what I'm saying."

"It's hard because you're making it hard," countered Rafia, who struggled to control her temper, knowing from past experience what would happen if she let it loose. "I am disagreeing with you because I have a different perspective from you. It's because we have different perspectives that neither of us can ever win this argument. Perhaps you should listen to me for a change rather than only to what you have to say."

"Always one to blame."

"And you're not?" snapped Rafia. "Didn't you just hear what I said?"

"I'm not blaming, Rafia, I'm explaining. I equate familiarity between two people as love."

"And that's where we disagree, Sirius, because I don't."

"Yes, that's the problem right there," complained Sirius. "You don't understand what I'm saying. Or if you do, you're ignoring the truth in my words."

"That's what I'm trying to explain, Sirius. This argument has nothing to do with truth and everything to do with differing perspectives. That's why ..." Rafia stopped herself, seeing the look that Sirius was giving her, one that made her feel like she was a young girl again who should stay quiet rather than share her opinion.

Before she screamed at the top of her lungs, needing to release the agitation that was threatening to explode within her, Rafia decided on a different course of action. Perhaps a new viewpoint was needed and could end this nonsense. Shaking her head in frustration, she turned her attention to Declan, who through the entire argument had kept his eyes focused on the fire, staring into the flames, trying to ignore the rancor circulating around him.

"Declan, what do you believe?" Rafia asked. "Is familiarity the same as love? Or is it something different? Something more valuable? Something less valuable?"

For several heartbeats it didn't seem like the Sergeant of the Blood Company was going to respond. There had been several times during the last hour that he could have injected himself into the dialogue, if only to make an attempt to shut it down.

He had held off. He had realized then, just as he understood now, that no matter what he said he was in a no-win situation. Why would either of them listen to him?

Neither of these two Magii had demonstrated any desire to listen to one another. They simply wanted to listen to themselves. Then again, Rafia had appeared to soften her position during the last few minutes, Sirius, as was his habit, ignoring the opening that she had given him to stop this foolishness.

Understanding that he was likely making a mistake, he stepped into the combat as if he was in the Pit, engaging if for no other reason than the realization that he didn't think that he could stand another hour of this useless chatter. So better to take a risk and hope that he might gain some peace and quiet for his efforts before it was time to turn in for the night.

"You two are arguing because you both enjoy arguing. You don't care what the other has to say, you just want to win. And it's because of that desire that neither of you is ever going to win this argument. What's more, you both know it. Or at least Magus Rafia reached that conclusion a few minutes ago. I haven't heard anything from Magus Sirius to suggest that he has. Regardless, neither of you has shown the courage needed to consider the other person's perspective in a more open manner."

"Really?" challenged Rafia, secretly pleased by Declan's comment, Sirius looking at the Master of the Gladiators as if he hadn't understood a word that he had said. "If we've both got it wrong, then please enlighten us. What's your take on all this?"

Declan smiled at that. He knew interacting with these two would be a mistake. He had done so anyway. Now there was nothing to do but say what he wanted to say and hope that it might shut the both of them up.

"In my experience, balance is always the most important factor in a successful relationship. If you don't have balance, you don't have anything."

"Balance?" asked Sirius. "What do you mean by that? It sounds like you're just trying to make everyone happy."

"I mean that familiarity between two people is a good thing," he replied. "There are times in a relationship when that familiarity is absolutely essential for that relationship to survive. It's that familiarity that can help you when times get tough, and there will always be difficult times to work through in any relationship."

Declan stopped then, his eyes still on the fire, seemingly lost in thought. Both Magii stared at him, assuming that he had more to say. Right before both Sirius and Rafia were about to restart the argument from their own viewpoints, neither able to contain themselves for long, Declan offered the rest of what was on his mind.

"You want to know the person. You should know the person whom you love," he clarified, a strangely wistful smile curling his lips. "But familiarity is not love. Love and passion are more than that. Without love or passion, familiarity eventually will breed contempt. Love and passion allow you to build something deeper, something more meaningful, something that will grow over time. Love and passion lead to excitement, to that spark that every relationship needs. Yes, familiarity is good, in fact it's critical if you really want to build a good relationship, yet without the passion, without the fire, you're not building anything that can last for the long term. You'll grow sick of each other before you can do that."

Declan could have said more. He could have said that

what he was explaining was directly applicable to them. But what was the point? Their argument wasn't meant to discover the necessary foundation for a good relationship. It was meant to determine which one was right and which one was wrong.

"Do you even know what you're talking about?" questioned Sirius, who wasn't certain whether what the Master of the Gladiators had said aided his argument or Rafia's, and in his mind, that was all that mattered.

"Actually I do," Declan replied with a grunt and a sad smile, finally pulling his gaze from the flames to catch Sirius' eyes and then Rafia's. "And I know that when you finally have that balance, when you have the familiarity, the love, the passion, all working together as it should, and then it's taken from you, that it hurts more than a Ghoule's claws in your gut."

When Declan's eyes captured hers, Rafia was barely breathing, and she could do nothing more than stare right back at him. That was fine with her, because that's all that she wanted to do. This man, who seemed so straightforward, so transparent, actually was more complicated than he appeared to be. The more time that she spent with Declan, the more intrigued with him she became.

"Declan, I don't know whether to disagree with you or not, because I'm not sure I understand your argument," began Sirius. "I am simply trying to gain agreement among us that ..."

"For the love of the sand!" shouted Declan, his stentorian voice capturing the attention of everyone else in the camp. "You two have been going on about this for more than an hour. Give it a rest. None of us want to hear it anymore."

Declan's unexpected outburst stunned both Magii, neither knowing what to say next. And that was fine by

Declan, because he didn't want to hear another word from either of them.

Before Declan returned his gaze to the fire, Rafia caught his attention. As he stared into her eyes, he didn't demonstrate a trace of nervousness. Instead he studied the Magus, just as she was studying him. There was a spark in the Magus' eyes when she looked at him that mirrored his own, and that discovery didn't bother either of them in the least.

AISLINN WALKED into the verge of the Dark Forest, allowing her smile to break free. She and everyone else in the camp had been forced to listen to the argument between the two Magii. They had no choice but to do so, the two voices drifting on the wind to drown out anything else that might be said by the soldiers relaxing around the fires. Declan's decision to engage the two, and then shut down the conversation after he said his piece, had been met with mumbled thanks from more than one of the soldiers of the Blood Company.

Despite the fact that the argument between Rafia and Sirius had been circular at best and mind-numbing at worst, the Magii's dialogue had gotten Aislinn thinking. And rather than sit at a fire and stew about what was going through her mind, she decided to try to obtain some closure if at all possible. She understood the risk involved, and how a negative response could affect her, that potentially upsetting result making her slightly nauseous as she contemplated its likelihood.

Still, better to know than not. Better to know if the balance that Declan had mentioned, that served as the point of integration between familiarity, love, and passion, could be achieved. And better to gain those answers now, knowing that each day to come held an uncertain fate because of the almost impossible challenge they were seeking to overcome and the deadly dangers presented by the Ghoule Overlord and his Legions.

So she continued to navigate the heart trees, walking past several sentries with a nod and a wave, to find Bryen about a hundred yards deeper within the grove. He was no more than another shadow as he stood among the huge roots that twisted and curled along the forest floor. It was so dark that she never would have found him if not for the connection that remained between them.

Even with the bonds of the Protector's collar completely severed, they could still sense one another, so she knew exactly where he was before she had risen from her seat on the log by the fire. For some reason that aspect of the magic had never faded, unless that link now was based on something else. Something that was more substantial. More meaningful.

That was an interesting thought, though she didn't have the time to pursue it having come to stand right next to her Protector, who hadn't bothered to turn at her approach, sensing that it was her.

"What are you doing?" Aislinn asked, giving her Protector a nudge with her hip. "If you are going to wander off into the woods, it's customary to ask a woman to come with you."

"Is that right?" asked Bryen with a smile. "I'm sorry. I wasn't aware of that requirement."

"You believe you know so much," she said with chuckle. "Yet you still have so much to learn."

"And you can teach me?" asked Bryen, giving her a

nudge with his hip to return the favor. "Is that what you're saying?"

"If you ask nicely," she said with a mischievous smile.

Bryen had to admit that she was right. He had learned quite a bit since leaving the Colosseum. Unfortunately, he still didn't understand much about engaging appropriately with a beautiful woman. It wasn't exactly something that Declan or any of the other gladiators could teach him in the Pit, and if they tried to give him advice on that topic he probably would have ignored it. He only had experience being direct with people, innuendo often leaving him confused.

"I'll keep that in mind."

"Good," replied Aislinn. "I'll be here when you need me."

She was certain that he had been about to say something more. Either he was nervous, didn't know what to say, or had thought better about revealing what had popped into his mind. Aislinn wished that Bryen had just blurted it all out, but she understood that wasn't how he worked. He had opened up to her quite a bit in just the last few weeks now that they were spending more time together again. Even so, his reserve usually slammed down as soon as he was uncomfortable and he would change the subject. Just as was doing right now.

"I was searching," Bryen offered, returning their conversation to safer, more serious ground.

"Are they close?" Aislinn didn't feel the need to identify her specific concern, as they faced only one real danger in this part of the Kingdom. A danger, in fact, that gave the conversation she wanted to have with Bryen a greater sense of urgency.

"A few Ghoule packs off to the north have reached the

Breakwater Plateau and are moving in this direction," he replied, "and there are a dozen more deeper within the Shattered Peaks. None are an immediate threat."

"That's good," confirmed Aislinn. "We can breathe a little easier for a bit longer."

"Yes, for now. A few days at least."

"So you were right," said Aislinn. "They know that you're here."

"They do," Bryen confirmed. "The Ghoule Overlord wants the Seventh Stone."

"The Ghoule Overlord wants you," corrected Aislinn.

"Yes," he agreed with a half-hearted grin, trying to alleviate some of the concern that he heard in her voice. "That's probably the best and most accurate way to put it."

Aislinn leaned against him again, and this time she stayed there. She reached around his back with her left arm, placing her hand just above his hip and hugging him to her from the side.

"Aren't you afraid? The greatest threat that Caledonia has faced not only has returned, but the beast needs you to have any hope of conquering the Kingdom."

Bryen thought about Aislinn's question for a moment, a bit distracted by how close she was to him. Her touch was pushing his mind down a road probably best left untraveled.

"No, not really."

"I'm supposed to believe that?" she asked in a challenging tone.

Still holding onto him, Aislinn gave him another nudge with her hip, what seemed to have become her preferred practice for poking fun at him.

"I don't say that just to say it."

"I know you don't," replied Aislinn, who pulled him into

her once again for another hug. "I just like to tease you when I can. I don't think that you have an arrogant bone in your body."

"Declan broke all of those years ago."

"Why am I not surprised?" Aislinn laughed.

"So why did you come out here?" Bryen asked. "I know it wasn't to talk about Ghoules."

"Actually, I just needed to get away from Sirius and Rafia for a time," she replied, delaying, as she still wasn't certain if she had the courage to engage in the conversation that she really wanted to have with him. That she needed to have with him as she felt the intense urge to achieve some clarity at least in regard to whatever this was between them since so much of what they would face in the days to come was uncertain.

"That I can understand," Bryen nodded. "You should have heard those two when I was at Haven with them. They bickered like an old married couple."

"Yes, it was becoming a bit much tonight. Thankfully, Declan put a stop to it."

"Did he? I guess I shouldn't be surprised. He doesn't have much patience for the same conversation being replayed time after time. Particularly one that he believes should remain private."

"Relationships?"

"Yes," Bryen confirmed. "He never had any time for discussions of feelings or the desire to be too close to another person. There was too much else to worry about in the Pit. Better to focus on that rather than on something that in his mind wasn't important or realistic."

"And what about you?"

"What about me?" asked Bryen, not understanding Aislinn's question.

"Are you willing to engage in a conversation of a more personal nature?"

There. She had broached the topic that had been bothering her since they had left Tintagel. Come what may, at least she had demonstrated the courage to try to speak to Bryen about it rather than let it lie.

Bryen, in turn, stared at Aislinn, a slow heat rising in his face that thankfully she couldn't see because of the dark.

"I could be. Although I still don't know what you're referring to."

Rather than continue to beat around the bush, Aislinn decided that Bryen's approach to most issues was best. Better to be direct and eliminate any confusion, now and in the future.

"I wanted to ask you about Lycia," said Aislinn. "She doesn't always look at you as she would if she were looking just at a friend. She looks at you as if you mean more to her. As if you're more than just a friend."

Bryen was going to respond immediately, then he stopped himself as he began to understand where this conversation was headed. He needed to step carefully, while still being honest with Aislinn.

"We are friends," Bryen finally said. "She liked to keep an eye on me when we were both in the Pit."

Aislinn frowned. Now she wasn't certain if Bryen didn't understand or he was simply trying to deflect and avoid entirely what she was getting at.

"What I mean is that the look she gives you suggests that you were more than friends in the Colosseum. Closer than that. Much closer."

A surge of heat rushed through Bryen, not sure how he should respond. Then he realized that his first instinct -- to be honest with Aislinn and with himself -- was the right one. She deserved nothing less than that. If what he said affected their relationship going forward, there was nothing that he could do about that.

"We were as close as we could be in an environment where death was a constant companion. Yes, we were more than friends."

Aislinn nodded. She had suspected as much. And she was glad that he had told her the truth, even though she didn't like the answer.

Now what was she supposed to do? Stop acting like a lovestruck teenager, she told herself. So she gathered the resolve that had pushed her into the wood after Bryen in the first place and plowed forward.

"Do you still have feelings for her?"

"Of course," Bryen replied softly, his voice barely above a whisper. "We went through a lot together. I will always care about her."

Aislinn felt the bile start to rise in her throat, and she began to wonder if this had all been a mistake. If it would have been better to simply not dig too deeply into his past. Then she realized that she did want to know. She had to know. She might not like what she learned. Still, she was glad that she had removed the uncertainty that had been troubling her.

Life didn't always work out as you wanted, so it was better to know the truth than not. And that's when she realized that if Rafia had asked her the question that she had asked Declan about what was needed for a good relationship, she would have agreed with the Master of the Gladiators except for one addendum. Passion, love, and familiarity were all important for different reasons, all needed to help achieve the balance that Declan mentioned.

She also would have included one other item. The truth.

There had to be truth, otherwise there could be no trust, and nothing mattered more than that.

"Although not in the way that I care for you," Bryen continued before Aislinn could pull away from him. "I will always be Lycia's friend. But the past is the past. With you, I see my future."

It took a moment for Aislinn to fully comprehend what Bryen had just said, and then she felt Bryen turn toward her, pulling her into his arms. When his lips touched hers, all her fears and worries vanished, burned away by a sensation that warmed her entire body.

21

RECEIVING THE CALL

South Cove, located on the southeast side of the Bay of the Dead, was a fairly large and quite prosperous town. It had been for centuries. A home to fisherfolk and a place to restock supplies and provisions when sailing south down the Three Tongue River toward Ironhill and Trader's Way or heading north through the Bay to the Burnt Ocean, few travelers stayed there for more than a day or two. It was simply a way station before people and goods went somewhere else.

That was fine with the residents of South Cove, such as Irelda. She taught at the only school in the town. She tended to keep her long hair tied tightly in a bun, which gave her a severe appearance. How she presented herself, though, didn't fit her personality. She had a quick smile, an even faster wit, and she loved working with her students, particularly her younger ones, doing everything that she could to make learning fun.

When she was growing up her best teachers had understood that the only way to keep her engaged was to help her see how what she was being taught had a practical application in the real world, and she aimed to do the same thing with her lessons, which might be why attendance at her school had improved year over year.

Although South Cove was a busy town, it tended to be fairly quiet, the city council, which was dominated by merchants, believing that good business required an environment that allowed for a focus on trade and making money rather than on the pleasures sailors so frequently desired after long spells on the deep blue, so even that profitable but potentially raucous and disruptive business was tightly controlled. Hence, the reason that those same sailors tended to move quickly through the town, never staying long enough to get themselves into any real trouble, the City Watch helping to convince those who might have something else in mind that it would be better for them to try their luck in another port.

Those who tended to ignore South Cove's business philosophy never lasted very long in the town, the merchants forcing them out either through legal or not so legal means. It didn't matter to them. Whatever was required to keep the wheels of commerce turning smoothly was always the deciding factor.

Irelda had known all that before she had arrived, having settled in the coastal town after moving around Caledonia quite a bit when she was younger. She had started her career as an educator in the western Duchies, beginning in Roo's Nest and then working her way through the many small towns along the coast of the Burnt Ocean before turning to the east and making her way toward Murcia and then north around the Flats until she had found herself on the shore of the Bay of the Dead.

She had never stayed in one place for more than a few years. In addition to teaching, she mixed herbs and other natural supplements to augment her income. Some of her concoctions worked with such great success that her abilities drew unwanted attention, so she kept moving. That's how she had been trained, and based on her experiences in life she believed that such a peripatetic existence was necessary if she wanted to avoid any trouble.

She was thinking about that as she walked out of the school, which was situated on one of the many hills that overlooked the Bay of the Dead. She was done for the day, the last child having just left for home. She had a few appointments that afternoon -- one with a woman struggling to get pregnant, another with a sick child whose fever had finally broken but was still in need of the tea that she had blended for him -- as well as a few additional orders to fill.

Yes, it was likely time for her to move on. She was coming up on three years now, and though it was easy for her to blend into South Cove because it was larger than most of the other places that she had lived and the population was more transient than most; still, she felt that her time here was coming to an end. Word of her cures was spreading up and down the coast, and that was beginning to make her uncomfortable. Besides, the teachers who had joined her at the school were quite competent and would be more than able to carry on her work when she left.

The question was, where to go next? North toward Tintagel or east toward Battersea? She ruled out going back to Murcia. No, never back to somewhere she had already been. No matter how much she might have enjoyed her time there. So either Tintagel or Battersea. But which one?

Having a few minutes to relax before her first appointment, she began to mull the decision that she needed to make as she walked down the street toward the plaza lined with small shops, taverns, and restaurants situated on long piers that extended out into the water. She turned to the right, taking the steps down to the beach so that she could walk along the shore for a time before she turned back up toward where her small house was located just a few hills farther north.

Lost in thought as she enjoyed the feel of the sand between her toes, the gentle waves of the Bay of the Dead lightly kissing the shore, she almost failed to see the younger woman coming toward her from the other direction before she ran into her.

The woman looked familiar for some reason. Irelda was certain that she didn't know her. She had the unique ability to remember the face of every person she had ever spoken with; nevertheless, the woman had a look about her that made Irelda think that she should know who she was. As they walked right by one another, no more than a few feet separating them, the young woman gave Irelda a bright smile and then nodded toward the sand.

She should have expected as much. Returning the young woman's smile, Irelda continued to walk along the beach, ignoring the steps that would have led right back up the street toward her home. Instead, she walked a bit farther down the shore, her eyes tracking the sand.

Then she saw it. The message scratched into the beach was made up of three short sentences that were arranged to look like a poem that would mean little to most. But she knew what the message meant, and it sent a chill down her spine.

She had hoped that this would never come to pass, yet in that instant the voice of one of her mentors played through her mind with one of his favorite sayings: "Hoping doesn't make it real."

Unfortunately, she had no choice but to agree with him.

She walked through the message, scraping away the lettering with her feet, and not continuing on her way until it was unintelligible.

Irelda would walk a bit farther on just to keep up appearances, then she would take one of the staircases up to the street and come back to her small house in a roundabout route. Once she was done with her appointments, she would gather what she needed. It wouldn't take long. She always had a bag packed specifically for this reason.

Once she left town, she would stop in a few villages that she was familiar with along the way. Perhaps she could catch up with the other Magii who would be heading toward the north and the Winter Pass before they reached the Northern Spine and she could travel with them.

It was not the best part of town. Of course, in Roo's Nest, there were very few neighborhoods that could be defined as safe. It only made sense. There were the docks and then not much else if you didn't live on the butte overlooking the harbor.

Maria had no desire to live there with those who so enjoyed looking down upon the other residents of the capital of the western province, both literally and figuratively. No, this was a good place for her. She could do the work that she wanted to do. She could help the people whom she wanted to help. And she could avoid the people whom she didn't want to deal with.

She lived just above her workspace in a cramped attic, and that didn't bother her in the least. It was certainly better than where she had just visited. She had just returned from a small, ramshackle house that could better be described as a hut that was only a few blocks away from her small shop.

The woman living there clearly was struggling to make ends meet, and Maria didn't want to think about what she had to do to keep food on her table for her three young children. The mother had taken her to a small room in the back, finding a boy of no more than seven lying on a dirty cot, his sweat staining the torn and worn blankets as a fever burned through him.

The mother had explained that her son had stepped on a sharp rock while climbing down by the harbor. It had been just a slight scrape a few days before. As time had passed, rather than healing on its own the wound had soured.

Maria hadn't been surprised. She had lived along the coast for years, becoming knowledgeable about the injuries and illnesses common to this part of Caledonia. She had taken one look at the boy and the festering wound, pus dripping down his heel, and had known the cause instantly.

Her ability to decipher the source of someone's ailment in just seconds certainly aided her as a healer. The mussels scattered along the rocks in the harbor often carried a bacterium that poisoned the blood, just as it was doing to the boy. Rather than scraping his foot on a sharp rock, he had stepped on a broken shell instead.

When Maria had told the mother what was needed to heal her son, the woman had worried about the cost of the medicine. Maria had told her to not be a fool. They would work something out when the time was right. Maria had not trained as a physick at the Royal Medical School only to be stopped from doing what she did best because her clients couldn't afford to pay.

Money wasn't her reason for doing this. She wanted to

help people. And she would, even if those same people couldn't help themselves.

As she worked at her bench, mixing various herbs to be added to an elixir that would help fight the infection and fever and get the boy back to climbing the rocks in the harbor in a just a few days, Maria almost dropped her mortar and pestle as a voice that she recognized but had not heard in quite some time filled her mind.

"The Ghoule Legions come. The Winter Pass. Ten days' time."

Maria took a deep breath to settle herself. She should have expected as much. She had heard the stories of Ghoules in the Northern Spine and the Southern Marches from some of the sailors in the harbor, though she had ignored them until now, not wanting to follow that information to the most logical, frightening conclusion.

Growling in irritation, she went back to her work. She liked it here. Even though she had been in Roo's Nest for less than a year, it felt right to her. Perhaps she would have the chance to return here when she was done in the Winter Pass, and if not, well ... if she didn't return, then she would be dead, and the Ghoules rampaging through the Kingdom would no longer be her concern. Then, rather than worrying about a fever or a broken bone, the people of Roo's Nest would be focused on more serious concerns, such as staying alive and off a Ghoule spit.

With those morbid thoughts drifting through her mind, she went back to her work. She would finish the medicine for the boy as well as the two other preparations that she needed to complete that evening and then deliver them while she was leaving town. She would just need to grab the bag that she always kept packed for this specific eventuality.

It would be difficult for Maria to get where she needed to be in only ten days since she was so far to the west.

Perhaps she could catch a ship sailing across the Bay of the Dead to South Cove or North Cove and then head northeast from there.

And if that didn't work, she would find another way. She needed to get there in the time that had been allotted. She would not let her brothers and sisters down. They were too few as it was, and the cost of not reaching the Winter Pass in time was too great and not something that she wanted to contemplate.

22

LEARNING SOMETHING NEW

The Company of Blood had traveled more than five leagues that day, pushing farther into the Dark Forest though always staying less than a league from the Breakwater Plateau to their east. They wanted to take advantage of the cover that the heart trees provided, recognizing that their choice of route would be slow-going because of the massive roots that were thicker than a man that wound and contorted along the forest floor.

They also wanted to preserve their options. If something unexpected happened while among the heart trees, they could head out onto the grassland in short order. So far, all had gone to plan, and they had very little to worry about other than the many obstacles that hindered their pace.

Maybe that was why Declan felt a little anxious. He had spent more than a decade in the Royal Guard, and he had learned quickly during his time as a soldier that nothing ever went to plan, that reality being reinforced time after time while he had been consigned to the Pit.

Of course, something else could be causing his uneasiness, such as the sharp-eyed, incredibly intense Magus who strode beside him as he walked the perimeter of the camp, checking on his gladiators who were now soldiers to ensure that they were doing as was required of them.

Not surprisingly, they were. Dorlan, Kollea, and all the others who had joined the Blood Company took their responsibilities seriously. They may have been freed from the Pit, but the attitude, commitment, and expectations that had helped them to survive in the Colosseum remained.

Those characteristics had become too much a part of them for these soldiers to simply put all that aside now that they no longer had to answer to the demands of the white sand. Instead, they had applied with a will all that they had learned to their new roles. Declan was quite pleased by that. He had hoped that they would. They were too well trained not to do so.

Declan was pulled from his thoughts when a hand that he could barely see reached out and grabbed onto his arm. Rafia had stumbled on a root, and she had used him to catch herself before she tumbled to the ground. As they moved deeper within the Dark Forest, the settling night was turning the deepening shadows an inky black.

"You all right?" he asked.

"Yes, thank you," she replied, perhaps holding on to his arm for a bit longer than she needed to. Declan didn't mind. If he was being honest with himself, he kind of enjoyed it. He rarely had the chance to spend time with a beautiful woman, even if she was a Magus.

They continued walking for another dozen yards as if they were on a stroll before she finally released her grip. They passed two more soldiers standing quietly and attentively among the trees, both nodding to their Sergeant and the Magus when they went by. It was just after that when Declan came to an abrupt stop.

"Any chance you could give us some light?"

Rafia nodded, though she doubted that Declan could see her acquiescence with the surrounding gloom. Reaching for the Talent, she produced a small glowing ball that flickered just above her palm. She then directed the light where he pointed toward the ground. At first glance, Rafia didn't know what had captured Declan's attention. Only after squinting and leaning down did she realize what it was.

"How did you see that?" she asked disbelievingly. "You couldn't have. It's too dark to see that."

"I sort of saw it," he replied. "I more felt it than saw it. At least, that's probably the best way to explain it."

"What does that even mean?"

"I started out as a tracker in the army. I picked up a few things along the way."

Rafia stared at Declan for a moment, the glow of the Talent just above her palm softening his craggy features. The Master of the Gladiators was just one surprise after another, and she liked that.

She turned her attention back to the ground, Declan running his fingers in the soft loam next to the marks that he had identified in the gloom. Four long scratches in the dirt. And then more about six feet farther on. Clear signs of the Ghoules.

"Recent?"

"No. They've had some time to set in the soil, and the roots protected them from the wind." Declan continued to stare at the tracks. "A day or two old at the most."

"A pack?"

Declan took a bit longer to answer this question than the one that had preceded it, pushing himself up from the ground and staring off in the direction the tracks led. He saw nothing but soaring trees with trunks a hundred feet wide and curling roots that dipped and rose and slowly blended into the darkness.

"I can't say for sure," he replied. "But no, I don't believe that it's a pack. Just a few scouts would be my guess."

"Looking for something," surmised Rafia, her eyes catching Declan's.

"Looking for us," he nodded.

"Looking for Bryen," she clarified.

Certain in her belief, Rafia reached for more of the Talent. Wanting to ensure that they didn't have anything immediate to worry about, she searched around their campsite just as she had done earlier that evening. She confirmed as she had before that there were no threats close to them.

Next, she extended her search to the very edges of the Dark Forest and then beyond to the Breakwater Plateau. From there, she expanded her search to the lower reaches of the Shattered Peaks. It didn't take her long to find what she was looking for.

"A pack on the northern edge of the wood. They seem to have settled in for the night." She took a closer look with the Talent, taking her time, wanting to make sure. Yes, a dozen Ghoules with one Elder. They had burrowed in among the trees, resting against the trunks and the roots. If not for the Talent, the beasts would have been invisible to the naked eye. "They're not coming any closer. At least not at the moment."

"That's good to hear. Even so, that doesn't mean they'll stay there."

"No, you're right about that. We've learned that the hard way too many times in the past. I'll keep an eye on them just to be sure."

"I don't like this," said Declan.

"What do you mean?" asked Rafia, not understanding

and fearing that perhaps the Master of the Gladiators was referring to the fact that she had joined him on his rounds that evening.

"I don't like waiting for something to happen." Declan shook his head as if he had a bad taste in his mouth. "When you do that in the Pit, bad things tend to occur. Usually you die."

"I agree with you about that," nodded Rafia. "Better to take the initiative. Did you have something in mind?"

"Perhaps we could take a more aggressive approach as we head to our destination."

"What are you thinking?" she asked, intrigued by how Declan's mind worked.

"If the Ghoules are hunting us, perhaps we should return the favor. Perhaps we should hunt them as well."

Rafia took a few heartbeats to consider what Declan was proposing. She certainly liked the direction that his thoughts were going.

"We can get started on that tomorrow," she agreed. "In the meantime, I can do something that might make us feel a bit more secure during the night."

Declan watched with a great deal of interest as thin strands of white energy sprouted from her hands and then twisted and turned haphazardly as they drifted out among the heart trees. At least that's what it looked like at the beginning.

As he observed more closely, he saw that there was a design in what Rafia was doing. The strands of the Talent that she sent out into the forest around them began to connect with one another, forming a papery web. When the threads linked together, they flashed once and then disappeared into the darkness.

"What are you doing?" he asked, intensely curious.

"Think of it as an early warning system," she replied as she rotated slowly, the threads of the Talent spreading around them in a broad circle that continued to expand so that it would protect the entire encampment for the night. "If any creature of Dark Magic tries to approach, we'll have the time to prepare our defense well before they arrive. And when any of the beasts walk through one of these strands, it will cut through them like steel."

"Quite vicious," Declan murmured, a smile loosening his normally stern expression. "I like how you think."

"That's kind of you to say," she replied with a broad smile. She then released her hold on the Talent, the web of energy complete and now positioned almost a league from the perimeter guards.

"I'm just speaking the truth."

"Do you always speak the truth?" asked Rafia, recalling the conversation of just a few nights before with Sirius, Declan, and everyone else in the troop who had the misfortune of having to listen. Declan hadn't mentioned this quality then, so now it was her turn to be curious.

"I try to speak the truth," he replied. "At least as I see it anyway."

Rafia nodded, appreciating how he had qualified his response.

"So you believe that there is more than one truth?"

"No," he replied instantly. "But we can't ignore someone's perspective. How someone has lived. How someone was raised. Their experiences. Their beliefs. Their fears. Their desires. All that and more will affect how they interpret the truth. Based on all that, the truth may be the same for both of us, yet how we view that truth, what we do in response to that truth, may differ."

Rafia nodded, thinking on what Declan had just said as

they continued to make their way carefully around the roots of the heart trees as they sought to complete their circuit of the camp.

"What if there is no truth? What do you do then?"

"You sound just like Petroklos," Declan laughed softly. "Questioning everything."

"You know Petroklos?" Rafia asked in surprise.

"Among other philosophers, yes," he confirmed.

At first, she was surprised. Then she realized that there was no reason to be. Not after the many conversations that she had engaged in with Bryen while they were on Haven. Obviously, the Protector was well read and extremely well educated, and Rafia was certain that had come about because of the man she was walking with now.

"And what if the truth frightens you?" asked Rafia. Why that question had come to mind, she didn't know. Yet for some reason she felt the need to ask him.

"It often does," Declan confirmed. "That still doesn't mean that we can ignore it. We must acknowledge that truth regardless of how it affects us. And if that truth frightens us then ..."

"Then we simply must deal with it," finished Rafia.

"Correct," Declan said. "Exactly what I was going to say. The truth is the truth. Better to believe it than to ignore it."

"A very stoic perspective, Declan."

"Were you expecting something different?" he asked with a tinge of amusement in his voice.

"Actually, no, I wasn't," she replied. "Not with you. You are probably the most straightforward and consistent person I have ever met."

Declan nodded with satisfaction when they reached the next sentry, who was exactly where she was supposed to be. Alert. Prepared for anything that may come. After a few words of greetings and praise, Declan guided Rafia back among the trees.

"You know, I'm impressed," she said. "Your Company of Blood has come a long way in a very short period of time."

"Thank you, Magus. You're very kind to say so."

"There's no need to be so formal, Declan. We've been through this many times already. Please call me Rafia."

Declan simply nodded in response.

Rafia assumed that he was going to say more and was waiting expectantly for whatever might be on the tip of his tongue. As the seconds passed, she realized that he had nothing to add. He was no longer looking at her. Instead, his eyes were surveying everything around him as they walked through the spreading dark, Declan continuing to check the location of the guards. She felt the need to fill the silence.

"Still, you should be proud. They are all quite disciplined and competent."

"Thank you. And I am proud ... Rafia," replied Declan, hesitating just a second before calling the Magus by her first name. "However, I don't deserve all the approbation. There are several others who have helped us. We couldn't have come this far this quickly if not for the leadership and guidance provided by Tarin and Jerad."

"You have an interesting habit of sharing credit," said Rafia. "When praised, you acknowledge it but give it to others. When there is blame, you accept it yourself, seeing it as a key responsibility of a leader. Not many are willing to take such an approach. Most only want the praise and want nothing to do with the blame."

"I give credit where credit is deserved," said Declan. "Besides, I prefer to speak the truth, whether good or bad." He offered that last comment with a broad grin.

"So I'm beginning to understand," replied Rafia with a

bark of laughter. This certainly was a clever man. "Still, it is a unique ability. Some would suggest that it's a weakness, though I believe that it's a strength that is rarely seen these days."

"Perhaps you've been spending too much time with the wrong people, Rafia. In my world, we have little time for games. We speak plainly. We accept praise when it is deserved, blame as well. There is no reason to hide from either."

"Perhaps you are right," answered Rafia, who nodded knowingly, her opinion of the Master of the Gladiators only improving with every word spoken. "You know, I have also heard that your gladiators would do anything for you. That you treated them like a family, getting them the best weapons, trying to get them better food, finding medicine when needed. Doing all you could to care for them despite the fact that their fate had been determined as soon as they set foot within the Colosseum."

"It's what they deserved, Rafia. To be treated with respect. They were required to sacrifice themselves for the enjoyment of others. They had no choice. They deserved a fighting chance. No more, no less."

Declan had spoken quietly but strongly. Rafia stared at him with a great deal of interest, clearly struck by his words. A man who cared about the people he was responsible for, who had a clear sense of what was right and wrong, and who tried to act at all times with integrity. A rare breed indeed these days. What was she to do with him?

She considered the question that she had raised for a few seconds. In part, because of her personal interest in the Sergeant of the Blood Company. And also because of what might be required of her with respect to Bryen and the Curse.

Declan cared about Bryen. He was a son to Declan in every way but blood. How would Declan react if his sense of right conflicted with his emotions? Would he stand in her way if she needed to do what was necessary to prevent Bryen from being corrupted by the Curse?

She didn't know the answers to those questions and she didn't want to know, at least not then, so she moved the conversation in a different direction.

"If I may be so bold, Declan, how was it that you ended up in the Colosseum?"

"You really want to know?"

"I do," she replied.

Declan could tell that the Magus wasn't interested because of a morbid sense of curiosity. Rather, something else drove her interest.

"I killed a man," he replied.

"Why? Who was he?"

"He was a lord's son who was trying to make a name for himself in the Royal Guard at the expense of others. At the expense of those who couldn't defend themselves or speak for themselves."

"And the father wanted you to hang. Your commanding officer disagreed with him."

"Correct, and so I ended up in the Pit."

"Why did you kill him?"

"He deserved it."

Initially, Rafia thought that Declan might be making a joke. She quickly realized that he was being completely serious. He was speaking the truth.

"I would think that there was quite a bit more to the story than that."

"There always is, isn't there," he agreed, though he chose

not to offer any more details on what had consigned him to the Colosseum for the last twenty years of his life.

Having completed their loop around the campsite, Declan steered Rafia back toward the small fires that dotted the wood, the glow of the flames visible now between the heart trees. Then he stopped abruptly and turned toward her, his eyes capturing hers despite the darkness. The spark that had been there just the night before had returned, and for a moment it took Rafia's breath away.

"What's your story, Rafia? You seem quite interested in me for some reason. I'd like to know more about you."

"Does that bother you?" she asked lightly, hoping that she hadn't pushed him too far and also wanting to keep the conversation focused on him rather than on her. She didn't like revealing too much about herself. "Being the focus of my attention?" Then she realized that her concern was groundless. Declan would say what he wanted to say and if he didn't want to say anything then he wouldn't.

"It makes me nervous."

"Always honest." Rafia smiled, her eyes still locked with Declan's. "In my experience honesty can often bite you in the ass."

"It can and it does," he said with a laugh. "Still, better that than having to lie to someone." Declan studied the Magus for several seconds. He was good at reading people, although there was something about Rafia that made it difficult for him to do so. He could see what she wanted him to see and no more than that. "Now back to my original question. Why are you so interested in me?"

Rafia smiled in surrender. She should have expected that Declan wouldn't give up.

"Two reasons."

"The first one?"

"I find you intriguing. I haven't met a man like you in quite some time."

"I'm sure that there are many more out there like me."

"You'd be surprised, Declan. And I've been looking for centuries."

Declan continued to stare at her, slightly uncomfortable. He decided to not ask the next question that came to mind, knowing that inquiring about a woman's age was bad form.

"And the second reason?"

She pointed behind him to where Bryen and Aislinn were working together with the Talent just a few yards away from the main campsite.

"Our former gladiator, former Protector, and now Captain of the Blood Company who also is the Seventh Stone and has the potential to become one of the strongest Magii in the history of Caledonia, if he lives long enough."

Declan nodded, turning for a few moments to watch Bryen as he practiced with Aislinn some skill that he likely wouldn't understand. Then he smiled and turned back toward Rafia.

"He does carry quite a lot on his shoulders," Declan said.

"You worry about him."

"All the time," he replied.

"He's more than just a ward to you."

Declan was reluctant at first to tell Rafia much, recognizing that she might be seeking information for her own purposes. He understood that even though she was naturally inquisitive, there was more to her interest in him than just the possibility that she might be attracted to a gruff and gritty gladiator. Yet the openness of her gaze and the warmth of her smile suggested that any of his concerns in that regard were misplaced.

"He's like a son to me." Declan immediately corrected himself. "He is my son."

"He does you credit."

"He does himself credit."

Rafia turned her gaze away from Declan, finding it difficult to pull her eyes from his, so that she could watch as the two young Magii continued their training. Yet even as Bryen and Aislinn added to the complexity of their practice session, she found it difficult to give them her full attention, her mind moving in a different direction entirely.

Everything about the Master of the Gladiators and now Sergeant of the Blood Company appealed to her. How he talked. What he said. How he looked at her. His lack of fear in speaking his mind. She was hundreds of years old, yet when she spent time with Declan, she felt young again. That was a wonderful feeling.

A dangerous one as well. And she needed to be wary of that going forward.

"That's it," said Aislinn, her smile illuminated every other second as a handful of shining orbs sped her way. "Make sure the size doesn't change. That's the goal. Maintain the size of the spheres no matter how much of the Talent is used to construct them."

She caught with ease the orbs that Bryen threw to her and allowed them to play across her fingers for just a flash before she flung them right back to Bryen, who snatched them out of the air, taking a few seconds to juggle the five gleaming balls with both hands before once again sending them back the other way.

"And this is supposed to help with what again?" he asked.

"It helps to refine your control. It improves your touch with the Talent. Power and precision. We know you have the former. You need to work on the latter."

"I take it that this is something that Sirius had you work on quite a bit."

"Yes, how did you know?" Aislinn asked.

"This exercise just seems like something that would germinate in his mind," responded Bryen, his eyes never leaving the balls of energy that traveled back and forth between them. "I assume that you began doing this right after you blew up his chamber."

"How did you know that when ..." Aislinn flushed red, slightly embarrassed by the memory of her losing control of the Talent and destroying Sirius' private quarters in the Broken Tower soon after she had met Bryen. "I did not blow up his chamber. It was no more than a small accident."

She had blamed her failure then on Bryen, trying to convince herself that his arrival as her Protector had thrown off her concentration. It had. She had realized soon afterward that it wasn't Bryen's fault. Rather, it was hers. She was the one who let her focus slip, and it had proven to be a costly mistake.

"Just a guess," replied Bryen with a grin. "No more than that."

He saw the value of what he and Aislinn were doing with the Talent, and he didn't disagree with her. Both Sirius and Rafia had been harping about his need to improve his exactness with the Talent since they had started teaching him. And he hoped that if he improved his precision, it would lessen his primary concern, because he still needed to be careful whenever he sought to facilitate the natural power of the world, especially when he was not holding the Spear of the Magii.

He still feared that if he took in too much of the Talent it would awaken the Dark Magic that resided within him. But so far, so good. His control appeared to have improved, and there was barely a whisper of the Curse in the back of his mind.

"You don't need to be smug about it."

"I'm not being smug about it. I was just confirming my suspicion."

"You're being smug about it," Aislinn protested. To emphasize her point, she began to throw the spheres of light toward him with greater velocity.

"And you seem to be getting angry," chuckled Bryen, "which I can't say that I find all that surprising."

"You think so, do you?" asked Aislinn with a raised eyebrow. "This is nothing. You'll know when I'm angry."

"That I will."

"What do you mean by that?"

"That I'll know when you're angry."

"You really think that you can tell when I'm angry," she said. "You are so smug."

"No, just being honest," he replied. "I know when you're angry and when you're just pretending to be."

Aislinn stopped herself from throwing the spheres back to Bryen, instead having the white orbs spin around the top of her right palm. She smiled at her Protector. He could tell that her expression held little in the way of humor.

"Because of the collar?" she asked.

"No," Bryen chuckled. "Because I know you."

"Really? You know me so well?"

"I believe that I do, yes," Bryen replied, his voice filled

with confidence. "Sometimes I think I know you better than you know yourself."

"Am I angry now?" she asked, the spheres of light spinning faster and faster around her hand.

Bryen took his time before replying, studying his charge. She painted quite a picture, the Talent whirling around her fingers, a cocky grin, her posture suggesting that she was ready for anything with her legs square to her shoulders, one foot slightly in front of the other, and her free hand resting on her hip. She was confident with just a touch of arrogance. He knew the truth, however, because he knew her.

"No, you're not."

In a flash, the five orbs of energy shot from Aislinn's palm straight toward Bryen. Rather than ducking, and despite the speed of Aislinn's throw, he snatched the five spheres out of the air, manipulating them so that they danced around his fingers now. He was quite pleased with himself considering the pace with which the energy had sped across the short distance between them.

He had little time to congratulate himself. In an instant, he transformed the Talent contained within the spheres into a small buckler that he gripped with his left hand, raising it just in time to deflect the dagger made of the Talent that Aislinn thrust at his side.

No, definitely not angry, Bryen believed as he pivoted away from her. Even though she was trying to make him think that she was. She certainly was motivated, though, as she continued her attack.

Aislinn ignored the sparks that flashed in the dying light of the day every time her dagger struck Bryen's shield. Her Protector blocked her first few strikes easily enough. Aislinn had assumed that he would, so she had choreographed in her own mind the sequence that she wanted to follow that she hoped would penetrate his defenses. Unsurprised that Bryen parried her jabs, she spun back around, seeking to catch him on his other side. Unfortunately for her, he had expected such a move, twisting around with her and catching her dagger once again with his shield.

Even so, she wasn't deterred. She immediately took a half-step back, then lunged forward, stabbing for his gut.

Bryen turned his body without even thinking, allowing the glowing dagger to slip by him. He then launched himself up into the air, jumping over Aislinn's attempted backhanded slash that sliced through the space in which he had just been standing.

And so it went for the next few minutes, Aislinn maintaining her assault, Bryen using his shining buckler to frustrate her. For every question that she asked with her blade, Bryen had the answer with his shield. Through it all, neither seemed to care that they were locked in a stalemate. Instead, they were both smiling broadly, enjoying the challenge of dueling with someone who was just as skilled as they were.

It all came to an end just as quickly as it started. Aislinn feinted a slash toward Bryen's shoulder, then rotated quickly so that she could bring the shining blade down across his side. Rather than blocking her strike as had been his habit since the start of the duel, Bryen spun away from her instead. He then reached blindly with his free hand, grabbing hold of Aislinn's hand that grasped the dagger, and whirled her about before pulling her in close.

The maneuver left the two combatants facing one another, arms crushed against each other's chest, dagger and shield blazing brightly in the fading light. Realizing that the combat had concluded, they both released their hold on the Talent, though neither made a move to disengage.

"This was your plan all along," accused Aislinn. She said it with a smile that clearly demonstrated that she was far from upset with how the duel had ended.

"To get you in my arms like this?" he asked in amusement.

"Yes," she nodded. "Exactly as you orchestrated."

"You give me too much credit," he replied with a grin and a wink. "You certainly do think quite a lot of yourself."

Bryen flinched unexpectedly, feeling a slap on his bottom courtesy of Aislinn's use of the Talent.

"It's not nice to tease a Lady of Caledonia."

"I'll try to remember that the next time I run into one," he replied.

Before Aislinn could offer a very pointed response, which she thought at least in her own mind was quite clever, she gasped, feeling a light slap on her backside.

"That's very fresh of you," protested Aislinn.

"I'm simply returning the favor," responded Bryen.

"Not very chivalrous of you," she said with a wicked grin.

"Perhaps not," Bryen agreed, who was enjoying the feel of Aislinn pressed against him. The Lady of the Southern Marches appeared to be quite comfortable as well, having made no attempt to free herself from his grasp. In fact, she seemed to be pulling him in even closer. "Then again, I've never been described as chivalrous."

"And clearly there's a reason why," Aislinn answered, enjoying the give and take between them. She couldn't do this with anyone else. She didn't want to do this with anyone else.

"Remember what we talked about in the training circle back in Battersea?" asked Bryen.

"What would that be? You had a lot of sayings that I tried to remember."

Bryen grinned, not rising to the bait. He saw the spark in Aislinn's eyes, which for a moment took him back to a few nights' past when their discussion had devolved into something far more interesting.

"Don't start something unless you can finish it."

Aislinn leaned into Bryen even more. A warmth had begun to spread through him, and it wasn't because of the duel that they had just engaged in. She captured his eyes with her own, then reached up with her hand to take hold of the back of his neck to pull him toward her until her lips hovered just a hair away from his.

"I have no concerns about that, Protector."

The way that Aislinn spoke, the underlying suggestion that was left unsaid, sent an enjoyable shiver down Bryen's spine. Before he could respond, however, he felt an unexpected pulse of energy surge through him that had nothing to do with his former charge.

Bryen felt as if he had been split apart, realizing that his very essence was hovering just above where he and Aislinn stood. Aislinn was staring at him with an expression of concern, sensing that something was wrong. Then, with a lurch his spirit soared into the sky. For a time, he saw little but the moon peeking out from behind the clouds every once in a while and a dark smudge when he looked down that he took to be the massive wood that he and the Blood Company were hiding in.

As he flew above the ground at an eye-watering speed, he realized that some power was pulling at him, taking him to the northwest, and all he could do was go along for the ride. Finally, the clouds fell away, allowing the moon to guide his way.

The dark of the night gave way to a shimmering light that revealed the long grass beneath him, which sped by in a blur. He recognized the Breakwater Plateau, which appeared to stretch off to the east and west for as far as he could see. It wasn't long before he was past the plain, into the lower hills, and then among the soaring pinnacles of the Shattered Peaks.

At the outset of this unexpected adventure, Bryen had thought that the Weir would be his final destination. Confirming that belief, the demanding pull turned him gently toward the west. The snow-capped summits of the mountains, shining brightly at the touch of the full moon, soon gave way to the rocky spires of the Trench, purple and white heather growing liberally along the sides and across the tops of the sandstone pillars that poked their heads above the ever-present clouds. Finally, Bryen came to a stop above a glowing dome, a broad geyser of glaring energy shooting up into the sky and illuminating the night for leagues around.

He could feel the heat of the power being employed, knowing that if he got too close it would sear his flesh until it flaked away from the bone. Luckily, whatever had brought him here kept him at a safe distance, though still close enough so that he could look down upon the top of the spire and see clearly all that was transpiring.

He should have assumed as much. The Sanctuary.

Then it all made sense. It was the Seventh Stone that transported him here. The Seventh Stone wanted him to see this. In fact, the Seventh Stone needed him to see this.

He realized as he stared down at the bowl-shaped depression in which the Seven Stones pulsed on their pedestals that he was not actually there. Rather, he was experiencing a memory captured by the Seventh Stone, the artifact giving him the privilege of looking into the past, of observing what had happened more than a thousand years before.

He watched keenly as the Ten Magii stood around the outside of the manmade cut in the base of the spire. The Talent surged from one Magus to the next in the form of blindingly bright swirling threads, and in the center of the hollow, standing adjacent to the pedestal upon which the Seventh Stone rested, stood Bryen's forebear, Viktor Keldragan.

Bryen noticed the resemblance immediately. Same height. Same build. Although his ancestor lacked the scars that marred Bryen's face and neck. Bryen guessed that Viktor was several decades older than he was, even though his ancestor appeared more youthful than Bryen did now. Maybe it was the sandy brown hair rather than the white that had spread across Bryen's scalp, a gift from his time in the Pit that Viktor never had to contend with. But, in that moment, it appeared that Viktor was dealing with a much more dangerous threat than any Bryen ever had to on the white sand.

Viktor was struggling to control the huge amount of power that churned around the Magii. What Bryen found most interesting was that Viktor and the other Magii weren't manipulating just the Talent, they were also making use of the Curse, courtesy of the Seventh Stone.

Bryen continued to gaze fixedly at the Sanctuary, trying to identify what it was that the Seventh Stone wanted him to see.

All of the Magii obviously had great skill in the Talent, doing their work with a precision that almost made Bryen jealous. That was to be expected considering who they were, the most skilled of all the Magii during that age when the Ghoule Overlord first attacked Caledonia. The fluidity with which the Talent circulated among them as they wove the magical barrier was impressive, even somewhat frightening, to behold.

Then he saw it. What the Seventh Stone wanted him to catch. There was a hitch in their work, an imperfection that couldn't be avoided based on their approach. And though they had missed it, it was exactly where Bryen assumed that it would be.

None of the Magii, despite their strength, adroitness, knowledge, and experience, could do with the Curse what they were doing with the Talent. There was a tainted darkness beginning to form around the Ten Magii. It was no more than a faint shadow. Even so, that was all that it would take to doom them.

He assumed that because the Ten Magii were so focused on their task that they hadn't identified the threat yet. But they would, he knew, and that discovery would lead to terrible consequences for them all.

Bryen turned his gaze away from that burgeoning gloom back toward the center of the Sanctuary, concentrating on Viktor Keldragan and the work that he was doing specifically. His ancestor played the key role in this entire endeavor.

Viktor was facilitating the release of the Dark Magic from the Seventh Stone, that artifact somehow linked to the Ghoule Overlord's black diamond. The stolen stone sat right next to the glowing white diamond, the two jewels flashing intensely in an alternating pattern, first white, then black, as the Ten Magii labored.

Through it all Viktor was the linchpin, because he was the one who sent the Dark Magic to the other Magii to do their work, and then once they were done entwining the two powers, the Magii around the outside of the Sanctuary returned the weave to Viktor and the Seventh Stone, that intricate, absolutely essential plait becoming the broad geyser of energy that shot up into the sky to form the shimmering barrier that would bridle the Ghoules' ambitions for more than ten centuries.

The Magii were working fast. Almost faster than he could perceive with the naked eye. So Bryen decided to use the Talent himself, though just a thin stream, so that he could sharpen his vision.

Bryen's eyes widened in amazement, not only impressed by the skill demonstrated by the Ten Magii, and in particular that of Viktor, but also by how much of the power, both the Talent and Dark Magic, that they employed to achieve their goal.

He could not imagine shaping so much energy at one time. Yet these Ten Magii had done it, and their creation continued to exist despite the passage of a millennium.

After watching for just a few seconds more, Bryen felt a little more confident about what he promised Rafia and Sirius he would attempt to do.

The Ten Magii were doing much as he had done in the Library of the Magii when Rafia and Sirius had tasked him with building a shield and then trying to make use of the Dark Magic of the Seventh Stone for the first time without corrupting himself with that evil power. The weave that the Ten Magii were employing to achieve their purpose was very similar to the one that he had used.

It was also unique. Thanks to the additional power offered by the Seventh Stone, Bryen had spotted the critical distinction, and he believed that that difference could be the key to this entire undertaking.

Bryen had a sense of what he needed to do now, what he could at least try to do, assuming, of course, that he and the

Blood Company actually reached the Sanctuary, which at the moment was not a foregone conclusion, not with the Ghoules dogging them.

Yet that was a worry for another day. Now, he simply appreciated the fact that for whatever reason the Seventh Stone had provided him with a glimpse of the past and given him some guidance for meeting a responsibility that when he really thought about it, he wasn't sure that he could handle on his own. Rather than allow that conclusion to weigh him down, he decided that that, too, was a concern for another day, and he'd keep that worry and all he just learned to himself, at least for now.

Just as quickly as this unexpected history lesson began, the action in front of him disappeared into a black mist. With a jolt Bryen came back to himself, the Seventh Stone apparently having decided that he'd seen enough. The shock of his return caused him to stumble just a bit.

Aislinn was still there, preventing him from falling by holding him up with her arms around his waist. She stayed with him, holding on tight, not certain that he could stand on his own without dropping to the soft loam of the forest.

"Are you all right?" she asked, the concern in her voice quite clear.

"Yes, I just got lost for a moment."

"Was it the Dark Magic? If it was, then we need to talk to …"

"No, nothing like that," he assured her quickly. "Sometimes the Seventh Stone does something within me that throws me off. This was just one of those times."

"You're certain that you're all right?" Aislinn didn't believe him, at least not entirely.

"Yes, nothing to worry about," Bryen confirmed. "I'm just tired." He then gave her a big smile when he straightened again to his full height. Recognizing the look in her eyes, he understood that she wasn't going to let this go. For now, perhaps she would. When she decided that he was feeling better, she would raise it with him again. Since he wasn't ready to discuss it with her, he changed the subject. "Why don't we see if dinner is ready? Your training session and then you attacking me so viciously has left a hole in my belly."

Aislinn stared at him intently. She knew that Bryen was keeping something to himself. She'd allow it for now. So instead of pursuing the several questions that had popped into her head, she simply nodded and, keeping an arm around his lower back, guided him toward the campfires that flickered not too far away in between the heart trees.

23

LETTING GO

The recently appointed General of the Army of Caledonia strode purposefully through the massive cantonment, Kevan Winborne right at her side. Noorsin Stelekel observed an orderly, disciplined scene as the soldiers of the Royal Guard and the Duchy Guards made camp for the night, raising tents, starting cook fires, and establishing picket lines for the horses, the sentries already having been set.

The combined forces of the Kingdom had made good time during their march, covering almost fifteen leagues as they headed east from Tintagel. Still, they would need to be careful. They didn't want to push their mounts too hard knowing that they still had more than a week before they reached their destination. Once they got there, they wanted to ensure that their horses were fresh. They would need them in their fight against the Ghoules, for if the beasts broke out onto the Breakwater Plateau they could rampage through Caledonia with little to stop them.

Noorsin understood the limitations that they had to work under. They could only push themselves and their mounts so hard if they wanted to arrive at the Winter Pass with the necessary fitness to challenge the Ghoules. Still, Noorsin's sense of urgency, the feeling that they needed to reach the Shattered Peaks as quickly as possible, nagged at her.

The Dukes were feeling the press of time as well. The longer it took them to get to the Winter Pass, the greater the threat their enemies presented to all of Caledonia. The greater the chance that the Ghoule Overlord would gain the initiative in the war to come.

"How goes it, Captain Klines?" called Noorsin as she maneuvered around the many tent lines that threatened to trip her. She had decided to get off the main path leading through the camp as she headed east, not wanting to get in the way while the quartermasters used that newly made trail of crushed grass to deliver that evening's food stocks to the various companies so they could begin to prepare their meals.

"As well as can be expected," replied Klines. "May I have a few moments of your time, Duchess Stelekel?"

"Walk with me, Captain. After such a long day in the saddle, I feel the need for some fresh air and some space free of unwashed soldiers and smelly horses."

"A person after my own heart," replied Klines. "It would be my pleasure to accompany you."

Noorsin led the two past the sentries and just beyond the camp, enjoying the light touch of the breeze on her face as the sun began to set behind her. The mountains of the Northern Spine soared into the sky to her front, the last rays of light glancing off the snow-capped peaks that were still several days' journey away.

Klines stood quietly next to Duke Winborne after they walked a few hundred yards beyond the camp, giving

Duchess Stelekel time to enjoy the peace and relative quiet, the rumble of so many soldiers compressed together dispersed quickly by the wind. Klines understood that as the commander of the thousands of soldiers marching toward battle, there were few opportunities to relax. So even just a few minutes now and then were to be taken and relished.

"You did not come looking for me for no reason," Noorsin finally said, feeling slightly rejuvenated as she turned her attention to the Captain of the Royal Guard. "What do you have for me?"

"Just as we did this morning, the advance guard will head out before the sun rises tomorrow, Duchess Stelekel. And as has been our practice, the bulk of the army will follow shortly thereafter, although this time one of the Duchy Guards will take the lead so that all of our troops have a chance to serve as the vanguard."

"Any suspected problems on our route for tomorrow?" asked Noorsin.

"No, Duchess Stelekel," replied Klines. "So long as the weather remains good, tomorrow's course should be much as it was today."

"That's good to hear," replied Kevan. "If we can keep this pace, we should reach the hills of the Northern Spine in three days' time."

Kevan's estimate was a good one, thought Noorsin. Once they got to the mountains, they would turn north and track the Spine until they hit the Shattered Peaks and then the Winter Pass. Another seven days at the least, assuming all went well along the way.

Of course, she wasn't one to lay all her hopes on what might or might not happen. She preferred to assume the worst instead. So she decided on twelve days at best, maybe as many as fourteen, before they caught sight of the southern tip of the Winter Pass. That much time to get where they needed to be worried her, only accelerating the sense of exigency that had set her stomach churning.

"It is indeed," said Noorsin, as she began to walk further east of the camp, enjoying the solitude of the plains, the two men following in her wake as she parted the long grass. Every so often during their journey that day, they came across small forests that broke up the monotony of the steppe. Those groves were few and far between and usually easily avoided. Who knew what could be hiding within them? Better to stay out in the open when traveling with such a large force that few would willingly challenge. "But you didn't come looking for me just to tell me that. What more do you have for us, Captain Klines?"

"I'd like to make a suggestion," Klines said with a smile.

Duchess Stelekel was quite sharp. He should have assumed that she would sniff out his true purpose for finding her. He hadn't worked with her for long, but he had to admit to himself that he was enjoying the experience. She was smart. Intuitive. Wasn't afraid to make a decision when one needed to be made. Even better, she never felt the need to make a decision simply to make a decision. In his mind, these and her many other positive characteristics testified to her skills as a leader.

"What would that be?" Kevan's question interrupted Klines' train of thought.

"That we place several lines of skirmishers on our flanks and stagger them so that the farthest is a league distant."

"You wouldn't suggest that tactic without cause," said Noorsin. "Your reasoning?"

"Our scouts have spotted signs of Ghoule activity farther west of the Northern Spine than we had expected," replied

Klines. "They found some tracks less than half a day from here."

"Large packs?" asked Kevan, a hint of concern in his voice.

"No, Duke Winborne. They appear to be no more than scouts, although we can't say for certain. So I'd prefer to be cautious rather than overconfident."

"Any contact with them yet?" asked Kevan.

"No, but I expect that it won't be long before the clashes begin. When that happens, the Ghoules will have the advantage because of the landscape. I'd like to mitigate that by strengthening our numbers along the flanks as we continue on our way."

"Thank you for the suggestion, Captain," said Noorsin. "Good thinking. I assume that you can put everything into place?"

"You're quite welcome, Duchess Stelekel," said Klines. "Yes, I can. I'll take care of it now."

"Thank you, Captain. I do appreciate you taking the initiative in this regard."

"Of course, Duchess Stelekel," replied Klines, another hint of a smile crinkling his normally stern visage. Another reason Klines liked and respected the Duchess of Murcia was that she was a leader who actually listened to what you had to say. That had been an uncommon occurrence during Marden Beleron's reign in Tintagel, so he certainly appreciated it now. "If you'll excuse me, I have a few other matters that require my attention besides getting the skirmishers in place for tomorrow. If the scouts discover anything else of interest, I'll let you know."

Klines then nodded to Noorsin and Kevan before striding back toward the quickly forming laager. Noorsin watched him go. A good man and an even better leader.

Aislinn had told her as much, explaining how the Blademaster befriended her and came to her aid despite great risk to himself, and it hadn't taken Noorsin long to discover it for herself.

She had noticed the change within the Royal Guard as soon as the Blademaster had assumed command. A quiet confidence had swept through the ranks, replacing the stench of corruption and privilege of which the former commander, Killen Sourban, reeked.

"I am glad that the Blademaster was on our side during the uprising," said Noorsin. "I would have hated to have him as an adversary."

"You can thank Aislinn for that," replied Kevan, who came to stand next to Noorsin, both of them watching the last rays of light dance off the mountaintops.

"Indeed we can," agreed Noorsin. "Captain Klines is much too competent a soldier to ever want for an enemy."

"I'd hate to cross blades with him," admitted Kevan. "Facing off against him is likely just as bad as sparring with Aislinn's Protector."

"That was an imprudent decision on your part, Kevan," scolded Noorsin mildly. "You're lucky Bryen decided not to take his anger out on you, because he would have been justified in doing so, and you had no way of knowing what he would do when you walked into the Pit. If I were in his boots, I probably would have at least marked you a few times with my blade just to demonstrate my displeasure with you."

"Believe me, his anger with me is quite plain," chuckled Kevan. "I find it surprising that you are less forgiving than he is."

"I'm just telling you how I feel."

"I appreciate that," said Kevan. "And you're right. I probably should have thought more about sparring with him before I walked out onto the white sand. I didn't calculate the potential risk very well, as I didn't know what would come from my visiting with him."

"Then why did you take the risk?" demanded Noorsin, having already taken Kevan to task as soon as she had learned of what he had done. He had no right to place himself in such a dangerous position. Not when she relied so heavily upon him. "I doubt that even Aislinn would have held Bryen accountable if he had decided to kill you when he had the chance."

"I didn't think that her Protector ..."

"Bryen, you mean?"

"Yes, Bryen," replied Kevan with a slight grimace. He still had trouble saying the young man's name. It was as if not saying his name lessened the impact of what he had done to the Protector, taking some of the sting out of it. He needed to stop doing that and acknowledge that what he had done, though quite expedient at the time, was wrong. "I didn't believe that Bryen, though he had every reason and right to do so, would do anything to harm me."

"And this wasn't your ego talking?" asked Noorsin. "I know you're good with a blade. No assumptions that you would be able to challenge the Volkun in a fair fight and best him?"

"Maybe when I was younger," replied Kevan with a grin that Noorsin didn't return, his attempt at humor falling flat. "But no. Remember, I saw him fight and kill a black dragon in the Pit before I took him with me to the Southern Marches. I could never have done that. No one else could have done that. Not even the Blademaster, as I'm sure he would readily admit. So no illusions of grandeur on my part."

"Then why did you do it? Why place yourself in a situation that could have ended so badly for you?"

"I had to do it," replied Kevan softly. "Bryen deserved no less. He deserved the chance to make his own decision about me and what I had done to him. And he deserved an apology."

Noorsin nodded in understanding. A courageous thing to do, though still not the best approach in her opinion. Kevan could have handled it in a way that didn't put his life at risk.

"Brave," Noorsin admitted reluctantly. "And I agree that it was the right thing to do. But still foolish. If you are to serve under me, Duke Winborne, I will not countenance such incautious behavior in the future."

"I will try to curb my reckless tendencies," said Kevan with a smile and a nod. "I enjoy serving under you, and I would like to continue to do so."

For just a moment, Noorsin stared at Kevan with an upturned eyebrow. She could interpret what he had just said several different ways, one in particular more enjoyable than the rest. A few possible responses immediately came to mind, none of them useful. So she decided to return to more professional matters, leaving the personal for later. She handed several small slips of rolled up paper to Kevan.

"Information from your eyes and ears?" he asked, although he already knew the answer as he started to scan the various messages.

"Yes, and they are all reporting much the same."

"They've burned a few villages, slaughtered the inhabitants, just as we expected that they would," he said, his anger dripping into his words as he flipped through the first few pieces of paper quickly. When he got through them all, he stood there deep in thought, realizing that what they had anticipated wasn't coming to pass. At least not entirely. Or at least not yet. "The Ghoules are not just raiding now."

"No," said Noorsin, shaking her head with worry. "It seems that they're clearing the villages on the southern slopes of the Shattered Peaks and fortifying the Winter Pass and the lower hills leading to it."

"They're preparing the way," said Kevan, his mind putting the disparate pieces of information together quickly, concluding that Noorsin had already done so as well and had reached the same conclusion. "It's not just packs now as we hoped. The Ghoule Overlord is already sending through his Legions." The Duke of the Southern Marches sighed in resignation. "We can take some solace from the fact that the Ghoule Overlord still will lose some of his beasts to the Weir. The Elders' ability to hold back the Talent in the barrier remains inconsistent at best."

"That seems to be the case," agreed Noorsin, "which means that what Aislinn, Bryen, and the Blood Company will be doing at the Weir has become all the more important."

"How much time do you think we have?"

"Until the Weir fails?"

He nodded. Kevan wasn't sure that he really wanted to hear the answer, though he still needed to ask the question. The response played a critical role in their strategy.

"I don't know," replied Noorsin, clearly frustrated by her reply. "I wish I could tell you. I just can't. No one can."

"Frustrating when you can't predict the future?" asked Kevan with an impudent grin.

"Don't be cheeky," chided Noorsin. "I don't have the patience for it now."

"Sorry. I was just teasing."

"I know you were, Kevan." Noorsin reached out a hand

and grasped Kevan's arm warmly. "You just hit a nerve. I do pride myself on my ability to predict the future."

"So I've finally identified a weakness in the Duchess of Murcia," replied Kevan, entwining his fingers with those on his arm. "Unable to predict the future. Even with all of her eyes and ears. Who would have guessed at such a failing?"

"You're incorrigible, you know that?"

"I try my best," Kevan said mischievously. "Now that we've confirmed that you can't predict the future, what's your best guess as to what might happen next?"

"Now you're putting me on the spot."

"I am," Kevan confirmed. "Although you can't predict the future, you have a talent that no one else can match for looking at the larger picture and figuring out how all the pieces fit together."

"You're being too generous," said Noorsin, blushing slightly but still pleased by the compliment. "Just a guess, mind you."

"A guess is good enough. That's the best that we usually have to work with, so we really can't ask for more than that."

"Based on the information that is coming in, it leads me to assume that if the Ghoules are digging in, then the Ghoule Overlord is preparing the way for his Legions as you've suggested," said Noorsin. "He likely believes that the Weir will come down soon or be weakened to such a state that the number of Ghoules and Elders that die attempting to cross the magical barrier are of no consequence. They're an acceptable loss because he knows that he doesn't need to bring his entire army through the Weir to defeat us. There are one thousand Ghoules to a Legion if I remember my history."

"That's correct," nodded Kevan.

"Then the likelihood of achieving his goal of conquering

Caledonia simply comes down to numbers. Get a certain number of Ghoules through the Weir and into the Kingdom, and his victory is almost certainly guaranteed. The Weir will no longer be relevant."

"As we discussed, the Ghoule Overlord needs maybe ten Legions," said Kevan. "Perhaps twelve at the most. That would be more than enough Ghoules to beat us. Our numbers would be comparable in a pitched battle, yet even with the new tactics that we've been employing to fight the Ghoules we'd still be at a disadvantage against the beasts."

"Agreed. To have any chance of success in an open battle we'd need twice as many soldiers. Three times would be better."

"Preferably four times," offered Kevan.

"That doesn't change what we need to do."

"No, it doesn't," agreed Kevan. "It does change how we need to do it."

"I'll invite Captain Klines, Cornelius, and Wencilius to dinner tonight," said Noorsin. "We can use that time to discuss how we'll need to manage this change in circumstances."

"I look forward to it," replied Kevan. "I'll draw up some proposals to discuss when we return to camp."

"Thank you," said Noorsin. That conversation completed, the Duchess of Murcia explored the Duke's often inscrutable countenance. "There's something else bothering you at the moment, isn't there?"

Kevan considered denying it, though there really was no point in doing so. Noorsin would get it out of him one way or another.

"How did you know?"

"Because I know you, Kevan. We spent a great deal of time together in the Southern Marches before Tetric so rudely interrupted us. While I visited with you, I learned more about you than you could possibly imagine."

"Should I be frightened?" he asked with a weak smile.

"Only if you try to keep anything from me," she replied. "Now what's bothering you? Aislinn?"

"You see through me too easily."

"I see a worried father."

"I am worried," Kevan replied. "She's heading off into an unknown danger. Taking more risks than she should."

"Similar in some ways to what her father is doing."

Noorsin's comment stopped him, their conversation about the Protector quickly coming to mind. So instead of protesting, he could only agree. "That's a fair point."

"And if she wasn't doing that," countered Noorsin, "she'd be here with us riding toward a known danger."

"I wouldn't have allowed her to ..."

"Save your breath, Kevan," said Noorsin. "You're just blowing smoke, and it's clouding your vision. You know as well as I do that that young lady will not be dissuaded from doing what she believes is right, no matter the danger."

"You're correct about that," Kevan sighed, acknowledging his daughter's hardheadedness.

"And you have yourself to thank for it. Aislinn learned a great deal from you. She's more than competent with both the blade and the Talent. She doesn't run from a fight. She makes good decisions. And clearly she understands the importance of and knows how to make allies."

"I can't disagree with you about anything that you've said," Kevan confessed reluctantly. "And I admit that I'm very proud of her. Without her who knows how matters would have played out in Tintagel with Marden and Tetric. Still, I worry about her."

"And you always will."

"Call it a weakness."

"I would call it a strength, so long as it doesn't affect your decisions," said Noorsin sagely. "And knowing you as I do, I'm sure it won't." Noorsin turned Kevan so that he was facing her, the Shattered Peaks no more than a dark smudge in the distance right over his shoulder. Then she pulled him close, giving him a long kiss before finally releasing him and taking a step back. "You need to give Aislinn more credit. When you were locked in your rooms under Tetric's sway, what was your greatest fear?"

"That Marden would take advantage of the situation and force Aislinn to marry him."

"Did that happen?"

"No."

"Why not? From what I understand Marden and Tetric were applying a great deal of pressure to Aislinn, even threatening to kill you if she didn't comply with their demand."

"You're right," sighed Kevan. "I know you're right. She can handle herself. She's proven that time and time again. She deserves more credit from me."

"And what was your greatest desire when you were locked in your rooms? When Aislinn had to fight your and the Southern Marches' battles within the halls of the Corinthian Palace?"

"That Aislinn's Protector was there with her. He could have helped her."

"Bryen," nodded Noorsin. "Exceedingly competent, very dangerous, even tempered, something of a mean streak, just like Captain Klines, though a bit rougher around the edges. Clearly a formidable opponent, as he has some skills that few others can lay claim to."

"Yes ... Bryen." Why he had so much trouble calling that

young man by his given name, Kevan didn't know. He promised himself that he'd break down that obstruction by the next time that he met Aislinn's Protector.

"She's with Bryen now," said Noorsin gently. "Regardless of the danger that she is headed toward, Aislinn is with the one person, even without the magic of the collar demanding it of him, who will do all that he can to protect her. You know I speak the truth."

"You're right. I know you're right. It's just hard to let go as a father."

"Of course, knowing your daughter I doubt that she'll need the protection that Bryen offers her," continued Noorsin with an impish smile. "From what Bryen has said, and has been confirmed by Captain Klines, she's likely better with a blade than you are."

"Now wait a minute," protested Kevan.

Before he could continue with his objections, Noorsin touched his arm again, though differently than she had just a few minutes before.

Kevan caught the look in Noorsin's eyes. Something was wrong. He tensed in response, his hand drifting to the hilt of his sword.

For almost a full minute, Noorsin stood stock still, eyes closed. She could sense a disturbance that sent a prickle of concern down the back of her neck. Not too far away. A feeling of decay. Of rot. Of evil. But shielded. Hidden in plain sight.

As the Duchess of Murcia continued to explore her immediate surroundings with the Talent, searching for a threat that she knew was there yet couldn't find, her mind drifted to the information that Captain Klines had just provided her and Kevan. Their scouts had identified tracks not too far away.

Maybe those marks were made for a reason. Maybe the Ghoules wanted them to find those signs. Maybe the Ghoules wanted them to think that there were only a few of their scouts tracking their movement. Maybe the beasts wanted them to focus on an envisaged threat rather than the real one. And maybe they had been about to fall right into that trap.

Finally latching onto the sensation that was bothering her, Noorsin seized more of the Talent and shot from her palm right over Kevan's shoulder a bolt of searing energy. The sizzling power slammed into an invisible barrier just twenty feet in front of them and burned right through, the strength of Noorsin's attack too much for the illusion.

The meeting of the two magics caused a temporary flashing that quickly dissolved to reveal an Elder Ghoule with a shocked expression on his face as he looked down at his chest, a charred hole larger than his fist running all the way through his body and out his back. The Elder Ghoule remained standing for just a few seconds more, then fell face first into the grass, finally realizing that he was dead.

Noorsin and Kevan stared at the smoldering body of the Elder just as those behind the dead beast did. Two more Elders stood there, along with a pack of Ghoules, who appeared to be dumbfounded, never having thought that they would be uncovered, much less have one of their Elders killed by a weak human Magus.

The beasts had little time to think on how they had been discovered, the Duke of the Southern Marches pivoting on his heel and in the same motion pulling his sword from the scabbard on his hip. With a roar, Kevan sprinted toward the Ghoules, seeking to profit from their indecision.

Noorsin's eyes widened at Kevan's audacity, although she couldn't say that she was surprised. He was his daughter's father, after all, and Aislinn was not known for being cautious.

To help clear a path as Kevan launched himself at the Ghoules, Noorsin ripped into the gathered beasts with the Talent. She targeted the two Elders, knowing that they posed the greatest threat with their ability to manipulate Dark Magic.

The creatures dodged to the side just in time, jolted into action upon seeing the first Elder fall dead. Instead, the half dozen bolts of energy that Noorsin threw at the creatures burned through two of the Ghoules who had been standing right behind the Elders, the beasts still trying to comprehend what had happened to the first Elder.

After that, any sense of order in the fight immediately disintegrated. Kevan cut as deeply into the Ghoules as he could, stabbing one through the gut who had been jostled and knocked off balance by the Ghoule standing right next to him. He then spun back around to slice across another beast's shin. Although his steel didn't bite deeply into the Ghoule's armored flesh, the blow was strong enough to knock the beast a few feet backwards right when the creature was about to stab Kevan in the back with his spear crafted from black steel.

Irritated that his strike hadn't done more, but pleased that he was still alive, Kevan continued his assault, leaping over the Ghoule who had fallen to the ground, a thick black blood seeping from the wound in the beast's stomach, and slashing for another Ghoule's neck. That beast ducked out of the way just in time.

The Ghoule standing right next to him wasn't so lucky. Kevan's blade sliced across his throat more because the creature was in the wrong place at the wrong time rather than it being Kevan's intention.

That didn't bother the Duke of the Southern Marches in the least. The Ghoule fell to his knees grasping for his neck, unable to stop the flow of blood down his chest.

A good start to the fight, Kevan thought. Yet even with so many Ghoules falling to his blade so quickly, he and Noorsin were still at a severe disadvantage fighting eight Ghoules and two Elders. Those were not just bad odds. They were likely fatal.

Realizing that the surprise of his initial attack had worn off, Kevan danced back from the several spears thrust at him to stand next to Noorsin. They would have fewer options now. The two Elders would hold Noorsin's attention, which meant that he would face the remaining Ghoules. He didn't doubt that Noorsin could hold her own against her adversaries. He did doubt that he could do the same against so many of the beasts at one time, fearing that the Ghoules would overwhelm him quickly.

"Come on you bastards!" yelled Kevan, refusing to go quietly. "I'm going to take as many of you with me as I can!"

The Ghoules standing in front of Kevan howled, displaying their sharp teeth as they smiled at what they viewed as an easy kill, preparing to launch themselves at him. Then much to Kevan's surprise, the Ghoules took a step back. And then one more.

What was happening?

The welcome sound that he heard right behind him sent a rush of energy through him.

Several squads of soldiers charged right by him, the Blademaster in the lead. Swords drawn, spears extended, the men of the Royal Guard crashed into the Ghoules with a savagery that warmed Kevan's heart.

He thought to join the fray, but decided against it. Noorsin had the harder fight, and he didn't want her distracted by any Ghoules that might slip by the soldiers. Better that he stay where he was to offer what little protection that he could and watch the Blademaster at work.

JURGEN KLINES RAN by Duke Winborne with no expression on his face, something that the soldiers with him were not surprised by as the Blademaster rarely showed any emotion during a combat.

He was focused. Intent on his prey. Looking forward to the challenge.

Klines was impressed that the Duke had killed two Ghoules on his own. After this fight he promised himself that he would speak with the Duke so that he could learn anything useful from the experience and employ it in the future.

"Groups of three!" shouted Klines, his soldiers responding instantly to his command and separating into eight distinct groups, each one targeting a Ghoule.

With the implementation of a tactic learned from the Battersea Guard, what had started as a large skirmish instantly devolved into a series of smaller combats. Klines watched carefully as his soldiers took their time, poking and prodding at the surrounded Ghoules, waiting for the creatures to make a mistake. And, inevitably, the Ghoules did.

Not liking how the odds had shifted against them, the beasts tried to break free of the soldiers penning them in. Most of the time, the Ghoules' impatience only ensured that they died faster. As soon as a Ghoule overextended himself, seeking to eliminate one or two of the soldiers who had placed him in a trap of steel, one of the other soldiers would slice across his hamstring or ankle to disable the beast.

Not an honorable way to fight, perhaps, though it certainly was effective. Klines had explained time and time again in the practice ring that the honorable fighters also often tended to be the dead fighters. Honor was a wonderful concept until you faced the possibility of having your opponent's steel slide into your gut. Then, honor usually lost its luster and the instinct to survive kicked in. So better to do whatever would improve your chances of success, especially against beasts as dangerous as these monsters.

Only twice did Klines need to step in to help his soldiers. Once when a Ghoule knocked down a soldier despite the fact that the man had spitted the beast like a boar. The Ghoule was pulling himself along the wood of the spear trying to get at the man with his claws, the soldier's comrades unable to stop the creature in time.

Klines made quick work of the beast, taking the Ghoule's head off with a single swipe across his shoulders.

The other time required a bit more effort. A team of his soldiers had done exactly as they had been taught. The Ghoule they had cornered hadn't cooperated, proving to be too much for them. In just seconds, two of the soldiers were down, mortally wounded, and the third was fighting for his life, a slash across his shoulder and a stab in his side slowing him down and virtually ensuring that he would be the third to die at the claws of this Ghoule, who had towered over all the others in the pack.

Before the monstrous Ghoule could finish what he had started, Klines was there, stepping in front of the beast before it could drive his spear into the man's chest. Parrying the lunge with his blade, Klines ducked, having expected the Ghoule to try a backhanded slash that would take him in the chest or neck. Because of Klines' quick thinking, the Ghoule missed entirely and threw himself off balance as a result, so certain was he of his success that he had swung with all his might.

Klines took full advantage of the gift offered to him, slicing deftly across the Ghoule's left hamstring, which elicited a shriek of rage from the creature, and then just as fast across the beast's right hamstring, which this time extracted a scream of fear as the Ghoule collapsed to the ground, neither of his legs working. Before the beast could attempt to rise, Klines drove his steel into the Ghoule's lower back, giving his sword a twist for good measure.

The Blademaster then had turned his attention back to the Ghoules that his soldiers had trapped, ready to assist if needed, instead spending more time offering support and guidance, knowing that these combats were exceedingly valuable to his soldiers. What he and his men learned could be shared with the rest of the Royal Guard, thereby improving the skills of all. And that was his goal, because the more skilled his soldiers were, the more likely they were to survive the battles to come.

In Kevan's opinion the fight seemed to be going well, almost all of the Ghoules dead or dying but for a few, and they wouldn't last for much longer. Those beasts still alive now faced overwhelming odds, the soldiers trapping them with their long spears, one man lunging forward first, a soldier on the other side taking advantage of the attack when the Ghoule tried to avoid the cut.

It was an excellent strategy and one that the Battersea Guard had employed effectively when combating the Ghoules. Even so, nothing ever went exactly to plan during a fight, and the unexpected expectedly occurred.

One of the Ghoules, already bleeding badly from a handful of wounds, feinted to the right before one of the soldiers could stab his spear into the beast's flesh. Before one of the soldiers on the other side could make use of the opening, the Ghoule leapt over the circle of soldiers and sprinted right at Noorsin, hoping to kill her so that the two Elders could turn their focus onto the soldiers who were slaughtering his brethren. The beast's clawed feet dug up the long grass as the creature closed the distance to the Magus at an impossibly fast pace.

Kevan took a handful of steps forward and to the left so that he could put some space between him and Noorsin and place himself right in front of the charging Ghoule. The Ghoule howled with pleasure as he saw Kevan get in his way, the beast lowering his spear so that he could impale him and then take Noorsin from behind.

Most sane people would wet their pants if a Ghoule sprinted toward them, spear lowered for the killing blow. Kevan wasn't worried. Remembering his sparring session in the Pit with the Protector, he used the trick that Bryen had taught him, pivoting to the side and at the same time sliding his sword along the spear and then twisting with his wrist.

The unorthodox movement caught the Ghoule by surprise, almost causing the beast to drop his spear. Trying to prevent that from happening proved more difficult than the Ghoule anticipated since he was running at full speed, his attempts to regain control of his spear actually bringing the weapon between his legs and tripping him inadvertently, the beast crashing to the ground in an undignified heap.

Kevan never let the Ghoule rise again, driving the point of his sword into the back of the beast's neck. The Ghoule quivered briefly, then lay still.

Kevan congratulated himself on his victory, but it was short-lived. He was now facing Noorsin, and he could see the fear in her eyes. Not because of the two Elders who she was continuing to battle. She was more than a match for the servants of the Ghoule Overlord.

Rather, her fear came from the fact that another Ghoule had jumped over the soldiers trying to kill the beast, following the example of the Ghoule who Kevan had just eliminated. This second Ghoule had approached unseen and was about to drive his spear into Kevan's back.

The Duke sensed the looming presence behind him, and he realized with a cold terror that he had no chance to turn around and defend himself in time. That belief was confirmed for him by how Noorsin's eyes widened with fright.

At the beginning of the fight, Noorsin had encircled the two Elders with a shield made of the Talent, fearing that the two would be stronger than she was and that they'd be able to break through the shimmering barrier with ease. That had not proven to be the case as the two Elders battered the barricade that had taken them out of the fight with little effect. Now the two beasts were spending more time screaming in rage at their unfortunate situation than seeking to destroy the power that held them, though their circumstances were about to change quickly.

Noorsin couldn't contain the two Elders and engage with the Ghoules at the same time. Now she had to choose.

It was an easy decision to make. Allowing the barrier that she had constructed to dissolve, Noorsin came to Kevan's rescue just in time, the charging Ghoule's spear shattering as it slammed into the magical shield that she placed around Kevan right before the weapon's steel tip took him in the back.

The Ghoule stumbled to the ground, and Noorsin realized that she did not have to worry about that beast any longer. The Blademaster had arrived, skewering the Ghoule with his sword.

She immediately turned back toward the two Elders, who, now free of their temporary prison, shot shards of Dark Magic straight toward her. Realizing that she had no time, she did to herself and Kevan what she had done to the Ghoules, a shield of the Talent taking shape around them.

The Curse struck her barrier with a thunderous force, swirling around it. When the Dark Magic finally dissipated the Elders stared in amazement. The Magus opposing them and the human with her still lived, their efforts failing to destroy the Talent that she had thrown up in her defense at the very last second.

The Elders howled again in frustration, then pulled in as much Dark Magic as they could, sending streams of the Curse from their staffs to crash again and again in a steady, deafening rhythm against the gleaming barrier, setting the ground rumbling.

The Curse whipped around the Magus and the human, seeking a way past the shield, the misty black spinning faster and faster until finally, unable to penetrate the barricade, the Curse slowly dissolved, the two Elders unable to maintain control over so much of their evil power for long. What they saw when the Curse cleared filled them with an unfamiliar and uncomfortable dread.

Noorsin stood within the dome of energy, her hands held down to her side. She stared at the two Elders with a wolfish grin. Then the shield blinked out, only a few dozen feet separating her from the beasts who had failed to kill her. The beasts who had demonstrated that combined they didn't have the strength to challenge her.

With the rest of the Ghoule pack eliminated, she was going to give them one more lesson. Right now. With an undeniable finality.

Raising her hands to the sky, the air filled with a static electricity, the charge surrounding her prickling her skin. In her last combat Tetric had defeated her in the library of the Broken Citadel. She had promised herself that would not happen again. That she would never be defeated by a practitioner of the Curse again.

Taking a page from Rafia's book, Noorsin whipped her hands toward the ground. For a split second there was nothing but silence. Then two bolts of lightning shot down from the sky, obliterating the two Elders and leaving nothing but a few scattered ashes to swirl in the light breeze that swept across the plain.

Kevan watched Noorsin employ the Talent against the two Elders, awestruck. He knew the power that she facilitated, remembering how she had protected him against Tetric until the very end of that fight. How she had just protected him. But what she did now ... it was truly impressive.

This was a side of Noorsin that Kevan had never seen. She was still calm. Still collected. Just as she always was.

Yet there was also a fire in her eyes now. A simmering but controlled anger. Her power was undeniable.

He had known that Noorsin was a formidable woman before this. He just had never truly known how formidable until this very second.

"Thank you for your help, Blademaster," said Noorsin, finally releasing her hold on the Talent now that she was certain that all the Elders and Ghoules were well and truly dead. "We would not have survived without you. How did you know?"

"Actually, I didn't," he replied, "until I was almost back to the sentries. Something just didn't feel right. I ran into some of the scouts who had just returned, and they reported that they had found no game in the direction that you and Duke Winborne had gone. That didn't add up based on what we've seen since leaving Tintagel, so I pulled together a few squads and decided to explore the anomaly a bit further. Apparently, my assumption was correct and my concern was justified."

"I'm glad you followed your instincts," replied Kevan, nodding to the Blademaster in thanks.

"So am I," said Klines, who nodded to the Duke and then headed toward his soldiers to check on their well-being.

A half dozen members of the Royal Guard wouldn't be rising from the long grass, and several more were badly wounded. For all of the soldiers who Klines had rushed into the fray, it had been their first time fighting the Ghoules, and for a few it would be their last.

"Thank you, Noorsin," said Kevan. "If not for you, I'd be where that Ghoule is, face down in the dirt." He motioned toward the beast that the Blademaster had killed after Noorsin had prevented him from stabbing Kevan in the back.

"You can thank me later."

"You have something in mind?" Kevan asked.

Noorsin's eyes flashed. "That I do."

Kevan nodded knowingly, then he grinned. "Duty carries a heavy responsibility, but I will endeavor to meet it."

24

SCOUTING FOR GHOULES

"Should we head back?" asked Lycia.

Night was falling, and the Dark Forest, murky to begin with, was becoming much more difficult to navigate. The massive heart trees were fading into the background, the roots that curled around the forest floor resembling huge sea serpents that twisted off into the gloom.

"Probably a good idea," said Davin. "The last quarter hour I've spent more time tripping than actually walking." He called back over his shoulder to the third person in their small group, though in a quiet voice because he understood how the slightest sound could travel a great distance within the wood. "Can't you do something about that? I mean, you are a Magus, so Rafia and Sirius must have taught you at least how to craft a magical light that would help us steer through this jumble."

"I could, yes," Bryen replied, his grin evident in his voice. "But if I did ..."

"I know, I know," interrupted Davin. "The light would ruin our night vision. And if anything was out there tracking us," continued the gladiator as he motioned to the surrounding trees, "and I have no doubt that there likely is, we would be placing a very large target on our backs. We've been through it before. I just like to ..."

"Complain," Bryen finished for him.

"You won't craft a light, but you will put words in my mouth. Not very helpful. Not very helpful at all."

"Don't forget that if there's an Elder about the beast could sense Bryen using the Talent and follow the trail right to us."

"I didn't forget, Lycia. I just didn't feel the need to offer a full, expansive explanation as appears to be the case with you."

"Seemed like you did," Lycia pushed.

"I didn't, Lycia," Davin confirmed with a sigh, realizing that he and his sister were once again about to tread the path that was so irritatingly familiar to them. "Leave off."

"If you know all this, then why do you keep asking?"

"Because I'm tired of stubbing my toe."

"For someone who used to terrorize the Pit, having earned the nickname the Crimson Giant no less, sometimes I think that you're just a big baby," challenged Lycia, having no doubt that her words would have their intended effect.

Before Davin could reply, his sister's needle striking true and setting his temper to a slow simmer, Bryen stepped in.

"Do you two ever stop arguing? You've been doing nothing but since you first walked into the Colosseum."

"Do you even need to ask the question?" suggested Lycia with a suppressed laugh. "Only when we're fighting someone else," grumbled Davin. "Still, should we head back? I am getting tired of stubbing my toe."

"Let's go just a bit farther," suggested Bryen.

"Do you sense something?" asked Lycia.

The Blood Company had instituted Declan's more

aggressive approach just a few days before, the gladiators extending their patrols farther out as they worked their way through the Dark Forest, not only to scout the way ahead, but also to seek any Ghoules who might cross their path and eliminate them. Rafia, Sirius, Aislinn, and Bryen had aided in that task, using the Talent to search around them on a regular basis so that the gladiators knew where they were going and what they could expect when they got there.

So far, the new strategy had worked well. At least one Ghoule pack and several scouts had been removed as pieces from the board with no loss of life for the Blood Company, a few cuts and slashes the only price paid by the gladiators.

When they began, Lycia and some of the others hadn't trusted what Bryen and the other Magii could do with the Talent to assist them in their efforts. Once they received a good explanation, and they saw how it benefited them with their own eyes, they came to appreciate the utility of the Magii's unique ability.

"Nothing close," replied Bryen. "They're out there, though, and remember that they can move fast."

"We should go after them," suggested Lycia, always ready for a fight, even though in the weakening light they were focusing more on where they were placing their feet than on what might be lurking in the woods around them.

"I don't want Davin to keep stubbing his toe," Bryen replied with a straight face that quickly dissolved into an impudent grin. "It sounds quite painful, almost a debilitating injury, in fact."

"Hey, now that's not fair," demanded Davin, turning to face Bryen. Upon seeing his smirk, Davin smiled as well, realizing that his friend was baiting him.

"You really can be a pain sometimes, you know that?"

"So I've been told," said Bryen. "Many times. And many more to come I'm certain."

"You've got that right," confirmed Davin.

"Are we going to go after them or not?" Lycia asked, her own irritation growing. She had been out on several patrols in the last few days and had not yet come across a Ghoule. She was getting antsy. She wanted a fight.

"We don't have to," answered Bryen. "I'll let you know when they're almost on us."

Davin nodded, understanding. The Ghoules were coming to them. The three gladiators continued to walk among the heart trees, though now Lycia and Davin were paying more attention to what was around them. They knew that Bryen would give them warning, but their many years in the Pit had ingrained within them certain habits that were not easily ignored. First and foremost, as Declan had knocked into their skulls time after time, was to always know the battlefield before the battle began.

"I've been hearing stories of your exploits at the Battle of the Horseshoe," said Davin, his eyes sweeping through the encroaching darkness, looking for any sign of motion, knowing that a moving shadow likely would be the only giveaway, if there was even that, before the Ghoules attacked.

"You've been spending too much time talking to Sirius. You can't believe half of what he says."

"I need to talk to someone. You know that. I wasn't made for the silence that you seem to enjoy so much, and Lycia and I tend to rub each other the wrong way if we spend too much time together."

"I hadn't noticed," Bryen offered sarcastically.

"Besides, Sirius is a good storyteller," Davin continued,

ignoring Bryen. "He always livens things up. He has a knack for making everything sound exciting."

"Particularly when he can make himself the center of attention," offered Bryen.

"That's to be expected," Davin acknowledged. "All good storytellers do that. How much time do we have?"

Bryen took hold of the Talent, extending his senses for several leagues around them. All was as it should be, nothing out of the ordinary, except for one spot in the darkening wood. A small cloud blacker than the night approached, the sickening stench of evil suggesting that an Elder was attempting to shield the beasts until they reached their prey.

"A quarter hour," Bryen replied. "Maybe a little bit less than that."

"Then we need to talk about something until the beasts appear."

"We could just keep our own counsel and enjoy the quiet of the wood," suggested Lycia, her voice hopeful though strangely resigned at the same time. She already knew how her brother was going to respond.

"We could, but that would be really boring. Nice try, Lycia."

"It was worth a shot."

"Now back to the Battle of the Horseshoe. Tell us about it."

"There isn't much to tell."

"Isn't much to tell?" Davin scoffed. "You fought and killed almost a thousand Ghoules and several dozen Elders. It was the biggest battle against the beasts from the Lost Land since the First Ghoule War."

"Sirius was exaggerating."

"Of course he was," agreed Davin. "As I said, that's what

all good storytellers do. He also said that you led a mounted charge to catch the Ghoules in a vise. Then you used the Talent to help him finish off the Elders. Chopping off heads, burning through chests with a scorching power. There's a lot to talk about."

"It was only several hundred Ghoules and about a dozen Elders," Bryen corrected.

"Maybe so. Nevertheless, several hundred Ghoules and a dozen Elders. It was still the largest battle against the beasts since the First Ghoule War."

"And still not much to tell. The Battersea Guard beat them. I was just along for the ride." Bryen really didn't want to share what had occurred during the clash. "Besides, it sounds like you've already heard it all from Sirius."

"Still not much to tell?" challenged Davin. "You cleared the Southern Marches of Ghoules for a time. A remarkable feat." Davin snorted in fake disgust. "You were like this in the Pit as well. Never wanting to be the center of attention. Never sharing stories. It's almost like you want people to think that you're boring."

"I am boring."

"You are far from boring," countered Davin, allowing Bryen's recalcitrance to frustrate him. "You're the Volkun!"

"Only when I have to be."

"You are always the Volkun," said Davin. "And what does that even mean? It makes no sense."

"It makes perfect sense," interrupted Lycia.

"Then could you at least explain since Bryen doesn't seem to want to?"

"The Volkun isn't who Bryen really is. It's someone he had to become so that he could survive in the Pit, just as you became the Crimson Giant and I became the Crimson Devil. He will be the Volkun if there's a need, but only if there's a need. Allowing the Volkun to become more of him than it already is could mean that over time he loses who he really is. He loses himself."

"Thank you, Lycia," said Bryen, nodding. She nodded to Bryen in turn, giving him a quick smile, happy to help.

Davin grumbled in disgust. All he had wanted was a story, just a story to pass the time, yet these two refused to accommodate him, simply adding to his frustration. He promised himself that he would seek out Sirius again tonight and see if he could pull out any more interesting details from the battle that the Magus may have forgotten to share the last time they spoke.

"At least tell us what we can expect when the Ghoules arrive," Davin said, not one to be put off entirely. "Neither of us have had the chance to fight the beasts yet, and we'd like to know what to expect."

Lycia perked up at the request. Finally, her brother was touching upon a useful topic.

"I'm sure that you've already spoken with the gladiators who have come up against the beasts."

"I did," confirmed Davin.

"What did they say?"

"Big. Strong. Aggressive. Armor on the shoulders, shins, thighs, and forearms. They can slice you with their steel or their claws. Just as interested in eating you as killing you. Not a shred of mercy in them."

"You got it all except for one other quality."

"What would that be?"

"Do you remember the giant scorpion that you and Lycia fought in the Pit? It was your first combat."

"How could I forget?" grimaced Davin. "It was the fastest animal we ever had to fight. Why Beluchmel made us do it the first time we fought in the Colosseum, I still don't know."

"Beluchmel did it because he could, and he knew that doing so would anger Declan," said Bryen. "So all the better for him."

"Doesn't take much to anger Declan," chimed in Lycia.

"You're right about that," agreed Bryen, who quickly returned to the topic that Davin had raised, knowing that time was running short. "When we face the Ghoules it will be a similar though more difficult experience as when you fought the giant scorpion. A Ghoule is faster than a giant scorpion with just as sharp a sting."

"Any suggestions, then?" asked Lycia. She had heard much the same as Davin, and she wanted to be thorough, understanding that any additional information, no matter how small, no matter how potentially innocuous, could be the difference between life and death.

"Nothing you don't already know," said Bryen. "My only suggestion would be to anticipate as much as you can."

"Anticipate?" asked Davin. "Could you clarify?"

"Yes, anticipate. Try to assume where their blade or claw will be, because if you don't, they might get you before you get them."

"That sounds kind of ominous."

"I'm just sharing what I learned. And, if at all possible, dictate the combat. Make the beast respond to you instead of the other way around. The Ghoules are not used to fighting on the defensive during a combat. Making them do so can throw them off."

Lycia nodded her thanks, allowing what Bryen had just said to sink in. She began to think about how she might put his advice into action.

"Wonderful," said Davin with a disgusted shake of his head. "Another challenge. I can't wait."

"Don't you want the challenge?"

"After fighting so long in the Pit, I'm done with challenges. I'd prefer an easy fight for a change."

"Hoping doesn't make it real," said Bryen.

"That sounds like something Declan would say," nodded Davin.

"It does, but it's not. I picked it up from Sirius instead."

"What was it like with him and Rafia?" asked Davin, seeking to keep the conversation going now that Bryen seemed willing to talk more than he had earlier. "Sirius can be quite engaging when he wants to be. I can't get a feel for Rafia. She appears to be quite serious, almost intimidating, in fact."

"That's about right for Rafia," confirmed Bryen. "She does have a good sense of humor, though she tends to keep it to herself. And if you show that you're not frightened of her, even challenge her once in a while, she'll respect you."

"Thanks for the advice, though I think that I'll just stay away from her," said Davin. "It's safer that way, her being a Magus and all."

Bryen shrugged, as if to say that was his decision to make though he didn't necessarily agree with it.

"With Rafia, you know what you're getting. There's little in the way of deception. With Sirius, it's harder to tell," observed Lycia.

"What do you mean?" asked Davin.

"Lycia is right," agreed Bryen. "Sirius comes across as a somewhat confused pedagogue who likes to tell stories and hear the sound of his own voice. Remember, he's the Master of the Magii. He's in that position for a reason. He's also one of the most powerful Magii in Caledonia, and when he gets angry, the real Sirius will come out. That can be a frightening sight."

"I'll try not to make him angry," responded Davin.

"A good decision."

"So not a lot of fun when you were with them?"

"Fun, no," said Bryen. "Particularly when those two got going. Bickering all the time just like they were earlier today, even worse than the arguments that you two get into so frequently. Your guess is as good as mine as to how they could keep it up for so long, because I found it all exhausting. Still, I have learned quite a bit from them regarding how to employ the Talent. I've also learned something critically important."

"What's that?"

"Don't get on a Magus' bad side if you can avoid it."

"Sage advice, thank you," said Davin. "Although I wasn't planning on doing that."

"Good decision, because with those two it doesn't take much. Their tempers can get the better of them at times. Just be careful with Sirius. If his eyes look as if they're suddenly filled with a clarity that's usually not there, watch out. Better yet, leave him be."

"I'll keep that in mind," promised Davin, although he had to admit that he was slightly intrigued. What did an angry Magus really look like? That was something that as dangerous as it sounded he wanted to see for himself.

"What went on between you and the Lady of the Southern Marches?" Lycia asked from out of the blue.

Bryen didn't reply immediately, continuing to focus on the roots obstructing the forest floor.

Davin stubbed his toe again. This time he ignored the pain that shot up his foot, instead staring intently at Bryen, curious as to how his friend would respond.

"She was my charge. I protected her."

"Obviously," she replied with just a touch of exasperation. "You were her Protector."

"Exactly so," confirmed Bryen. "There wasn't much else to it."

"Are you trying to be difficult?" she demanded.

"No more than usual."

"Why do I even put up with you?" she wondered, a touch of aggravation seeping into her voice.

"My winning smile and personality," Bryen offered with a grin and a wink.

Lycia found it extremely difficult not to smile at Bryen's remark. Why did he have this unique ability to do this to her? She wanted to be angry with him, yet all he needed to do was give her a look or say a few words, and he would defuse the tension that built up inside her.

"No, definitely not that," Lycia finally said when she was certain that she wasn't going to laugh. "I'm not going to let this go. There's more between you and Aislinn Winborne than just the fact that you were her slave."

"Protector," corrected Davin, trying to be helpful, though his efforts only earned him a dirty look from his sister.

"Protector. Slave. Is there really any difference?"

"Well, they're clearly very different words with very different connotations ..."

"Davin, you're not helping," interrupted Lycia. "Feel free to join the conversation when you have something useful to offer."

"I was just saying that ..."

"Davin." Lycia stopped walking and turned back toward her brother, who had no choice but to stop otherwise he would have run into her, which then required Bryen to stop as well. After giving her brother a pointed look that resulted in him raising his arms in submission, she turned her attention back to Bryen. "Regardless of the words used, a Protector is a slave and a slave is a Protector. You know it. You lived it."

"You're right, although to clarify, Aislinn didn't enslave me. Her father did."

"Be that as it may," Lycia said through gritted teeth, "you answered to her. You were with her all the time."

"Being with the Lady of the Southern Marches," began Davin, the statement having piqued his curiosity, "what did that really entail ..." Davin immediately stopped talking when he saw the murderous look that his sister gave him.

"Yes, although that was unavoidable," said Bryen, motioning to the silver collar he still wore around his neck. He should have expected that Davin's mind would wander in the direction that it did, and that was information that his friend didn't need. "With the collar I had no choice ..."

"I know how the collar works, Bryen. You don't need to explain it to me. Something happened between you and Aislinn Winborne, and it had nothing to do with the collar. It's written all over your face when you two are together."

Bryen stared as Lycia for several heartbeats, glad that the falling darkness prevented her from seeing the blush that he felt spreading across his cheeks. Then he shrugged his shoulders again.

"I don't really know what happened," replied Bryen, having a difficult time explaining, his emotions a mess, not prepared to have this conversation with her, even though he knew that he couldn't avoid it for much longer.

Lycia stared at him with an expression that demonstrated that she wasn't convinced by his response. Every so often, she caught the white spark in the back of his eyes in the fading light. Bryen had explained what it meant. Even so, seeing such an obvious reminder of the power that he wielded still unsettled her.

"You were fairly dense about these matters in the gladiators' compound," Lycia said finally. "I guess not too much has changed since then."

"What are you doing with Jerad?" asked Davin, seeking to change the topic of conversation as it was beginning to make him uncomfortable. And as was his practice, when faced with situations that were making him uncomfortable, he tried to make his sister uncomfortable in his stead.

Davin realized that he probably should have thought about it a bit more before trying to turn the focus to Lycia. He had caught the pained expression that had crossed Bryen's face, and he wanted to help his friend. He recognized now that he may have made a mistake when he saw his sister's entire body become tense. Clearly, he had struck a nerve. Too late now, though.

"What are you talking about?"

"You know exactly what I'm talking about," replied Davin, thinking that if he stayed on the offensive, it would prevent Lycia from changing the focus to him.

"You have no clue what you're ..."

"Lycia, it's obvious," continued Davin. "The looks you give him. The smiles. As soon as he demonstrated an interest in you, you started to play him."

"I was not playing him," protested Lycia, although her words sounded slightly hollow in her own ears.

"Then what are you doing?"

Lycia was about to defend herself, a natural reaction when she argued with her brother. However, she didn't know what to say. What was she doing with Jerad? Because she had already told him in no uncertain terms that he needed to look elsewhere for someone to return his affections, starting with the Corporal of the Battersea Guard.

"I don't know what I'm doing," she admitted. "I like him, all right. Or maybe it's the attention that he gives me. It's nice to be the object of someone's affections. Be that as it may, I've kept him at a distance. There's someone else with a stronger claim on him, and I don't want to get in the way of that. He deserves better than what I can give him right now, and I've told him as much."

"You think that Jerad could do better than you?" asked Bryen.

"That's what I just said," she snapped through gritted teeth, her irritation rising again because clearly Bryen had no clue that Jerad and Lycia had been dancing around one another for quite some time.

Lycia was going to say more. Instead, she held back. She didn't want to make things any more awkward than they already were. She didn't want to have the conversation that she knew that she needed to have with Bryen. She wasn't ready for it, especially not with Davin there. In fact, she wasn't even sure that she wanted to have the conversation at all.

"Sorry, Lycia," said Bryen. "I wasn't trying to make you angry. That wasn't my intention."

Bryen then gave her another grin, which just like the other one helped to ease some of the anxiety that she was feeling. Then Bryen's eyes and expression changed, his temporary levity replaced by his normal seriousness.

Davin was about to offer his thoughts when a hand signal from Bryen that he almost missed stopped him, silence falling among the three friends. Bryen issued a series of additional instructions, his fingers flashing furiously.

Davin and Lycia moved quickly to obey. Davin stepped

away from Bryen, holding onto his spear with two hands now, and turned in the direction that Bryen nodded toward. Lycia stepped several feet behind the two, drawing her preferred blades from the scabbards across her back.

No one moved. No one made a sound. Their breathing slowed. Their senses sharpened. It was just as if they were about to walk out into the Pit for a combat, yet here a dark loam with huge tree roots disturbing the soil had replaced the white sand.

The three friends didn't have long to wait. Less than a minute, in fact. Bryen detected it first, then Davin and Lycia. A flash of movement to their front that they could barely see in the smothering gloom. Then another. Followed by two more.

Bryen communicated again with Davin and Lycia, his fingers flicking a message that made them both grasp the hilts of their weapons just a little bit tighter. Without a word, Bryen launched himself from the root he was standing on, slashing with the Spear of the Magii toward the neck of the Ghoule who had just glided into the small clearing that he, Davin, and Lycia had been waiting in.

The Ghoule was fast, faster than Bryen had expected truth be told. The beast responded instinctively to the movement that he had sensed off to his side, raising his spear just in time to catch Bryen's steel. The Ghoule's only mistake was to assume that that was his opponent's real attack and not a feint.

Before the Ghoule could open his maw to shriek a challenge, the other blade on Bryen's spear sliced across his throat, the Ghoule dropping his weapon and falling to his knees, his sharp claws going to the wound that spilled his life onto the roots of the heart trees.

For just a moment, the other Ghoules stared in shock as

their leader collapsed to the ground with barely a sound. Low growls then emanated from all three, the Ghoule closest to Bryen digging his clawed feet into the root he was standing on to propel himself toward the human who so foolishly chose to fight rather than run or hide.

Bryen turned to face the beast. He did so not to fight the Ghoule. Rather, he just wanted to keep the creature's attention focused on him.

Before the Ghoule could attack, the tip of a long spear slid into and then through the beast's neck, Davin having charged forward on silent feet to stab the creature with fatal precision. The Ghoule instantly became a dead weight, and Davin tried to pull the spear free with a sharp tug.

Much to his dismay, Davin realized that the steel was stuck in the creature's vertebrae. There was no easy way to pull it out, and certainly not in time to defend against the Ghoule who was flying through the air toward him now, the beast using the dead Ghoule's attack to mask his own.

Davin released his hold on the haft of his spear, the dead Ghoule falling to the dirt to join his compatriot. He reached for the long dagger on his belt, but he realized with a slight tinge of nausea rising in his throat that he wouldn't be able to pull the blade free in time to block the sword that was streaking toward his own neck.

For just a split second, Davin considered the whole situation to be quite unfair. To kill his first Ghoule and then be killed by another seconds after that just wasn't right. Of course, some would argue that there was a certain kind of sick symmetry to it all, and that concept strangely appealed to him.

His thoughts were pulled back to the present when Davin heard a grunt and then a crash, the Ghoule who had been about to take his head soaring backward through the air, his sword spinning away into the darkness. The beast landed heavily against the trunk of a heart tree and remained there, the hilts of two swords protruding from the Ghoule's chest and pinning the beast to the bark.

"That was one of your better throws, Lycia," said Davin, a sigh of relief escaping him.

"I thought so myself," she replied. "A good thing that I've been practicing."

"A good thing, indeed," he agreed. "My thanks."

The brother and sister then turned their attention toward the last Ghoule standing.

The creature watched unmoving, astounded by what he had just witnessed. Humans were soft creatures. Easily killed. They were no more than food. The Elders had told the Ghoules so, and the Elders never lied. How could these humans have done this? In just a few heartbeats, three of his fellow scouts were dead. And now he stood alone against these humans who had just accomplished what should have been impossible.

Realizing that these humans were more dangerous than he possibly could have imagined, the remaining Ghoule decided that there was only one course of action that made sense. He could run and report what he had seen or fight. Better to fight. Better to kill these three humans. He would earn his bone knife today if he was fast enough, and then he could rise in the eyes of the Elders for killing the three humans who had somehow killed three fellow Ghoules.

Pleased by his decision, ready to put his plan into motion, he realized that he was no longer alone on the root that arced well above the forest floor. The human who had killed his leader stood right in front of him, no more than a foot away, his dead eyes staring up into his own. With a grunt, the Ghoule doubled over as he felt the steel of a long dagger slide into his chest and then cut downwards toward his belly, the sensation sending waves of debilitating torment throughout his body.

"You should never have come through the Weir," the tall human said, his white hair his only easily seen feature in the gloom. "You die now because of that decision. You die now because you don't belong here. This is not your land."

"You are right," said the Ghoule in his guttural language, struggling to get the words out because of the pain of his wound. "It is not our land. Not yet. But it will be soon. We will take your land, and we will feed on you."

"It will never be your land," said the human with a sharpness and certainty that almost made the dying Ghoule believe him.

Before the beast could respond, the light left his eyes, and he slid back off the dagger to fall from the twisting root to the black dirt of the Dark Forest.

"How did you do that?" asked Lycia, who had come to stand right below Bryen, not too far away from the shadowy heap that was the Ghoule her friend had just dispatched so easily.

"How did I do what?" asked Bryen in some confusion.

"You spoke to the Ghoule."

"So?"

"You spoke to the Ghoule in his language," Davin clarified.

"I did?" asked Bryen, his confusion obvious on his face.

"You did," Davin confirmed.

"How did you do it?" asked Lycia.

"I didn't even know that I was doing it."

"That's not an answer to my question," said Lycia, who scampered over the tree roots and with one hard tug followed by another pulled her blades from the chest of the dead Ghoule, the creature sliding down the tree trunk to the ground in a tangle of arms and legs. When she turned back around, she saw that her brother had retrieved his spear from the Ghoule's neck. "I didn't ask if you knew that you were speaking to the Ghoule in the beast's language. I asked how you were able to do that. No human can speak the Ghoule language, no human should be able to, yet you can."

"Are you sure you heard me correctly?"

"Bryen!" Lycia said sharply. She refused to be put off by his attempt to avoid her question.

Bryen looked at Lycia sheepishly as Davin joined them. The expression on his face suggested that he was just as curious about his newfound ability as his sister was. How much should he reveal? His friends had learned just recently that he was a Magus, that he could use the Talent. That was a big adjustment to their relationship. So perhaps now was not the best time to reveal all that had happened since he had left the Pit.

"When I was at the Aeyrie ..."

"Where you became a Magus?" asked Davin, his interruption earning him an angry look from his sister.

"Yes, when I became a Magus at the Aeyrie, it didn't go exactly as planned."

"What do you mean by that?" asked Lycia, her eyes narrowing.

"I didn't go to the Aeyrie to become a Magus," he said. "I did become one, though that wasn't the plan. While Aislinn was passing the Test to become a Magus, we were attacked by Elders and Ghoules. I was wounded ..."

"We know all that," said Lycia, her impatience getting the better of her. "You were wounded by one of the Elders and Sirius had no choice but to put you through the Test to become a Magus. It wasn't enough to heal you. Sirius needed the Seventh Stone to do that, and as a result you are the Seventh Stone now ..."

Lycia stopped herself midsentence. "The Seventh Stone," she whispered. She was beginning to understand. The Seventh Stone had done more to Bryen than just allow him to heal himself.

"The Seventh Stone," Bryen confirmed with a nod. "Ever since it became a part of me, I've been able to understand the Ghoules, and apparently I can speak their language as well. It's not me, it's the Seventh Stone."

"It is you," said Davin. "You are the Seventh Stone."

"You're not helping, Davin," said Lycia, seemingly deep in thought. She wondered if Bryen had picked up any other unique abilities as a result of his joining with the Seventh Stone.

"I am helping," Davin grumbled in irritation, shaking his head. Why was Lycia worried about Bryen being able to speak and understand the Ghoule language? It wasn't going to hurt him. At least he didn't think that it would. It was a good skill to have now that they were fighting the Ghoules. It would give them an insight that they hadn't had before.

Silence once again descended over the three, all of them lost in thought. As Lycia continued to stare at Bryen, Davin took stock of his first combat against a Ghoule, pleased with the result. Still, he couldn't take these new enemies for granted. Bryen had been right. They were fast. Faster than the giant scorpion just as he had said. If not for his sister, he'd be lying dead on the ground right now with the Ghoules. He would need to be more careful during his next combat to avoid such a fate.

Davin was about to ask Bryen if he had any suggestions on how he could improve his performance against the Ghoules when he caught the look on Lycia's face and then

Bryen's corresponding nod. Slowly, Davin turned back around.

He watched more of the beasts emerge from between the heart trees and out of the gloom. The Ghoules came to a stop in a semicircle. They hadn't been tracking just scouts as they had thought. They had been tracking an entire pack and three Elders to boot. Wonderful. Just wonderful. Then Davin heard the maxim that he had heard so many times before, which helped him to hone his concentration in an instant. Because the real fight was about to begin.

"Death doesn't choose us," Bryen began.

"We choose our death," finished Lycia and Davin.

They knew that if they didn't kill the Ghoules, the Ghoules would be feasting on them that evening. The anticipation, the excitement, the fear of the combat about to start vanished in that certain knowledge. It was exhilarating and terrifying both at the same time.

Several of the Ghoules stared at them in obvious hunger, a few others with hatred as they identified the remains of their scouts scattered around the small clearing that had served as the site of the initial skirmish and would now become a larger battlefield. Once again, Bryen gained a step on the beasts, putting his own hard-won experience of fighting the Ghoules to use.

Reaching for the Talent, the two blades on the ends of the Spear of the Magii began to glow brightly, setting the small clearing alight. He then used his weapon as his focal point so that he could pull on more of the Talent than he could without the Giant-crafted weapon, shafts of blazing energy streaking from the tips of the blades toward the Elders.

The servants of the Ghoule Overlord responded immediately, joining their power together to create a shield that protected them from Bryen's assault. That was fine with him. His goal was to keep the Elders busy. And he did that with a will as he spun the Spear of the Magii in front of him faster and faster, the bolts of light bursting from the blades so swiftly that they soon appeared to be two continuous streams of energy. Now that Bryen had the Elders' full attention, it would be up to Davin and Lycia to challenge the Ghoules.

Following Bryen's example, the brother and sister attacked with a ferocity that was reminiscent of their time on the white sand. They were often paired when fighting in the Pit, and they put that experience into play now as they sought to make use of the fact that the combat between Bryen and the Elders forced the Ghoules to shield their eyes with their claws as the Talent struck the shield of Dark Magic with a frightening force.

Davin started with the Ghoule closest to the Elders, the beast no more than a few feet from the shield that flickered incessantly, the Elders already struggling to maintain control of their power under Bryen's onslaught. The Ghoule dodged out of the way of Davin's first lunge, having seen the steel spearpoint coming at him from the side. Unluckily for the Ghoule, Davin didn't do what the beast anticipated that he would do next.

Rather than pull back and lunge again, Davin stepped into the Ghoule, kicking forward with his right leg, his boot crashing into the beast's left leg and bending it backwards with a sickening crunch, the ligaments torn and the kneecap shattered. The beast fell to his good knee, Davin already standing above him, using the haft of his spear to knock the beast to the ground. Before the Ghoule could push himself back up, Davin plunged his spear into the back of the Ghoule's neck, severing his spine.

The Ghoule right next to the fallen beast tried to exploit the opportunity, targeting Davin's exposed back with his spear. The beast failed to take Lycia into account, who with two economical slashes across the creature's throat, ensured that he would bleed out in less than a minute.

Lycia immediately turned toward the Ghoule who was closest to her, the beast already bringing his sword down in a vicious stroke that would split her in two from head to toe. She didn't even worry about it, knowing that Davin would be there in time.

And he was, holding his spear with both hands above her head, parrying the blow, which gave Lycia the blink of an eye that she needed to thrust both of her swords into the shocked Ghoule's groin and gut.

Leaving the wounded Ghoule for dead, Lycia whipped the sword in her right hand toward another Ghoule's hip. The beast caught the strike with his spear, although he wasn't fast enough to stop Lycia from cutting across his other hip with the blade in her left hand.

Enraged by the wound, the Ghoule reared up, his anger driving him forward as he took a step toward Lycia.

He didn't get any farther as a steel spearpoint slammed through his teeth and into the back of his throat. Davin held the beast there for just a moment, giving Lycia a few seconds to drive her steel blades into his heart, before he ripped the steel free.

Davin and Lycia then stepped back, taking stock of what they had accomplished in less than a minute. Four Ghoules down, never to rise again. Not bad. But four Ghoules still left to fight.

The Ghoules spread out, seeking to come at them from the four points of the compass. Davin and Lycia immediately settled back to back.

They were surrounded.

It didn't bother them in the least. They were comfortable with this situation. They had faced it countless times before in the gladiators' compound under Declan's close supervision.

This time, the twins allowed the Ghoules to make the first move, the two gladiators circling slowly just as the Ghoules moved around them in a larger circle. Lycia and Davin didn't have long to wait.

One of the Ghoules facing off against Lycia lunged forward with his spear, yet it was only a feint as he stopped his progress after just a few feet, expecting her to prepare to meet his attack, thereby giving the Ghoule to his right the chance to take her in the side.

It didn't work. Lycia had expected that they would employ such an obvious tactic, and she quickly turned it to her advantage.

Seeing that the first Ghoule who lunged at her had dug his claws into the soft earth after taking only a few steps, she ignored him, sprinting several steps toward the Ghoule who was now coming toward her from her side. Before the beast's spear sank into her flesh, she twisted her body and ducked beneath the lunge, her legs sliding across the ground and slamming into the Ghoule's legs, sending the beast head over heels to the turf.

Before the Ghoule could rise, Davin was there, driving his spear through the beast's heart. He then tore his weapon free from the dying Ghoule's chest, turning in the same motion and swinging the haft of his weapon with all his might. He caught the Ghoule who had been approaching him from behind across the shins, the creature tumbling to the ground.

Davin ignored the fallen beast, charging instead toward

the other Ghoule on his side of the clearing, the Ghoule never expecting such an aggressive approach from a human. That brief moment of surprise was all that Davin needed. He used the haft of his spear to knock the beast's sword from his claw, then drove the butt of his spear into his gut, knocking the breath from the Ghoule. When the beast doubled over, desperate for air, Davin rammed his spear through the back of the creature's head.

He then whipped around, wanting to aid his sister. He wasn't surprised to discover that she had been just as efficient with her kills as he had been.

When he had left the Ghoule that he had knocked to the ground lying there, Lycia had slipped in behind the beast, slicing across his throat with both blades from the inside out so that the Ghoule would never rise again. She had then returned her focus to the last Ghoule on her side of the clearing.

With all the other Ghoules dead or dying, she thought she caught a glimmer of fear in the beast's eyes. She didn't pay any attention to it, intent on her task. Wanting to end this combat as quickly as possible because of the danger presented by the Elders and her desire to help Bryen, she charged toward the Ghoule, blade in her right hand raised above her head.

The Ghoule responded by bringing his sword up to block the blow. He succeeded, catching the strike. Smirking at the thought of biting into the human, the Ghoule saw too late that he had made a terrible mistake.

Lycia slashed with the blade in her left hand, which sliced off the beast's forearm, the severed extremity dropping to the soft loam with the creature's hand still gripping the hilt of his sword. Before the beast could even scream in shock and pain, Lycia drove both blades through the

Ghoule's neck, a thick streak of black blood spurting from the wound as the creature collapsed to the forest floor.

Lycia immediately spun toward Davin, relieved to see that her brother was all right. She was frustrated as well, realizing that the fight with the Elders wasn't something that she or Davin could assist Bryen with as their friend continued his assault on the shield of Dark Magic.

The two streams of energy slammed into the barrier with a power that demanded that the Ghoules do nothing but defend themselves. They didn't have the strength to do anything else. Even so, the beasts were holding their own, maintaining their shield despite the tremendous effort required, and that was beginning to irritate Bryen.

So Bryen decided to employ a method that he had learned while fighting the Ghoules on the pier at Haven. Using the Spear of the Magii, he opened himself to the power of the Seventh Stone, which surged through him, scouring him clean with an almost painful heat.

He could sense the Curse within him, struggling as it always did to break free from the barrier that contained it. Before he had acquired the Spear, this endless demand by the Dark Magic would have terrified him. Not now, however. Now he exercised a level of mastery that he had never imagined that he could attain, and he put that hard-won skill to use.

Maintaining control over the two streams of the Talent shooting from the blades of his Spear, instead of seeking to break through the billowing shield of Dark Magic, Bryen adjusted his focus, connecting the two streams to the Curse. Then, using the potency of the Seventh Stone, he began to drain away the power that the three Elders were using to defend themselves.

It was a slow pull at first, the Elders not even noticing

what was happening. Once Bryen was certain that what he was doing was working as it should, the Curse flowing back into the Seventh Stone within him, that tainted energy pooling behind the barrier that kept the Dark Magic's corruption from harming him, he accelerated the flow, the streams of white shifting in color as a pitch black pulsed within them.

Bryen need only watch the expressions of the Elders to know that he was succeeding. At first, he saw looks of surprise, which quickly turned to shock as the shield began to weaken and then flash dangerously. Those expressions of shock turned to horror as the shield splintered with a resounding crack, the streams of energy that Bryen had been using immediately clamping onto the Elders instead.

In seconds, it was over. The Seventh Stone bled the Elders of the Dark Magic within them along with their spirits, leaving behind three withered husks. Satisfied that the skirmish had concluded, Bryen released his hold on the Talent, inordinately pleased that his friends had survived the fight unscathed.

Unable to restrain his curiosity, Davin walked over to the mummified Elders, even giving one a nudge with his boot. Davin jumped back quickly when that modest touch caused the dead Elder to disintegrate into a fine dust that slowly settled onto the dirt.

"You know, as I said, I always wanted to see what would happen when a Magus got angry."

"Was it what you expected?" asked Bryen.

Bryen had come to stand next to his friend, Lycia now on his other side. His use of so much of the Talent, and then using the Seventh Stone the way that he did, had tired him. But in a good way. It felt like he had put in an honest day's work.

Davin took a moment before responding, the image of what he had seen burned indelibly into his memory. He had watched in horror, although also with a touch of satisfaction, when the Elders slowly shriveled in upon themselves; however, what he had found even more terrifying was what he saw when he looked at Bryen.

His friend radiated a power that Davin couldn't even begin to comprehend, a power that frightened him in a way that he couldn't explain. Threads of energy had sparked off Bryen's hands, a glowing nimbus surrounding him. And his eyes. Davin, just like his sister, had noticed that every once in a while when he was looking at Bryen's eyes a white spark flashed behind them. When he was fighting the Elders, though, Bryen's eyes had turned completely white, as if that spark had expanded, flashing with the power that had consumed him.

"Yes and no," Davin replied carefully.

"What do you mean?" asked Lycia.

"I had expected it to be impressive, and it was."

"But?" prodded Lycia.

Davin shrugged, not sure how to say what he wanted to say next, then deciding that there was nothing for it but to simply spit it out.

"When I saw you fight in the Pit, when I saw the Volkun fight in the Pit, I always felt a shiver run up and down my spine. I never wanted to fight you on the white sand, and I'm glad I didn't, because you were more chilling than any of the beasts we ever had to fight, including the giant scorpion that Lycia and I started out with. But here, now, watching you do whatever you did to those Elders, that was the scariest thing I've ever seen. And I definitely don't need to see it again, because Bryen the Magus is much more terrifying than Bryen the Volkun."

"Thanks," replied Bryen, not really knowing what to say, "I think."

"You're welcome," replied Davin, "and I meant that as a compliment, just so there's no confusion between us."

"I wouldn't take it any other way," confirmed Bryen.

"Good," said Davin with a nod. "Now could we head back to camp? Watching Bryen's demonstration, I think I wet myself, and I'd like to change my breeches."

25

A MENACE

"That was impressive."

"Frightening as well," replied Sirius, both he and Rafia releasing their hold of the Talent at the same time.

The two Magii, during their search for threats within the Dark Forest, had caught the end of the clash between the three gladiators and the Ghoules and Elders.

"Bryen certainly has perfected his use of the Seventh Stone, at least with respect to his dueling with Elders," said Rafia. "He used the same approach against these beasts as when they attacked us on the pier at Haven."

Sirius nodded, agreeing with Rafia's comment and recalling that previous engagement. It was a good sign. Bryen learning to use the power offered to him by the Seventh Stone was critical if they were to have any chance at all of rebuilding the Weir. It was worrisome as well because a mistake would be deadly. It was something that Sirius didn't want to contemplate, yet he had no choice but to do so.

"Yes, Bryen truly is a menace," Sirius finally said, his

tone suggesting that he viewed that as a positive development.

"Hopefully he remains a menace just to the Ghoules and Elders," offered Rafia.

"So far, so good. Of course, hoping doesn't make it real."

"You know," said Rafia, "I thought we might be able to have at least one conversation when you didn't work in one of those sayings that you enjoy so much and repeat so often."

Sirius grinned. "That saying is right on target. It needed to be said."

"If you say so."

"I do," Sirius harrumphed, knowing that Rafia was trying to get a rise out of him and not wanting to give her the pleasure of that success. So he stayed on topic, which often was a challenge for him. "If the time comes when we must do something about Bryen, if the Curse gains control, if there's even the hint that the Curse is gaining control, then we will do what is necessary."

Rafia hated the finality of Sirius' tone. The coldness. She couldn't fault it, however. In this matter, they were of the same mind.

"But not yet," she clarified.

"No, not yet. And with any luck, never. Still, we will need to keep a close eye on him. Just in case."

"We will," promised Rafia. Understanding that part of their conversation was complete, she wanted to move on to a more immediate concern. "Did you sense it to the north?"

Sirius nodded, his mouth twisting with displeasure, as if he had just tasted something sour. "I didn't get a good fix on it. It was there and then not."

"Same for me," agreed Rafia. "A cloud of evil, much like when we search for Ghoules and Elders."

"Yes, but different. Older. Almost primeval."

"Do you know what it could be?" asked Rafia.

Sirius wanted to say yes. He had an innate desire to answer any question put to him, trusting in his knowledge and experience. Yet with that desire to respond was mixed an even greater aspiration to never be wrong.

"No," he said finally. "I can't tell for certain. A sense of corruption, rot, decay. Beyond that, I don't know. It's masked too well."

"If you were to guess?" asked Rafia.

"Something worse than Ghoules and Elders," Sirius muttered in disgust. "If I'm right, we need to pick up the pace. Even with Bryen learning how to master the Seventh Stone, I'd like to avoid these monsters at all costs."

"Why are you so worried?" asked Rafia, never having seen fear cross Sirius' face before.

"Because if I'm right, these monsters are quite good at killing Magii."

Rafia nodded, thinking about what Sirius had just revealed. If he was right, that could mean only one possibility. So be it. Their fight would continue.

Still, she couldn't help but smile. Because with Bryen they might be able to end this fight once and for all.

EPILOGUE

Bloody Slaughter

The shadows created by the heart trees had lengthened, extending for several hundred feet across the long grass of the Breakwater Plateau. The Shattered Peaks, though far to the north, were still visible just above the horizon. It was late afternoon, the sun falling in the west and setting the billowy clouds afire in bright oranges and reds.

Smoke drifted into the sky from the chimneys of the small cottages that made up the village nestled along the eastern outskirts of the Dark Forest. Hampden served as a waypoint for the merchants and tradespeople who traveled between the mines on the southern edge of the Shattered Peaks across the Breakwater Plateau -- this being the shortest and fastest route for crossing the dangerous plain -- to Tintagel, which was south of the wood, and points beyond. Several blacksmith forges lined the main street along with a few taverns, two inns, a general store, and even a house of ill repute.

Although the dozen miners coming back after their six-month shift in the mountains certainly had no qualms about visiting the large, two-story building that was set a bit off the street on the southern border of the town and in among the first of the heart trees that served as the boundary between village and wood. No, they had been looking forward to this visit, not having enjoyed the company of the opposite sex for quite some time. What they found peculiar was how quiet it was when they rode into the village and stopped in front of the brothel with half a dozen wagons filled to the brim with iron ore that was bound for the foundries at Ironhill far to the south.

"Something doesn't feel right, Jaxon. Doesn't feel right at all."

The foreman pushed himself up from the wagon seat, then jumped down to the ground, landing deftly for a man of his size. After having spent more than a decade in the deep tunnels that peppered the Shattered Peaks, digging out the iron that the Dukes and Duchesses paid a premium for, his broad shoulders and muscular arms testified to his strength and the work that he had done, yet he still retained a surprising nimbleness for someone so big.

"Why do you say that, Nelsin?" asked Jaxon, who walked slowly along the side of the wagon toward the back, his eyes never leaving the large building that appeared to be deserted.

"There's no one about. There's always someone about in Hampden, particularly here. Usually two or three women standing right there on the porch telling us to come in and have some fun. Not a soul in sight. And look," Nelsin said, pointing to the sky. "The fires are going in many of the homes and the forges. Where there are fires, there are people. But no one passed us by when we came into town. There's not a person to be seen."

"Thanks for the explanation, Nelsin. I was being facetious."

"Being what?" asked Nelsin, not understanding the word his foreman had used.

"Facetious," replied Jaxon. "It means ..." The foreman shook his head, realizing that an explanation would have to wait. "Never mind. I'll tell you later."

Because Nelsin was right. Something was amiss. They could all feel it.

Every other time that they had ridden into Hampden the shops had been open, the fires in the blacksmith forges had been burning, and the streets had been lined with townspeople and travelers. Not now. Other than the few wisps of smoke drifting into the air, there was nothing to suggest that anyone still lived here.

That made Jaxon extremely nervous. No people. No movement. No sounds. Just an eerie silence and smoke from the evening's cookfires.

He was a cautious man by nature, which was why any miner fortunate enough to be added to his team did all that he could to ensure that he stayed on his team. Working in the mines was a dangerous business. Cave-ins, floods from hidden underground rivers, deadly gases, broken machinery, and accidents were constant concerns.

Jaxon always had the highest producing team at the mines, which meant a nice bonus at the end of each month. Yet he didn't take risks to achieve his success. He rarely lost a miner because he always looked out for them. He didn't rush. He took his time. He made good decisions. And he listened to his instincts, which at that very moment were screaming at him that something very bad had happened in this town.

With that worrisome thought in mind, Jaxon pulled a key from his pocket and unlocked a strongbox bolted beneath the wagon between the wheels. He then pulled down the lid and pulled out a pickaxe. It was a common tool in his trade and a handy weapon if ever there was a need.

The feeling that tickled the back of his brain, warning of danger, suggested that there was a need. He nodded to the miners who had been watching him, and then they all scrambled down from their seats and grabbed hold of a pickaxe, placing themselves around the wagons as if they were about to be attacked.

For several minutes the miners just stood there, watching for any sign of movement around them. Listening for any sound. They were patient men. They had to be to work in the mines.

Nothing.

Jaxon didn't like it. He didn't like it at all. It was much too quiet, and they couldn't stand here all day. The sun was beginning to set, and he needed to make a decision.

Stay or go. Stay in a village that the last time he was here was filled with noise and merriment and good food and beautiful women but now only reminded him of a ghost town, or go and hope that whatever had happened here didn't find them farther down the road. Not liking either option, he decided that he needed more information before he made his decision.

"Nelsin," said Jaxon, nodding toward the entrance to the bordello. "Why don't you have a look. Just a quick glance."

Nelsin gulped, stared at the double doors that normally had two very large men standing there to ensure that nothing got out of hand, and then nodded reluctantly. The young miner's first few steps toward the brothel were hesitant. He gained greater confidence when he received several nods of support from his friends.

When Nelsin reached the double doors, he used the head of his pickaxe to open them slowly, wincing when the door on his right squeaked loudly thanks to a rusty hinge. When nothing happened, he stepped through quietly, the doors swinging shut behind him accompanied by a soft clap.

Several of the miners held their breaths, waiting for Nelsin to reappear, their worry growing as the seconds passed.

In less than a minute, Nelsin burst from the building, slamming the doors open and then sprinting out into the courtyard. He came to a stop right in front of Jaxon, who danced back a few feet when the young miner spewed the contents of his stomach on his boots.

"They're all dead," Nelsin finally said in a whisper, wiping away several strings of spittle with his sleeve. "They're all dead."

"What do you mean they're all dead?" asked Jaxon, that feeling of fear that had started in his belly upon entering the village now spreading into his spine, and then into his arms and legs.

He got this feeling from time to time in the mines, and he always listened to it. Usually, it meant that he should pull his miners farther back because the scaffolding was about to collapse or some other mishap was about to occur.

He was beginning to think that he didn't need to find out what happened here. He needed to pull his miners back from danger. He just needed to take his miners and go.

"Just what I said," Nelsin answered, groaning, a few

more dry heaves keeping him bent at the waist, hands on his knees. "They're all dead. Dozens of them. Men. The women. Some were torn apart, you can't even recognize them. And the blood. The blood is everywhere. I've never seen anything like it, and I don't want to see anything like it again."

Nelsin's description of what he saw made the miners grip the handles of their pickaxes just a little bit tighter, several looking around nervously, shifting from one foot to the other. They hadn't seen any sign of bandits or soldiers along the way or hiding in the wood around the town.

What could have done this?

"And there was a shadow," Nelsin continued. "A shadow in the very back. I couldn't see what it was, but it was big, and it had large eyes, red eyes that glowed in the dark."

"What do you mean a shadow?" demanded Jaxon.

"I have no idea what it could be," Nelsin said, finally able to stand straight again. "It was a shadow, big, and when it looked at me, my entire body went cold. I just ran. I don't know what it is."

"Just one?"

"Yes, just one."

Before Jaxon could ask any more questions, the double doors of the brothel swung open, attracting the gaze of all the miners. The foreman couldn't get a good look at what stepped out, the shadows of the porch hiding whatever it was. When the monster jumped off the steps and landed in the fading sunlight no more than twenty feet away, Jaxon could understand why Nelsin had exited the building so quickly.

The beast was huge, standing taller than a draft horse. Jaxon caught glimpses of its armored skin, short spikes protruding from the creature's shoulders, thighs, and forearms, those spikes extending all the way down its spine and tail. Yet even with its size, he was having a hard time focusing on the monster, its mottled grey and black skin fading in and out of the gloom.

"What is it?" whispered one of the other miners.

None of them had ever seen anything like it, and with the encroaching darkness, the only features that they could see clearly were the blood-red eyes and the creature's fang-filled maw, which was streaked with the blood of its many victims.

"I have no idea," answered Jaxon. "I've never seen the like."

"What do we do, Jaxon?" asked Nelsin.

The monster stood there almost perfectly still, only its tail swishing back and forth. Jaxon guessed that the beast might be doing that to maintain its balance, although he didn't know for sure. Whatever the thing was, it didn't seem to be in a rush to do anything to them.

Then again, maybe the monster didn't view the twelve of them as a danger. In Jaxon's opinion, it appeared to him as if the monster was studying them, waiting to see what he and his crew would do.

"There was only one in there, Nelsin?"

"Yes. Just this one. I didn't see any others."

Jaxon nodded, making a decision that he hoped he didn't come to regret. "We kill it."

The miners moved quickly upon hearing their foreman's instruction, his voice strong and confident, the one that he used so that all of them could hear what he had to say no matter how deep they were in the mines. Although they weren't soldiers, they all liked to think that they knew how to fight.

The men spread out, surrounding the monster, though

not coming too close. Several of them stared at the beast in confusion, having assumed the creature would have moved by now, the monster only turning its head, watching as the men shuffled around it, still unconcerned, almost amused.

Oddly, it was Nelsin who was the first to attack, charging toward the monster with his pickaxe held above his head, swinging with all his might. Unfortunately for him, instead of digging into flesh, the steel point of his tool smashed into the packed down dirt of the courtyard. The monster side-stepped the miner with ease, even giving Nelsin what Jaxon took to be a grin, but he couldn't be sure with all the teeth in its mouth.

Nelsin scuttled back quickly, concerned that the monster would strike at him while he was pulling his weapon from the ground. He had little to fear. The beast simply stared at him, seemingly bored by his action.

Another miner behind the beast decided to try his luck next, charging forward with his pickaxe, aiming for the creature's lower back. When the steel swept through the space, the monster was no longer there, having dodged out of the way with a surprising agility for such a large beast. Then another miner came forward, and then another, until all of them at once desperately tried to kill the huge fiend.

No matter what they did, the miners failed to strike the creature. It was too fast, spinning, jumping, and gliding out of the way with a grace and dexterity that Jaxon found almost captivating if it wasn't so scary to watch. Through it all, the monster's sickening grin broadened, the beast obviously enjoying this test against the miners. That was until Nelsin actually managed to slice the tip of his pickaxe across the monster's forearm, for the first time drawing a thick, almost oozing black blood.

Nelsin's shout of triumph turned into a sickening gurgle

as the beast's tail whipped out from behind its back, the sharp spike at the end punching through Nelsin's chest. The miner's terrible scream of fear and pain brought a temporary end to the combat.

The miners pulled back in horror as the beast used its tail to bring Nelsin close enough so that it could rip out the man's throat with its claw. Then the beast lifted Nelsin higher with its tail, tilting the dying young man so that Nelsin's blood flowed into its gaping maw.

Jaxon knew that this was the perfect time to attack again. But just like the other men with him, he couldn't get his legs to move, his feet rooted to the ground. What he saw stunned him. Terrified him.

He and the other miners had tried to kill this beast, all of them attacking at once, all their efforts for naught, and all the creature had done in turn was play with them. Now Nelsin was dead, the creature's latest victim.

What was he supposed to do now? They could continue the fight, although Jaxon had little doubt that even with their greater numbers, the miners were no match for this monster. They could try to escape. Maybe the beast had been satiated and wouldn't feel the need to pursue them.

Stay or go? The same question of just a few minutes ago, his first decision leading them into this mess. What was it to be now?

Two low growls made Jaxon's decision for him. Closing his eyes in surrender, when he opened them again, Jaxon saw a second monster on the far side of the circle, right behind his men. A third stood just behind him, catching the beast out of the corner of his eye.

Nelsin had been wrong. There had been more than one monster, and these two had little interest in playing with the miners like the first one had done.

The beasts leapt at his men faster than Jaxon thought possible, sharp claws ripping through flesh, spiky forearms and shoulders blocking the miners' steel weapons, whiplike tails lashing out to puncture chests and slice open bellies.

Right before Jaxon died, a clawed hand digging deeply into his gut, he realized that he had made a mistake. Stay or go. That was always the key question in the mines. He hadn't listened to what his instincts had been telling him.

He should have gone.

Immediately.

He shouldn't have stayed here, trying to figure out what had happened. If they had gone, the beasts might have let them be, and now he and his men were dying because of that one mistake, because of his failure to listen to his instincts.

Once Jaxon died, the remaining miners didn't last long against the beasts. When the Slayers finished killing these fresh humans, they feasted upon them, draining their blood before tearing into their tasty flesh.

They were hungry. They needed to eat. Their Master had kept them in their cells for far too long.

And now they could feast again. Now they could hunt again. Now they could find the prey their Master so desperately wanted.

After leaving the Shattered Peaks and crossing the Breakwater Plateau, finding this small village was a good start to their search. The men who had appeared unexpectedly were nothing more than an additional, delicious treat.

Yet for the Slayers to continue their chase they would need sustenance again soon. They would need blood and flesh.

The Slayers could feel the Seventh Stone. They were

getting closer. They should catch up to the artifact by nightfall of the next day at the latest.

When they did, they would take the Seventh Stone just as their Master required.

Then they would feast once more on the tasty flesh of the soft humans.

BONUS MATERIAL

If you really enjoyed this story, I need you to do me a HUGE favor – please follow me on Amazon and BookBub. And if you have a few minutes, consider writing a review.

Keep reading for the first two chapters of Book Five of *The Tales of Caledonia, The Protector's Reckoning.* Order Book 5 on Amazon.

THE TALES OF CALEDONIA
BOOK FIVE
THE PROTECTOR'S RECKONING
PETER WACHT

THE PROTECTOR'S RECKONING

BOOK 5 OF THE TALES OF CALEDONIA

By Peter Wacht

Cover design by Ebooklaunch.com

Published in the United States by Kestrel Media Group LLC.

ISBN: 978-1-950236-26-8
eBook ISBN: 978-1-950236-27-5

1. A TASTY TREAT

Mottled grey and black skin blended perfectly into the surrounding gloom. The only visible signs of the monsters were the blood-red eyes that burned through the murk, devoid of any emotion but one.

A desire to kill.

They were made for a singular purpose.

They had no choice but to obey the Dark Magic from which they were created. To obey their Master.

When the Slayers emerged from the Shattered Peaks and then stalked across the Breakwater Plateau, they had entered the Dark Forest hopeful that they would have the chance to fill their aching need. To find their quarry. To satiate their hunger.

Within a day the beasts had stumbled upon a small village that served as a waypoint between the mines in the mountains and the iron foundries in Ironhill. It had been a fortuitous discovery for the Slayers, though not for the people living in the village.

The monsters had been starving then, ravenously so, just as they were starving now. They were always hungry, rarely able to recall a time when they weren't a victim to the compulsion that they feed. An urge that they could not ignore, the pain of attempting to do so too much even for them.

It was a pain that they hated. A pain that was all too familiar. A pain that they could rarely escape.

A pain that could only be alleviated by obeying their Master. By obeying the Curse that flowed within them, that gave them life. That gave them reason.

Because for these monsters, for them to live, there had to be death.

The villagers had filled a need, satisfying their yearning briefly, reducing the pain so that it was more tolerable.

But only for a time. Much too short a time.

For them to live, for them to soothe the pain that was so much a part of their existence, they had to kill their prey.

Once the monsters had slaughtered and eaten their fill of the villagers, they had gone west, moving deeper within the Dark Forest, searching for the one so important to their Master that for the first time in centuries he had released them from beneath the Temple of the Ghoules.

Within hours, the Slayers began looking for another small village along the way, needing to satiate their rapacious craving once again. Yet they had found little sustenance.

The soft humans and their succulent flesh that would placate the gnawing need within them were nothing but taunting memories, the grim, silent wood empty. Even the few large animals they sensed within the forest eluded them, staying well clear of the hunters.

With few other options, the monsters had no choice but to make do with the quarry they did locate. It wasn't what they wanted, but it would do.

This meat, stringy and tough though it was, would sustain them for a day. Maybe two. No more. That was all right.

The Ghoule Overlord's creations expected that they would be feeding again on something more succulent by then. That they would catch the prey their Master had sent them after. Once they did, they could gorge on the tasty meat of the humans.

The largest of the Slayers, the beast well above nine feet tall, crouched in the darkness, leaning his spiked spine against the trunk of a heart tree. The monster took his time. Despite the remarkably bitter taste, he savored what they had come across hidden within the wood, noisily slurping with its split tongue the marrow from the bones that he had arranged into a small pile in front of him.

Having sucked the fluid from the vertebrae of the spine, the Slayer picked up a femur, strings of mottled green flesh still hanging from it in several places. Not as delectable as the humans. Still, it satisfied his need. For now.

With little effort and a quick twist of his massive claws, the Slayer cracked the bone in half, then tilted one side toward his gaping maw. His long, snakelike tongue shot out to dig the marrow free from the bone. Finishing with one half in just seconds, the Slayer turned his attention to the other half of the femur, engaging in the same process to extricate the fatty tissue.

That done, the Slayer lifted the skull that lay just off to the side of the pile in one large, razor-sharp claw, the head already scraped clean of flesh thanks to his sharp teeth. He had been saving this delicacy for last. With just a touch of pressure, the top of the head cracked and then split apart, a grey mass appearing beneath the thick bone. The Slayer dug his claw into the skull, picking out the brain and then chewing on the delectable morsel for quite some time before allowing it to slide down his gullet. A tasty treat to complete his meal.

Two other Slayers on the other side of the small clearing growled at one another, just as they had been doing since they had settled down to eat, tugging on the remains of the last of their kill. One of the Slayers gripped tightly to an arm, the other to a leg, neither willing to let go as they pulled with all their might, both wanting as much of what was left of the corpse as they could take for themselves.

With a sickening snap and crunch, the monsters ripped apart the body at the hip, one of the Slayers dragging the upper torso farther among the heart trees, the other Slayer pleased to have the two meaty legs to feast on. What had once been a Ghoule was devoured quickly. The two Slayers bit into the flesh with their sharp, serrated teeth, four fangs, two on the upper jaw, two on the lower, helping to rake the meat clean from the bone.

The Slayers were fortunate to have come across the Ghoule pack as they headed toward the northeastern corner of the wood. The Ghoules had been sleeping, unafraid of any predators that might be in the Dark Forest, believing that they had little to fear in the land of their prey. Until the Slayers fell upon them.

Just like the Slayers, the Ghoules were touched by the Curse. They obeyed the same Master.

The Slayers didn't care. The monsters viewed anything living as food, even another Slayer if they were desperate enough.

If the Slayers had discovered an Elder with this Ghoule pack, they probably would have avoided the beasts as they rested within the wood. Because there were no Elders to be found, because their hunger felt like a burning hole in their stomachs, they gave in to their craving.

Ghoules feared nothing, except for the Slayers, and these Ghoules, although they fought bravely -- at least the ones who even realized they were under attack, more than half of their number killed before there had been a shout of warning -- had not lasted long against their formidable foes. Slayers could only be killed with the Talent or Dark Magic. Even the blackened steel of the Ghoules skittered harmlessly off their armored flesh.

The Slayer who had been eating on his own, after finishing with the brain, rose from where he crouched in the darkness, kicking through the pile of bones in front of him to see if he could find anything else worth eating. Nothing piqued his interest, having picked clean the flesh, so he sniffed the air, searching for a particular scent. A magical scent that had been inscribed within him by the Ghoule Overlord.

The other two Slayers soon joined him, having eaten the last of their bounty. Mimicking his action, they sniffed the air, seeking the scent that thanks to their Master they could find even from several hundred leagues away.

The minutes dragged on, and during that time the Slayers remained perfectly still. Perfectly silent. Perfectly focused as they sought their prey. Then they growled in unison.

The largest one, the leader, raised his maw to the sky. He couldn't see the light of the moon because of the branches that intertwined above him. Still, in the deepening dusk he howled with pleasure.

The Slayers had located their prey. They were certain of it. They could sense the huge quantity of Dark Magic that was being used in the northeast section of the Dark Forest no more than a few dozen leagues away. They could sense the Talent as well. More important, they could sense the artifact.

They were closer than they expected, which was a good thing. Because their hunger already was beginning to gnaw at them despite their recent kill. They would be ravenous again soon.

Their hunger was a gift from their Master. It gave them an even greater incentive to fulfill his commands. It was also a curse they could never evade.

The Ghoules were a necessary meal. But it wasn't enough for the Slayers. They had been locked in their cells for a thousand years. Their craving knew no bounds as a result. They would feast again when they caught their Master's quarry.

And when they did, they would take the Seventh Stone, just as the Ghoule Overlord required. Then, their Master would set them loose in this land and allow them to feed on the humans until they had finally eaten their fill of soft, tasty flesh. Until they had finally met the demands of their voracious hunger.

2. BATTLE IN THE GLOOM

"It's unnerving how they can sense the Seventh Stone," said Sirius. "There are thirty or more Ghoules and Elders about to walk right into us."

"They won't walk right into us," growled Rafia. "They'll walk right by us."

"Quiet," whispered Bryen, who stood next to Rafia and Sirius at the head of the Blood Company. "They're almost upon us."

This was one of the reasons Bryen had balked at asking the gladiators to join them on this mission. The Elders could sense the Seventh Stone because of the Dark Magic that it stored. That meant that the Elders could sense him. Vaguely, at best, though well enough for the beasts to narrow their search to less than a league.

Bryen had thought that perhaps he could try for the Sanctuary on his own because of his desire to put as few people at risk as possible. He realized after several long discussions with the two Magii that he'd never make it by himself. He wouldn't get there even if he took just the two Magii with him.

He wasn't just squaring off against the Ghoule Overlord, although that was certainly a distinct possibility. He was going to have to fight his way through whatever obstacles the Ghoule Overlord erected in front of him. Because the Magii were certain that the Master of the Lost Land would do all that he could to prevent Bryen from reaching the Sanctuary.

So no matter how much he disliked it, he needed to take with him people whom he could trust to help him, and that meant putting their lives at risk. Just as they were doing for him now. He hated being in this position, although he understood the necessity of it all.

Bryen and the Blood Company were close to the north-eastern boundary of the Dark Forest, not too far from the Breakwater Plateau. They had covered a good bit of ground that day, halting a few hours earlier than usual because Aislinn had detected several Ghoule packs coming in their direction across the long grass from the Shattered Peaks.

No one doubted that the beasts were searching for the Seventh Stone. Searching for him.

The Company had no chance of escape, so they had done the only thing that they could. Rafia and Sirius used the Talent to blend the warriors into the Dark Forest, using the wood's natural pall to aid the deception so that any of the beasts who walked by saw nothing but what they were supposed to see.

Heart trees soaring into the sky. Roots thicker than a man was tall worming their way along the forest floor. Shadows and gloom everywhere else because the sun couldn't break through the latticework of branches that had become intertwined into a haphazard web as the centuries passed.

The Company of Blood had lost their disciplined order

to a certain degree because of the width of the heart trees and the many roots, their preferred marching column unavoidably breaking down into smaller groups and individuals as they maneuvered through the obstacle course that was the Dark Forest.

Even though they were somewhat separated from one another, all of them remained silent. All of them stayed still. All of them barely breathed. They knew what was required of them for the illusion to work. They had gone through this same exercise several times upon entering the wood just a week past.

Within just a few heartbeats of Bryen shushing Sirius, the Ghoules appeared to their front. At first, there was no way to tell what was approaching. Just a few flits of movement that broke the gloom of the grove. Then, as they came closer, the Ghoules took shape, their mottled green skin and brown leather armor merging into their surroundings with frightening ease.

As the beasts drew parallel on their western side, striding by in a single file, the fighters of the Blood Company watched nervously, only their eyes tracking the creatures, none of the soldiers willing to move their heads for fear that such a motion would untangle the magical deception.

So far, so good, thought Tarin Tentillin. The Captain of the Battersea Guard stood in the back of the scattered column, Jerad right next to him. They both gripped the hilts of their drawn swords tensely.

They trusted in the power of the two Magii positioned at the head of the column. Still, they wanted to be ready. You never knew what might happen. And they found it quite unnerving to be standing so close to their enemies, even catching the faint, rank odor of the beasts, yet unable to press the advantage the Magii had given them.

The Ghoules glided past the concealed soldiers, calling to one another in barks and hisses. The beasts saw nothing other than the forest around them, even though they were no more than a few feet from men and women who stared at them with undisguised hatred mixed with a healthy dose of respect.

The Blood Company had fought the Ghoules several times now. They respected what the creatures could do with their blades and their claws. Yet they saw them as no more than another enemy to be defeated. All of the gladiators had spent too much time in the Pit to allow the Ghoules to frighten them in any way.

From their time on the white sand, they also had learned to approach every combat with the beasts by acknowledging their abilities -- their own and their adversaries -- knowing that if they failed to do so, that if they demonstrated any overconfidence whatsoever, they were the ones most likely to color the white sand red rather than the Ghoules.

Tarin believed that they just might have dodged what would have been a difficult fight, the several dozen Ghoules and Elders likely testing the gladiators to their limits if they crossed blades. He was about to take a real breath for the first time in the last ten minutes when the unexpected happened, just as it always did.

One of the Ghoules in the middle of the column stumbled on a root, falling to the side and through the illusion that Rafia and Sirius had created so painstakingly. The Ghoule landed on his back, his chest disappearing, his legs remaining outside the boundary of the sham, leaving only his lower body exposed to the other Ghoules.

The silence of the Dark Forest reigned for just a second more before the Ghoule behind the one who had fallen reached through the deception to pull his comrade up, still trying to understand how a part of him had disappeared entirely in the gloom.

The Ghoule's eyes widened in surprise when he gripped his comrade's leather armor. The fallen Ghoule was a deadweight, his throat a bloody mess from the spearpoint the soldier standing above him had driven through with such force that the tip had dug into the soft ground beneath the beast.

Before the Ghoule who had tried to aid his comrade could screech a warning, Dorlan, the large gladiator who was slow to anger but fought with a terrifying ferocity, lunged with his spear, driving the sharp point through the Ghoule's eye. Kollea, who had killed the first beast, patted his arm in approval. Two quick kills. A good start to the battle that was just moments away from exploding.

When the second Ghoule collapsed, he fell entirely through the illusion, making the magic shimmer for no more than a flash, though that was just long enough for the Ghoules to see what was hiding from them just a few feet away. With growls and roars, the Ghoules leapt past the mirage, destroying the illusion entirely to reveal the Company of Blood standing ready.

In seconds, the soldiers were engulfed by the Ghoules, the bloody skirmish erupting up and down the column. The gladiators knew how to fight the Ghoules. They knew how to kill them. They also knew that they needed to kill them all, because if just one Ghoule escaped, the Company would never make it out of the Dark Forest.

All the other Ghoule packs would learn where they were. Then the beasts would come for them with a renewed vengeance, and their critical expedition would come to an end before it even really began.

Declan parried the Ghoule's slash, catching the beast's steel with his own, before spinning away and leaping backward. One foot hit the bark solidly, the other slipped, and for a very tense few seconds Declan fought to maintain his balance, knowing that if he fell he was dead. Finally, he got both of his feet back under him, coming to stand on top of a large root that rose five feet above the forest floor.

Now he could finally see the Ghoule eye to eye. The Master of the Gladiators kept his footing as he twisted his core to the left, and then just as fast to the right, avoiding by no more than a hair the two thrusts the Ghoule attempted, the creature trying to stick him like a pig with his blackened spear.

Frustrated, the Ghoule jumped up onto the root with him, forcing Declan to take a few steps back. It wasn't in Declan's nature to give ground willingly, so he launched himself toward the Ghoule, his blade a grey blur as he cut, slashed, and sliced, so fast, in fact, that the beast failed to parry all of his attacks, the evidence of Declan's success demonstrated by the thick black blood that oozed from several deep slices across the Ghoule's forearms, hip, and thigh.

The Ghoule was an excellent fighter even with the many wounds he received. Nevertheless, Declan wasn't worried. He had fought many warriors who were more skilled than he was. The difference was that he was still standing, and those others were buried six feet under the ground.

Despite the skill of his opponent, Declan felt good. He

was in his element, and it was so much better to be fighting for a reason other than the amusement of the rich and privileged. It was so much better to be fighting somewhere else, anywhere else, than the Pit.

Live or die, he was just glad to be free of the white sand.

Declan took a quick look around him when the Ghoule stepped back a few feet, putting some distance between them so that the beast could examine his many wounds. He was pleased to see that his gladiators were performing well ... his soldiers actually. He needed to remind himself of that daily. They were no longer gladiators, although he doubted that any of them would ever be able to look at themselves in any other way. They were all free now, fighting because they chose to. Fighting because they believed in the Volkun and the mission that he had set for them.

His gaze returned to the Ghoule when the beast charged at him again. The Ghoule clearly wasn't happy that he had gotten the worst of the combat so far, his expression murderous.

Declan smiled maliciously, pleased that the beast allowed his anger to drive him forward, obviously furious that Declan was able to score his flesh so frequently. Declan was more than happy to challenge the beast's assumption that humans were soft and that he should already be dead. It only made the combat more pleasurable for him, and it improved his chances of winning.

The Ghoule growled louder as he swung down with his blade, irritated even more when Declan parried the blow aimed for his neck and then twisted the handle of his weapon so that his sword slid off the Ghoule's spear and sliced across his ribs. The beast hissed in both pain and rage, doing his best to ignore the burning of this new wound, blood now seeping down his left side as well.

Pleased by his success, Declan continued his attack, noting how the beast's eyes changed when he cut across the creature's left side. The Ghoule's anger had transformed into a fiery rage. That was something that Declan could work with. He had seen it thousands of times before in the Pit.

Once you gave in to your anger, you gave control over to your opponent. Your decisions were no longer driven by cold reason and a phlegmatic calculation of risk, but rather by your emotions. Declan meant to use that change within the Ghoule against the beast.

And he did with a devastating finality. Enraged by his latest wound, the Ghoule rushed toward Declan, caring less about protecting himself and more about killing his opponent.

Declan backtracked along the root, giving ground. Each time the Ghoule swung his blade, Declan parried it, and then when he neared the trunk of the heart tree he added an unanticipated twist, pulling the dagger from his belt and striking faster than a cobra.

Now, every time the Ghoule swung his spear, fixated on driving the steel into Declan's flesh, Declan blocked the blow with his sword and punched his foot-long dagger into the Ghoule's flesh instead. The beast was so enraged that at first he barely noticed the new wounds, the Ghoule's attention so focused on Declan, his eyes never leaving his, that the beast didn't even register the additional damage that Declan was inflicting upon him.

One stab, then a second. A third. A fourth followed just as fast. The Ghoule's movements were slowing, although the beast's strategy hadn't changed. A fifth jab with Declan's dagger, this time straight into the beast's gut. Then a sixth into his groin.

The Ghoule was becoming sluggish now, the beast's agility disappearing, replaced by a disjointed stumble that reminded Declan of watching the marionettes in the marketplace shows when he was a child. It appeared that he had cut almost all the Ghoule's strings. Then came the seventh strike, Declan's dagger sliding straight into the beast's heart.

The Ghoule stood there for a few seconds, Declan's dagger keeping him in place, the creature holding his spear across his chest. After just a few heartbeats, the spear slipped from the Ghoule's claws, the light leaving his eyes as the beast fell back onto the root and then tumbled off and fell to the ground. Declan watched his enemy die with a cold satisfaction, yet he had no time to savor his victory.

Declan ducked, almost losing his balance on the root, one foot sliding off. Once he had both feet back under him, he jumped several feet into the air, then again, and a third time for good measure, avoiding a twisted black staff that was swung with an incredible force, buffeting him with a gust of air every time it passed by him. Landing on the bark and realizing the difficulty of his position, Declan jumped backward and onto the soft loam, the black staff slamming into the tree root right where he had stood just a second before.

A dark shadow jumped over the arcing root to stand in front of Declan. An Elder. The evil breast grinned at him, revealing his sharp, sawtoothed teeth.

The Elder swung his staff at Declan a fifth time, aiming for his head. This time, Declan ducked, and once clear of the stave, missing his head by no more than the width of a finger, he lunged for the Elder's side with his sword.

The Elder caught the blow with his staff, bringing the twisted wood back around with remarkable speed, jabbing with the sharpened tip for Declan's stomach. Declan pivoted to the side and sucked in his gut, the rough, hardened wood scraping across his leather armor rather than through it and into his flesh.

Before the Ghoule could pull the staff back, Declan swung down with his sword with all of his strength, the steel cutting deeply into the black ash. He wanted to break the staff in two. Bryen had told him how the Elder he had fought on the coastal road had lost control of his Dark Magic when he fractured the beast's staff, and Declan was attempting to eliminate his adversary's greatest advantage the same way now. Unfortunately, unlike Bryen's combat, although Declan chipped a huge chunk of wood from the Elder's staff, the twisted black ash remained intact.

The Elder stumbled back a few feet in shock, realizing just how close he had come to losing the Dark Magic that the Ghoule Overlord had bestowed upon him. The beast examined the staff frantically, both terrified and enraged by the large gash about halfway down its length, the scar setting off a low snarl within the beast.

The Elder had wanted to play with the human, to make him experience a long, slow death for what he had done to the Ghoule. The beast realized then that he had made a mistake. This human was more skilled with the blade than he had anticipated, and he could not risk his hold on the Curse just to teach him a lesson.

Turning his black eyes back toward Declan, he grinned. A black mist began to seep from the top of his staff, spinning faster and faster as he gathered more and more of the Dark Magic for his use. He would still make an example of this human. The Elder would simply do it in a different way. In a way that demonstrated the power that he wielded.

Declan shook his head in irritation, knowing how close

he had come to destroying the Elder's staff. One more good blow and the Elder would be nothing more than another Ghoule, a beast that, as he had demonstrated just minutes before, he could kill.

When he saw the Dark Magic beginning to revolve around the top of the Elder's staff, he resigned himself to his fate. Their combat had come to an end, because Declan had no way to protect himself against the Curse.

A sphere of incandescent energy shot from Rafia's palm, slamming into the trunk of a heart tree right where an Elder's head had been just a second before. She tried again and missed again, another ball of fire spinning from her palm, the Elder too quick, the beast diving behind a root that resembled a corkscrew before she could strike him with the Talent.

Rafia enjoyed games, just not in circumstances such as this. As they had been trained, the Company of Blood focused on the Ghoules, leaving the Elders to her, Sirius, Aislinn, and Bryen. At the start of the fight, the dozen Elders had not expected to find so many Magii in one place. They had paid the price for that, half of their number flaking away into a black ash in just seconds thanks to the Talent. The Elders who survived that initial assault proved harder to kill, particularly this one.

While the battle raged around her, Rafia had spent the last five minutes trying to destroy this beast. He was fast. Faster than she anticipated. So far, he had either dodged out of the way or used his Dark Magic at the very last second to construct a shield that prevented Rafia from hitting him with the Talent.

She was getting frustrated. Unlike most people, however, she wasn't predictable when she became aggravated. Her exasperation instead helped her to achieve a new level of focus.

She had been trying to hit the Elder where he stood. He had escaped every one of her attacks. So time for a new strategy. She decided on one similar to what she did when she wanted to flush out a hare. To improve her chances of success, she couldn't focus on where the hare was, rather she needed to anticipate where the hare would be.

With that in mind, a dozen bolts of energy shot from her palm in just a few seconds, one right after the other. The Elder had pushed himself up from behind the corkscrew, preparing to send a shard of Dark Magic toward Rafia. Her latest attack caught him off guard.

Rather than ducking back down behind the tree root, the most sensible move, he sprinted to his left, Rafia's bolts following him, slamming one after another into the trunk of the heart tree as the Elder used his impressive speed to stay just a step ahead of the sizzling energy that tracked him.

The Elder responded exactly as Rafia hoped that he would, because just as the last bolt of power slammed against the bark behind him, so did the Elder, a spear crafted from the Talent impaling the beast through the chest and pinning him to the trunk of the heart tree. A blinding white light pulsed from the spear as it slowly dissolved, burning through the Elder from his core to his extremities, until there was nothing left but a swirl of cinders.

It was just a matter of timing, and hers had been excellent, aiming her throw for where she anticipated the Elder to be.

Nodding with the satisfaction of a job well done, Rafia

surveyed the rest of the skirmish. She could only see so much of what was going on, the heart trees and roots hiding several of the combats that flowed around her. What she did see required immediate action.

Why Declan had decided to challenge an Elder, she didn't understand. The man was either stubborn, unlucky, or a fool. Probably not a fool, she corrected, though definitely stubborn and unlucky.

The beast was about to kill the Sergeant of the Blood Company, Dark Magic forming just above the cap of the Elder's staff. That was something that she simply refused to allow.

Using what just had proven to be so effective in her duel with the now destroyed Elder, she shot a dozen bolts of power from her palm, the blazing energy streaking through the gloom and slamming into the back of the unsuspecting Elder right before he sent his Dark Magic streaming toward Declan.

One second the Elder was there. The next, he wasn't. The power of Rafia's strike left behind nothing but a swirling cloud of black ash.

Peering through the cinders, Declan caught sight of his rescuer, giving her a nod of thanks before he jumped over a tree root and drove his sword into the side of a Ghoule who was coming at Asaia from behind.

The gladiator had just used her barbed whip to decapitate one of the Ghoules, which was an impressive feat. Although she might have recovered in time to take on the stealthily approaching beast, Declan hadn't wanted to take the chance.

Rafia watched Declan in action for just a moment more, impressed by his handiwork. Then she began walking among the trees in search of any other Elders who may have escaped her notice.

Davin and Lycia had cleared their small part of the battlefield with an efficiency that mimicked their time working together in the Pit. Fighting back to back, Davin with his spear and Lycia with her twin blades, they had taken on the handful of Ghoules foolish enough to challenge them.

The results of their work lay at their feet. Three dead Ghoules, one missing his head because he underestimated Lycia's skill with a blade, not thinking that a woman could hold her own against the likes of him and paying for that miscalculation with his life.

The Ghoule who Lycia fought now was not as foolish as the last, taking her seriously from the start because he had seen what she could do with her steel. Still, that knowledge hadn't helped him all that much. Lycia had wounded the Ghoule four times already, and she wasn't done with him yet.

The Ghoule tried to rotate away from the slash that Lycia directed toward his midsection, realizing almost too late that he could not get his sword up in time to parry the cut. His several wounds were affecting him badly, the worst of them a slice across his gut that was bleeding profusely and forcing him to keep one claw against his belly, as he feared that the wound would rupture if left unattended.

Lycia took full advantage, the blade in her left hand cutting from the top of the Ghoule's chest down to his groin, taking the beast's claw with it. The wound now resembling a cross, and the beast down to one claw, the Ghoule's guts inevitably spilled out onto the forest floor. The Ghoule stood there for just a moment more, staring in horror at what had happened to him, before he crumpled to the ground, bleeding out.

Lycia spun around immediately, the Ghoules facing her dead or dying, to check on her brother as the sound of steel striking steel rang in her ears just behind her. Recognizing that Davin would be finishing the Ghoule he faced in just a few more moves, his spear a blur in front of him and the Ghoule already bleeding from a handful of serious wounds, Lycia scanned around her to see how the rest of the skirmish was playing out.

Aislinn Winborne fought two Ghoules just a dozen yards away from her, the Lady of the Southern Marches caught in a vise between the beasts. Lycia judged that she was more than holding her own. Lady Winborne had gotten several good strikes in, streaks of blood apparent on both Ghoules, and she had yet to be wounded. Still, the Lady Winborne was stuck between them with no easy way out.

Lycia growled in anger. A small part of her wanted to leave Aislinn Winborne to her own devices and allow her to extricate herself from the dilemma she faced. A larger part of Lycia, the compassionate part that she tried so hard to suppress most of the time, wouldn't allow her to do that.

Sprinting across the soft earth on silent feet, Lycia swept her blades from the inside out, two deep cuts leaking a thick black blood from the back of the neck of the Ghoule closest to her. His spinal cord severed, the beast collapsed, no longer able to move any of his limbs.

The Ghoule attacking Aislinn from the other side was distracted by the surprise attack, and his moment of hesitation gave Aislinn the opening that she needed. With a quick feint toward the Ghoule's leading thigh, she adjusted her grip on her sword and slashed upward with a backhanded movement, her sharp steel slicing through the beast's neck to the bone. With a soft gurgle, the Ghoule fell to the ground to join his brethren.

"My thanks," said Aislinn, turning toward Lycia. "These two were putting up quite a fight."

"I didn't do it for you," Lycia grumbled. "I just wanted to kill another Ghoule, and this one was the closest."

"Of course," nodded Aislinn, not believing a word that Lycia said.

Aislinn's gaze then shifted to a series of small explosions just past the heart tree a dozen yards to her front. Both she and Lycia sprinted through the gap, coming to a stop at the edge of a small clearing. Bryen stood in front of them, several dead Ghoules lying around his feet. The last Elder opposed him, and they were engaged not only in a combat of steel, but also of the Talent and the Curse.

Both were wounded, Lycia judging the Elder to have absorbed the worst of the fight so far, though the blood running down Bryen's side worried her. Bryen had infused the Spear of the Magii with the Talent, the two blades glowing brightly. Even so, he was having a difficult time breaking through the Elder's shield of Dark Magic, which swirled around the beast in a mist that solidified every time Bryen cut toward the Elder, keeping the shining blades from striking true.

Not one to give up easily, Bryen stepped back and instead of slashing toward the Elder with his Spear, he instead shot two streams of energy toward the barrier, the power proving too strong for the beast as the Dark Magic began to waver. Then, with a blinding flash and a resounding boom, an explosion ripped through the small clearing, kicking up a storm of dirt. When the grit finally began to clear a few seconds later, Bryen hadn't moved, the Spear still in his grip, but the Elder was gone.

Catching a flash of movement about fifty yards in front of him, Bryen sprinted after the beast, refusing to let the Elder escape, knowing and wanting to avoid the cost of doing so.

"Bryen, wait!" both Aislinn and Lycia shouted at the same time as he chased after the bolting Elder and lost himself among the heart trees.

Bryen sprinted around a heart tree, vaulted over a root that twisted almost five feet off the ground, cut to his left to avoid another root that had shattered into dozens of sharp spikes, then curled back around to his right. He stopped for just a moment, searching to his front.

The slice across his chest from the Elder's staff had scorched his flesh just like the mark that he had received on his cheek from the Ghoule Overlord when they met for the first time in the Sanctuary. He did his best to disregard the pain of his wound. He could deal with his injury once his opponent was dead.

Where was the Elder? He was certain that the beast had come this way. Bryen might not have gained on him because of all the obstructions in his path. Still, he couldn't be too far behind.

Bryen caught a flash of movement no more than a few dozen yards ahead of him, just off to his right. The Elder was fast. Very fast. Bryen caught a glimpse of him through the ragged breaks in the trees and the roots.

He was staying with Elder, he just wasn't gaining on the

creature. Not willing to risk losing the beast, Bryen decided that he needed to do something to slow his target down.

Grasping hold of the Talent, Bryen shot a streak of energy from his palm that blazed through the gloom of the Dark Forest and slammed into a root that was just a few feet in front of the Elder. The blast of shattered wood, thousands of jagged splinters bursting into the air, caught the Elder from the side, throwing the beast off his clawed feet. The Elder landed hard on his back, skidding to a stop against the trunk of a heart tree.

The Elder tried to push himself up. He couldn't, his strength failing. Looking down, he could understand why. Hundreds of shards of the destroyed tree root had shredded his chest just as well as if not better than a steel blade could have. The Elder realized that his end had come, so he settled back against the tree, waiting for the world to fade around him.

Bryen appeared before the Elder just a second later, taking in the result of his efforts. He held onto the Spear of the Magii tightly, the double blades glowing with the Talent. Bryen realized that he would have little need to finish the beast. It was only a matter of time before the Ghoule went to the other side.

"You will not escape, human," whispered the Elder in a raspy voice, a thick black blood beginning to bubble out of the creature's maw. "You will not escape."

Although the Ghoule spoke in his guttural language, Bryen understood every word.

"We come, human," continued the Elder. "We come for you. Your death is certain."

"Yet I'm the one still standing," replied Bryen in the Ghoule's language, not making the conscious decision to speak in the creature's tongue, never having learned how to speak it, yet knowing exactly what he had said, thanks to the Seventh Stone and the Dark Magic within him.

The Elder lying against the tree chuckled at that, the flow of blood running out of the beast's mouth accelerating.

"Not for long, human. We know who you are. We know what you have become. We come for you." The Elder then became silent for a time, Bryen staring down at him, thinking that the beast might have died, the pain of the burn across Bryen's chest becoming more insistent. Then with a start the Elder's glazed eyes gained a startling lucidity for just a few seconds more. "We come for you, human. We are here."

At the same time the dying Elder drew his last breath, a shard of Dark Magic slammed into Bryen's chest, knocking him off his feet. He ended up on his back lying in the dirt ten feet from where he had been standing. His entire body burned with a cold fire, the Curse surging through his blood.

What had happened? It couldn't have been the Elder he had been speaking to. That beast didn't have the strength to call on his Dark Magic, not with his staff shattered by the blast of the Talent that also had killed the creature.

Bryen tried to push himself up, finding the task too much for him. He was only able to raise himself to one elbow and shakily at that before he dropped back onto the dirt.

Then two pairs of clawed feet appeared just to his side, and he realized that he had made a terrible mistake. He had focused so much of his attention on the escaping Elder that he had never considered that there might be others coming his way. He had run right into a trap, the wounded Elder nothing more than bait.

With the Dark Magic rushing through him, staining his

body with an oily filth, Bryen knew that he couldn't make use of the Talent on his own. Not now. If he did, he'd resign himself to a fate worse than death. He turned his head to the side, finding the Spear of the Magii just out of reach.

If he crawled just a few feet, he could grab the Spear. With the Spear, he could dispatch these two Elders. But when he tried to flip his body over so that he could dig his hands into the dirt and pull himself in the direction of his weapon, Bryen's strength failed him.

He was about to try again when his greatest fear came to pass. The Dark Magic that he had gained through the Seventh Stone and had locked away was reaching for the Curse that had just struck him, trying to bring the two together.

The Dark Magic was pushing from both sides now against the barrier that he had created within himself to keep free from the taint. And as Bryen's stamina waned, his ability to maintain control over the barrier wavered.

Once the shield collapsed, he would be lost to the Curse forever.

He desperately sought to maintain the barricade, even though he knew that without the Spear he didn't stand a chance. And if that wasn't bad enough, an even more immediate threat approached. Tilting his head forward, Bryen watched as one of the Elders approached.

His first thought was that he was about to die, something that he didn't fear, though certainly regretted. Then he saw the second Elder call on his Dark Magic, the tainted black energy spinning across the top of his staff, the beast manipulating the cursed power to form a portal.

The Elders didn't want to kill him, he realized. They wanted to take him. Now Bryen truly was afraid. The Elders wanted what was in him, which could mean only one thing.

They wanted to take him to the Ghoule Overlord, who could extract the Seventh Stone from him. Once that was done, the commander of the Ghoule Legions could then destroy the Weir.

The faint mist that had been spinning behind the second Elder slowly coalesced into an opaque disk of black large enough for a Ghoule to walk through. The portal was ready, the Elder closest to Bryen reaching down with his claws to throw him over his shoulder.

Desperate, Bryen reached for the Talent, just a trickle, any power at all, now more fearful of being brought to the Ghoule Overlord than being touched by the Curse. He cursed silently in frustration. There was nothing for him to grab hold of, the fight within him between the Talent and the Curse consuming all the strength and energy he had left.

As the Elder's claw grasped Bryen's arm, a streak of scorching energy sizzled through the air, slamming into the other Elder from behind. The beast screamed in agony, his shriek cut short as his body turned to ash in just moments, the portal that he had created winking out as his staff fell to the ground.

The Elder who had been reaching for Bryen snapped back up with his staff at the ready, seizing the Dark Magic that flowed within him. He was fast, just not fast enough. Another bolt of energy burned through the beast's chest and flung him back against a heart tree in a heap, his body a smoking ruin.

The next time Bryen looked up, Aislinn was there, her face staring down at him and a welcome replacement for that of the Elder's.

Rafia stood next to her, using the Talent to search the area around them and ensure that it was free of any other

Elders or Ghoules. Once she was satisfied, she released her hold on the natural magic of the world and she knelt down next to Aislinn.

"That was quite impressive," complimented Bryen in a weak voice.

"Rafia taught me," replied Aislinn distractedly as she examined the wound on Bryen's chest. "Rafia, please take a look at this. I don't know what to do."

Fear filled Aislinn's voice. She remembered what Bryen had looked like after being wounded by the Elder just outside the Aeyrie, and this injury appeared to be much worse, streaks of black already stretching from where he had been hit in the chest out to his arms. She assumed the Dark Magic had seeped down his legs as well. The Curse was moving more swiftly than she ever imagined possible to make Bryen its own.

Rafia bent down for a closer look, ignoring the burn across Bryen's midsection. That was nothing compared to the thin tendrils of black that wormed their way up and down Bryen's body.

Davin, Lycia, and Declan appeared next, followed by Tarin, Jerad, and Sirius. No one said a word as Rafia took hold of the Talent once again and scanned Bryen, trying to figure out if there was anything that she could do to help him.

She identified the source of the infection almost immediately, a sick feeling in the pit of her stomach telling her that there was nothing that she could do about it. She couldn't help Bryen.

"Bryen," Rafia said in a quiet, calm voice that she hoped hid her fear. "You need to heal yourself. Just as you've done so many times before. I can't help you. None of us can help you. You need to cleanse yourself of the Dark Magic the Elder struck you with."

"I know," Bryen replied through gritted teeth, his body beginning to shake uncontrollably, frightening all the people surrounding him. "I know. I just don't know if I can. The Dark Magic is calling to me. It wants me."

"Fight it, Bryen," said Sirius, who knelt next to the Protector and grasped his hand. "Fight it. You must."

Bryen looked up into Sirius' eyes, realizing that the real Sirius was with him now. The Master of the Magii, not the somewhat addled instructor. His eyes blazed with anger, and Bryen detected a hint of terror worming its way into his gaze. At first glance, Bryen thought that was likely because of what Sirius needed him to do with respect to the Weir, and that if he was taken by the Curse, Sirius would have to kill him.

But the look in Sirius' eyes suggested that there might be more there than just that. That Bryen perhaps was more to the old Magus than just a tool to be used.

"The Seventh Stone, Bryen," said Aislinn, her words pulling his eyes to hers. "Use the Seventh Stone, just like when you were at the Aeyrie. It will give you the strength that you need. You must use the Seventh Stone."

"I can't," Bryen whispered, finding it harder and harder to talk. The Dark Magic within him continued to spread rapidly, weakening him, the boundary that separated the Curse contained within the Seventh Stone fraying, thread by thread. If he tried to use the Seventh Stone now, the barrier would unravel completely and the Dark Magic would gain dominance. When that happened, there would be no return.

It wouldn't be long now. It wouldn't be long before he was gone. Before the Curse stole who he was.

"You must!" shouted Aislinn, tears forming in her eyes. "You must at least try."

Bryen stared at Aislinn, seeing nothing else. He could let go right now. All the pain. All the fear. All the anger would disappear. He would be free from it all. Then a few soft words behind him shook him from the haze that threatened to engulf his spirit.

"Death doesn't choose us," whispered Lycia.

"We choose our death," finished Davin.

"The Spear," Bryen mumbled, his breath increasingly difficult to come by now, clarity returning to his thoughts if only briefly. The shield within him was about to crack. Despite that, or maybe because of it, Lycia and Davin were right. He needed to fight until the very end. If he was going to die, it would be on his terms and no one else's. It would be with his weapon in his hands. "I need the Spear."

Lycia dashed to her left then was back at Bryen's side in less than a second, placing the Spear of the Magii on Bryen's chest and then helping him wrap his hands around the steel haft of the weapon.

In a flash, the Talent surged within Bryen, the Spear serving as a focal point, augmenting his strength a thousandfold, giving him a way to push back against the Dark Magic that was so close to consuming him. But he needed to do something else first.

Connecting the Talent that flowed through the Spear to the Seventh Stone within him, Bryen concentrated on the barrier that was only a few heartbeats away from fragmenting. He was done in an instant. The vault that he had constructed in the back of his mind to contain the Curse gifted to him by the Seventh Stone was made whole again. Strong. Solid. Unbreakable. For now.

That done, Bryen turned his attention to the Dark Magic

that flowed through his veins because of the Elder's attack. Thanks to the power and unique qualities of the Spear of the Magii, the next change was almost instantaneous, the weapon helping Bryen to pull the Dark Magic from his body and destroy it in the welcome fire of the Talent.

Those surrounding Bryen watched in wonder as the entire Spear glowed a bright white, and as it did, the threads of black crisscrossing Bryen's body dissolved into nothing. When Bryen took a deep breath and then pushed himself up into a sitting position, Aislinn and Lycia both helping him, they all breathed a sigh of relief.

"Didn't you learn anything the last time you chased after a Ghoule on your own?" asked Tarin, not expecting an answer from Bryen, his words simply a way to release some of the tension that had been building within him.

"He's done this before?" asked Aislinn, her voice sharp because of the rawness of her emotions.

"After you left for Tintagel, Lady Winborne, Bryen pursued a Ghoule right into a trap just like this," confirmed Jerad. "He received just a scratch then."

"This was not just a scratch," Lycia said, her face red with anger. Not because of what Jerad had said, but rather because Bryen clearly hadn't learned from his previous escapade.

"I might have said too much," Jerad murmured, seeing both Lycia and Aislinn staring at him with daggers in their eyes.

"Perhaps you did, Sergeant," said Tarin. "Come on. Let's leave Bryen so that he can pay the piper. We need to check on the Blood Company."

"Sarcasm from the Captain of the Battersea Guard? I never would have guessed."

"Nice try, lad," said Tarin in response to Bryen's whispered comment. "You can't turn the conversation that easily. You made your bed. Now you get to lie in it."

"I think I'll go with them," said Sirius, who pushed himself off the ground, giving Bryen a companionable pat on the shoulder before he left.

"Definitely a death wish," murmured Rafia to no one in particular. "I knew it the first time I met him."

"You did this before?" demanded Aislinn. "When we were training in the practice yard at the Broken Citadel, what was the one thing that you kept telling me?"

"I'm not sure," said Bryen with a sheepish grin. "We talked about a great many things."

Bryen was tired, but he was stronger now. He felt more like himself. The Spear of the Magii had rejuvenated him to a certain extent, though he knew that he would be feeling the effects of his wound and the healing process for the next several days.

"Don't try to distract with humor," growled Lycia.

"I wasn't trying to be funny, it's just that ..."

"You can make a mistake, but you can only make it once. If you make it twice, you're dead," cut in Aislinn.

"Sounds just like Declan," confirmed Lycia.

"Good advice, don't you think?" Aislinn asked heatedly. "Why didn't you follow it?"

"It was just that ..."

"Why didn't you listen to your own advice?" Aislinn interrupted again, not having any patience for Bryen's attempted deflections. She had something to say, and she was going to say it. "You almost died because you made the same mistake twice."

"I didn't want anyone else to be hurt or killed because of me!" shouted Bryen. Although his tired voice wasn't very loud, it did stop Aislinn's diatribe. "Too many of the

Company fell today. I didn't want that last Elder to hurt anyone else. To reveal where we were. I thought I could take him."

"Clearly that wasn't the case," said Lycia quietly, her eyes still blazing with anger at her friend's foolishness, though understanding his motivation.

Aislinn offered her hand to Bryen, who accepted it. Then she helped him to his feet and she didn't let go. Instead, her grip tightened as she pulled Bryen close to her.

"You are the Seventh Stone. You are the only one who can repair the Weir."

"Yes, even though I don't even know if I can do that."

"That doesn't matter," said Aislinn, her voice returning to a less agitated level. "We believe in you even if you don't. And even if you fail, it doesn't matter. You're the only one who gives us a chance to hold back the Ghoules. You. Just you. We are here to help you get to the Sanctuary. Succeed or fail, we are only here to help you try to repair the Weir. If we fall, we fall. If we fall, you continue on. We don't matter. Only you do."

"That's not true ..."

Lycia cut him off, agreeing with every word that the Lady Winborne had said.

"She's right. We're here for you, not the other way around. Don't do something that stupid again, or I'll kill you myself."

With that, Lycia nodded to Aislinn. Then they both turned and followed after the others back toward the Company. Lycia grabbed Davin by the arm to take him with her, the Crimson Giant shrugging his shoulders apologetically to Bryen as he trailed after the two women.

Watching them go, Bryen didn't know what was worse.

Being chewed out by both Aislinn and Lycia or the two women agreeing with one another.

With everyone else gone, Declan finally came up to Bryen. He could see the emotions raging across Declan's normally taciturn features. Anger. Irritation. Fear. Relief. Apparently even some satisfaction at the lecture that Aislinn and Lycia had just given him.

"You acted the fool," admonished Declan, now that it was finally his turn. "You're not the only one here who can fight. You're not the only one here who can take risks and get things done. Don't do that again. The Lady Winborne is correct, whether you like it or not. All of us can die, and it won't matter. The only thing that matters is that you stay alive and do whatever it is you need to do at the Weir. Are we clear?"

Bryen nodded, feeling like when he was a child and he had first entered the Pit, the Master of the Gladiators taking him to task for the tiniest of mistakes that he had made while he fought on the white sand.

"Yes, Declan."

"Good." Declan nodded grouchily, not feeling the need to say anything else as he struggled to hide the terror that had surged within him when he'd seen the wound that Bryen had received. Declan cared about fixing the Weir, but not as much as he cared about Bryen. With that in mind, he shifted his focus to their next challenge. "Once the wounded are cared for, we'll get moving again. We need to assume the Ghoules know we are here."

"You're right about that," agreed Bryen, as he and Declan started to walk slowly back to the Blood Company, Bryen taking his time as his legs felt a bit wobbly. Declan stayed at his side just to make sure he was there if the young man he viewed as his son needed his help. "I'm beginning to worry that we won't be able to make it to the Sanctuary. We're less than a week out from Tintagel, and the Ghoules have already found us. I knew that this would be difficult. I knew that we would face challenges. I just didn't expect to face those challenges so soon."

"Could I offer you one piece of advice?"

"I doubt I could stop you," Bryen replied with a grin. "What would that be?"

"We've been hit in the mouth and knocked to the ground a couple times. When that happens, there's only one thing to do."

"What would that be?"

"You get back up."

"And you hit whoever hit you harder than they hit you."

"There you go," confirmed Declan. "I guess you did listen to me on occasion."

"How could I not?" asked Bryen with a short laugh. "You make it very hard not to." Bryen reached across and grasped Declan's arm warmly, nodding his thanks for his guidance. "On to the Sanctuary?"

"On to the Sanctuary."

LOOKING FOR MORE ...

I hope you enjoyed the first two chapters. To keep reading *The Protector's Reckoning*, Book Five of *The Tales of Caledonia*, order your copy today on Amazon.

Made in the USA
Las Vegas, NV
28 August 2022

54157027R00236